About

Laura JK Chamberlain lived most of her life in Colorado but has recently moved to the Pacific Northwest to be near family. If she is not writing, she can be found hiking in the mountains, working in her gardens, or visiting her grandchildren.

Laura began writing after giving birth to undiagnosed triplets (instantly changing the family dynamic from two children to five). Journalling about the entertaining escapades of five-against-one motherhood provided plenty of material to compile into a manuscript. She entitled her work *No Rest for the Fertile* and submitted it to the National Writers Club Book Manuscript Contest, which won an honourable mention.

She is the author of an illustrated children's book, *The Story of Norman* (Donna Brooks, illustrator, and Heart to Heart Publishing, Inc.), which was chosen as a winner at the third Annual International Book Awards competition.

The book *This I Believe On Love* (John Wiley & Sons) included her essay, *They Built a Family*. Ms Chamberlain is an oral storyteller and has been a member of and past president for Spellbinders of Littleton Oral Storytellers.

Pillars for the Gods

TO: Elisa,

I love watching your little family "grow up." I enjoy how you interact with them and help them blossom!

I hope you enjoy this story about Persia back in the day!

Laura
July 06, 2024

Laura JK Chamberlain

Pillars for the Gods

Vanguard Press

VANGUARD PAPERBACK

© Copyright 2024
Laura JK Chamberlain

The right of Laura J. K. Chamberlain to be identified as author of
this work has been asserted by her in accordance with the
Copyright, Designs and Patents Act 1988.

A CIP catalogue record for this title is
available from the British Library.

ISBN 978-1-83794-139-1

Vanguard Press is an imprint of
Pegasus Elliot Mackenzie Publishers Ltd.
www.pegasuspublishers.com

First Published in 2024

Vanguard Press
Sheraton House Castle Park
Cambridge England

Printed & Bound in Great Britain

To Lily, Elden, and Lhally

"Without God, we cannot. Without us, God will not."
Saint Augustine

Thank you, family and friends, for listening and encouraging me to see *Pillars* through. I especially want to thank Kathleen Odefey, Charline Richardson, Annikki Chamberlain, Christine King, and Kurt Loth Langland.

Thank you, Cezmi Çoban, Mahmut Turgut, and Archaeologist Bahadir Berkaya, for sharing your knowledge of ancient Halicarnassus and the people who lived there.

And a special thank you goes to Marek and Heather Aquila, owners of Imperial Combat Arts, and Heidi Jo Chamberlain – my faithful traveling companion, events coordinator, chaffer, navigator, and fellow explorer on our trip to Turkey.

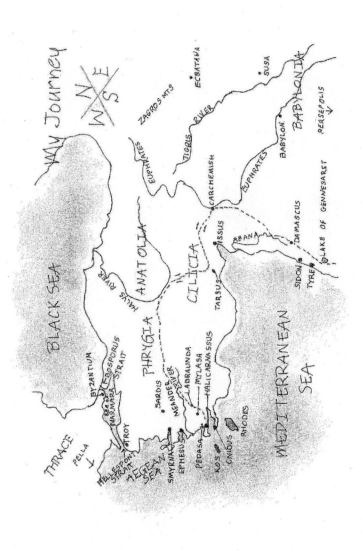

Prologue

The year is 279 BC. The Colossus of Rhodes, one of the Seven Wonders of the Ancient World, has recently been completed. Rising from its white marble pedestal standing proud above Rhodes Harbor, the bronze masterpiece greets a steady stream of ships. Every day, droves of tourists arrive on the island, anxious to view the tallest statue in the world. Ethan, from the Land of Israel, is among the sightseers.

Nearing his ninety-fourth year, this aged gentleman joins the migration of curious travellers for reasons all his own. He comes to Rhodes seeking atonement – to make amends for his deceptive part in history. Viewing the Colossus is brief, the first leg of his mission. Returning to Halicarnassus is his eventual objective and is meant to be his final act on Earth.

The story begins on board a Greek sailing vessel underway in the Aegean Sea.

Chapter 1

The Colossus of Rhodes

"Captain! The old man who boarded with us in Rhodes is dead!"

"Dead?"

"Yes, my Captain! He is below deck, sprawled across one of the cots. I assumed he was sleeping, but when I tried rousing him, he did not awaken," the chief officer reported.

"Did you find assault marks or blood from a wound?"

"Nothing, Captain. I checked him myself. He appears to have died while sleeping."

"Is this man Greek?"

"Most likely Jewish. I found a staff ornamented with Hebrew words lying on the floor beside him. His head rests on a ragged travel satchel, and I removed this small stone from his hand – a polished piece of chert."

"By the gods, even now, we lag behind schedule. I cannot afford another delay on this crossing. Bring me his property and prepare for burial," the captain ordered.

Before rummaging through the dead man's possessions, Captain Dareios first examined the staff and the fragment of chert – a light green oval stone polished to a high sheen. The timeworn satchel, a strange design unlike any bag he had seen, was secured with a bronze ring looped around a mushroom shaped stud. Hoping to find identification papers, Dareios lifted the triangular flap and removed its contents. He found a purse filled with coins, a pen and a bag of ink powder for writing. There were also a box of spices and some fritters purchased from an island bakery. A silk robe lay folded on top of an old pair of Persian trousers. Digging deeper, he discovered numerous scrolls, rolled tight and secured with braided cords.

"Manuscripts?" Dareios said to himself. "It appears the old man writes a historical account. Perhaps he worked as a chronicler documenting the completion of the Colossus."

Further investigation would have to wait since Dareios was summoned on deck to conduct a brief interment ceremony. Calling all hands to reverence, the chief officer directed passengers and crew toward the ship's stern. Performing burial at sea was the one task this Greek captain most disliked. He felt releasing someone's loved one overboard deprived their family of saying a proper farewell or praying for their upcoming journey, not to mention robbing the deceased of a marked burial site. Bereft families often struggled to find closure when there was no grave to visit. For such reasons, Captain Dareios approached each burial as a sacred trust, carefully giving the deceased a respectful and courteous funeral in their family's stead. The worn-out old man dying in the hull of his ship was no exception, although no one knew his name, from where he hailed, or why such an aged gentleman travelled unchaperoned in this part of the world.

One sailor approached with information; he had observed the old man on Rhodes viewing the Colossus. "Surely daft, my Captain, and a disordered fellow. With my own two ears, I heard him rambling, talking to the statue as if it would answer him. Finally, he laughed and said, 'There you are, Goliath. I have sorely missed you, my friend.' I watched him mumbling to himself, hobbling along, viewing the statue from every angle, then he chuckled louder and said, 'After all these years, your legs still look like trunks of a gnarled oak tree.' When he tired, he sat on the bench where I sat. As soon as he noticed me, he slid closer and initiated a most unusual conversation.

"He told me that years ago, the people of Rhodes commissioned a temple of pure white marble to grace the harbour in the exact spot the Colossus stands today, but treachery on the part of Persia prevented its construction.

"The old fellow added, 'Tiny Rhodes garners tremendous wealth with no strength to defend her prosperity from the eyes of greedy tyrants. To be sure, my heart soars watching these people celebrate their Colossus. Seventy-two cubits of justice, that is what this statue amounts to.'

"His conversation jounced around with odd comments and wistful thoughts, but he did say he once lived in Halicarnassus and, as a young man, had the opportunity to visit Rhodes. He said, 'Save for the Colossus, the place has changed little during the seventy years of my absence.'

"Pointing to the city square, he continued, 'Except the queen is gone. I do not begrudge the Rhodians that; I expected as much. Undoubtedly she got smelted with other bronze items needed to build the statue. To be sure, returning to this area bewilders my soul. I am conflicted with difficult memories and secrets of shameful incidents, while at the same time, I rejoice in remembering the people I love. And most unexpectedly, a pledge I swore to myself many years ago has grown unkind. I fear I will burst if I do not speak the one name I promised to forever block from my lips, Jaleh. While looking out across the sea, I realize I still yearn to know what happened to beautiful Jaleh. I pray she married a capable man and gave him many sons – perhaps twins as her mother had done.'

"Through tears, the old man smiled while talking about this girl. Then he looked straight at me and said, 'In truth, I fear Jaleh and her family met with a terrible demise in the City Which Is No More. Ho, to be sure, the most imprudent and senseless act in all of history was Alexander setting fire to Persepolis. I thought I knew him better than that.'

"I cannot say for sure, my Captain, what his scattered mutterings meant, and I avoided giving him much consideration. How would a daft old Jew know of such matters?"

Passengers and crew stopped their tasks and gathered on deck. With bowed heads, they listened as the captain spoke a kind tribute honouring the elderly stranger. He finished by praying, "Known only to the gods; we commend the body and the life of this unknown man into the silence of a watery grave. May he find acceptance in the next world." With that, two sailors lifted the shrouded corpse and dropped it overboard, sending a spray of cold water onto the crowd of peering observers.

The white shroud, floating atop the surface, remained visible when contrasted against the azure waters of the Aegean Sea. For a moment or two, choppy waves seesawed the body back and forth in a lullaby motion until a white-topped surge grabbed the veiled corpse, shaking it in a tightened grip. Unpredictably, the shrouded body broke free. The corpse jetted forward as though darting through an open window, then lingered a bit, riding the rise and fall of ripply swells. Before long, another wave hurtled over the corpse. Still protesting, it refused to sink. Despite further jabs from watery arms, the mutinous old man remained buoyant, drifting in wavering tides as if mocking the cruel summons of Hades.

Captivated by the strange sight, passengers pressed tight against the rail, trying for a closer look. Still bobbing, rocking to and fro, the corpse continued skittering along the surface of the water as if basking in the warmth of the sun-drenched day. Escaping the thrust and grapple of each wave brought forth a crescendo of jubilant cheers with vibrant applause from frenzied passengers eager to bolster the old man along in his heroic effort. Then, as if showing off, the corpse waggled headlong through another barrage of waves, lapping and grabbing for him. And yet, the wilful body refused to concede to the beckoning call of the deep.

Despite their cheers, the beaten old man had no chance. With no place to go, he conceded to his worldly fate. Onlookers stared in eerie silence, saddened as the lifeless body surrendered its mortal right, sinking deeper and deeper until disappearing, another lost and nameless soul pulled into eternity by the merciless arms of the Aegean Sea.

People stood transfixed, looking deep into the water while whispering, discussing the peculiar sight they had witnessed. When words ran out, the crowd dispersed, and their lives returned to normal. Captain Dareios barked orders, heading the ship toward its designated stops throughout the Dodecanese Complex.

Come evening, the ship moored in a crumbled marina beside the virtually deserted city of Halicarnassus. With the crew gone ashore for entertainment, the captain settled in for the night, enjoying the hush of his private cabin. Thoughtful of the dead man, he opened the timeworn satchel and removed the delicately tied manuscripts. Laying them across the table before him, Dareios pondered the row of rolled papyrus.

Chapter 2

The Scrolls of Ethan

Unfurling the first scroll revealed a map followed by a meticulous script written in the flowing penmanship of an apparent scholar. Across the top was written, 'A Chronicle of Historic Concern.'

It began with these words: *I write my final words during the third year of the reign of Ptolemy II Philadelphus. I am Ethan, son of Zuriel, a Jew born of the tribe of Benjamin in the land of Israel, raised in the city of Jericho during the reign of King Artaxerxes II Arsicas of Persia.*

Dareios paused. "Ethan. So, now I know your name," he said. "I am sorry to tell you this, Ethan, but you died today. I had to bury you in the sea. While trying to identify you, I came across these scrolls. To be sure, they have piqued my curiosity. Please forgive the intrusion into your private thoughts; I only seek to discover what was so important that you carried these manuscripts. Did you have a certain destination for them? What is their intended purpose? Perhaps by reading them, the answer will reveal itself." Reaching for his pipe, the captain settled in and continued reading.

My father named me Ethan for an Ezrahite, a musician, and a cymbalist who played in the courts of King David. Ethan means energetic, optimistic, enduring, and permanent. My father bestowed this name upon me as a blessing, and today, being over ninety years of age, I have lived longer than anyone I know.

During my life, I worked as a stonemason, a spy, an arbitrator, a model, and an engineer owning my own business. I served my country during two world governments, witnessing the birth of a new political era after one feeble king, lacking in ambition and aptitude, destroyed the largest empire the world has ever known. I have sat at the tables of kings and queens, rulers and conquerors, warriors and renegades, and worked beside gifted craftsmen and the world's most renowned artisans. I have been a prisoner, a prince, a warrior, and a murderer.

God blessed me with a wonderful wife, but she has since died. Her name was Hadassah, daughter of Maath of the tribe of Judah. Her birth happened on the anniversary of Purim inspiring her father to name her Hadassah after the Jewish girl later called Esther, Queen of Persia. Hadassah and I raised six sons and enjoyed thirty grandchildren.

I loved my wife, but before her, I loved another – a Persian girl named Jaleh. I called her Jaleh Joon because she was the one who held my heart. We were young then with hope and spirits full of wonder. The sweetness of life had brought us together, and the world was our friend. How easily we laughed, frolicking away the days with fanciful dreams and plans for the future. We never imagined the vindictive spirit of a jealous man would one day shatter our lives and callously sweep aside our broken hearts like shards of worthless pottery. To be sure, it is a pitiless wind that blows away the innocence of young love.

Perhaps in error, I hid the events of my Persian life from Hadassah. I avoided telling her of my time with Jaleh. Neither did I mention killing a man and causing the death of another. Hadassah would have insisted on knowing details; she would expect me to be sorry, but I felt no remorse. Besides, how does one explain killing a man, placing his head in a basket, and gifting it to the most beautiful woman in the world?

Like skeletons resting undisturbed in the recesses of forgotten tombs, I ordered my memories to remain hidden in the dark shadows of my mind. This continued silence has served me well. But, today, my conscience is at war against me and will no longer permit the comfort of dormant quietude. Each morning I awaken in startled awe, realising I am still alive. Without my consent, time draws me closer to my final moments, but before my life ends, I must tell my story. I must share unusual yet historical events I have seen – marvellous but also shameful things; secrets of fraud, unethical profit, and murder.

Theopompus was an excellent historian, I knew him personally and still enjoy reading his works, but as a Greek, he writes with the bias of an ancient rivalry that favours the Greeks. My portrayal of events may contradict his well-established narrative, but I have no political views to slant or attitudes to steer. The singular purpose of my account is to write an addendum to history *by sharing what I know. I include facts and details revealed to me by others. Still, most of this chronicle is based on personal observations while living as a reticent spectator during the last gasp of the Persian Empire, an energetic time of innovation and expansion ending in shocking tragedy.*

Only by fortuitous accident did my life intersect with some of the most dynamic people of Persia – people somehow chosen for greatness, glory, and grief. While the blessing of this accident obligates me to pen their unique histories, it also breaks my heart anew.

Before it is too late, I must return home to Halicarnassus, the grandest sun-kissed city on Earth – a kingdom without equal, soaring in radiant heights somewhere between heaven and Persia. Once the most affluent town on the Aegean coast, shimmering with gold and pure white marble, Halicarnassus was built by a loyal satrap during a matchless era of prosperity and splendour. Ho, to be sure, I stand as a witness to the unprecedented Age of Mausolus.

My story begins when my oldest brother, Sakeri, died during the first year of the reign of King Artaxerxes III Ochus of Persia.

Chapter 3

Halicarnassus, Persia

Queen Artemisia sensed the figure hiding behind her bedroom tapestry seconds before he leaped at her. Shrieking maidens, stricken with fear, recoiled as the queen unsheathed her dagger while positioning herself in a fighting stance. Unafraid and confident, the warrior queen leaned forward; circling her weapon, flicking her wrist in a jabbing motion. Trained for combat under the tutelage of her father, King Hecatomnus, and his elite squadron of Zoroastrian priests, Artemisia aimed her fit body toward her wily opponent.

The queen smiled, snapping her dagger, mocking her adversary as though playing a game. Then, light on her feet, she sprang forward, skirting the assailant's initial charge. He turned to pounce. She ducked and rolled, sweeping her drawn blade with one quick strike. Then, bounding to her feet, she wheeled around, ready to inflict the next offensive wound. Startled by the swift jab into his calf, the intruder let out a stifled whimper of pain and anger.

The queen's mind fixed, circling her opponent; she zig-zagged her weapon, slicing it through the air. Within moments, her guards crashed through the door. Unwilling to concede the fight, Queen Artemisia stepped forward, wielding her sharp blade in front of her body. The wounded assailant moved backward, plying his weapon in beckoning motion. She charged.

Two guards intercepted the move by pulling her into a thicket of wicker shields and surrounding her with their armoured bodies. Having secured the queen, the third guard heaved his javelin. The shot came off awkwardly, allowing the assailant an easy sidestep. Then, with the thunderous roar of a stampeding bull, the rear guard charged forward, brandishing his sword. Expecting a counterattack at the patio archway, he spun around a support column, slicing his heavy weapon upward through the air. Empty.

Had the queen not interfered, the lethal tip of a Persian javelin would have this man haplessly pinned against the palace wall. But, instead, the intruder slipped away, vanishing into the night.

Chapter 4

Sabbath

Trekking alone in the wilderness, I knew nothing of this offence. With Sabbath approaching, my main concern was to find a suitable place to rest in Persia's rugged countryside. After traveling for months, trekking over 350 parasangs, my once-exciting adventure had grown tedious, and I welcomed the Sabbath rest. According to my calculations, the capital city of Halicarnassus lay ahead, about a half day's hike. That is where I hoped to find my older brother, Caleb.

I discovered an ideal campsite on an elevated flat with a slight outcropping of rocks. Green and wooded, terebinth trees offered cooling shade from the afternoon sun and protection from the wind. The rise afforded a panoramic view of the sprawling hill country which, several parasangs ahead, joined the Aegean Sea.

While my evening meal simmered, I collected tree sap to repair a shoe mishap. Sitting beneath a cloudless sky, warmed by a small fire, I smeared copious amounts of the sticky fluid across the sole of my torn sandal. Finally, with sandal drying and my belly full, I stretched out to admire the brilliant night sky laden with a million stars, each vibrant, twinkling a unique cadence from its divinely assigned place in the universe.

Contemplating those unfathomable stars hanging in an infinite space of time and eternity reminded me of my family back home in the province of Judah, and my people living in the land of Israel, including the multitude of Jews scattered to the four corners of the Earth. Father Abraham, my ancestor, predicted the children of Israel would flourish, reaching beyond the number of stars in the sky, and it appears we have.

My dwindling food supply offered up the last of the figs. Impatient for its honey-like sweetness, I removed the stem. Just then, a faint rustling in bushes caught my attention. I was not overly concerned; chasing away rodents attempting to steal my food was a nightly occurrence. With quiet stealth, I set down the fig, grabbed a smooth stone, and loaded it into my sling while soundlessly rising to my feet. Waiting, listening, surveying the darkness, I briefly considered the crackling noise may be from a larger animal, something ferocious, maybe a lion or a wild boar wandering in the darkness. In that case, I would shinny up a tree. I have had to do that before, too. Nevertheless, I stood ready, unafraid, and determined to defend my camp.

Instead of the nocturnal creature I expected, a man wielding a dagger leaped from the ledge above. He landed hard on the ground in front of me. Covered in the sweat of a wayward traveller, he stood frozen in terror. His amber eyes bulged with panic, and his mouth fixed in a twisted sneer of crooked, yellow teeth. Injured and losing consciousness, his hand slackened. When his dagger fell, I lunged at him as he toppled forward. Guiding this unsteady visitor onto my bed of woven linen, I observed blood flowing from a jagged wound in his leg. He had tried dressing the injury with strips torn from his cape, but his effort to stop the bleeding proved unsuccessful. Without my assistance, this man was going to die.

I knew what to do and prayed he would stay unconscious while I cauterised the wound. After heating his dagger in the flame of my fire, I laid the red-hot blade directly into the cleft of his calf while gasping against the repugnant odour of burning flesh. Searing is always a brutal remedy, but the treatment worked, and his bleeding stopped. To safeguard against infection, I coated the damaged tissue with a healing salve my mother packed for my travels, then wrapped his calf with strips torn from the edge of my tunic.

Shaking the dust from his cloak, I covered him, tucking the edges around his body for warmth. Moaning, he mumbled strange words in a tongue foreign to my Aramaic dialect. I initially thought he spoke Akkadian or a close derivation, but I could not be sure. Soothing his angst, I pressed a moist cloth against his flushed face, rousing him several times to coerce sips of water from my drinking gourd. He grimaced and struggled against me until weakness forced him to accept several swallows. He drank and sputtered, mumbled, then drifted off again.

Having done my best, I prayed for Yahweh's healing hand and divine watchfulness over this man with no name. Then, sliding away, I considered the peculiar circumstance of our meeting, studying my mysterious guest in great detail. His arrival fascinated me, as did his appearance and the strangeness of his costume. Perhaps he served in the army; scars on his arms and chest suggested he had been in combat. Someone had inked a most intriguing monster onto the skin of his right shoulder – a chimera, part lion, part goat, and part snake. The unusual colour of his hair reminded me of a burnt orange sunset. Traditionally, the reddish hail from the northern territories of Scythia and Thrace; I imagined this fellow received much attention in Mediterranean regions with his ruddy thatch of messy hair.

I also noticed the man had the slightest disfigurement, a minor tear in the flesh of his earlobe, a ragged saw-toothed slit from a wound poorly healed. My stealthy guest intrigued me, and I hoped to get acquainted with him when he awoke in the morning. But, warmed by the night fire, the day's events overwhelmed me, and I drifted off into an exhausted sleep.

During the night, I had a strange dream. I dreamt I worked as a master stonemason in the employ of King Solomon, tap, tap, tapping away at slabs of marble being dressed and fitted to restore ancient stones in temple walls compromised by war, settling, or minor earthquakes. While working, chipping away with my carving hammer, I dreamt tiny flecks of airborne stone kept landing on my feet.

Startled, I awoke with the morning sun shining in my eyes. At first, I failed to recognise my surroundings. On noticing the blood-soaked linen, I recalled helping the wounded man, except he had vanished, taking my drinking gourd and entire food supply. Just then, a tiny pebble sailed past me from above, landing in a pile mounting at my feet. Glancing up, I found myself surrounded by the King's Guard.

Chapter 5

Arrested

Fierce Persian Dathaba, or a detachment of ten foot- soldiers, rudely set upon me, bound my wrists, and, using the stinging point of a spear, herded me forward as though a helpless lamb headed for the butcher's shop. I protested my arrest, asserting my innocence, but every objection proved futile and my protests fell on deaf ears.

One proud soldier – the apparent commander of this unit – used a long strap to tether me to his belt. This fellow was the largest man I had ever seen. Standing beside him made me feel small, like a puny insect fun for squishing. His muscles bulged on top of more muscles, with legs measuring the diameter of oak trunks wider than the thickest part of my gangly body. My entire head fit into the cup of his iron hand. His neck, thick with corded tendons, merged into brawny shoulders, becoming rock biceps before connecting to bulging forearms of rippling sinew. His intimidating size made me feel bitty as a pitiful grasshopper; the story of David and Goliath came to mind.

At the time of my arrest, I was a boy – a boy who brazenly imagined himself a grown man. But, in truth, I was callow, a blundering mix of eager and impetuous, barely realising a world existed beyond my small tribe in the central city of Jericho. Jericho's underground streams transformed our town into a lush oasis in an otherwise barren desert. With so much beauty and abundant natural resources, pride became a bit of a regional pastime.

My father Zuriel, son of Palti, worked as a stonemason, as did his father before him and his father before him. "And each generation going back to the construction of the Great Pyramids of Ramses of Egypt, making us the reason those pyramids still stand," my grandfather would state with considerable satisfaction. Whether his musings were my actual heritage or the ramblings of an old man, one fact remained: stonemasonry was the profession chosen for me.

Unlike other boys in my clan, I grew tall and muscular in my early teens. This developing physique greatly pleased me, and I eagerly awaited a fitting beard complementing my fine form. Working in my brother's business as an apprentice stonemason under the directive of Hezekiah, governor of Judah, I managed every style of hammer. With equal proficiency, I could swing the largest sledges in broad sweeping arcs and manipulate iron-tipped tackers using either hand. Such strenuous labour bulked me up with a man's body, firm and well-defined. Still, my physical form was inconsistent with my foolish adolescent naïveté and overconfident outlook.

Seventeen years of age with the body of a man, I had smooth skin back then, olive-coloured, and dark, wide-set eyes highlighted by long lashes and thick brows. My high cheekbones sprouted an uneven growth of facial hair burgeoning down my jawline. Even today, my nose is slightly crooked, as it has been since a lively boy back home re-sculpted it with a misguided rock. However, my nose was not the issue; the nemesis of my vanity proved to be my dark curly hair. I imagined myself a grown man, but the thick piles of soft ringlets foisted upon me at birth produced a delicate boyish look. And now, contrasted against my captors' imposing appearance, my scrubby beard and flowing ringlets of curls turned into an instant scourge. Compared with their sharp features and swarthy skin, my shiny complexion gleamed as a spring lily from the Plain of Sharon.

Worse yet, my worn-out sandals and pitiful clothing – a simple linen tunic covered by a robe of mourning tied at the waist with an artless sash of braided cloth – became an embarrassment when measured against the military uniforms of this elite force.

Despite the distance these men must have travelled during the night, the Dathaba presented in a crisp, well-ordered fashion. Under their fluted headdresses of stiffened felt flowed bushy hair, flaring out and merging with oiled beards cascading to their chests in rows of stylish waves. Their lightweight uniforms, designed for manoeuvrability and rapid travel, consisted of loose-fitting silk shirts worn under sleeveless, mid-thigh tunics. An embroidery across a linen breastplate displayed a Faravahar amulet – Persia's Zoroastrian symbol representing 'good thoughts, good words, and good deeds'.

Wide bronze bazuband bracelets protected their arms, and each wore trousers with baggy legs tucked inside ankle-high sandals. I shuddered to imagine wearing such heavy gear on a hot day, but wearing trousers intrigued me – silky fabric brushing against my legs with every step. Right then and there, I determined that if I managed to survive my present situation, I would try a pair of silky Persian trousers.

The colour and style of a military uniform signified which king each division served. The unit capturing me wore regimental outfits of saffron-coloured tunics and dark brown trousers; I was unsure which king governed this Dathaba since none shared a single word of information with me.

Maintaining the swift marching pace set by the soldiers was a challenge. Before finding a rhythm, I lost my footing several times. Despite falling, bruising myself, scuffing my knuckles, and skinning both knees, Goliath –the name I secretly gave my gigantic captor – remained unconcerned about my welfare. He continued his rapid gait, dragging me, thumping, bumping, and tumbling off balance at the end of his leash.

Ho, to be sure, you overgrown Persian thug! I said to myself. *The more you try humiliating me, the more determined I will become to thwart your loutish pleasure!* I resolved to appear unmoved by his callous harassment. Projecting an aura of confidence, I held my head high, squared my shoulders, puffed out my chest, and tried matching him stride for stride as we navigated wooded hills and mountainous landscapes. The effort was exhausting.

Each soldier, equipped with a wicker spara (or lyre-shaped shield), carried a long spear. Back then, Persian spears were massive. A counterweight was required to balance the extra-large metal tip – a tip I had grown tired of jabbing me in my backside. Over their left shoulder, the Dathaba stowed a bow and quiver filled with cane arrows, and from their leather belts hung a sling, a short knife, and a sword housed in a decorative sheath.

I could not help but notice that the curved sword attached to Goliath's belt had dried blood smeared on the sparkling pommel atop its full tang blade. Strips of leather wrapped the grip, and a metallic cradle connecting to a crosspiece protected the hand. His simple scabbard had a gold Faravahar amulet attached at the top and a wrap of golden lace encircling the tip.

Considering the sophisticated manner in which this band of soldiers marched, dressed, and carried themselves, I believed them to be a special force of highly trained fighters. But what interest could they possibly have in me? Regardless, I fumed with outrage. Trussed and off-balance, it was all I could do to remain vertical while keeping my eyes fixed on the giant's hand, fearing he may move it toward that sparkling, blood-smeared pommel.

Chapter 6

My Journey

You may be curious how I happened to be camping alone on a remote mountain ledge of the Anatolia Plateau. Family business: my father needed me to find my older brother, Caleb, and send him home.

I embarked on a long and arduous journey, heading out on the first day of spring. My father, Zuriel, escorted me from Jericho to the city of Lod, where I joined a caravan heading north toward Carchemish. I had never ridden a camel and wished to walk, traveling alone, but my father adamantly denied my request for safety reasons. The land of Israel abounded with lions and prowling leopards, not to mention heartless bandits lying in wait to prey on isolated travellers. Besides, traveling required sharp navigational skills for locating wells and skirting unfriendly territories. I resented my father's over-protectiveness, but considering my sudden arrest, I figured his growing list of dangers would now include ruthless soldiers.

Traveling from Lod to Carchemish required two weeks, considering we stopped to pick up additional passengers and rested for Sabbath. Our caravan was small, consisting of 150 camels following in a single line, one behind the other, connected by a cord tied to the camel walking in front. Most people taking lengthy trips wait for the longer trains offering comfortable two-humped Bactrian camels. Given the urgency of my mission, I boarded the first available train, one using dromedaries or the one-humped camels of Midian. Sitting on a padded saddle made for a pleasant enough ride; I figured out how to lean forward to catch a quick nap by situating my gear and bedroll against the saddle bar. Persian passenger trains are designed for safety and durability, not speed. We only travelled about ten parasangs each day.

Riding in the saddle, rocking back and forth, and watching scenery match scenery in rhythm with the camel's gait left me heavy-eyed and lazy, so I chose to walk beside the caravan whenever possible. The exercise alleviated stiffness, and exploring off-trail prevented boredom. Above all, walking gave me an escape from the women on the train. Girls must ride at all times since they are forbidden to walk, but there is no law against them talking. Sitting on cushioned furniture beneath their shading canopies, the women chattered nonstop. Parasang after parasang, they babbled on with uninterrupted giggles and endless fuss punctuated by emotional gasps when learning a bit of exciting gossip. How did they find so much to say about nothing?

Our camel master, a Rechabite, had travelled this route numerous times. He knew where to find freshwater, shade, and favourable settlements willing to sell us necessary provisions. My favourite part of the caravan was when we arrived in a new village, and people ran out to greet us, hurling question after question, curious to learn the latest news from the south.

Several families from Egypt travelled with us. Egyptian independence from Persia was always a sizzling topic and promoted many discussions marked with mockery and biting criticism against the other person's point of view. Arguments usually ended with blaming and criticizing either the pharaoh or the king. This grudge against Persia is centuries old and originated when Persia conquered Egypt in the Battle of Pelusium. My youth forbade me from commenting during these heated debates, but I learned plenty about ancient and ongoing political issues by listening to their arguments.

Our third evening, still within the borders of the land of Israel, found us camping along the northwest shore of the Lake of Gennesaret near the town of Capernaum. Gennesaret is famous in my country. It is the largest freshwater lake and a renowned fishing spot. I had never been there before, so after making camp, I ventured along the shore to watch the endless parade of narrow fishing vessels gliding across the surface; their white sails stretched full against the breeze.

Fishermen lugged in nets bulging with musht and biny, violently flipping their tailfins and arching their backs in a vain attempt to escape their destiny. A tasty musht met his demise in a hurry when an older woman operating a lakeshore booth roasted him for my evening meal. I also purchased silver-coloured sardines –pickled and smoked – a delicacy I anticipated snacking on in the days ahead.

Our first Sabbath layover was in a caravan camp on the outskirts of the ancient city of Damascus, the oldest city in the world, with structures, homes, and agoras built by people long forgotten. Walking down those ancient streets overwhelmed me when I realized I was walking on paths others had walked as long ago as Father Abraham.

Imagining the many cultures of Damascene civilisations, I wondered how closely the lives of our prehistoric forbearers, the sons of Shem, compared to ours today. The ancient race undoubtedly shared similar ambitions and worthy goals as our modern society – bountiful harvests and authentic friendships while worshiping gods and dreaming dreams. Their days were probably the same as today: loving and laughing, enduring heartaches and failures, birthing their families, and burying their dead. Yet, I had to wrestle my mind away from the grim reality that those once robust citizens of ancient Damascus, whether wealthy or poor, loved or despised, kind or cruel, are now virtually forgotten characters, just nameless, faceless souls with no story.

Considering a similar fate befalling me or my people gave me pause. Are we nothing more to this world than a shadow, mere guests passing through time? And what about nations? Mighty Persia is more powerful than any empire in the history of the world. How could a nation with such a powerful army and advanced scientific knowledge cease to exist, wither like an apple overlooked by pickers, and left to fall to the ground? I promptly put such dread out of my mind knowing our modern society is unmistakably more elaborate than the nominal societies of ancient Damascus; we today are much too sophisticated to face extinction.

After spending time on the banks of the Abana River, we pushed north for Carchemish. By week's end, we came upon a large monument marking a massive burial ground called the Field of One Hundred Thousand Corpses. An eerie silence settled over the caravan; no one spoke a word while crossing this sacred ground. It was the site of a massacre known as the Great Battle of Carchemish. I knew the story; rabbis include this gory account in their pastoral teachings. The most significant battle in history was fought on this plain between three contenders – Assyria, Egypt, and Babylon.

Rabbi Efrat said whether we knew it or not, most likely we had ancestors killed in that battle: "By the time the gruesome slaughter had ended, the world was forever changed," he said. "From the blood of annihilation, Babylon emerged as the decisive winner and seized the world.

"Ah, but greed is a bottomless pit, impossible to fill," he added. "The savage conqueror of Babylon, a prince named Nebuchadnezzar, next turned his attention toward a sparkling gem, our nation of Judah. With callous disregard, he destroyed Solomon's Temple, robbed the treasury, razed Jerusalem to the ground, and carried away thousands of our fellow Jews into slavery."

I never imagined visiting this historic battlefield; truth be told, I did not enjoy the experience. The area felt shadowy and strange, perhaps inhabited by one hundred thousand ghosts. I was glad when we reached the city.

Caravan access into Carchemish was through the Gate of Yariri, a towered gate in a double-thick limestone wall. Once inside, we merged into the congestion of the outer city populated with immigrant settlers bustling along a wide avenue leading to the central agora.

An ancient shrine honouring Kubaba, the patron goddess of Carchemish, stood in the centre of a courtyard paved with alternating black and white marble squares. Beyond that, a towering wall encircled the wealthy inner city.

Our caravan master settled us along the west banks of the Upper Euphrates near an encampment of fierce mountain people known as Uxians. Employed by the empire, this tribe of nomadic people earned a handsome living by guarding and patrolling the high-country passageways of the Zagros Mountains. Besides their garb of deer hides, leopard pelts, and feathered caps, their rugged manner fascinated me. Eager to make the acquaintance of an actual Uxian, I approached the camp bearing gifts of fresh figs. Bad idea.

They reciprocated my attempt at neighbourly etiquette by shouting terrifying foreign words and pointing a wall of sharp spears at vulnerable parts of my body. Perhaps I should have offered my sardines; maybe their culture prohibited eating figs. Regardless of their issues, I meekly backed away, weak-kneed with feeble steps, forever averting my eyes whenever those frightening people passed in my direction.

Camping on the Euphrates for an entire week allowed ample time to explore the diverse city while inquiring about Caleb. No one had seen him, though.

Carchemish was my crossroads – the junction forcing a change of direction. My choices were to go east or go west. Should I journey east following Persia's Great Royal Road or travel west into rugged terrain toward Sardis? Eastward lay the cities of the capital district - Babylon, Ecbatana, Susa, and Parsa.

Joining an eastern caravan, traveling the Great Royal Road toward these governmental cities meant traversing the terrible desert. Parasang after parasang of sterile, pallid, barren terrain in an expanse offering venomous sidewinders, scorpions, and sharp stones projecting from arid landscapes in salt-saturated ravines void of water, where caravans hid from blazing heat by traveling during the coolness of night. Dreadful thought. That miserable route held no fascination for me, yet Caleb's occupation as an interpreter for the empire may have sent him on assignment to one of the prominent eastern cities.

On the other hand, traveling west would mean crisscrossing varied pathways throughout Anatolia. This direction promised pleasant temperatures, plenty of water, and shady forests. While that route began on a well-maintained spur of the Great Royal Road known as Sardanapalus Way, the landscape eventually changed into a rugged, inhospitable passage through the Taurus Mountains, a section known as the Cilician Gates.

My father was legendary for quoting proverbial texts – he could not help himself. If he thought I was lazy, he would say, "Consider the ant, you sluggard." Or if I misbehaved, he would say, "A foolish son brings grief to his mother." I often heard this one, "Each heart knows its own bitterness." When we parted company in Lod, my father reminded me, "Ethan, a man is a fool to trust himself. But those who inquire of the wisdom of the Lord are safe."

In the days of my youth, I was much too invincible to regard my father's words as anything other than daft. So, after brief consideration, I decided on my new course. I would trek the westward route, but I am embarrassed to admit wisdom had nothing to do with my decision. I chose west because that direction sounded easier.

Looking back on that, traveling west instead of east cost me my sole opportunity to visit the terraced city of Parsa. The legendary capital of King Darius I, built two centuries earlier, had grown into the most prosperous city under the sun. Ho, to be sure, Parsa, which means the city of the Persians, would have been an extraordinary sight to behold. (The Macedonians call it Persepolis; in their language, the word pólis implies city, and perse means Persian.) After Alexander destroyed the wealthy city of Parsa, the once affluent capital became known as the 'City Which Is No More'. But that is enough of my wistful meandering.

The next day, I joined a different caravan. This one was specially outfitted to cross the craggy mountains. We left Carchemish and headed toward Kastabala then down to Tarsus. I chose a position at the caravan's hindmost perimeter despite the fine mist of airborne grime stirred up by the line of camels walking in front. I was curious about the spotter posted at the rear and wanted to watch him work. This sentinel was to scan the road behind, survey the horizon, and watch for angaros riders.

On spying a distant speck so trivial no one else would notice, he stiffened in the saddle and spurred his horse forward while blowing a signal trumpet. He shouted, "Get out of the way! Move right! Move right!" Travelers scrambled off the road giving ample room for the angaros to race past, galloping at breakneck speed on one of the finest horses in the world.

Angarium was an organized company of imperial express couriers called angaros. In the service of the Great King, these commissioned cohorts delivered pouches containing essential documents intended for prominent people throughout the empire. Nothing mortal moved faster, and nothing knit the empire tighter than this rapid communication system continually transporting vital information. Angaros held proud their ritó inscribed above the door of every relay station: 'We are stayed neither by snow, nor rain, nor heat, nor darkness from accomplishing our appointed course with all speed'.

Under the direction of Darius I, Persians built the incredible Great Royal Road, sometimes called the Royal Highway, and later broadened its function by forming the Royal Angarium System. The elaborate transport technique operates like the torch-bearing relay popular at the Olympics, a sprint where cadence is crucial to success.

Once dispatched with official documents, the angaros sets off at high-speed, galloping toward a specific station where he transfers the sealed pouch into the care of a waiting rider. After securing the bag, the new courier bursts forth as suddenly as a summer squall, transporting the vital package further along the route. Finally, arriving at his intended stop, he tosses the document bag into the hands of the third carrier, who then races toward the fourth man, already mounted and eager to assume his leg of the cross-country journey.

On and on, fearless couriers ride, racing from station to station; gifted equestrians in synchronised rhythm traversing the continent from Susa to Sardis. Civilians required three months to travel such a distance while faithful angaros, traversed the entire course in seven days.

Straining my eyes, I, too, scanned the serrated fringes of the vast countryside until, at last, I spotted a faint cloud of dust forming on the horizon. Whipping up a haze of dirt, racing closer and closer, growing larger and larger, the outline of a noble figure soon came into full view. Then, in a blur of speed, the uniformed man appeared directly in front of us, leaning parallel to his stallion's neck, streaking past at unimaginable speed.

Swish! The blur whirred past, pelting us travellers with tiny pebbles as we waved and cheered, urging the rider along. Children ran into the road, chasing behind while prancing delightfully in the falling dust. Observers watched the sight in awestruck wonder, instinctively bending forward, straining to see the waning figure become a distant cloud on the opposite horizon before vanishing.

How daring! I began to consider this impressive occupation for myself – the Empire holds its army of angaros in the highest regard, but most notably, so do its fine-looking young women. Both were pleasant incentives.

When our caravan reached Tarsus, we resupplied before entering the low plains of Cilicia. The route took us into the Tarsus Mountains, through the Cilician Gates, and then onto the Anatolian plateau. This part of the journey amounted to five harrowing days of constant vigilance against rough Cilician bandits while traversing a landscape of steep, narrow passages on a snaking trail of sharp, loose limestone slippery in places where gentle streams trickled from canyon walls and across our path. Even the practised camels found this rugged, inhospitable corridor a complicated trail to navigate.

Veteran caravan masters disconnected camels from each other to prevent a disaster should one beast fall and pull the entire train over the edge. Single file, the animals walked along the narrow rock ledge. From time to time, their full packs scraped against the canyon wall, dislodging rocks, tumbling them past whoever hiked on the lower trail. It took several moments before hearing the splash from the rocks landing in the gorge below.

We proceeded tenaciously, creeping along steep, treacherous ravines, pressing forward day after day through the narrow gates until arriving safely in Thoana. To be sure, our safe arrival on flat terrain was nothing short of a miracle.

Firsthand experience of the treacherous Cilician Gates caused me to marvel at the ambition of King Cyrus, the Persian. Advancing to subdue the nations before him, he marched his entire army, including all their equipment and war machines, over this perilous terrain and through the gates, giving his army a tremendous advantage since no enemy anticipated such a reckless manoeuvre. By now, we know that centuries later, another daring conqueror succeeded by using the same tactic of marching his army through the strategic pass in the Taurus Mountains; we know him today as the young Macedonian Alexander the Great.

Each time our caravan arrived in a new community, I asked other travellers about Caleb. Finally, one evening while resting in a settlement on the plateau of Phrygia, another procession came in from the west. An older Jewish rabbi told me of a young fellow named Caleb serving as an interpreter in the Persian city of Labraunda. Indeed, this had to be my brother. At first light, I left the comfort and safety of my caravan and set out alone for the remote town in the district of Caria.

I crossed the Maeander River and then lumbered several days through rough country, until reaching the terraced city of Labraunda - the great mountain city of Zeus nestled in a sacred grove of plane trees. To my disappointment, my arrival proved ill-timed; Caleb had been there but had since left.

On my first evening in Labraunda, a prominent Jewish family kindly invited me to stay with them. One common occurrence in my travels was receiving an invitation to share a meal or lodge with a Jewish family. Jews everywhere share the same heritage and serve the same transcendent God, so our race functions as a global community where we accept one another as brothers. At times arguments erupted when neighbours fought over me, each insisting on having me stay in their home.

Despite diaspora forcing many to live in foreign countries, Jews remained interested in events involving the land of Israel, especially any news about Judah and Jerusalem. I expected the barrage of questions launched by faithful Hebrews eager to learn of issues regarding their native land.

"Is the temple being cared for?"

"What instruction does Governor Hezekiah hand down in his latest edicts?"

"How is the health of the high priest?"

"Please, has God sent us a new prophet?"

"Is there any information concerning the promised Messiah? Has he arrived?"

Regrettably, we Jews are in a time of God's silence, receiving no fresh words or added prophecies concerning the Saviour – nothing new since the writings of Malachi. Not knowing the day or the hour of the promised

Saviour's appearance made me anxious to find Caleb and return home before completely missing his prophetic arrival.

Caleb was lodging with this family when, four days earlier, he received transfer orders reassigning him to the port city of Halicarnassus. Four days. I missed connecting with my brother by four days.

Halicarnassus, a name I had never heard before, was the capital of the district of Caria. My hosts shared plenty of tales describing this enchanted kingdom by the sea. "Ethan, you will be visiting an intriguing world never before imagined," the father told me. "While the city offers many good things, it is also filled with idol worshipers.

The grandfather added, "Halicarnassus is a community of wealthy citizens and prosperous merchants. It boasts the prestigious reputation of the most affluent region of the Aegean coast. One could easily become seduced by its pleasures. "

The father added, "True, the burgeoning resort town shines like a jewel on the sea, attracting wealthy nobles, powerful kings, and progressive thinkers. The empire's leading orators and famous philosophers gather more admirers with every visit. But do not be misled; these patricians bring many factions to the city, each espousing mysterious ideologies. Beware the subtle trap of allurement."

Another man in the room warned, "You will be fine as long as you steer clear of the king. Mausolus, the dreaded satrap of Caria, is both tyrannical and self-seeking. He reigns as a ruthless shah. He and his wife, the harsh Queen Artemisia, govern the district with punitive judgment. So keep your head down; get in and get out of the city as quickly as possible."

The grandfather joined again with, "Did you know the city is walled? Has to be. Every building is lavish and built on streets of marble slabs trimmed in gold. Free citizens live in fabulous homes filled with furniture upholstered in vibrant silks and accented with gold and silver. Pleated draperies embellish walls along with muraled paintings."

"And heaven to walk on floor coverings with colourful designs adorning every room," the women swooned.

Folly, to be sure! Folklore! Fabrications; mere stories growing with each new telling. I did not believe any of it, yet the idea of such extravagance intrigued me. I wished to visit the place to see for myself. Halicarnassus lay eleven parasangs southwest of Labraunda. I set out at first light and, upon advice from my host, utilized the little-known forest route to bypass congestion in the town of Mylasa. The following day is when the Dathaba appeared.

Chapter 7

Enduring the Dathaba

Struggling to ignore the tight leather straps cutting into my wrists, I mentally prepared a legal defence – if granted such an opportunity. Bewildered, the lone infraction I imagined warranting my arrest might be trespassing on the king's land. With no signs posted, I hoped to receive leniency. Unfortunately, by refusing all conversation, my straight-faced captors made understanding the severity of my situation impossible. They gave no hint of my crime and spurned my inquiries about our destination with aloof dismissal.

Depending on their accusations, I could lose an ear or two – perhaps my nose. I tried visualising life with one ear. I might manage a productive life after losing an ear, but heaven help me if I lost my nose. Castration was another loss that came to mind. And such horrors were the kinder forms of punishment. Persians had at their disposal any number of slow, painful, and altogether horrible methods of execution – with political prisoners receiving the worst possible deaths.

Imagine this gruelling death: the Tower of Ash. A tower, 30 cubits high, filled with fine ash powder and revolving wheels used for churning noxious clouds of choking dust. Here is how it works. After being dragged up steps to the top of the tower, the condemned stands on a drop door. The executioner operates a lever that opens the door, haplessly dropping the condemned into the ash heap below. The worst part, most victims survive the soft landing. Death comes when the executioner orders the 'turning of the wheels'. Large rotating wheels roil up lethal clouds of powdery ash to suffocate the conspirator as he chokes and gasps for air. Death in the Tower of Ash negates the right to a proper burial.

Gross disfigurement or agonising torture, both prospects seemed equally demoralising. Consoling myself, I prayed Moses' tribal blessing to us Benjaminite's, 'May the beloved of the Lord rest secure. May Yahweh protect him all day, for the one the Lord loves rests safely between His shoulders.' After praying it, I prayed it again.

As the landscape changed from rock-strewn paths, I kept a better pace on the softer trails padded with pine needles. Shaded woods filled with honeybees and flitting nuthatch smelled of wildflowers and herbs. Dark purplish pinecones littered the ground, and I mindlessly entertained myself by squishing them beneath my sandals.

Anticipating a brief rest somewhere along the way, I needed to stop for food or a drink of water. Still, the unrelenting soldiers pushed onward, traipsing through the hill country, ignoring gurgling brooks hidden in the dense floral undergrowth. I wanted to argue, "Summer foliage receives water; I deserve at least the courtesy bestowed to a crocus or a crambe." But, while considering this a logical argument, I remained silent, anticipating their callous response.

Compensating for my thirst, each time we encountered a cold spring trickling across our path, I bent forward and splashed my feet, hoping for even a drop of water to land in my mouth. My diminishing strength, hunger, thirst, and fatigue did nothing to appease the Dathaba. Did no one require relieving themselves? I sure did!

The shade canopy of tall trees eased my discomfort by offering a reprieve from the oppressive heat. After entering the lowlands, the scenery changed into stumpy evergreen shrubs or the occasional hornbeam, myrtle, and some arbutus trees. Losing our canopy of shade had no visible effect on the Dathaba. The giant showed no reaction to the warming temperatures and never slowed his pace. Despite the sweat dripping down my face, I matched his stony demeanour and refused to react to the insufferable heat. *Hey, Persian Goon! Look at me!* I said to myself. *Ah, I feel cool as a cucumber.*

As we dropped in elevation, a pungent odour of rich dark soil rose from the fertile valleys that stretched like giant fingers, straining toward the blue waters of the Aegean Sea. We pushed through groves of olive and almond trees, passing branches heavily laden with pods not yet ripened for harvest. Vineyards of Shiraz grapes abounded, and small farms grew black cumin, emmer wheat, and barley.

Vigilant shepherds and goatherders, armed with swords and spears, studied us with suspicion as we skirted their pastures. The quirky beasts looked like nothing I had seen before. Thick-bodied Israelite sheep have long legs and produce a decent amount of meat; a large family would barely find a full meal eating one of the slight Persian ewes I observed grazing in the meadow.

Curious looking goats grazed among the sheep. I later learned these floppy-eared creatures were Angora goats with highly prized fleeces. The creamy white ringlets of luxurious mohair fibre were popular commodities highly coveted by royalty and aristocrats. The twists of soft wool also fetched a handsome profit for merchandisers in the dye industry.

Gradually, meadow-filled land transformed into fields rife with lemon and lime orchards, figs, walnuts, peaches, and apricots. The sweetness of their bouquet pooled around me, reminding me of my hunger. Our intrusion through trees and myrtle brush roused nesting birds. At this point, I knew the Dathaba were not human; they were creatures visiting Earth from one of the five planets. Human beings do not stride along oblivious to a fiasco of rebuking fowl screeching half a span above their heads.

Mimicking stony Goliath, I tried giving no heed to the onslaught of air assaults lofted against us by annoyed fowl, but I could not manage it. Ducking and dipping, I covered my head with my bound hands, protecting myself against the swarm of angry warblers filling the sky, scolding our rude presence by swooping and squawking us away from their nests.

I was exhausted by this time, parched, and done in, yet we began climbing again. Marble signposts displaying a bust of the district's ruling satrap began appearing – an indication our destination was near. By the time the Dathaba prodded me up the final hill, shadows had grown long, and the temperature was favourable. Cresting the ridge top brought a gust of air blowing off the Aegean, whooshing across my body, cooling my skin, and filling my nostrils with the freshness of the sea. From such a height, I observed white flecks skipping across the dazzling blue sea, resounding with the bickering caws of contending seagulls. Sails fluttered as scores of fishers cast nets over the side of their boats and laboured in their weighty hauls. Pelicans swooped past them, trying for an easy meal. Beyond, streamlined and graceful dolphins manoeuvred their way through the water.

On a distant hill top, I noticed rows of impressive stone windmills lining the cliff in such a way as to catch coastal airstreams. On another hill, sat a Greek-style theatre built entirely of stone. The multi-tiered seating swept around a circular slope and melded into a grand platform of marble slab directly in front of a large orchestra platform. In the middle section of seats were two thrones, grand chairs no doubt to ensure an unobstructed view for the king and queen. Seeing these thrones made me recall the warnings I had been given about the satrap's unfairness. "Steer clear of the king. He governs the district with punitive judgment." But presently, I had enough troubles to manage and wished to avoid even the slightest glimpse of these sovereigns.

From the ridgetop, I cast my eyes on the city below; the sight took my breath away. Dazzling in brilliance and splendour lay a glistening city cradled between the hills as if burrowed in the arms of glory: gilded Halicarnassus! One glance at that enchanting kingdom by the sea told me the stories I had heard failed to capture the city's full elegance. Halicarnassus stretched across a broad wooded peninsula where scores of vessels sheltered in a busy harbour bordered by glossy buildings clasped in rays of shimmering sunlight reminiscent of golden halos. The glistening pride of the Aegean, this wealthy metropolis of King Mausolus and Queen Artemisia, was a city graced by polished white structures capped with red tile roofs, immaculately nestled in a botanical garden facing the bluest water on Earth. Cresting that hilltop and beholding Halicarnassus for the first time remains among my fondest memories.

Forgetting my restraints, I gazed at my captor with an awed gawp. Slicing his calloused finger in mocking jest across his throat, the glare of a surly-faced brute met the silly grin of an awestruck boy. I broke eye contact straightaway, squared my shoulders, and acted unmoved by the captivating new world stretching before me.

While searching for Caleb, I never anticipated arriving in the acclaimed city of Halicarnassus as a tethered prisoner under arrest by the Imperial Guard. Yet, it all happened just as I have said.

Chapter 8

The Capital City, Halicarnassus

As we descended into the city, the air became fragrant, sweet like a bouquet. This particular woodland path took us to the city's Mylasa Gate, where stunning lilac and bougainvillea trees lined the roadway. Walking among the clusters of pink and purple blossoms felt like a noble dignitary entering the city beneath a ceremonial canopy of colour – until the cloying aroma of lilac made my head swim.

Suspicious sentries peered at us from behind their tower embrasures as we neared the checkpoint. The thick wall encircling Halicarnassus supported fortified watchtowers woven into the composition of stonework. Massive bronze and oak gates restricted entrance to one of six garrisoned access points. Each access routed visitors through an ingress station where a superintendent questioned foreigners about their business, length of stay, and reason for visiting Halicarnassus.

On recognising the Dathaba, gatekeepers waved Goliath onto the footbridge, over the moat, and through the gate. The limestone blocks forming the vaulted passageway created an echo, making it sound like a battery of soldiers was about to emerge. Something happened inside that musty corridor of the Mylasa Gate. I was transported to a distant realm. Somewhere between the entrance and the exit, I entered a different world - a celestial estate, bounteous and as affluent as a luxuriant vine laden with desirable fruit.

We made our way to a broad avenue paved with smooth white stone. Achaemenid Street, named after the Persian Royal Dynasty, was the main thoroughfare running through the town centre. Halicarnassus was laid out in a grid zone, segregating the town according to administrative, public, religious, and residential usage. Even though no two structures were alike, Greek styles coordinated with other architectural themes, resulting in an elegant-looking town with a stylish flair..

Narrow streets, charming and curved, wound in and out of residential areas filled with impressive homes, each sturdy built with support beams of solid timber and limestone walls overlaid with white marble or decorative brickwork. Rounded roofs embellished with painted tiles covered living spaces and large porches.

Water flowed abundantly through the Qanat system – a most impressive Persian invention for bringing groundwater to the surface and then channelling it through an underground tunnel. Clay pipes ushered freshwater to gardens and ponds or into homes for drinking, therapeutic pools, and private baths. In addition, the network of underground pipes kept the city clean and odour-free. All these comforts and luxuries made it apparent why highborn nobles and kings chose Halicarnassus as a preferred holiday spot.

We passed unnoticed behind planters labouring in the central parádeisos. Gardeners adorning tiered beds around the commons area knelt beside handcarts filled with tools for pruning and raking and spades for planting shoots and seedlings. Other workers cleaned freshwater pools and cleared debris from elaborate cascades.

During the empire's heyday, ostentatious gardens were a Persian lifestyle. Properties with meticulously cultivated grounds lent status and signified nobility. Affluent cities throughout the empire prided themselves on landscape architecture by showcasing one-of-a-kind horticultural displays. The gardeners' rallying cry was, 'Go one better!' In other words, Persians everywhere intended to outmatch and outclass King Nebuchadnezzar's legendary Hanging Gardens of Babylon. Flashy gardens of class wittingly delivered a condescending slap to the ungodly Babylonians.

In ancient times, Royal Hanging Gardens – the pride and showpiece of the mighty Babylonian World Empire – symbolised the determination of an ascending people. Rising from the sand of a sterile desert, flourishing under a scorching sun, they grew a world-famous botanical parkland. This marvel symbolized the scant nation's rise to absolute power, with the garden becoming an icon of ascension – from scavengers of parched ground to masters of world supremacy.

I earlier mentioned Babylon; the harsh and undefeatable owner of the world. Yet today, Persia owns that world. How did that happen? Cyrus.

Using exceptional prowess and perfect timing, General Cyrus engineered a sneak attack on the capital of Babylon by diverting the aqueducts, allowing his army to slip under the walls and move unnoticed into the city. In a single night, the entire Babylonian Empire collapsed. This fortuitous annihilation gave birth to the kingdom of Persia. General Cyrus earned the eternal name King Cyrus the Great of Persia, King of Kings, and Owner of the World for his ingenuity and stealth.

That clever takedown accounts for Persia's audacity and arrogance in most things, including populating the modern world with tiered botanical wonders. 'Go one better' diminishes the achievements of Babylonian inferiors by suggesting it took the Persians to refine and perfect the art of gardening and all that goes with it.

Not to be outdone, Halicarnassus held her own when it came to floricultural accomplishments. Dazzling arrangements of vibrant blooms and ivy tendrils spilled from windowsills. Fragrant jasmine and wisteria vines crept along walls and partitions or overflowed from balconies. Bougainvillea wrapped porticos and covered building fronts in red, pink, and purple blossoms. The city was a rainbow of colour woven with blossoms decorating their homes, businesses, estates, and avenues.

Tiered flowerbeds, rising and expanding in dimension, alternated ornamental designs with varying arrays of multi-coloured blooms interspersed among the rows of redbud trees, pink oleander, and hydrangea bushes outlining both sides of Achaemenid Street. Decorative grasses highlighted landscaped waterfalls channelling water through angled slopes into rock-lined ponds filled with heart-shaped leaves and orangish-red lilies. Indeed, Halicarnassus was a city in bloom.

Most breathtaking about Halicarnassus was the way inbound rays of sunlight ricocheted off polished marble buildings, scattering shafts of radiant light, immersing the city in the brilliance of an incandescent sheen. This luminosity merging with a deep blue sea nestled between the forested arms of distant mountain peaks earned Halicarnassus royal honours and legendary distinction for her unsurpassed beauty.

Smartly dressed people mingling throughout the squares visited with friends beneath shaded magnolia trees or sat together on marble benches near the sundial by the Spring of Salmacis. Distant calls from merchants advertised their imported wares while soft sounds of the lyre, tambourine, and harp accompanied singers worshiping in nearby temples.

The sight of armed Dathaba marching a tethered felon through town caused folks to stop and stare. My face melted with embarrassment as conversations abruptly ended, followed by an uneasy hush where gawking citizens stood motionless, wide eyed, and curious. Heads swivelled in unison as we passed, and when out of earshot, they huddled together, no doubt with discussions about my criminal-looking facial features.

Continuing through town, I noticed an unkempt, sparsely wooded knoll of imposing size dominating the middle of the city, yet without buildings or structures. *Strange*, I thought. *Why build a lavish city and leave the scar of undeveloped acreage looking as conspicuous as a blemish on flawless skin?*

Navigating a stepped path, guards descended, dragging me into a busy agora, the city's main convergence point. A public sign hung over the entrance. We passed under in a hurry, but I managed to read the first sentence: 'Notice of City Law: public debates, speeches, political announcements, and peaceful demonstrations shall remain limited to the Stoa of Aegea'.

The noisy agora, lined with fancy vendor booths and wooden market stalls, tortured me with intoxicating aromas of roasting vegetables and baking bread. Haggling customers and harried people scurried chaotically throughout the square causing Goliath to rein in on my leash, keeping me away from citizens and their booths, primarily booths selling blade works.

He also kept me away from a cluster of tables cordoned off and reserved for conducting business. Brokers watched while record keepers wrote agreements, then servants poured hot wax for imprinting stamps bearing a legal signature to finalise the deal.

Energetic music near a pottery booth contributed to the frantic mood of buying and selling. The continued fragrance of steaming food caused my stomach to growl wildly with hunger.

More stares followed as we walked through the agora. Cautious citizens gawked and glared, whispering their suspicions concerning the notorious prisoner. I wanted to scream my innocence but ignored their wary glances by looking at the ground. My ears, glowing red with embarrassment, gave away my shame.

Considering my filth-crusted condition, I found no fault with the fine citizens of Halicarnassus; I would stare at such a sight myself: grubby and dirty in threadbare clothes, dry, cracked lips, knuckles bleeding, scraps on my knees, and streaks of blood hardened down both shins. The sap repair loosened on my sandal, causing a flapping noise each time I stepped. And I stank. Raising tethered hands to preen my snarled hair revealed chalky wet circles under my arms. Embarrassed by my state, I kept my elbows tight against my sides and looked at the ground.

With whispers from the agora behind us, we descended another flight of stairs following a path along the waterfront. Unaffected by our passage, dockworkers concentrated on their duties and strenuous tasks. I saw one worker toss a freshly severed fish head into a collection of eager cats. Ferocious screeches and sharp yowls accompanied an explosion of claws and airborne fur, allowing a line of mice to scurry unnoticed toward several morsels of spilled grain.

When I arrived in Halicarnassus, modernisation of the ancient settlement was recent – completed within the last decade. I later learned about Mausolus relocated the capital from Mylasa to Halicarnassus because of the protective geographic features and to have access to the sea.

During Artaxerxes' time, the world's network of sea routes was smaller than today; ships mostly steered from Egypt to ports along the Mediterranean coast, then westward to Cyprus and Rhodes. Logistically, Halicarnassus made a convenient stop before vessels continued to Ephesus, Ilion, and the Black Sea. The problem was that large merchant vessels could not navigate the shallow marina of Halicarnassus, so real progress bypassed the city.

Mausolus commissioned a substantial deepening of the inlet and enticed seafaring traders by redesigning the primitive harbour into one of the most advanced ports of the era. As a result, Halicarnassus burst onto the world scene as a major commercial hub. Besides building a seawall with sweeping arms capable of sealing the channel entrance, Mausolus created a double harbour by combining the natural features of the shoreline with silt dredged from the seafloor. Merchant ship access was limited to the outer marina. This area, known as the Commercial Harbour, had newly built wharves well positioned to accommodate easy loading and unloading of cargo.

Then, an additional hedge of silt formed the interior marina, called the Naval Harbour, which held military vessels. These warships docked in parallel columns for quick mobilisation of troops.

The popular Stoa of Aegea overlooked the harbour area. This ornate porch, painted in bright colours with an arched roof supported by sturdy columns, was a popular haven for meeting friends, garnering local news, sharing political opinions, or discussing weighty topics with orators and philosophers.

The palace was built on Zephyria Island – Zephyria was the settlement's original name. This palatial fortress, covered with tiles and polished stucco, glistened like radiant light from heaven. Constructed to capitalise on panoramic views, its strategic position allowed for easy monitoring of the sea, harbour activities, and events in the Stoa of Aegea.

Mausolus used dredged silt to form a land bridge connecting the island to the city. In addition, he built a private marina with a secret passageway in case a hasty escape became necessary.

The clam-shaped city hugged the marina and included a neck of land extending on either side. I can best explain this layout if you imagine a bull with two horns protruding from its skull. One horn held the palace estate. The main town was spread out along the bull's forehead; this includes the courthouse, several governmental offices, the stoa, and the agora. Residential structures, the public garden, and the commons area filled the area toward the bull's neck. The neglected hill I called a blemish was also in this area. The other horn held the citadel, barracks, arsenal, water clock, and spring. Finally, the famous double-harbour filled the space between the horns and opened into the Aegean Sea.

The Dathaba had marched me through much of the city, and when we reached the waterfront, I did not think there was anywhere else to go, yet they continued prodding me. Then I understood! My stomach flipped with nausea! They were taking me to the Naval Harbour!

This band of militants had not arrested me for some infraction of the law; they had kidnapped me. They planned to castrate me and then brand me as a slave to serve as an oarsman aboard a Persian fighting ship or, worse, hard labour on a penal island. My grief-stricken parents would never learn of my demise. Until the day they died, they would be haunted, wondering about my fate. I predicted a grievous conclusion to my earthly existence was drawing near.

Surveying available options, I began formulating my chances of a death-defying escape, but at that moment, the Dathaba turned into a narrow aisle. Instead of taking me to the Naval Harbour, they marched into the Enclosure of the Guard directly behind the courthouse. We stopped.

Chapter 9

My Day in Court

A pleasant arrangement of shrubs and colourful flowers surrounding the polished white marble walls of the classical-style courthouse made the place look innocent enough. Artistically positioned fountains gurgling among the gardens soothed like a lullaby. Painted columns supported an arched roof of red tiles shading a semi-circular staircase accessible from three directions. The atmosphere inside the courthouse was dramatically different, though. Within those walls, people's lives hung in the balance with pronouncements and edicts deciding their fate. And now, I was to be counted among their number.

A small army of soldiers patrolled the halls and scrutinised visitors; two guards stood beside the heavy oak doors leading into the courtroom. The continuous hallway, wrapping three sides of the building, had ingress coves opening into private offices used by the city's most prominent figureheads and chief officials. At the end of the hallway, a private office and lavish apartment were reserved for the special inspector when he came for a routine visit. The most trusted eyes and ears of the Shahanshah, the Great King Artaxerxes III, the special inspector travelled throughout the realm, checking on conditions in each satrapy along with the imperial vassals managing them.

Respected guests, honoured visitors, and valued staff entered the courthouse through the welcoming front doors. But not me. Prisoners entered from the back courtyard through a narrow passageway between steep stone walls leading to a guarded entrance. Laws and Persian statutes were etched into marble plaques and carved around the doorpost supporting an iron door. Once inside, murals painted on both sides of the hallway showed the district satraps on their judgment thrones. A guard ushered me through another iron gate and coldly deposited me in a holding area lined with dingy booths.

After a brief wait, the same guard reappeared and roughly escorted me from the prisoner block, through another gate, and into the stylish, brightly lit courtroom, smelling sweet and musky like saffron incense.

Curious spectators had already filled every seat in the legislative hall by the time the guard shoved me forward and pushed me into a kneeling position in front of an emblem tiled into the marble floor. The symbol, a pair of rising branches, encircled a muscular lion holding a curved sword in his right paw. A blazing sun rose behind. I guessed the sign represented a Persian god or perhaps signified the authority of the king.

Creative weaving and artwork filled this courtroom revealing an accumulation of cultural identities – ostrich plumes of gold from Egypt, ivory fans carved with the standard of Cyrus, and tapestries from the Orient. A sweeping Faravahar covered one entire wall; on another were murals and golden reliefs of Mesopotamian ziggurats.

Marble columns topped with ornate capitals supported a prestigious vaulted ceiling of cedar panels outlined with gold trim. Expertly painted in garish colours, the panels depicted compelling scenes of famous battles, noble kings, and significant events in Caria's history. Inert in stone, Grecian deities stood guard at the front of the room.

More gods and idols, I thought. Ho, to be sure, numerous gods occupied temples and homes throughout the empire, all taking on different forms and religious rituals. The harsh gods reigned over their subjects with a taste for blood. Many governed in silence, while others contented themselves with regular offerings of grain or votive coins. The many different idols confused me. To this day, I cannot remember which gods possessed which capabilities and who worshiped whom.

We Jews worship a single God who exists as the invisible Almighty One, Yahweh. He is neither wood nor stone. Instead, he is our trustworthy source of blessings now and for future generations. Yahweh is the Creator of everything, including Persia. His most endearing characteristic is the love he has for flawed humanity and his willingness to forgive transgressions, restoring the broken-hearted when they pray the prayer of King David: 'O God of unfailing love, cleanse me from my sins. Wash away all my iniquity, cleansing me with hyssop so I may be joyous once again. According to your tender compassion, blot out my transgressions so I may rejoice again in gladness.'

From my kneeling position, I noticed two goddesses of marble posed on pedestals at the front of the courtroom. I recognised Themis because she held a set of balanced scales indicating divine law. The other was Dikē, the Greek goddess of justice and fair judgments.

Ample seating for spectators was provided by semi-circular rows of benches that faced carpeted steps ascending to the spacious platform holding two extraordinary thrones. Each was built of acacia wood, trimmed in white ivory, and accentuated with red and green rubies ornamenting silver side panels. Side by side, their chairs touched feet – the clawed feet of a lion – after which the legs curved away before reconnecting with lion-headed armrests. A lover's knot blended the two thrones into one, putting the king's armrest on the queen's side and the queen's armrest on the king's side. Tassels of golden thread dangled from cushioned seats and overhead stretched a silk canopy embroidered with the same lion and sun emblem as on the floor. Behind the thrones, folds of colourful silk draperies hung from rods suspended between vertical marble pillars.

On these lavish thrones sat King Mausolus and his wife, Queen Artemisia II – satraps of Caria, imperial vassals to the King of Kings, governors of the district. Armed guards remained on either side of me, and four surly-looking guards monitoring the audience stood behind the imperial couple. On the carpet beside the queen's throne sat a long-haired cat licking his front paw and then rubbing it across his face and around his ears. Off to the side were official record keepers preparing their papyrus and ink.

If the satraps required refreshment during the proceedings, an official cupbearer stood nearby, holding a golden rhyton ornamented with the forefront of a rearing Nisaean stallion. Court officials wore a pleated cap with a long, impressive robe tied at the waist.

Also present was the ring bearer, a Zoroastrian priest commissioned to safeguard the satrap's official signet ring. The priest's role was supervisory, ensuring that dual rulership of the district remained a joint effort, not a solo venture. In addition, he presided as a neutral party during all bureaucratic functions. After the satraps jointly sealed a document or decree, the ring returned to a protective location with the Zoroastrian.

I wished to inspect every inch of that fascinating legislative chamber, but one of the guards beside me jabbed me in the back and snarled, "Head down! Eyes down! And keep your murderous hands hidden behind your back!" He reinforced his instructions with a crude description of the severe bodily harm he intended to inflict if I disobeyed. I was tired of being roughed up by these people but complied by staring at the ferocious lion on the floor.

To open the proceedings, official translators began speaking in different languages – Akkadian, Arabic, Egyptian, Macedonian, Attic Greek, and a variation of broken Hebrew. Fearing their tactic was a possible test, I remained silent until addressed in my native Aramaic tongue.

After establishing a common language, King Mausolus, speaking Carian through an interpreter, hurled a barrage of questions at me. His deep voice reverberated effortlessly to the back of the room. "Do you admit to passing through Phrygia?"

Another irritating jab in the back hurried my answer. "Yes, my Lord, after exiting the Cilician Gates. But not myself alone. The entire caravan travelled the mesa near the Lycus River; we passed through the area quickly, within a few days."

"Tell me of Mithridates! Did you confer with him while you rested? Has he sent you here?"

"My Lord, I know of no such man."

"Perhaps you work as an accomplice, hired by Araissis, the conspirator? Has my old enemy sought vengeance against me by attacking my wife?"

Exasperated with the proceedings and her husband's line of questioning, Queen Artemisia pulled a dagger from the folds of her throne and then sprang to her feet. Alarm rippled through the courtroom. *So this is it,* I thought; *my death is imminent right here, right now. Death by dagger – death by a stunningly beautiful woman with a jewelled dagger, no less.*

"Give the boy a weapon!" Then, motioning, she held out her dagger to the guard.

Bowing while accepting the jewelled blade from her hand, the soldier leaped off the carpeted steps, forcibly jerked me to my feet by one arm, and handed me the blade. A stampede of wild horses thundered through my chest as I crudely fumbled with the knife.

"Boy!" she yelled. "Kill my guard!"

This woman terrified me worse than Goliath. The room spun in a woozy light, and my voice cracked. "How, ah…"

She screamed, "Do it! Kill him, or he will kill you!"

Appearing glad for the excitement, the guard beckoned me to stab him. Therefore I did. Positioning the dagger in my hand, I raised the blade above my head and charged. Without the slightest effort, he straight-armed me, holding me off with one hand over my face. I hoped to stab his arm by swinging the knife around but bungled the move and dropped the weapon at such an awkward angle it skittered across the marble floor. The entire courtroom erupted in laughter. The guard released my face, collected the weapon, returned to the platform, and presented the queen with her dagger while bowing low.

Impatient, she spat, "Enough! He was not involved. Just look at him! He is just a clumsy boy. I fear this child's biggest threat is stabbing himself in the foot."

Ho, to be sure, her ridicule cut deep as gales of laughter again filled the room. My ears burned red with embarrassment.

"Ask him his business in Halicarnassus," she demanded.

Respecting the imperial couple and the head attached to my shoulders, I timidly explained that my parents, Zuriel and Ruth, lived in the Land Beyond the River – the official Persian name for Judah was the Satrapy Eber-Nari. Then, I related how they dispatched me to locate my brother Caleb. After traveling a long distance and making inquiries in every city, I learned he might have received a commission to Halicarnassus.

Through the interpreter, the queen asked why I sought my brother. "Yibbum," I said.

"Infidel! Explain yourself!" The unexpected outburst of indignation came from an elderly court usher.

Flicking her hand, the queen indicated displeasure. The sudden flash of annoyance sent an array of golden bracelets clattering down her arm, piling against her wrist. Spooked by this sudden movement, the preening cat bounded onto the queen's lap. After calming her furry companion with long smooth strokes, Artemisia motioned me to continue.

The sheer terror of this ordeal sent my voice into a quiver. And I did not want to humiliate myself further, so I fought hard to hold back the tears. "According to our Hebrew beliefs, when a man dies before producing a child, his succeeding brother must marry the widow, thereby producing an heir for the deceased."

Bypassing the mediator, the queen spoke directly to me using Aramaic. "You have lost a brother?"

Waiting for a wave of grief to wash past, I answered. "Yes, my Queen. Sakeri, my older brother, died in an accident while working on a portion of Jerusalem's outer wall."

"A stonemason?" The king asked me directly, choosing to forego the protocol of the mediator.

"Indeed, my King. My family has worked as stonemasons in the land of Israel ever since the great Persian King Cyrus personally commissioned them to oversee the restoration of Jerusalem after its destruction by the barbarians of Babylon." I hoped bringing up an enemy in common might divert some of their ire away from me.

Taking a quick gulp of air, I continued. "When I became old enough, I began an apprenticeship under my brother, Sakeri. My grandfather says our family's masonry occupation began at the building of the great pyramids of Egypt, making us the reason they still stand."

Revealing some of my family's eccentricity to an imperial official embarrassed me, but at least people in the courtroom laughed. Relieved by the reprieve from the king's harsh interrogation, I dared a glance, half expecting a stiff jab in the back.

Ho, to be sure, grand King Mausolus looked magnificent, poised as a distinguished ruler of apparent nobility and authority. He was the first king this trifling boy from the land of Israel had ever seen.

Meeting an actual king astounded me; Mausolus acted entertained by my boyish gawp. The king possessed a deportment overwhelming the throne upon which he sat. His dark brown body, heavy-built with broad shoulders, revealed athletic arms bulging beneath the loose hanging sleeves of his long purple robe. His saffron-coloured tunic, trimmed in purple braids and sewn snug across his muscular chest, hung long to his knees – the Persian custom for nobility.

Golden thread embroidered designs on his dark brown trousers complemented ginger-coloured stockings, and leather shoes – tapered at the toe – were laced tight and tied at the ankles. His array of royal finery included a bejewelled diadem resting atop thick waves of trimmed black hair. Instead of wearing a false beard, he grew whiskers – a thick moustache with a beard trimmed tight against his chin, accentuating fleshy lips and a sharp jawline.

Beneath a pair of wilful eyebrows glistened distinctive eyes, bluer than any eyes I had ever seen! Royal adorners artistically enhanced them by applying black cosmetics to broaden and highlight their unusual sapphire colour. Around his neck, a collar of twisted gold mingled with thin braided chains. Also, thick bands of gold clasped both wrists.

As a display of wealth, a golden loop pierced his right ear, and on the left side of his girdle, he wore a jewelled sheath from which protruded the cross-bar of a dagger. His strong hands resting on his knees showed adorners had clipped and shaped his fingernails. He wore several rings, including his official bronze signet ring.

Sitting beside him was the lovely Queen Artemisia II. I forgave her earlier humiliation of me once I beheld her seductive beauty.

Makeda! I thought,

You may remember Makeda, the Arabian beauty from the desert kingdom of Sheba who profoundly enchanted Israel's King Solomon. As a child, I heard stories about her and dreamed of someday meeting such a woman. But the instant I laid eyes on the satrap queen of Caria, Makeda vanished from my thoughts. Sitting before me was the most splendid-looking woman I had ever seen, a beauty radiating elegance and grace. That was the day Queen Artemisia II captured my hapless young heart – it was love at first sight.

Sparkling eyes, dancing beneath arched brows, were enhanced with delicate black cosmetics and applications of violet shade. Plump lips, the colour of pomegranate, held a mysterious grin, and that soft, smooth skin glistening with oil was brown as a walnut at harvest time. Gracing the woman's lovely neck was a collar of purple gemstones gathered by chains of gold to a central tear-drop pendant.

The luxurious white fabric of her dress was painted in violet designs, delicately accentuating the neckline of her sleeveless gown. A matching sash of violet silk wrapped her tiny waist, and a robe of royal purple draped her arms. At her hip, she wore a jewelled sheath housing her bronze-handled akinaka – a short sword used by many Persians at that time.

Bejewelled and ornamented from head to toe, she wore a string of pearls woven into the dazzling braids of her thick dark hair. Jewelled rings adorned her slender fingers. Bracelets decorated her willowy arms, and anklets of pearl rested above the petite sandals slipped onto her lovely, manicured feet.

Halting the laughter, King Mausolus resumed control of the courtroom. "Do you deny all knowledge of the recent attack against the queen?"

Returning my eyes to the yellow sun, I focused on its blaze glowing behind the warrior lion. "I have no reason to harm the queen or any person. Today is my first time in Halicarnassus, and I know nothing of your people or the issues surrounding your district."

"My men found you hiding in the hillside with blood-soaked linen, evidence of a wound."

Choosing my words with the utmost caution, I explained the precise details of my night in the wilderness.

"Describe this man!" King Mausolus demanded.

"He stood half a span taller than me, was clean-shaven and fair complected with a body hard-built and muscular. He carried a rounded shield with a scoop out of the top, looking like a giant creature had helped himself to a bite.

"A broad belt, patterned with yellow and blue ikat, wrapped his flax-linen shirt; he wore the waist-hem tucked inside a grey thigh-length skirt lined with red cloth inside the pleats. A band of yellow trim rounded the edge of his felt cap, which rose into an elongated cone and tilted toward the brim." I demonstrated the tilt.

"A Thracian peltast!" Mausolus appeared thunderstruck.

"Reddish hair protruded from under the cap, scraggly over his ears and long on the back of his neck."

Alarmed by this new information, the king leaned forward on his throne. "A Thracian peltast and a reddish! To be sure, scholars have long theorised that the reddish are men of bad character, but this man sounds like a hireling from the northern realm. That is preposterous! The idea makes no sense. Continue at once!"

"He wore sturdy traveling shoes of quality leather. Maybe goat or fawn-skin. A long black cloak fastened with an acorn shaped broach gathered over his shoulder. Oh yes, that was another thing, his shoulder. Beneath the skin on his right shoulder, I noticed an ink drawing."

"What words did he speak?" he asked.

"No words, my Lord. Events occurred in haste, and he fell unconscious before speaking. In his delirium, he mumbled indistinct words."

"What else?"

I had to think of something, so I blurted out, "His dagger! He had no weapons with him other than the knife he brandished. After he fainted, I used the blade to scorch a deep wound in his calf but returned it to the sheath – which was leather and painted with a symbol resembling the sun. The curved blade, the span of a man's hand, had a beak at the end."

Still fearful, I qualified my description. "I cannot be certain about the sheath, my Lord; maybe not an image of the sun; maybe an icon of a starburst."

"Do you swear you have told me the truth and revealed every detail?" the king asked me.

"I swear, as the Lord lives, I studied him with much attention," I told him.

"No doubt someone recruited this man," Mausolus said, "but why send a mercenary peltast to kill somebody in Halicarnassus, let alone the queen?" King Mausolus became suspicious and flashed a questioning glance toward his wife, but I noticed she averted her eyes and acted bored with his concerns.

Turning to face me – the condemned – the court usher belted the verdict using his best governmental monotone. "Ethan, son of Zuriel, of the Satrapy Eber-Nari in the land of Israel, this court finds you innocent on all charges."

Closing my eyes, I exhaled, desperately trying to stifle an involuntary tide of giddy laughter. Not only was I going to live, but I was also free to leave. A broad grin spread across my face

King Mausolus added, "My custodian will show you to your quarters for the evening, but we have more business to discuss. I will send someone to fetch you in the morning."

A strike to the gong sent vibrations across the marble floor and up through the soles of my feet. The imperial couple rose in unison, exiting the gallery through long drapes hanging behind their thrones.

With the court adjourned, I wanted to run out of that room and enjoy my rights as a free man. But when I turned to leave, Goliath stepped in front of me to block my path. He stared down at me with the most deadly Philistine snarl. Perhaps the fellow misunderstood King Mausolus had exonerated me! Freed me! I was no longer a doleful prisoner. Goliath broke out in a loud hoot of laughter and lifted me off my feet, embracing me like I was a doll sewn of rags. Then, slapping me on the back with fondness, he said, "Come."

Chapter 10

Return to Court

Exhausted and no longer caring about anything, I followed Goliath in docile submission as he escorted me through a grassy courtyard strewn with children's toys and onto what appeared to be a training area with climbing walls, wooden figures, and a sandpit. A long row of the servants' quarters ran parallel to the military barracks, and at the end were guest huts. That is where we stopped. Goliath opened the door and motioned me through. Drained from the day's events, I headed straight for the luxurious bed covered with silken blankets, dropped face first in a crumpled heap, and fell asleep.

I awoke in the same position the following morning when something roused me. My tired brain tried focusing. It sounded like giggling, more like the high-pitched twitter of an embarrassed girl.

The unmistakable chortle reminded me of my younger sisters back home tittering while attempting to sneak up behind me. Then, barely able to open my eyes, I observed something colourful in the middle of the room, maybe a dress – yellow and orange, something else apricot- coloured.

As my eyes adjusted, I saw a young maiden holding a tray of food. Glossy apricot-coloured sashes hung from her waist, and a long dark braid woven with orange silk draped attractively over her shoulder. Her smile revealed a row of straight white teeth. Attempting to return the polite gesture, I managed a faint smile. Her pretty face reddened, and my head flopped back onto the bed.

Hours later, I awoke again to find a tray of food on the side table, but no twittering girl. Perhaps she lived in my dreams, yet someone had left me a meal. Wasting no time deciphering the foreign cuisine, I broke off pieces of flatbread and scooped cold grains with bits of spiced fruit into my mouth. I stopped long enough to guzzle mulberry water, then wolfed down every morsel. Wishing for another bowl, I sat on the edge of my bed, unsure what to do. A moment later, the door flew open – I jumped! Goliath stood at the entrance blocking inbound light with his massive frame.

Sparsely dressed in trousers and sandals, visible scars across his torso indicated he survived several vicious combat injuries. Thin wisps of hair lay like slivers across the top of his bald head. Above his ears, a heavy grey fringe fanned into voluminous waves of black and grey hair reaching the back of his neck. This time he was beardless. That made sense since the Special Forces Militia wore false beards instead of growing whiskers. This prevented the enemy from grabbing a tuft of beard with one hand and slaying with the other. With no beard in the way, I noticed his broad, full lips covered a large portion of his lower face, but considering his immense head and jaw, the spread of his mouth complemented the size of his face.

Goliath motioned for me to follow. Suspicious of his intentions, I unwillingly trailed behind. Opening a door, he directed me inside. With tentative steps, I entered the room – a bathhouse! Goliath motioned me toward a pool of water and left. Out of place and intimidated, I focused on the door while peeling off drab and worn-out Hebrew linens.

Lowering my stiff, grimy body into a pool of warm water made it clear why Persians are infatuated with their baths. With pure delight, I sank deeper and deeper, splashing balmy water over my dry, dusty skin, soothing cuts and bruises on my buttocks, still aching with welts. Sinking beneath the surface, I held my breath as long as possible before popping up and inhaling gulps of steamy air. Dipping and plunging, slipping and sliding, I splashed and floated carefree.

Bars of soap lay on a marble ledge. I sniffed each one. Their sweetness overwhelmed me. Floating in the warm pool, I tried visualising the giant Goliath sitting neck deep in warm water, scrubbing his muscular physique in the syrupy fragrance of flowers. Surely not! I declined the actual washing of my skin with soap, perhaps another time.

Goliath abruptly stepped into the room, again startling me. This guy scared the wits out of me! As I flinched to cover myself, the giant grinned at my shyness while bundling dirty clothing and dropping a clean outfit on a nearby stool. He walked out. Estimating how much time I had before he again barged in, I soaked another moment and then begrudgingly climbed out. I grabbed the towel and hurried to cover myself.

Ho, to be sure. Trousers! The giant had left a pair of silky yellow trousers. I finished dressing just as the door flew open, again causing me to jump. The giant appeared dressed for duty, wearing linen armour, a sword and akinaka, ankle-high sandals, and a stiff headdress. Leaning his shield against the wall, he shook his head at my disorganised effort to dress. Untangling me with a chuckling grin, he pulled off my awkward clothing, turned the trousers around, and had me step into them. I observed as he knotted the belt around my waist. I most admired the cut of the vest; the style revealed the strength of my arms and showed muscular definition across my chest.

I squatted and crouched, then strutted around the room, allowing silky Persian attire to slide against my body. Goliath shook his head at my self-admiration. Wearing bright clothing was new to me, but becoming a connoisseur of colours did not take long.

Now footwear was different; the stiff, constricting shoes caused me to walk as though wooden blocks clung to my feet. Goliath laughed and motioned for me to follow.

Feeling rested, well-fed, clean, and dressed in proper attire, I followed as the giant escorted me to the courthouse. Kneeling on the hard marble floor, I again found myself in the presence of Mausolus, the satrap king of Halicarnassus; the second throne was vacant, and the entire courtroom was empty save for Goliath. Staring at the tiled lion, I remained unsure why the king had summoned me back to court.

"Rise," Mausolus commanded.

Kneeling on that cold marble floor hurt my knees, so I favourably obeyed.

"Come forward," he told me.

The intimate overture surprised me; I managed one hesitant step.

"Closer," he ordered in his stentorian voice.

Nervous, I moved to the edge of the plush carpet, standing close enough to detect the smell of myrrh and cassia dusted onto his clothing – a most pleasing mix like liquorice and cinnamon.

He asked, "The man, the Thracian, you aided in the hills; you mentioned you studied him."

"Yes, my Lord." Nervousness tempted me to start my mindless blathering again.

"Would you recognise him if you spotted him again?"

"Without a doubt, my Lord. How will I forget such an unusual person?"

"I want to hire you to work for the empire. To work for me."

Ho, to be sure, yesterday ruthless Persians called me an infidel, threatened to cut off my nose and both ears before leisurely killing me for sport, and today the king of Halicarnassus sought to employ me.

"I want to hire you as my spy," Mausolus said.

"What! A spy? But, my Lord, I am…" I protested.

"A spy with a specific duty. I want you to observe."

"Observe?"

"Yes. I want you to linger near the gates, move around the city, Stoa of Aegea, temples, and agora, casually and inconspicuously observing people. Listen to conversations, learn faces, meet people, notice groups, specifically watch men huddling in clusters.

"Learn every bit of news, listen to the slightest whispers, and inform me if you discover the slightest detail revealing this assassin's intended purpose. I want to know if you detect the smallest hint of subversion or catch even a glimpse of someone looking like the man from the hills. Blend into the community yet remain vigilant and aware of activities around you. Go unnoticed, but be cautious that no one follows you."

When I opened my mouth to speak, nothing came out.

"I will pay you a fair wage," Mausolus continued, "and provide comfortable quarters with meal arrangements. I will start you with an ample purse, a robe, and several changes of clothes. Use this money to merge with the public by purchasing food and items from the agora. If questioned, say you await the arrival of your brother. Avoid detection and maintain alertness without causing suspicion. My guards will be informed and allow you to pass without question. Trust no one and tell no one of this assignment, no one."

"As you say, my Lord," I answered.

"Young Ethan, you must swear an oath to me. Knowing the penalty is death, you must swear never to disclose this arrangement with anyone – especially not with the queen."

Such an intimidating alliance stunned me, but how does one say no thank you to a king? So I agreed to his terms. "I swear by my God, Yahweh. As the Sovereign Lord lives, I will protect the secrecy of this treaty between you and me."

With a wave of his hand, I became a spy, an official infiltrator for the king of Caria. Mausolus flashed a glance at Goliath, and both men nodded in agreement. Goliath backed his way out of the room, bowing low.

The king clapped his hands twice, and with the deep timbre of a gong, a man emerged through a side door. Dressed in a fluttering Persian robe and matching felt hat, the court official bowed to the king.

Mausolus directed the official's attention toward me. "Do you recognise this man?"

We were unsure which one of us was more shocked. "My brother, my Lord!" Caleb's eyes welled with tears. His questioning voice quivered with confusion as we embraced, then my eyes welled with tears.

Discovering Caleb alive and well brought such immense happiness that I feared releasing him for even a moment. Instead, I squeezed tighter.

"Ethan, stop! You are crushing me!" In my mind, I saw our father beaming with pride, pleased with my success.

"You two must talk." Mausolus gazed at me with a piercing stare. Our eyes locked. Without a word, his agonising glower reaffirmed my promise of utmost secrecy. Acknowledging my oath, I gave a slight nod; the uncomfortable transaction passed by Caleb unnoticed.

I kept my promise to Mausolus; I never discussed our transaction with anyone. Neither did I reveal my role of aiding the man in the wilderness. Later, I made more promises. My faithful silence prevented me from betraying a trust, but one day, that silence became a hiding place, an excuse for closing my eyes, making me a bystander to injustice.

Chapter 11

Heroes Amongst the Tombs

Echoing across his estate in Labraunda, Mausolus' voice thundered with anger. "I gave clear orders to take these rebels alive! Do these bloody corpses look alive to you? How am I to gather information from dead men?"

The king burned with anger, levelling the brunt of his fury against the humiliated troops he had commissioned for additional security at the annual festival of Zeus Labrandenos in Labraunda. Believing this well attended holiday provided an easy opportunity for another act of violence against Artemisia, Mausolus took precautions by dispatching a select unit of Dathaba on a two-day 'scout and secure' mission.

The satraps' holiday tradition was no secret; after leaving Halicarnassus, the couple first visited their family at the imperial palace in Mylasa before making the annual pilgrimage along the holy avenue to Labraunda, where they would remain for several weeks before following the same route back home. Mausolus had ordered a thorough sweep of the winding roadway, Mylasa, the festival grounds, and the wooded hills surrounding Labraunda. His orders were clear: "Arrest anyone who acts even a little suspicious or cannot account for their presence in the area. Bring all prisoners to me for interrogation."

Chastened troops stood at attention as Mausolus grabbed a clump of bloody hair and drew back a lifeless head. Speaking to the corpse, he sarcastically said, "Good day. I am told you are Thyssos, son of Syskos! Oh? What is that, you say? My apologies to you, sir." Looking at his embarrassed men, Mausolus said, "This man tells me he is not called Thyssos."

Pulling harder on the bloody tuft, he asked, "Well then, what is your name? So you are Manites! I have heard of you, Manites, son of Pactyas! At last, we meet, but I am curious; why have you determined to kill the queen? Strangely, Manites, you do not appear to have anything to say for yourself?"

Turning again to his men, Mausolus mocked. "It seems Manites is shy; he refuses to discuss his plans for killing my family." Then, after allowing the dead man's head to flop hard against the ground, Mausolus grabbed a tuft of hair on the second man.

"Then you must be Thyssos, son of Syskos. What do you have to say for yourself, Thyssos? Your partner appears unwell today; perhaps you can share information with me instead. I am curious, what are the names of those involved in your murderous scheme? Was the failed assassination attempt of an imperial vassal your idea? Speak up, Thyssos. I cannot hear you. Perhaps these many arrows my men fired into your body prevent you from telling me why you seek to kill my wife?"

Seething with anger, Mausolus dropped the lifeless head of Thyssos and turned to the lieutenant who led the sweep. "Roozbeh, what happened out there?"

Roozbeh snapped to attention. "My King." His right arm crossed his chest. "We caught the conspirators by surprise. Our investigation uncovered a plot to assassinate you and the queen during the festival's opening ceremony. Without having complete details, I initiated a tactical squeeze manoeuvre by positioning my men around the city's perimeter. We moved in, working in stealth, toward the temple, where we discovered these men laying an ambush between the temple terrace and north stoa.

"Realising their attack had been discovered, the men fled and barricaded themselves inside the weaver's shop. We surrounded the shop to block their escape. I called for their immediate surrender, but the hostiles resolved to kill every soldier possible before dying a martyr's death.

"They were heavily armed, my Lord. When I again called for their surrender, they burst through the door, hurling spears and arrows. They left me no choice but to stop their assault and prevent our troops from suffering unnecessary casualties."

Losing Thyssos and Manites in such a dramatic standoff was a hard blow to Mausolus. Their deaths prevented him from obtaining the information he needed to make sense of the late night attack against Artemisia. He could not understand the reasoning behind the confrontation with the peltast, this uprising in Labraunda, or if Thyssos and Manites were allied with other militants. As if blindfolded in a fight against a skilled adversary, Mausolus felt unprepared and exposed on all sides.

"Why? Why? Why?" he yelled at no one in particular. "Why now? Why her? Why a mercenary? Nonsensical! I am living in an absurd nightmare of nonsensical drama."

Mausolus soon recanted his anger against his men. He understood the rebels had placed his troops in an impossible situation. Roozbeh was a skilled fighter and a qualified lieutenant; after offering a weak apology and no penalty, the satrap dismissed them.

In truth, the root of Mausolus' frustration lay with his wife. Worshiping Zeus Labrandenos in Labraunda was a holiday they both anticipated attending. But with the Thracian at large this year, Mausolus wisely advised against travel. Journeying to Mylasa, then making the traditional family pilgrimage to Labraunda along the steep, winding Holy Avenue, posed unnecessary risks to the satraps and their troops. Mausolus suggested a travel postponement until the apprehension of the Thracian. This suggestion infuriated the queen.

"What! Cower in my palace? Do you dare insult me with this absurd proposal? I refuse! Refuse! You would ask me to live as a prisoner in my own home?" Artemisia fumed, appalled at the idea of forfeiting her cherished celebration. Worse still, relinquishing an occasion for sacred worship paled compared to the disgrace of being left out, unable to join her friends during days of high-spirited merry-making.

Hard pressed to understand why his wife made protecting her such a difficult task, Mausolus offered a half-hearted objection knowing the futility of reasoning with her. "Mesia, this situation reaches beyond us; it involves the lives of others. We have a responsibility to protect the citizens of this district. And I refuse to endanger our troops, treating them as disposable commodities casually sent to a senseless death."

Mausolus suspected Artemisia knew more than she let on; the peculiar way she reacted to threats against her life bothered him. During the festival week, he barely ate and hardly slept. He forced a smile while acting as master of ceremonies and feigned a light-hearted mood to avoid alarming citizens, but his joy came off as fabricated. Preoccupied, the satrap mindlessly fidgeted with unruly wisps of brow errantly straying above his right eye.

On the other hand, Artemisia frolicked in merrymaking, unaffected by the earlier massacre in the city square. Joining with her ladies, she cheered at the athletic games, applauded equestrian competitions, and celebrated the holiday to its fullest measure.

An uneasy spirit hung over Mausolus. His inability to defend his family left him feeling a way he did not usually feel: vulnerable. The satrap sought much needed advice from his father.

After relocating the capital halfway across the district, Mausolus rarely visited his family, who still resided at the imperial palace in Mylasa. But when life became difficult, Mylasa's Garden of Tombs became the satrap's spiritual oasis and private sanctuary for communing with his father, heroic ancestors, and notable satraps who ruled Caria in the distant past.

Mausolus' lineage was powerful, militaristic, and well-blessed. He was one in a long line of warrior satraps who lived extraordinary lives with triumphs and accomplishments while garnering abundant wealth and royal acknowledgments for contributions to the empire's expansion. Successors following in the footsteps of these powerful satraps lived under a daunting obligation to advance their satrapy by increasing previous acquisitions while leaving behind outstanding contributions.

Loyalty and allegiance to Persia warranted rewards unaffected by death. The faithful pledges of his predecessors entitled Mausolus to receive an endowment known as the Blessing of Ancestral Knowledge. This endowment meant no satrap would be left alone to rule. A spiritual class was available to guide their descendants with accumulative wisdom from centuries of experience.

Mausolus' ancient benefactors were impressive, reaching as far back as the district's first satraps, Lygdamis and Pisindelis, on down the line to the strong matriarchs of his era, Grandmother Bahar and his mother, Aba, and especially his father, Hecatomnus. At his death, King Artaxerxes II bestowed a special honour on Hecatomnus by dispatching an official emblem to be placed on his chest before sealing the sarcophagus. It read, 'Hero of the Empire'.

If Mausolus remained loyal to the Shahanshah, he would become a Hero of the Empire. His legacy would merge with his predecessor so he could strengthen the dynasty from beyond the grave. Disloyalty meant breaking the Chain of Knowledge, depriving the new satrap of needed assistance.

Unbeknownst to Mausolus, the political deeds of his predecessors were fast turning against him, as their previous actions now silently steered the Hecatomnid Dynasty toward a crushing defeat. Preoccupied with his wife and the Thracian sent to kill her, Mausolus remained oblivious to warning signs as, day by day, his bright spot on the Aegean Sea inched closer to its ultimate defeat at the hands of an unsuspected contender for world power.

Mausolus was a young boy when his father (the successor of Satrap Tissaphernes) gathered a large army to war against Cyprus and its rebel forces led by the dissident, Evagoras of Salamis. As a result of his daring military offensive, King Hecatomnus defeated the rebels and annexed Cyprus again under Persian rule.

King Artaxerxes II was so pleased with Hecatomnus' competence and swift action that he handsomely rewarded him with ownership of the wealthy settlement of Miletus. The distinct and culturally rich Greek city fuelled Hecatomnus' passion for Macedonian art, literature, and architecture – a fascination later embraced by his favoured son, Mausolus.

However, victory over Cyprus created an undercurrent of suspicion against King Hecatomnus. Rumours circulated, suggesting he planned to build an army large enough to rebel against the Achaemenid Empire. When no revolt materialised, Mausolus concluded such lies sprang from jealous subordinates. With continuing overtones of rebellion after his father's death, Mausolus worried the accusations might have validity. Recent events involving Queen Artemisia revived his uncertainties, and he feared there might be a connection.

Regardless of these murmurings, King Hecatomnus became a stalwart hero of the Persian Empire. He received a distinguished burial with full military honours, endowing him with the status of a brave warrior. Such respect guaranteed his successful crossing through the Dark River and into the Kingdom of Yama. Favour and acceptance by the world of the dead assured this victorious warrior eternal life as a god.

Housed in a sealed chamber beneath the temple of Zeus laid King Hecatomnus' ornate tomb - his coffin of love, a large sarcophagus filled with extravagance, sealed by mourners and surrounded by family. Once he was sworn in as the district's new king, Mausolus commissioned a mural painting and sculpted family portraits on a sarcophagus overlay. He trusted the faithful gesture would comfort Hecatomnus during his travels to the Kingdom of Yama. Sarcophagal carvings showed Hecatomnus reclining on his banquet couch with an outstretched hand, offering a golden vessel to his widow – the majestic yet mournful Aba. Such a gesture symbolised his property belonged to her, and he willingly allocated all his wealth to his wife.

The carving included Hecatomnus' children parading before him, bearing precious gifts – Mausolus, Roxane, Idrieus, Ada, Pixodarus, and his most favoured daughter, Artemisia. In a bold move, newly appointed King Mausolus restored Roxane as a legitimate family member and included her in this portrait. Roxane was not just Mausolus' sister; she was his one-time fiancée. Long ago, Hecatomnus believed the Fates had intervened to forbid his first-born daughter, Roxane, from reigning as queen of Caria. The Fate Sisters prevented the marriage by sending an illness to render the girl deaf. Hecatomnus then dismissed Roxane as an heir, dispatching her to live out her defect in seclusion at the furthest edge of the world, a barren region in the twelfth satrapy of Bactria. Afterward, all mention of her ceased in the Hecatomnid lineage. Mausolus disagreed with his father's harsh decision and secretly ordered reports about Roxane's care and wellbeing. He stopped worrying about her after she married and had children with a powerful man named Oxyartes. If nothing else, Mausolus at least re-established Roxane as a legitimate member of the family by including her image with the family on their father's funerary chest. I do not know if she ever learned of this.

The king's favourite possessions were nestled around this tomb – purple tunics and gold crowns, pearl-inlaid goblets, golden collars, and precious gems from across the empire. Also, his favourite weapons – his gold-handled dagger, hunting bow, and quiver filled with arrows. There were bronze, gold, and marble sculptures, along with the choicest foods such as wheat of Assos, wines of Helbon, and salt of Ammon – all necessary items to sustain a worthy king on his long journey.

Once, when referring to what he called "the flaw of life," Mausolus told me, "Tombs of the underprivileged are filled bones and left undisturbed. Precious items fill the tombs of the wealthy. My father's most favoured belongings have turned to cold, dormant objects surrounding his fragile bones in a stony sepulchre beneath a temple ornamenting a stunning garden protected by a feeble old priest. As with the great pyramids of the pharaohs, I suspect these items will one day succumb to thievery." He added, "To be sure, Ethan, this fact is true. The flaw of life is that the world continues despite the pain of its greatest losses."

Endless conspiracies plagued satraps, commanders, and generals of the Achaemenid Empire. Tissaphernes was not immune despite winning spectacular victories in battle, elevating him to the commander-in-chief of the entire Persian army. In addition to ruling as Satrap of Caria, he gained the appointment as ruler of Lydia. His undying loyalty to Persia at the Battle of Cunaxa angered the Greeks. Motivated by revenge, a group of conspirators led by Xenophon of Athens later murdered him in Colossae. His men buried him there in a secret grave. In Mylasa, a Persian sphinx of glazed panels meticulously painted with the winged body of a lion and a human head marked the empty tomb of Tissaphernes.

Before kneeling beside the grave of his grandfather, Hyssaldomus, Mausolus placed flowers for Bahar, his beloved grandmother – King Artaxerxes II's beautiful and spirited daughter who moulded Mausolus' life in extraordinary ways to ensure his success and endowment of the Blessing of Ancestral Knowledge.

Interestingly, Hyssaldomus served a dual role – he was the satrap of Caria and a priest. The man gave his life to the worship of Zeus.

Mausolus explained the story to me. "My grandfather lived a fully surrendered life to the ruler of Mount Olympus and Lord of the Sky. I have long suspected his devotion to Zeus was an act of self-punishment. He believed his penance appeased the gods for certain atrocities, releasing future satraps from warranted malediction."

"What atrocities?" I asked.

"For one, Hydarnes. He was the commander of the infamous ten thousand Immortals. During King Xerxes' reign, Hydarnes led the charge against three hundred Spartans – devout worshipers of Zeus – in the legendary Battle of Thermopylae. Hyssaldomus' sacrificial devotion is thought to have finally broken the curse incurred by Hydarnes.

"There is another reason for Hyssaldomus' years of penance; it has to do with the daughter of Lygdamis – Lygdamis was personally appointed to his position by King Cyrus and became Caria's first Persian satrap. At Lygdamis' passing, his daughter, Artemisia, ruled as Caria's first female satrap. But I caution you, Ethan, never discuss these things in the presence of my dear wife. Such a reference is awkward for her as it concerns embarrassment surrounding her forbearer Artemisia the First."

I swore an oath, and he continued.

"You see, Ethan, Hydarnes' Persian victory at Thermopylae only rallied the Greeks for warfare. Weeks later, they retaliated in what became known as the Battle of Salamis – Persia casualties ran high, and they lost most of the navy.

"The wish-to-be-forgotten scandal happened when Artemisia the First enlisted herself and five of her battleships in the Salamis fight, except she became an ally to the Persians. But, of course, things were different in those days, loyalties got blurred, yet this alliance was taken as a treasonous act and viewed as a slight against her Grecian heritage. Moreover, her actions were perceived as an unforgivable snub to Artemis, the most widely revered Greek deity from whom Artemisia received her name."

I asked, "Your ancestor, Artemisia the First, died in a battle against the Greeks?"

"Not at all; she made sporting humiliation of the Greeks. Her ship was the first to ram a Calyndian vessel – a betrayal that caused the Greeks to place a sizeable price on her head. To be sure, Persian King Xerxes was pleased. He viewed the battle from a mountaintop, spellbound by Artemisia's dangerously close manoeuvres and artful escapes. Xerxes said of her, 'My men have become women, and my women men.' Her tenacity and heroism impressed him so much that he handsomely rewarded her. Legend has it they became lovers."

"And then what happened?"

"Fawning over an enemy king was the shameless catalyst fuelling Artemisia's insolence and galvanising her arrogant choices, further enraging the Greeks. As a result, her life was never the same; she became apprehensive with no one to trust and seldom left the palace estate."

"Do you know whatever became of Artemisia the First?"

"She ruled as satrap of Caria for more than a decade – until unrequited love for a man named Dardanus pushed her to commit suicide. She jumped off the cliffs on the island of Leucas."

I asked, "What about Hydarnes? Do you know of his fate?"

"Persia left Greece alone after the embarrassing loss at Salamis and another defeat in the Battle of Plataea. With no wars to fight, Hydarnes retired from military service and lived a secluded life with his harem.

"King Xerxes' obsession with Greece cost the empire far more than his preoccupation was worth. In humiliation, he limped back home to Susa and focused on life with his new wife."

"Indeed, I know of her, a Jewess named Esther from the tribe of Benjamin. The same tribe as me."

"Loyalty and royalty," Mausolus said. "The two are a dangerous combination. Xerxes' confidant, a man named Artabanus, later murdered him."

Mausolus was correct about loyalty, but I have noticed another affliction of royalty –grudges. Greece by no means forgave Xerxes nor forgot Hydarnes' brutality at Thermopylae, and at that very moment, unsuspecting Halicarnassus lay in a deadly crossfire of revenge.

Still lingering among Mylasa's tombs, Mausolus knelt in prayer, imploring the divinities he believed most likely to stand by him – Ares, Athena, Hera, Hermes, and Zeus. Then, after sharing details with his father about the Labraunda assault, he asked for help to protect Artemisia.

Fixing his eyes heavenward, he cried out, "Father, noble King Hecatomnus, loyal satrap of the Great Shahanshah, possessor of accumulative wisdom from all others, tell me now, who is at the root of this great evil against my family? Am I to fight as a blind warrior? Surely not! Enlighten me, Father, lead me to the one who has set his hand against my wife, your daughter, the queen you chose for Caria. Guide me this day with the Blessing of Ancestral Knowledge."

Despite his impassioned pleas, the heavens above felt like iron, and the ground beneath him was like bronze. Such devastating silence left Mausolus wondering if help would come in time.

Chapter 12

Artemisia's Heroines

Mausolus honoured his ancestors and other remarkable men who helped advance the Achaemenid Empire, while Artemisia created goddesses from her heroines and then worshiped their audacity and fierce legacy. Mausolus surrounded himself with wise advisors and prudent counsellors, and for the most part, he respected the thoughts of others. Artemisia was the opposite; she designed a hierarchy, placing herself at the top while fitting gods and people into subservient roles. Whenever she felt stuck, she implored her gods for help while seldom heeding their advice.

Her favourite heroine was her namesake, the eccentric warrior queen Artemisia I. Thinly documented, the annals of history hardly mention the escapades and daring feats of the ancient satrap. Artemisia II depended on oral stories handed down throughout the ages to learn of her ancestor's bold life. The populace heard similar stories. Despite living a century apart and in strikingly different eras, comparing Artemisia II with Artemisia I became a typical exchange for the nattering women of Caria. With no historical records to contest the fertility of their growing imaginations, Artemisia I developed talent and unrelenting bravery. At the same time, Artemisia II dwindled as passive and, at times, ordinary, achieving no real legacy for herself. Unfair comparisons drove Artemisia II to risky acts while obsessively reflecting on history's most aggressive women.

I can attest that the queen was not ordinary and displayed no characteristics of passivity once stepping into her gymnasium. Trained by champion Zoroastrian warriors, their gruelling regime of calisthenics combined with the mental practice of yoga strengthened her concentration and physical agility, thereby sharpening her fighting skills. Daily she rehearsed combat techniques developed by Amazon women. These ancient strategies perfected the queen's proficiency with distance weapons – the javelin and bow

– and the vicious Persian sword—her ability to master every combat style put to shame the most skilled Dathaba.

Hand-to-hand weapon-less grappling was her weakest field, but when wielding a blade, she exhibited incredible nerve emulating the fighting style of another heroine, Pantea Arteshbod. A wife and a mother, this chief commander of Cyrus' Special Forces Unit served the king throughout his entire reign, playing a pivotal role in silencing Babylonia after its conquest. History immortalized Pantea as a symbol of female bravery by publicising her valour and legendary life.

There was also Queen Aegea. Artemisia often spent hours on the balcony of her palace communing with this Amazon sister. Hoping for a whisper from a distant land, the satrap would lean into the railing, willing the waves to roil in echoes of thundering hooves from the cavalry of Amazon women riding hard to Halicarnassus, wielding bloody clubs while rallying sisters everywhere to arms.

She mused, "Unspoiled beneath these rugged waves is the hallowed arena where you, my sister Aegea, queen of the Amazons, died in noble victory. Within this azure expanse is where your beating heart persists, the heart of a leader, a warrior, and one of history's truly courageous women."

In Artemisia's mind, Aegea still lived beneath the waves, holding a crescent-shaped shield before her body, defiantly grasping the shaft of a lethal spear. She imagined dampened feathers ornamenting a scuffed bow and her fleece-lined quiver teeming with choice arrows blood-soaked from a thousand battles; a frayed sling dangled from her well-formed waist. Her spirit-sister, enduring at the bottom of the sea, was all the more proud, ever radiant in burnished armour. Beneath her battered helmet glistened golden hair, fluttering like a windblown scarf, washing softly across the motionless face of a woman at peace for having died in battle.

Celebrated tales of wars fought, battles won, honours conferred, and deaths endured excited Artemisia's hunger for military involvement. Finally, she whispered to the sea, "My dear Queen Aegea, you now live in the timeless expanse of eternity. Your name, along with Pantea and a legion of our other sisters, will forever remain the measuring standard for history's valiant fighting women."

The list of fierce women and Amazon warriors Artemisia hearkened to was a lengthy record of reputable names. She trusted each to guide her spirit and contribute to her personal life by weaving their fiery essence into her mortality. The opportunity to lead a charging cavalry of fierce women, heavily armed and seeking blood, was her unrequited quest – the reason for her emptiness. Artemisia's spiritual restoration did not come from Mylasa's Tomb Gardens but from her dream – her vision of fighting, conquering and accomplishing impossible tasks made possible through her bravery.

Oh, how I adored her. From the first moment I laid eyes upon Artemisia sitting on her throne in that courtroom, I loved her. I expect she knew as much, but my fondness for her came from an unmapped place in my heart that I cannot explain. Even now, I sometimes ponder beautiful Artemisia, the satrap queen who, striving after the elusive wind, captured a savage whirlwind and brazenly clutched it tight against her bosom.

Obvious barriers stood between us, her world and mine, but once I held her in my arms. In her deepest pain, she sought to cry upon my shoulder. Safe in my arms, she became vulnerable as an abandoned child, afraid and seeking protection. Shielding her, soothing her against the searing pain ravaging her heart forever joined my soul to the queen of Caria. Exquisite sorrow rent my heart in two the awful day I caused her death.

Chapter 13

A House Divided Cannot Stand

"My Queen, you must decide! Spies have infiltrated the city, searching for their property. The Rhodians demand the return of their cargo. By the gods, those islanders will attack us. Hostile forces will launch their ships," General Orontobates pleaded.

"Leave me!" Artemisia ordered.

"Heed their threats; I beg of you, my Queen. Islanders have discovered your fraudulent seizure; they scream in outrage calling your deed an unforgivable offence! Return the ships at once before a war—"

She cut him off. "Remember your place, General," she warned. "You work for me and serve at my pleasure, now leave me. Guards! Remove this man!"

"War, my Queen! War is imminent! Your unreasonableness places Halicarnassus in danger." His frantic pleas echoed off the corridor's marble walls.

Retiring to the cool of her favourite patio, Queen Artemisia calmed herself by scooping Miut onto her lap and stroking his long dark fur.

Earth holds myriad unseen boundaries set in place by Wisdom to preserve harmony between the elements and creation. Imagine the vast waters of the Aegean, refusing to obey restrictions, thereby freely moving beyond its borders. Halicarnassus would fail to exist. While Nature accepts her boundaries, Queen Artemisia placed no such confines on herself. She supposed her position as queen of Caria entitled her to the generosity of the sea and the bounty of the land – including the wealthy assets of Rhodes. As a warrior queen, a self-proclaimed tessellation of fierce and influential women, Artemisia obligated the entire satrapy to acquiesce to her point of view and careless demands, bestowing respect for her regardless of merit.

Reaching her hand out to touch the alabaster vase on a stand beside her, she ran her tapered fingers around the edge until landing on the inscription. This ancestral treasure, her most prized possession, was a gift from King Xerxes to her great-great-grandmother Artemisia I, warrior queen of Caria.

"Hear me, Ahura Mazda!" Then she prayed each word of the inscription. "'You, the one uncreated creator. Of all the gods, Great King Xerxes has exalted you. No one will remove your sanctuary from Persia, neither from the world nor from among the gods in heaven.' So listen to me now, do not delay in unlocking the door of my future. Illuminate my path so I might fulfil the extraordinary destiny you have determined for preserving my place in history."

Leaning against her couch, Artemisia willed her mind back to happier times. She would dismiss General Orontobates scathing words and harsh warnings by recalling pleasurable things. She was the queen and refused to be frightened by a pitiable general lacking in vision with no courage to seize assets for the Shahanshah.

"Unusual eyes! Enticing eyes! No, inviting eyes!" A reminiscent smile softened her disposition as she remembered her fifteen-year-old self in Mylasa; that was the day she met her brother. "Homecoming day!" she said out loud, broadening her smile. She behaved giddily that day, enchanted by the sharpness of Mausolus' eyes, sapphire blue eyes, dancing with the vitality and wealth of a Persian prince.

King Hecatomnus had arranged a grand feast for his entire family and ordered everybody to attend this joyous occasion. After an extended stay in Susa, his first-born son Mausolus, prince of Caria, was returning home.

And no one wanted to miss the king's special announcement. Hecatomnus was about to proclaim the woman he had selected to become Mausolus' wife. Contenders for the honour would hail from within the family; Hecatomnus' way of ensuring the dynasty's wealth, both the dowry and the inheritance, remained protected in the Hecatomnid House Treasury. Artemisia giggled, knowing her oldest sister, Roxane, was the probable candidate.

Young Artemisia had yet to meet her older brother since, at age five, Mausolus left Caria to begin his education. Artemisia's birth occurred several months later. Their grandmother, Bahar, the daughter of King Artaxerxes II, recognised a light in her grandson, a striking aptitude she wanted to foster. Thus she commissioned her eunuch, Moza, to superintend an extensive education preparing her progeny and heir to the Hecatomnid dynasty for a life of administration and leadership.

During the empire's zenith, Persian boys automatically received fifteen years of education, grooming them to serve the king as accomplished soldiers and capable equestrians. Rigorous training came from endurance exercises: running, slingshot, archery, javelin, and hunting, with most drills executed on the back of a galloping steed.

Valiant-minded thinkers of the Persian World Empire considered the art of study a waste of valuable resources. Why invest young minds and capable bodies in manufacturing, commerce, or the foolhardy pursuit of science when innovations built by other nations would inevitably belong to the empire through the art of war?

Persian males, students of aggressive tactics, were taught, "Meagre subordinates exist to labour at meagre tasks, freeing superior Persian intellectuals to develop as tactical geniuses of war. The Shahanshah permits any means necessary to defend and preserve our world dominance." (Despite developing the most fearsome military in existence, the Persian Empire crumbled within 200 years.)

Bahar sought worthier goals for her precious grandson; she had aspirations beyond mere physical performance. Therefore, she meticulously devised the next fifteen years of Mausolus' life around an extensive regimen with just enough physical performance to satisfy the Shahanshah. Her academic program included world travel designed to immerse Mausolus in vibrant cultures, along with experiencing the empire's diverse provinces.

Twice he visited Peloponnesus, sitting with royalty in front of the ivory statue of Zeus, cheering national heroes competing for Olympic honours – his favourite events were Pankration matches, quadriga chariot races, and Hoplites sprints. He visited the ancient pyramids, floated the Nile, toured Ethiopia, and spent time in Jerusalem viewing the second temple of the Jews. Mausolus admired ancient King Solomon, a king hailed by nations as the wisest man ever. Once, Solomon threatened to cut a newborn baby asunder to reveal the child's actual birth mother. Those extreme gambles, and clever judicious acts by King Solomon, earned him Mausolus' respect.

As a prince in Susa, Mausolus' formal instruction was provided by the empire's most exceptional mathematicians, poets, artists, musicians, astronomers, equestrians, and general educators. Initially, he behaved as an unwilling captive of Queen Bahar, but after maturing, Mausolus craved enlightenment and became a most appreciative student.

Delighted with his progress, Bahar proudly watched her grandson outshine every peer. Then, the day arrived for Mausolus to return to his father's house. Leaving Mylasa as a boy crying for his mother, he returned accomplished, sophisticated, and an advanced scholar ready to marry and begin managing his father's holdings. In addition, he would utilise his education as a city employee by collecting taxes, presiding over civil and criminal cases, maintaining district roads, and commanding a division of militia to keep the peace. By law, Mausolus' duties required quelling any rebellion against the reigning king of Persia.

People gravitated toward Mausolus. I know I did. Captivated by his handsome good looks and jovial personality, folks wanted to be around him and instinctively placed their confidence in him. I cannot say he enjoyed such a liability, but he prided himself in following examples of honourable men when handling people. Explaining his perspective on governing, he said, "Ethan, to be sure, the measure of a man is what he does with power. His excellence is not a gift but a skill requiring practice. Refuse to act right because you think you are excellent; instead, achieve excellence by acting rightly; then, your good actions will strengthen yourself and inspire good actions in others."*

My characterisation of Mausolus is that he was two people combined into one body – Mausolus, the uncompromising king capable of carrying out severe requests in service to the empire, unafraid of striking fatal blows against all adversaries. Then there was Mausolus the inquisitive commoner. A civilian with a futuristic outlook, uninhibited by his playful spirit, entirely fascinated by others, and unafraid to enjoy their unique cultures. Over time, Mausolus became my beloved Persian father, an example, and a pattern for my life.

Accomplished in several languages, Mausolus spoke Carian and used the sanctioned Imperial Aramaic but preferred Attic Greek to satisfy his love of Greek literature, architecture, and design. In addition, Mausolus had a voracious appetite for prose despite living in an era where Persians viewed reading with minimal importance.

"Immature and pointless," he said about Persian writing and poetry. Preferring leisure time reading Greek classics, he praised them as "Timeless masterpieces, each intelligent, profound, and brimming with passion."

Above all, he treasured Homer's epic poems, *The Iliad* and *The Odyssey*. He also read the tragedies *Oedipus the King* by Sophocles and *Medea* by Euripides, the comedies of Aristophanes: and the verses of Archilochus and Sappho. He studied Thucydides' history of the Peloponnesian War and military accounts written by the famed historian Herodotus, Caria's celebrated hero.

Herodotus lived in Halicarnassus over a century ago. Some say he conceived the phrase we hear nowadays, 'Great Wonders of the World'. Imagine if Mausolus' tremendous improvements to Herodotus' hometown met his standard for a world phenomenon. Historical accounts would read, 'Halicarnassus, one of the Great Wonders of the World'.

Mausolus' homecoming feast was his first introduction to Artemisia, a scrawny girl with walnut- brown skin, pillowy lips reddened by youth, the nose of a Greek goddess, and a thick black braid casually tossed over her dainty shoulder. For the banquet, she wore a jewelled headpiece of opal stones.

His first impression? "Beautiful as a clump of buttercups." After conversing with the reckless princess, he included, "Spirited as a Persian warhorse."

Introducing herself, bowing with the customary swoop showing respect to a prince, she said, "I am your sister, Artemisia the second. Welcome home to Caria; to be sure, you will find life boring in Mylasa after living in the capital district and spending years traveling to exceptional places."

"In truth," Mausolus said, "I view returning to a quiet, modest part of the empire as a refreshing change."

Artemisia disagreed. "When I grow up, I will leave this pitiful district."

Mausolus, entertained by her, asked, "Where will you go?"

"I will travel to Themiscyra in Scythia and reign as queen of the Amazons. I shall have scores of daughters ruling beside me. I will name my first daughter Penthesilea after the great warrior queen of the Amazons. The second will be named Hippolyta, and she shall rule as mighty queen over all the mountainous territories."

"Will you fight against such warrior men as Hercules and Achilles?" he asked.

"To be sure! A warrior queen lives for such militaristic contests," she answered.

He toyed with her further. "Pardon me, Mesia, what will you do if the Amazons refuse you, barring you from becoming their queen?"

"I shall form a cavalry and fight against such a dissident group. After assuming my well-earned place on the Amazon throne, others will join me, and we will set out on a ruthless campaign, adding borders to my kingdom, including yours, my brother."

Mausolus bonked her impishly on top of the head. "Mesia, the Amazon women will be proud to have you as their warrior queen." He walked away, laughing to himself.

Artemisia stood frozen with infatuation. Feeling the top of her head, she brought her fingers against her fluttering heart, secretly preserving the keepsake of Mausolus' touch. "Mesia," she swooned. "He called me Mesia."

Unbearably smitten with Mausolus' charm, his easy laugh, and princely confidence, young Artemisia called her brother a 'half and half.' With his muscular build and lion's mane of flowing hair, Artemisia imagined him one-half Hermes and one-half Ares, the two handsome sons of Zeus.

The month following Hecatomnus' announcement proclaiming Roxane as Mausolus' betrothed and future queen of Caria, the elated girl became gravely ill, postponing their wedding. By the time she recovered, the sickness had destroyed her hearing. Plans changed for King Hecatomnus. He refused to permit such a person to marry his son, the future king. Instead, Hecatomnus sent Roxane away and arranged for Mausolus to marry Artemisia on her sixteenth birthday.

'Mausolus iriti sunki parki: the wife of Mausolus, daughter of a king.' This envious chant, spoken by the women in the district, fell short of Artemisia's deepest longing. Despite receiving her name from Artemis, the Greek goddess of fertility, Artemisia could not give Mausolus the children he desired.

Barrenness, the root of Artemisia's greatest fear, became the source of her extreme angst. In her mind, dying childless, and leaving the district with no heir, was nothing short of removing a valuable manuscript from history's eternal library – the manuscript about her. With no offspring and nothing measurable to pass on to future generations, she feared disappearing, evaporating as a faint mist burnt off by the morning sun.

The law entitled Mausolus to produce an heir, a prodigy, and a successor to his life by taking a second wife or even a third, but he rejected the option for unknown reasons. Nor did he procure a harem or a single concubine. Here is a possible reason, he once told me, "Ethan, do yourself a favour; avoid painful disturbances of the genitals by cleaving to one wife."

He added, "I fail to comprehend how achieving sovereign status entitles a man to amass countless women when the female collection merely dilutes his focus while exhausting his life. Once effective in noble endeavours, the man shrivels into a puny arbitrator quelling constant disputes between squabbling wives and bickering concubines."

Childless meant future leadership would one day pass to Idrieus or Pixodarus. Idrieus, the second son of Hecatomnus, held lofty ideas and ambitious visions for the dynasty's expansion of territory. He urged Mausolus to skip across the Aegean, confiscating additional islands, using them as stepping stones to inch closer to the island of Chios. Occupying Chios would handily position him within range to seize the riches of Greece.

Being an active builder like Mausolus, Idrieus regularly pestered his older brother with drawings and concocted ideas. His sights were set on the vacant mound in the centre of Halicarnassus. Wanting to build a Doric–style temple, he tried pressuring Mausolus with a variety of proposals. But despite their potential, Mausolus refused to endorse any of his brother's notions.

When the time came, no doubt Idrieus, first in line for the throne, would rule as a team with his sister-wife, Ada, the way Mausolus and Artemisia governed together. But Ada lacked the fire of spirit, and Artemisia feared her sister's attempt to reign would discredit the dynasty.

Mausolus had grown up enriched by his grandmother's wealth and influence, encouraged by her aspirations. Artemisia grew up emboldened to conquer, pushed hard by her father's cunning sway. Together, the husband and wife satraps held dreams of spirited and noble accomplishments for the district, Persia, and themselves. On the other hand, Ada had grown up as a victim, intimidated and mentally tortured by her insecure and jealous brother, Pixodarus.

Pixodarus, the youngest son, saw himself as an insignificant piece in the powerful dynasty, someone with no influence, valueless in any official capacity or significant military position. Such rationale led him to recklessness and indulgence in hunting, drinking, and with women.

Lacking the character of Mausolus, his insecurity drove him to target the weakest member of the dynasty: Ada. To be sure, Pixodarus ruined plenty of family gatherings with his sudden bombardments of twisted scenarios, pointless blame, and disparaging remarks pulled from thin air to undermine others. However, Ada internalised his rants until the weighty shame of her soul became evident in her timorous carriage and faint voice.

Given no other choice, Artemisia accepted her sorrowful barrenness, but she refused to relinquish her place in history – especially to Ada. Defying Fate, she determined to create a historic splash of a different nature. And it involved the vacant hill in the middle of the city.

She proposed a daring venture - regardless of the expense – a plan that would set the whole world abuzz. The absence of children did not mean the absence of legacy. Artemisia would build an immortal legacy all her own. A transcendent structure of such magnitude it would forever link her name with the majesty of her creation. She intended to commission the world's most talented architects, artists, and craftsmen in a way never before attempted. She would bring them all together for one project, creating the greatest aesthetic triumph the world has ever seen.

The problem was that Mausolus did not know her plans; he missed the warning signs of his wife's emptiness and troubling fears. After all, royal bards had written much about him, recording his brilliant triumphs, military prowess, and victorious commandership in the Ten Year Revolt of the Satraps and the intense conflict against his nemesis, Ariobarzanes. And Mausolus did not rest after the exhaustion of war. Instead, he added to his infamy by building a legendary city with an influential community unlike the region had ever seen.

What Mausolus built in Halicarnassus was more than a productive urban centre. By combining what he loved - diversity, expansion, and luxury - he created a vibrant lifestyle of freedom and excess, gradually replacing the worn-out traditions of Persia with the artistic styles of Hellenism. He ushered in a neoteric standard of culture and lavish living, propelling Caria into a new dimension: the unencumbered Age of Mausolus. Unparalleled in his day, it was as if the satrap rode atop an unstoppable surge – like balancing on the crest of an epic wave.

He relocated the capital city from Mylasa to Halicarnassus to protect the Carian way of life. Utilising the natural features of the sheltered cove on the gulf, Mausolus built a fortress, a gated community for preserving their rights, freedoms, and affluence. Steep slopes to the north with gnarled hills on the peninsula protected the city from capture by land, and the channel of its natural harbour and fortified port safeguarded citizens should there be an attack by sea.

Here I mention Mausolus' most ingenious invention, a configuration of stone walls encircling the city. He built an impregnable fortification using a unique layering system: walls measuring four cubits deep and 13 cubits high with watchtowers and locking oak and bronze gates woven into the formation. Mausolus believed his design would withstand attacks from any foe, especially Grecian ultramodern assault weapons of propulsion warfare - ballista engines and catapults.

Years later, my heart soared when I learned Mausolus' walls indeed held against attacks from the Grecian catapult. In the end, the fortress city of Halicarnassus surrendered, but not without first inflicting heavy casualties on the astonished Macedonians.

When I arrived on the scene, Mausolus' interests had shifted. He was getting older and sought to enjoy the fruits of his labour by spending leisurely days with friends, in recreation, and breeding horses. He was satisfied. Artemisia was not. She had grown fanatical, fearful of jeopardizing her extraordinary destiny. In her mind, failure to carry out the self-perpetuating assignment ordained through astonishing architecture was to ignore a request from the gods.

But money was a problem. People of Halicarnassus opposed giving further financial support to sustain the satraps' expensive lifestyle; Artemisia feared an uprising should she demand higher tariffs, levies, or crippling taxes to finance her ambitious aesthetic triumph. So instead, she used her power to carry out an unethical action against the wealthier community of Rhodes and then rationalised her larcenous tactics by saying, "A certain amount of female cunning is an admirable trait, a skill openly practised by the gods, and most ardently necessary to succeed in the empire."

There was more; Artemisia's vulnerable legacy and her doddering quest for recognition required help. She needed someone clever to influence her husband, someone with a passion for construction and a knowledge of stone building, yet filled with the contagious enthusiasm of youth. She sought a gullible sort to comply with her need to reawaken ambition in her unsuspecting husband.

And like unexpected snow, I, a naïve Jewish boy, happened to appear in Halicarnassus.

Chapter 14

Caleb

Emotion overwhelmed Caleb, and he wept. First, he wept with joy at my unexpected arrival. Then, he wept with grief as I explained the tragic fall that killed our brother, Sakeri. Faulty scaffolding collapsed beneath a crew of stonemasons repairing the wall near the Gate of the Spring. Several men held on until help arrived; of those who fell to the ground below, Sakeri alone died.

Realising his vibrant life as an interpreter for the Persian Empire had abruptly ended, Caleb wept for himself. Because he placed family values above himself, he accepted the obligation of honourable marriage to Huldah, Sakeri's grieving widow who had yet to produce a child. He wanted his brother to have an heir; he owed Sakeri such a blessing. Submitting to the Hebrew law of Yibbum, Caleb chose to obey our father's wishes and return home, but a large part of his heart desperately wanted to stay in the service of the Shahanshah. Overwhelmed, he wept.

We two resembled each other through the eyes and have the same shape mouth, but he received the blessing of straight hair. His fine-boned stature, comparable to our mother's side of the family, might explain why she favoured him. Priding himself as the family intellectual, Caleb found no joy in hard physical labour like Sakeri and I did.

Building his career as a roving translator for the Empire of Persia suited his linguistic aptitude and propensity for philosophy and principles. Depending on the region's political climate, his assignments varied between Persian cities and outposts, exposing him to diverse cultures and consequential ethical dilemmas.

"What?" Caleb shouted. "Remain in Halicarnassus! You jest!" Expecting to travel home together, Caleb was not pleased with my plans. "To be sure, you have no reason to stay behind in Halicarnassus. With no family and no occupation, how will you sustain yourself? Working as a stonemason in a city with no construction?"

This awkward position crushed me as if wedged between colliding boulders – telling Caleb the truth meant betraying the king's trust in me and lying to Caleb meant betraying our bond as brothers. Wishing to explain every detail involved in searching for him, I longed to share my dangerous encounter with the dagger-wielding stranger and explain how I tended his wound, became arrested, and ended up in court. I wanted to tell him about Goliath, my first steam tub bath, and how I loved wearing trousers. But, each time I opened my mouth with a plausible explanation, I recalled the stabbing eyes of the king swearing me to secrecy.

Otherwise, I would have said, *Don't worry about me, Caleb. I have employment; I am working in the service of the king. I am a spy, but the queen remains unaware because Mausolus wants his investigation to be kept a secret. I will work with the Imperial Guard, tracking down a dangerous assassin because I am the sole person able to identify him. Brother, you will not believe this, but I saved the man's life before he bled to death in the wilderness, and then I was arrested, but I still have both ears and now am a valuable asset to the king. Oh, and remember those stories we love listening to about Makeda, well I just met…… Perhaps I will keep that part to myself.* Ho, to be sure, the ridiculous words sounded nonsensical to me, and I knew them as true.

Instead, I told Caleb I was drained from my long journey and would head home after a much needed rest. I added that I might try a new trade by hiring myself out as a fisherman. My reasoning satisfied him, thus ending our discussion.

Mausolus showed compassion for our bereavement by securing passage for Caleb on a trireme, the Paralos III. The swift vessel sailing at top speed across the Mediterranean Sea cut months off an overland journey and eliminated the threat of highwaymen. The Greek ship, laden with Persian exports and foreign diplomats, readied her course for the famous port city of Joppa. From there, he would take whatever overland transportation he could find to Jericho.

Hugging in tearful departure, we brothers encouraged each other, and I assured Caleb I would be home soon. "Give my love to Father," I said. "He will accept my delay. Give my love to Mother and our grieving sister, Huldah.

May you produce a strong son for our brother, Sakeri. May you and Huldah have a quiver filled with sons - nineteen sons like King David." We both laughed.

Watching from the end of the seawall, I waved until the *Paralos III* disappeared over the horizon. Despite the clamour resounding from the waterfront, the world grew silent and strangely empty. Staring into the vastness of the azure sea, I wiped away my tears and, with a heavy heart, returned to life in Halicarnassus.

Chapter 15

The First Dispatch

Dawn exploded as if birthed for a single purpose: to advance a cast of characters across a supernatural game board, inching human players unwittingly caught in a global game of Technê ever closer to irreversible doom.

Enjoying brunch on their favourite midday patio, Mausolus and Artemisia discussed the previous evening's loud and boisterous celebration honouring their sister Ada's birthday. Before his death, Hecatomnus bequeathed his daughter Ada to his son, Idrieus.

"Ada enjoyed herself last night; the number of guests attending her party pleased her." Mausolus held a deep affection for Little Ada, as he called her.

"Our sister is an embarrassment," Artemisia responded. "She behaves like a mouse with her timidity." Then, with a mocking gesture, Artemisia brought her hands in front of her face and pretended to groom tiny paws. "Squeak. Squeak." She gazed around the room nervously like a fearful mouse and returned to her mocking gesture. "Squeak."

Mausolus disagreed by defending Ada's weak spirit. "She may improve, Nooré cheshm-am." (Mausolus used touching expressions of love when addressing his wife, this phrase meant she was the light of his soul.)

Artemisia argued, "Chances of her sitting as queen of Caria remains a distant possibility, but I fear if placed in that position, her attempts will fail miserably, and she may singlehandedly topple the Dynasty."

Mausolus continued with his defence. "The outcome of one's life remains a mystery until all circumstances have transpired. Consider the goddess Nemesis. One may believe Nemesis is stalking them to deliver bad luck. But then Tyche may intervene to bring about fortune and prosperity. The two look so much alike from a distance that one cannot know which goddess they have encountered until either good or bad circumstances reveal themselves.

Perhaps Tyche will remove Little Ada's timorous spirit and bless her with a voice of authority."

"I find your recitation of the gods unpleasant and unnecessary. I have tried but cannot find patience with the quivering mouse, and Pixodarus worsens the matter. His cruelty equals that of the god Antaeus. I wish Pixodarus to leave the district. Send him away to Parsa or give him an assignment in Susa, anywhere but Caria."

"Nooré cheshm-am, harken to the god Kairos," Mausolus said. "Perhaps Kairos will bequeath vitality to Ada as he has to us. Has this god ever failed to favour the Hecatomnid Dynasty? Has he abandoned the district of Halicarnassus? Perhaps one day he, too, will bless Little Ada."

Interrupting their conversation, Moza brought an urgent dispatch delivered by angaros. Reading the news flashed alarm across Mausolus' face.

"Terrible news concerning Ephesus!" he said.

"Oh, Mausolus, not another earthquake?" Artemisia asked.

He read on. "Worse, Nooré cheshm-am! Someone has destroyed the temple! Set it ablaze!"

"What! Arson?" the queen responded. "Why? Who would dare wreak such an awful offense? And on a sacred house of worship! No doubt a foreigner! Which country has claimed responsibility for this reprehensible act?"

"No, an Ephesian citizen unleashed this calamity. A young man named Herostratus. The message reads, 'In the act of maliciousness, Herostratus set fire to the wooden roof, which burst into flames, collapsing the entire structure along with its statues and every column. Nothing remains; the building has crumbled to the ground.'"

"Draw your sword! What you say cannot be!" Artemisia seethed at the appalling concept. "Such Grecian magnificence, gone? This pride of Ephesus, ruined? One hundred and twenty columns, razed? Ephesus is the grandest of the empire's majestic cities; what will such a loss mean for Persia? Where was Artemis? What all important event prevented her from protecting her temple? This reprobate, Herostratus, do we know this man?"

"Caution, my Queen! Attached is a statement released by the Council of Ephesus." He continued reading out loud. "'The infidel, captured and duly tortured, admitted his treasonous act before a legal tribunal, confessing the reason for his insanity: fame. He would stop at nothing for the opportunity to become included in history and chose this enormous atrocity to ensure time preserves the name Herostratus. Be warned; from this day forward, history will forget this man. Certain death awaits anyone speaking the name Herostratus.'"

A sickening aura hung over the room as the couple struggled to assimilate the seriousness of the Ephesian situation. Stabbed with guilt, Artemisia subconsciously turned her eyes away from her husband. She knew he would disapprove of what she was doing behind his back. For a moment, she questioned whether her daring scheme for securing a self-written tribute in the annals of history might be entirely noble.

Artemisia saw Mausolus' mouth moving, but she heard no words. Alarming dread had seized her as she realized how this unforeseen tragedy in Ephesus jeopardised her secret building plans. She would need to launch her project months ahead of schedule to retain its most essential feature. Imagine an inverted pyramid balancing on a tenuous point; Artemisia's grand design for achieving world recognition depended on a single aspect: hiring Satyros and Pythius of Priene as her architects and commissioning Scopas, Bryaxis, Leochares, and Timotheus as her sculptors. She needed them; she needed their collaboration; she needed the world's most prominent artisans in one spot - Halicarnassus - working concurrently on one project - her project.

Artemisia made a dim excuse for leaving the breakfast table; she urgently needed to communicate with Otis, her trusted personal servant. "This cannot be happening!" she said. "Since the beginning of time, no structure has claimed the distinction of the one I am planning. Otis, there is no time to waste. I must act now to prevent the Ephesians from snatching my builders over to their project; without these six men united in solidarity on one project, Halicarnassus can forget realising world fame.'

Nervously pacing back and forth, she talked more to herself than her servant. "Otis, do you understand how the name Pythius of Priene can bring legendary status to any structure regardless of its function? He could build a temple, a shed, or even a public húdōr, and it would become famous. Imagine six of the most important names in the world working together! Unthinkable that an arson fire, smouldering twenty-seven parasangs up the coast, could jeopardise my mission."

Knowing his response was unnecessary, Otis remained silent while listening to his mistress rationalise her dreams. "You may think us similar,

Herostratus and me, but I am nothing like this status seeking man. No! I plan to build something magnificent and lasting, a grand structure renowned for its beauty and richness. My ideas are beneficial, as are my endeavours. May it never be said that my plan is comparable to this radical's ambition. He is a thief and a traitor, illegitimately famous. My dreams are founded on conviction and an authentic desire for the glory of Persia."

Otis responded, "Indeed, fire is an unforeseen occurrence, my Lady."

Artemisia did not acknowledge his comment; he already knew she would not. Instead, she continued, explaining her dilemma out loud to herself. "I am counting on scores of skilled craftsmen across the Empire, clamouring for my Halicarnassus project, hoping to work alongside these prominent men. This operation is a remarkable chance for thousands of unskilled labourers to work on a famous site. They will scramble to Halicarnassus to join my army of workers. I refuse to lose them over to Artemis. She can find other men to rebuild her temple. Pythius of Priene is mine!"

She quickly penned a note, disguising her penmanship as a precaution, then dispatched Otis to deliver it to a specific drop spot. Who retrieved Artemisia's secret messages that Otis regularly left in locations throughout the city? He never found out; that person remains a mystery to this day.

Her message read: 'Destruction of Temple of Artemis unfortunate. Loss leaves Ephesians stunned. Must use their shock to our advantage. Move project forward at once. Secure masters and professional team before Ephesians recover and organize rebuilding efforts. Act in haste before possibility of bidding war.'

After sending Otis on his way, Artemisia casually re-entered the room. Mausolus had not noticed her departure. He sat in the same position, still stunned and processing the fire's ramifications for Ephesus and the empire.

Working a new conversation to satisfy her curiosity, Artemisia asked, "What has happened to the boy from court?"

Mausolus had his reasons for evading her. "Which boy?"

"You know which boy. The Hebrew! What has happened to the Hebrew boy seeking his brother?" she snapped.

Mausolus abbreviated the story. "He found him."

"And now?"

"They must have returned home."

"How is this possible when yesterday I observed the boy near the harbour?" the queen scolded.

"Did you?" Mausolus grabbed his favourite rhyton, the silver one decorated with the head of the mythical griffin, and sipped hot herbal tea while watching the soft ripple of waves across the sea. He had a way of avoiding Artemisia's searching stares when he needed to hide something, but this time, his casual manner piqued her suspicion.

"No matter," she said, "the boy seems resourceful enough; he will manage."

"To be sure." Mausolus fumbled with his rhyton as though paying no attention.

Chapter 16

My Spying Mission

Ho, to be sure, working in the king's employ was a grand way to earn an income. Incredibly, I received a wage for visiting the market square. According to Mausolus' instructions, I melded into the whir of the city, appearing as an average citizen following its labyrinth of interconnecting avenues, winding paths, and steep alleys leading to the shops, businesses, and the commons area. I strolled along Harbour Street and covertly listened to conversations in the Stoa of Aegea while feigning interest in the water clock.

I also visited the Spring of Salmacis - I did not drink the water, though. Most folks in Halicarnassus have avoided drinking from the spring ever since Hermaphroditus, the son of Aphrodite and Hermes, drank its water and, just like that, became thilyprepís -transformed into a girl while still being a boy.

My favourite part of the job was exploring the exciting booths at the agora. Tables displayed silk clothing and headdresses sporting white plumes of the cormorant bird, distinctive jewellery made of turquoise or amber beads, also decorative artifacts of copper, ivory, gold, attractive furniture, glazed tiles, and famous Persian carpets. Inspecting the springy pile of colourful yarn, I promised myself I would buy a grand rug for my mother.

Opulent bolts of purple silks and linens caught my eye. Loose ends of cloth fluttered like kites in the breeze as preoccupied merchants folded and rearranged their tussled wares. Tyrian purple! Ridiculous! Royalty, including the Jewish high priest, adores this colour. But no, thank you. Not when Carthaginians extract the dye from a murex shell. Splendid linen drenched in snail innards. Such goes against my taste, but few would agree with that opinion since the people of Halicarnassus sought flashy, pretty, and purple garments.

Carians sold distinctive wines from local Shiraz vineyards, but the highly favoured wines arrived from Phoenicia. World-renowned as masters of winemaking, Phoenicians dominated the wine business. They claimed the secret to their nectar was a gift from their god El who personally nurtures each fermenting kvevri. Phoenician wine was sold at inflated prices to fashionable communities across the empire. Regardless of the cost, generous amounts were purchased every day in Halicarnassus.

Merchant ships crisscrossing the world's oceans carried strange and exotic products to eager consumers. Vessels delivered sophisticated items such as frankincense from Arabia and cloth from Ethiopia; gold and ivory from Africa; blackwood and ebony from the Land of Punt; silk from China; and mysterious cooking spices from India. Metals like copper and silver came from Cyprus, and fragile glassware from Syria. It seemed the world's most lavish products found their way to Halicarnassus. But I was not interested in obtaining fancy baubles – my mother called them expensive gewgaws. She referred to such luxury as frippery.

Nice for some, but ostrich plumes and showy feathers from a cormorant bird, even coveted robes of purple cloth, held no temptation for me. Instead, I remained focused on the exotic cuisines for sale at the food booths.

Fish abounded in this anchorage where the Mediterranean Sea meets the Aegean Sea. Along with the tasty bluefish migrating from the Black Sea, merchants sold freshly caught sardines, mackerel, flounder, seabass, and bream.

Holistic consumers, typically Greeks, included leaves and petals in their food choices. Opposite to what they called 'the omnivorous and gluttonous diets of the Persians', Greeks focused on the advice of Hippocrates for improving health through a strict diet of fruits, vegetables, poultry, herbs, and seeds, preferably spiced with mixed petals and blossoms of roses for strengthening both mind and body.

Strengthening my mind and body did not concern me once an aromatic whiff of freshly baked bread caught my attention. Heading straight for a bakery stall, I observed women weaving braids of dough with nuts and raisins and topping rounded sponge cakes with ribbons of golden honey. Moist loaves of almond bread cooled on racks beside simple flatbreads – sangak and barbari – but the aroma wafting from the dessert items particularly aroused my appetite. I selected an apricot loaf with cinnamon crust and a pastry filled with grape molasses and bergamot paste. My daily routine included a stop at this bakery from that moment forward.

The world's newest cooking techniques captivated Halicarnassus, transforming everyday staples into an absolute dining pleasure of unusual flavours and tantalising sensations. Buffets consisted of meats and poultry, greens tossed in olive oil, roasted vegetables peppered with herbs, and sprinkled in spices: parsley, basil, mint, cumin, cloves, saffron, or coriander.

Baklava cooked with rose water was a popular choice. Customers favoured roasted duck, lamb-stuffed cabbage rolls, and tender veal kabob with noodles. I discovered a wonderland of delicious food –regular fare for fashionable Persians but all new to my humble palate.

After moving the flower petals off to the side, the eggplant dish with dumplings I selected was superb. The meal came with a slice of quince cheese. I scooped up bites of the walnut, pistachio, and berries cooked in pleasant-tasting spices using flatbread pieces. Afterward, I purchased an unusual beverage squeezed from lemons and limes. Gladdened by my delicious food choices, I procured a plum and salted green almonds to save for later, then hurried along to the public húdōr.

Another fabulous experience! Glitzy Halicarnassus overflowed with excesses and comforts, but none more glorious than their public húdōr. This luxurious facility, a place to relieve oneself, became known as the húdōr because of the streaming water transported through a system of clay pipes buried beneath the floor.

Since this contrivance is a rarity, I will explain how it works. Two long rows of side-by-side gourd-shaped holes face each other, allowing easy conversation across the aisle. After positioning over the hole, one can nestle into the sculpted contour of a seat designed for comfortable lingering. Excrement drops into the furrow below, where streaming water moves it along, sending it out the other end of the pipe. Relieving oneself in such luxury is a remarkable pleasure. I prized my regular trips to the public húdōr.

Drowsy from overeating, I tried shaking myself awake by strolling around a commons area where unchaperoned women visited friends or tended to errands. Their expensive attire and confident posture suggested they were neither slaves nor servants but lived as free women. I admired Empire women for their frankness, influence, and economic independence. Women in Halicarnassus were active in politics, ran their own businesses, rented properties, and managed large companies for influential nobles.

Here women could own anything – homes, fishing boats, flocks, orchards, and windmills – they could sell their crafts in vendor booths at the agora or work in the quarries. If a woman in Caria paid her taxes, she warranted the status of 'free citizen' and was permitted to make her own decisions. I observed a handful of women with veiled faces, but they hailed from different regions with different customs where veils symbolise respect.

Making my way to the circular Temple of Ares, I sat on a vacant bench under the shade of a wild maple. From there, I continued my secret mission of spying for the king.

Groups of people exchanged pleasantries while their children played nearby. As couples strolled past, I observed each face, searching for my nighttime visitor and would-be assassin of Queen Artemisia. I saw nothing unusual until a man named Otis appeared.

The queen's attendant approached me. "Go at once to the Harbour Garden." Saying nothing else, he walked away. I followed his route from a distance. Weaving in and out, the eunuch passed chattering people and preoccupied shoppers while dodging slow moving carts laden with cargo. Finally, he disappeared through a gated alcove somewhat hidden by an overgrowth of greenery.

I followed him through the gate into a sweetly scented tunnel arbour covered with Wisteria and white roses. The passage led into a splendid garden, a small scale Persian Parádeisos. Artemisia stayed in current fashion with Persian royalty by investing much time and money in her plants and garden architecture.

Novel growing techniques or evolving new plant varieties garnered the highest esteem from the King of Kings. And the Shahanshah had personally congratulated Artemisia for her plant genus, Artemisia Powis Castle. After giving his stamp of approval and an honourable commendation, Artemisia's silver-grey foliage became popular throughout the empire as a favourite ornamental border along city streets and walkways. Bold flowerbeds along Achaemenid Street incorporated this ornamental sage to accentuate colourful blossoms. And physicians were thrilled with the genus once they discovered the leaves produced a calmative reaction and provided medicinal remedies against liver infections.

I heard faint, melodious dings and followed the sounds to clusters of shells, bones, and hollow wood hanging from tree branches. Soft breezes collided the dangling objects into each other, creating a soothing chorus of tinkling and dinging. Peacocks in full plumage strutted among decorative grasses, alighting on barrier walls thick with vines of goji berry.

Sculpted busts mounted on pedestals stood beside statues of nymphs or wild animals and rearing warhorses. A double-headed griffin gazed both east and west. Considering the king's love for the Olympics, I imagined he particularly admired the bronze statue of the muscular Olympian poised to launch his spear at the sun.

Overlain on an inner wall, a bronze Faravahar spread its wings alongside a carving of a jinni – a Marid jinni ascending in erupting flames, escaping imprisonment in his bottle. The curious creatures, appropriated by Persia from the Babylonians, had wish-granting capabilities.

A tall statue of Hercules in the centre of the garden spewed a cascade of fresh water from his mouth, which accumulated in a clear pool before overflowing into angled rivulets and limestone basins. Decorative fountains doubled as an ingenious system for watering beds of greenery and the varieties of colourful flowers and bushes of peonies.

Shaded benches arranged among the colourful Callas encouraged visitors to relax beside the showy beds. Marble strolling paths wound through rows of orchids and manicured bushes of black roses. I heard the trill of a kingfisher but could not spot him among the trees. The eunuch stood nigh. I wondered what I was doing there.

Then, stunning as an angel, the last person I expected to see stepped into view – Queen Artemisia. On the day of her birth, I imagine a star from heaven bent low to kiss her brow. As a teenage boy, I had no power to combat the effect this erotic, dramatic, and remarkably exhilarating woman had on me.

Gliding toward me, the diplomat walked gracefully as a gazelle, barely touching the ground. The spans of her silk dress clung against her attractive body, and the slight sway of her shapely hips unduly tortured my soul. A subtle grin breaking across her crimson lips carried a hint of mischief, and I heard the faint jingle from her array of golden bracelets.

"Are you enjoying our fair city?" the queen asked.

Mesmerised by her scent, blue butterflies fluttered around, landing on her elegant shoulders. My mouth went dry as a desert wind. "To be sure," I managed to say but stood frozen, paralysed like a garden statue, while the most sensual creature I ever dreamed possible stood talking to me. To me! A mere Hebrew peasant!

Escaping wisps of soft dark hair fluttering beneath her royal headdress blew off her face as a gentle breeze floated the fragrance of her body around me – a provocative perfume of ginger oil. Today, a mere whiff of that fragrance sends my mind back to Artemisia and me together in her lush green garden.

"I expected you to be on your way home," she said as a sudden gust pressed her dress tighter against her body. I wanted to dance, scream, or run to escape the excitement I found in this woman's presence.

Squirming awkwardly and clumsy, unsure how to stand, where to put my hands, or where to cast my eyes, I glanced away, trying to spot that noisy kingfisher. I tell you the truth! While the beautiful queen of Caria spoke to me, I stood looking about like a witless fool.

Oh, Lord, I prayed. *I need your help. I am but a blundering donkey.*

Returning my attention to the queen, I focused my eyes on a safe place, her crescent necklace of bluestone and the dainty earrings tastefully accentuating her loveliest feature, her ears. Intrigued by the array of jewels, my attention became diverted to tiny golden flakes dusted across her neck. With my eyes, I followed the sprinkling of golden specks powdered along her neck and shoulders, continuing their course downward onto her chest, where the array stopped at the bosom of her dress. *Imagine,* I thought to myself while staring at her chest, *she has sparkling golden flakes on her—*

Aghast, I averted my eyes straight away. *Father in heaven, forgive me. But notice for yourself; she has golden powder above her… As you live, Lord, I was admiring the gold.*

Despite the cooling breeze blowing from the sea, I grew hot inside and feared my ears might glow red. The knife! I would keep my eyes fixed on the jewelled dagger she wore at her waist – such a trim waist. *Oh, Lord, forgive me. I am helpless; this time, I am most desirous of her perfect form.*

Uneasy and fidgeting, I crossed my arms, tucking my hands into my armpits, but my thumbs betrayed me by nervously rubbing back and forth across the silkiness of my yellow vest. Those flirty eyes of hers were driving me wild.

If there were a nearby hole, I would have gladly crawled into it. But, unfortunately, I had no choice but to ask, "My Queen, will you please repeat the question."

"Why do you remain in the city?" she asked.

Her inquiry raised a twinge of guilt; how could I speak in a forthcoming manner and protect my agreement with the king? Nevertheless, I stuck to the story I used with Caleb to avoid creating inaccuracies for myself. "Making the long journey home required me first to rest."

"And your brother?" Artemisia asked.

"He departed on a merchant ship to Joppa."

"My husband has taken a liking to you," she said,

Ho, to be sure, such a comment came without warning; I had no response, but what followed next staggered my mind even more.

"I have an assignment for you, requiring you to remain in the city until completion. I want to hire you to work for me. Indeed, I will pay you a handsome wage."

Wedged between a king and his queen! I opened my mouth but had nothing to say.

"My husband, at times, grows dreary when preoccupied with trivial matters of the district – foolish concerns amounting to nothing more than inconsequential drivel. The dullness of his routine robs him of creativity, and he forgets to dream the way we once dreamed. I have found that during these times of tedium, he requires a nudge from someone with zest and fresh new ideas. Someone with marked passion and contagious enthusiasm. My husband requires inspiration from a sprightly youth such as yourself."

My mouth felt dry as a sponge from Kalymnos while listening to this exotic creature wangle my adolescent ego against me. Like a ravenous wolf, I devoured every glorious morsel of her adoration.

"I know you have witnessed the advantages of having a prominent sanctuary. Such a place is a point of convergence for travellers and locals, not to mention it generates public revenue, which benefits the entire community."

She was referring to the Temple of the Jews in Jerusalem. "You are experienced in stonemasonry, true?"

"Yes, my Queen. I have a keen interest in original design and structure." I tried to sound cultured, hoping to impress her.

"Notice there, in the middle of the city." Then, with her eyes, she indicated the direction of the unkempt hill I noticed on my first day in Halicarnassus. The garden wall prevented me from seeing it, but I knew the place she implied.

"Imagine a landmark standing on this hill, a sanctuary as prominent and distinctive as King Solomon's Temple, lofty and elaborate, admired by ships sailing into our harbour. Picture an alluring place for presenting Halicarnassus to the world while honouring my dynasty – the Hecatomnid Dynasty. Close your eyes, Eeeethan. Can you see my vision?"

Ho, to be sure, a tingle shot straight down my spine as she seductively stretched out my name, "Eeeethan." After that, I became unsure of anything she said – something about ships.

Again she said, "Eeeethan, visualise marble, glistening and pure white, rising heavenward from a spacious courtyard surrounded by statuary of historic grandeur. Picture such a sight here in Halicarnassus to honour Persia and revere Mausolus as the great King of Caria."

"You intend to build a new temple here in Halicarnassus?" I asked.

"The gods have enough temples!" Her tone became abrupt. "To be sure, must every temple honour a deity? I envision building a sanctuary."

"A sanctuary?" I asked.

"A meeting place requiring a membership based on elite criteria. An inner sanctum where a league of privileged people will be granted special privileges and entitlements. An extravagant place to convene for play and leisure and to share ideas while feasting with friends."

Membership? Such a foreign concept piqued my interest. "Indeed, my Queen, I visualise a showpiece for the highborn as dazzling as you explain. Will common people of the district contribute their means to such indulgence with no personal advantage?"

Again her tone became abrupt. "Such a worry is no concern of yours, Ethan. I merely require your assistance in helping my husband desire this excellent idea for himself; I trust your youthful excitement will boost his waning enthusiasm. Tell me, does Halicarnassus appear to be the perfect city?" Before I could speak, she answered the question herself. "To be sure, it does not." Again with her eyes, she indicated the hill. She said, "You can see it remains unfinished and is lacking. However, a stunning showpiece will glisten like a magnificent crown of achievement resting on the head of an already beautiful city. Such a work of genius will complete our efforts here."

I had no interest in memberships or a Persian building project, but like a doomed musht, I had been hooked by her charms. I selfishly wanted this woman's attention and longed for the thrill of hearing her say, "Eeeethan."

"Do you understand my request, Eeeethan?"

More shivers. "Yes, my Queen. You desire to build a monument or a sanctuary in Halicarnassus to honour King Mausolus, and you ask me to trick him—" I stopped mid-sentence, horrified at myself. "Please forgive my naïve choice of words. Not trick, my Queen, I meant to say convince the king his important and virtuous ideas will improve the district's future."

"Correct. You are a wise boy, Eeeethan, very discerning." So there it was, my reward for answering correctly. Eeeethan rolled off her lips like kisses dipped in honey. "Above all, you must not raise suspicion; allow this dream to come from Mausolus. Be clear; no one must know of our arrangement."

I wondered, *if Artemisia reigns as queen and desires to build an inner sanctum, why must she wait for Mausolus' approval before initiating her project? They are the rulers, so why do I need to be involved?* I remained silent with my curiosity, though, assuming the matter exceeded the ability of my peasant's brain.

Continuing with her proposition, she forced me to swear. "You are sworn to secrecy, my dear Eeeethan. It will not go well with you should you humiliate King Mausolus by revealing our arrangement."

By now, I would swear to anything; I was malleable clay in her hands, and she knew it. After giving me names and keywords to use, she further explained her ideas, enlightening me on her vision and dreams of transforming the hill into an astonishing sanctuary for the privileged.

Confident I understood her plan, she added, "I forbid you to approach me concerning this matter. However, should you find it necessary to communicate with me, or if you have important information to share, show this stone to Otis and await instructions."

I asked, "How will I, a Hebrew peasant, talk to the king? Should I perhaps..."

Impatient, she cut me off. "Ordering such details belongs to me, Ethan. I will arrange for you to be invited to social events. You will have access to the king, prominent nobles of Halicarnassus, aristocrats, and influential court executives there. Talk of economically strengthening Caria and advancing the prestige of the Empire will greatly interest them. You will have plenty of opportunity to plant seeds at these gatherings."

After her final instructions, she turned and walked away. The abruptness of her departure hurt my feelings. It was as if she had poured cold water on me, cooling a curious pressure heating up within me. I wanted her to stay. I wanted her to take my breath away and consume me again with her delicious scent.

I struggled to regain my senses once she snipped the strings manipulating me like a puppet. At last realizing the stone clutched in my hand, I examined its shape and texture. It was a simple piece of chert, light green, polished into a perfect oval. *Sly. She is brilliant,* I thought, applauding her cleverness. I wondered if this sort of thing was typical in the spy game. Placing the stone in the breast pocket, I exited through the tunnel arbour onto the streets lined with trees, then walked along the beach, trying to sort through the strange new predicament taking over my life. I thought I heard a voice of gentle silence, "Beware allurement."

Chapter 17

The Second Dispatch

Returning to the palace after setting her secret plan in motion, Artemisia arranged white, yellow, and orange tulips in vases around the room. The king suspected nothing since his wife frequently spent afternoons in her favourite garden near the harbour.

Mausolus' mind remained preoccupied with his thoughts – arson in Ephesus, the incident in Labraunda, and the mercenary's assassination attempt. Dark thoughts plagued his mind, circling around and around as he re-analysed the few details he had. In the end, he was left with the same two thoughts: who and why.

Tentatively, he broached these fears with his wife. "The events of late concern me. Two offences against your life, and now a wanton act of destruction against the temple of your patron goddess, Artemis. I sense these are warning signs. We may unknowingly be on a collision course with tragedy. Perhaps the gods are pleading with us to change something. Or stop something. Or start something. Perhaps there is still time to prevent a calamity, maybe alter the course of history. Why else would the gods sound the alarm? Am I failing in some vital matter? If I knew a different path, I would gladly change my course to divert a misfortune.

"When last we travelled to Mylasa, I implored a sign from our forefathers, earnestly praying for guidance, but the heavens remained closed, hard as bronze. Heed my words, Nooré cheshm-am; I see a dangerous sky blowing in a foolish wind, billowing with blackened clouds. I wonder, which direction will this wind blow?" Mausolus had no way of knowing an invisible cord tied him to the tragic loss in Ephesus.

Artemisia set up the board for a game of Technê. She used this tactic to divert her husband's attention away from matters she wished to keep secret.

Right now, she wished to distract him from his probing questions by suggesting his premonition was nonsensical.

After marrying, Mausolus taught his wife to play the Technê game, which he learned while living in Susa. This game is so new, its legitimate name is debatable. Some refer to it as Strategy; others call it War; it has also been called Chess. But I like the Persian word, Technê, because playing it requires the same creative techniques used in the art of war. The game involves marble pieces (some use ivory) carved into military characters that get moved one by one across a cedar board with lines indicating obstacles, such as rivers and mountains. The end goal is to take down the opposing team's generals and imprison their king. It is an enjoyable game of cunning, strategy, and patience for outmanoeuvring the other's military generals and ultimately annihilating their army.

Moza interrupted their game. He had received a second dispatch. Artemisia held her hand out, indicating she wanted to receive the message. After lifting the scroll from a silver tray, she unrolled the communiqué and read.

"News from Macedonia," Artemisia said. "How grand! King Phillip II of Macedonia and his wife, my dear friend Queen Olympias, have birthed a son. His father calls his name Alexander III of Macedon."

"A Macedonian prince born as the Temple of Artemis burns? Peculiar timing," Mausolus said. "Perhaps this baby is preordained. His noble birth might explain why Artemis did not protect her temple; perhaps she was away guarding Alexander's arrival into this world."

"And by further happenstance," Artemisia said, "he arrived on the birthday of our sister Ada, surely a well-meaning sign from above. Great is Tyche, goddess of good fortune and good messages; we must honour her by sending lavish gifts to the child. We must plan a sailing trip to Pella."

Mausolus agreed. "A stallion will be a suitable gift for a young prince."

"My Lord, the child is a newborn. Such a gift, I fear, sounds excessive."

"Nonsense!" he said. "A boy requires early exposure to achieve mastery in handling animals of exceptional quality. Therefore, I will select my finest colt, bold and beautiful, yet spirited and built for speed. Yes, I know the very one! I will send the black foal of the Thessalian mare, the one sired by Idreius' chestnut-brown. Remember, I showed him to you last week; he has a large white star over his brow. I have decided to call him Bous, given the unique marking of an oxhead on his hindquarters."

"An animal of such heft seems remarkably spirited for a young child. Perhaps something smaller and easier to manage, perhaps a foal from the Caspian breed. My Lord, send something of a smaller class if you must send a horse."

"A spirited colt such as Bous will teach young Alexander valuable lessons – given he has the will to learn. The gods know the depleted Argead Dynasty needs a dose of vigour. Indeed, Bous is a superb choice for a young prince."

"As you wish, my Lord. I concede to your wisdom in equestrian matters."

"Then we agree; I will ship my best foal to Pella." Mausolus beamed, proud of his decision and his generosity.

He added, "Today's mood has grown even stranger; it feels like a contest between Eris and Harmonia. One god sends a disaster; the other god sends a triumph. A mysterious meaning exists when rival gods send opposite events in a single day. My mind has grown weary. Let us sleep now, Nooré cheshm-am."

Chapter 18

Harmonia and Eris
Goddess of Harmony, Goddess of Chaos

At about this time, the new Shahanshah, King Artaxerxes III Ochus of Persia, began making enemies across the empire. Murdering every member of the Persian royal family had unleashed a barrage of scrimmages, uprisings, and revolts led by angry protestors. The king's unreasonableness and insecurity plunged his government into chaos, straining the administrative abilities of royal strategists and military advisors. With anarchy rippling across the empire, panic spread throughout the outlying satrapies.

Persians anticipated war – both foreign and domestic – and a war would obligate each satrapy to rally behind Artaxerxes with financial assistance and enlistment of soldiers, a strain crushing the weaker, financially strapped districts.

Caria was one of the empire's most distant satrapies. While technically under Persian sovereignty, the great distance (more than 400 parasangs) and lack of prying eyes afforded the district excuse, liberties, and the flexibility to rule independently. Like most Persian cities along the coast of the Aegean Sea, Halicarnassus was culturally more Grecian than Persian. Artaxerxes had no way of knowing the goings on in any of his remote districts without the investigative skill of his special inspector. Mausolus proceeded cautiously, anticipating the inspector would arrive with an ominous report concerning the realm's political climate. He feared war was coming to his corner of the empire and expected mandates restricting expenditures. He would not risk disgrace and humiliation from financial overextension should the Shahanshah demand aid.

Not only Mausolus, no satrap in the empire was foolish enough to risk even minor construction projects during such economic and civil unrest. Yet, Artemisia continued unabated with her plan to erect an overly ambitious engineering marvel. Once convincing herself she was on an errand for the gods, she would not be dissuaded. Instead of turning back, she wildly moved forward with preparations. Her timing could not have been worse.

Violence marred the celebration in Labraunda. A tragic arson fire destroyed worship in Ephesus. Threats of war rippled across Anatolia, and instability rocked Persia's fledgling government. Mandatory financial obligations loomed large, and in Halicarnassus, the special inspector was due for his annual visit. All this was happening with an assassin at large.

Despite chaos on every front, Artemisia persisted, working secretly behind the scenes while relying on me to convince Mausolus this was a great time to build an ostentatious sanctuary.

And here I will tell you why Artemisia chose to weave me into her plan. Two words: dual leadership. Dual leadership forbids either vassal from enacting new regulations or structural developments without agreement from the other. Artemisia, legally prohibited from proceeding with her building project, required Mausolus' consent before initiating construction. The special inspector was proficient at spotting infractions, especially something as apparent as an absent or forged signature. And Artemisia did not want to incur a stain on her record by receiving a reprimand.

With underhanded plans for construction already in motion, she felt pressured to gain that consent. Why the urgency? Delays brought danger, and danger brought risk, and protecting her assets became progressively more difficult.

Unbeknownst to Mausolus – to any of us, for that matter – a secret treasure lay hidden on a lonely Persian island. Uninhabited. Desolate. Unpatrolled by military vessels, ignored by traders, and skirted by shipping lanes. This unimportant island offered one valuable amenity, a hidden cove. Difficult to spot and difficult to navigate, once through the tricky channel, ships found a safe harbour protected from wind, rough seas, and eyesight.

Hidden within the anonymous bay, a fleet of ships anchored, heavy laden with quarried stone, limestone, and premium Athenian marble. Smaller vessels held various tools, hardwoods, construction equipment, pumice barrels, tin oxide, and precious gold, silver, and bronze alloys. Artemisia needed these materials to build her magnificent sanctuary for the privileged. Once she had Mausolus' consent, these ships would bring her precious cargo to Halicarnassus, and work could begin.

At times Mausolus and Artemisia were as opposite as Harmonia, goddess of harmony, and Eris, goddess of chaos. Mausolus wisely halted all enterprise and proceeded with caution. Artemisia, on the other hand, relentlessly pushed onward in foolhardy abandon. Close by, the Fates spun their thread of human destiny.

Chapter 19

Life at the Palace

Ho, to be sure, Queen Artemisia kept her word; within days of our meeting, I received an invitation requesting my presence at a dinner party hosted by the satraps.

In giddy disbelief, I left my quarters and headed toward the imperial palace. Eagerness put a skip in my stride as I walked along Harbour Street, then over to the street called Anáktora. But the closer I got to my destination, the more my boldness turned to terror bordering on panic. Impossibly nervous, I fidgeted, adjusting my costly new outfit, smoothing my trousers, and rearranging my vest. I ran my fingers through my hair while rehearsing an invitation speech.

"Most gracious King Mausolus, thank you for..." No, too thick.

"Your humble servant thanks you, oh wonderful King Mausolus..." No, too grovelling.

Practising politeness, including several flowing bows, brought curious stares from confused passers-by. Apprehensive about first impressions, I feared I might miss a critical signal or break some royal protocol. Guests may laugh at me or my peasant background; I may say something daft or grossly incorrect, forcing Mausolus to cut off my ear.

After arriving at the arched entrance of the land bridge, I stopped. Overwhelmed by such majesty, I surveyed the sweeping palace and found it necessary to have a discussion with myself. "Lunacy! Wake up! This idea of dining with the rich and famous inside their luxurious white palace is unsettling. You are dreaming or suffering from heatstroke hallucinations. After all, Eeeethan, you are a peasant, a boor, and a borderline dolt. You have no right to accept an intimate gesture of fellowship with nobility, let alone dinner with Persian satraps. Fly to the moon; that would feel less awkward."

Standing motionless as a tree stump, staring wide-eyed across that bridge, I tried to muster the courage to proceed. I wanted to turn around, run, and keep running far away from people who dress in beautiful silk and wear jewelled crowns. "No!" I said. "I am not going in there! I cannot go through with this absurd idea!" There is no explanation for what happened next other than to say an unexpected peace washed over me as a quiet fascination beckoned me to proceed. I accepted the challenge and walked into a bold new life.

Fingering through my windswept curls one last time and straightening my clothing, I encouraged myself over the bridge and up the broad drive of polished masonry blocks. This approach, outlined with fluted columns, led to a wide staircase beneath a stucco-laden colonnade painted deep porphyry red.

Two armed sentries watching my hesitancy at the bridge stood before the bronze palace doors. They intercepted me at the top of the steps. With ridiculing pleasure, they demanded to know what I was doing, loitering in front of the palace. They accused me of looking suspicious and asked if I was a lunatic who talked to himself. My nervousness made my voice squeak, coming off high-pitched and shrill, which gave them much cause for laughter.

One tried to mimic me by squeaking, "I received an invitation to dine with the satraps!"

The other answered with a high-pitched inflection, "Ooh, fancy! Dining with the satraps! Well, la-dee-da! Come right on in, my Lady!" They granted me entry with a sweeping gesture, then burst out laughing. I hurriedly stepped through the stone archway before the glowing red of my ears inspired further mockery.

The entranceway opened into an open-air aíthrio or an indoor courtyard with an opening in the roof, allowing daylight to shine through. As the sun followed its course across the sky, beams of light washed over the walls and, one at a time, illuminated murals as if telling a story episode by episode. Paintings told of mythological creatures, sea battles, and action scenes from famous plays. Warblers sang from their perches atop bottle-shaped palm trees, and a pleasant fragrance of vanilla emanated from rows of orchids. The sweet air, joyful chirping, and soft murmur of fountains spilling into clear pools produced a most welcoming atmosphere, and I began to relax.

The enchanting white polished palace, surrounded by a thick stone wall, was built high in the centre of rocky Zephyria Island, which was naturally edged by large jagged rocks protruding disorderly above the soil. The terrain varied between a wooded area growing beside jagged rocks filled with rock roses and green clusters of samphire, then to a section of manicured ground plants and limestone statuary, then more craggy rocks, and back to lush greenery and colourful flower beds with marble benches overlooking the sea. Amid an orchard of pink, purple, red, and white bougainvillea was an ornate fountain filling a large pond. Additional bougainvillea trees were scattered throughout the island, adding splashes of vivid colour to the drabness of the rock.

The enormous, rectangular-shaped palace overlooked the sea on three sides – it looked like it had two levels, but there were three. The lower level was mostly below ground. A semi-circular portico sheltering the staircase to the servants' quarters, kitchens, and laundry protruded into a yard with vegetable gardens, animal pens, a fish house, and shelter for Mausolus' chariot.

Inside the palace, broad staircases provided easy access between the upper two levels. The uppermost level accommodated the satraps' residence, which included two lounges; one was private, and the other was for entertaining. Also on this level were the satraps' private chambers, a dining hall, a library, a workroom, and a meeting room for conducting business. Their private quarters, which occupied the extravagant pinnacle wing overlooking the sea, had individual bathing and dressing rooms, shared married quarters, sweeping porches with flower gardens, Mausolus' private den, and a gymnasium used each morning by Artemisia.

Large windows all around provided panoramic vistas allowing bright sunlight into each room. Servants closed the curtains at night and burned oil lamps to keep the chambers well-lit.

The middle story was reserved for visitors, Artemisia decorated this level in deep colours, richly painted murals, tapestries, and decorative statues. In addition to a lavish parlour for receiving high-ranking officials, this tier included sleeping accommodations, rooms and halls for gatherings, entertaining friends, or hosting special dinners.

The entire west side of the palace was one large room. Artemisia called this room the apādana, although it was nowhere near a true apādana where the great Shahanshah banqueted. But it was by far Anatolia's most impressive hypostyle hall. This one was built with forty columns – instead of seventy-two like the one in Susa – and had an exquisite floor of multi-coloured tiles. The vaulted ceilings were carved of cedar. Double doors opened onto a sweeping patio letting in the freshness of the sea and providing views of the gardens and verdant lea below. I fondly remember every grand party celebrated in that apadana.

Never before or since have I endured such a terrifying social visit as I did on my first visit to the satraps' palace. Gradually, I became more comfortable and spent much of my free time in the couple's home. Better still, I was permitted to explore the entire fortress; my favourite area was Mausolus' private den, where he displayed fascinating collectibles, relics, and trophies, including a collection of exotic animal furs.

Curious to know of such beasts, Mausolus explained, "Ethan, my boy. You are looking at the hides of creatures existing only in the jungle, a remote land parasangs from Caria where black people are neither Persian nor Macedonian. This stripped hide is called a zebra. But feel this; it is called a monkey – and over here, a gorilla. There is a giraffe, a capybara, and a wildebeest. Go ahead, stroke them." The jungle was unknown to me, but I found each hide irresistible for stroking and occasional nuzzling when no one watched.

Mausolus unrolled his map to show me the location of the jungle compared to the rest of the world. Ho, to be sure, how could there be a drawing of the whole world? Mausolus taught me how to read maps with symbols and codes. His maps came from the prominent mapmaker, Anaximander of Miletus.

"Notice, Ethan. The Earth is like a pie, cut in half through the middle of the Mediterranean Sea. The northern piece of pie Anaximander calls Europa, and the southern piece he calls Asia. Since the dividing line practically touches the district, Caria barely fits into the south portion."

"Where is the Land of Israel?" I asked.

"Israel is here; it resides well within the southern section."

"And this area is the Aegean?" I asked.

"Excellent!" he said.

"I thought the Aegean was a boundless sea, but Anaximander's map shows it as a large bay extending off the Mediterranean Sea. It looks small by comparison, like a bubble suspended between Greece and Persia in this area called Europa," I said.

"These modern maps detail information about other countries. See this triangular symbol? That indicates a mountain, whereas several triangles mean a mountain range. And these lines show important river systems in each half of the world. Best to avoid those places beyond this thick border, Ethan. These lands are unexplored; mysterious creatures lurk in this dangerous domain."

I thought, *How grand an adventure to use maps and traverse unexplored lands filled with mysterious inhabitants.*

The satrap proudly displayed his unusual finds and intriguing objects on tables and in nooks and crevices throughout his den. Enamoured with the amount of information he possessed, I revered his lessons, viewpoints, philosophies, ethics, and principles. Like dough leavening on a hot day, my trivial world expanded beyond measure because of my association with Mausolus.

Life with the satraps was filled with festivities at the apādana, meeting influential people and making new friends, dining with distinguished visitors, listening to famous theorists and philosophers, eating exotic foods, wearing fine clothing, and frequenting the theatre. I had no trouble adjusting to palace life or basking in the affluence of Persian luxury while continuing my dual assignments, spying for the king, and what should I call my service for the queen? Contriving?

Chapter 20

Swords, Spears, Fists, and Daggers

Faithful to his word, Mausolus provided me with an income. I received double pay, a wage from the king, and a wage from the queen. Moreover, neither knew of the other, and both paid me handsomely since both depended on me. As promised, Mausolus provided a room for me at the barracks and arranged my meals... with Goliath.

Entering Goliath's home for the first time, I subconsciously ran my hand across my buttocks, remembering the welts inflicted there and my annoyance at him for doing so. Annoyance? No, absolute outrage is what I felt toward him. Annoyance is what I felt toward Mausolus for making this arrangement. I planned to ask him to place me with a different family.

Goliath ignored my presence in the doorway as he reclined at a table, waiting for the evening meal.

Unsure of myself, I stepped forward, but before finding an opportunity to speak, four boys resembling a cavalry charge crashed into the room and attacked him. My heart froze. Roaring the deep thundering roar of a hungry lion, the giant struggled to his feet while the boys laughed and jumped on him, pushing him back. Then, breaking away, the oldest boy grabbed a small wicker shield with a mock spear, spun around, and charged.

Seizing the boy's leg, Goliath laughed while flip-flopping him in the air like a freshly caught fish. Then, grabbing another boy around the waist, he suspended the giggling youngsters high above the table and roared, "Behold, my dinner!"

Screaming boys ran around in a circle while the two captured boys laughed and batted each other mid-air. Finally, Goliath set the children on the floor and prepared to go after the other boys standing a span out of his grasp. I watched in stunned silence, wondering how this scenario would play out when a middle-aged woman carrying a tray of food walked into the dining hall and called the room to order.

"Enough. Play with your father later; now we eat." She arranged the food on the table and straightened the cushions.

What! Father? The giant has children! Impossible! He must have stolen this brood from a village in the province to work them as slaves!

Next, she walked in. Carrying dishes and a tray of food, the girl in my dream entered the room, the giggling girl from my first morning in Halicarnassus. I recognised her pretty face with rosebud lips and straight white teeth. The long dark braid hanging over her shoulder had been woven with a ribbon of pale green silk, matching the sash of her Persian dress. She wore several bracelets and a toe ring on her pretty bare feet. Praise heaven, her petite frame and smooth tan skin resembled her mother instead of her father.

Like the morning she served my food, the maiden's face reddened at my presence. Setting the tray on the table, she turned to leave but first eyed me with the coy glance of an interested woman. My heart skipped like a spring calf let out to pasture. Her fleeting gaze did not go unnoticed; in childish banter, the boys taunted, "Jaleh loves a boy!"

Ho, to be sure, Jaleh was her name. Their lovely daughter had a beautiful name, Jaleh. It sounded to me like a song – Jaleh!

Goliath's eyes followed his wife, Simin, around the room while she flitted past preparing the family meal. Leaning across him to place a basket on the table, I heard his tender whisper. "Jeegaram." She smiled at his affection. Goliath settled the boys and invited me to their table. Returning with cups for our drink, the girl sat across from me.

Simin appeared younger than the giant and deeply loved her husband and children. Settling around the table, she welcomed me to the family, and after reciting a strange blessing, she passed a bowl to me first.

I accepted the honour.

The room grew strangely quiet. Fearing to break the silence, I focused on eating.

Simin continued, "My husband tells me you come from Eber-Nari, in the Land of Israel."

"Yes, ma'am." I tore off a piece of bread.

"Tell us of your land far away from Caria." I heard a soft voice speaking words sweetened with the nectar of an angel. Everybody stopped eating and looked at Jaleh. Her face turned red as a vegetable root, mine also. We locked eyes from across the table and then self-consciously looked back to our plates.

Cas, the oldest boy, said, "Oh, nobody cares about Eber-Nari. Do you have a dagger?"

I was grateful for the diversion and told him no, but I planned to purchase one and promised to show him. He acted pleased.

Lifting a basket of vegetables from the middle of the table, Goliath suspended the item above him, examining the quality as if he expected the bottom to fall off. The boys burst into laughter at his mischief. Patting her daughter's hand, Simin scolded her husband. "Aziz, my beloved husband, how will our daughter improve her talents with your continual teasing?" Apologising, he told Jaleh he much admired her art. I became aware of different projects in various stages of completion strewn around the room – mats, vases, bowls, boxes, and simple pieces of furniture.

"You wove this lovely basket?" I asked. Jaleh's face reddened, and the boys punched each other while laughing.

Simin smiled. "Thank you, Ethan. Jaleh studies basket-making from women in the city; she enjoys experimenting with different patterns and is learning complex techniques. One day, she will acquire a booth and sell her wares for profit in the agora. We are proud of her tenacity and creative abilities." Jaleh kept her eyes focused downward, self-conscious of the attention.

To be sure, I enjoyed spending time with this family; I felt a strong kinship with them. I particularly enjoyed the hardy romps and grappling matches with those rowdy boys. Twelve years of age and already a miniature Goliath, Cas wanted nothing more than the opportunity to be a soldier, following in his father's footsteps.

The middle boys – twins, Farzin and Gulzar – looked about ten years of age and stuck together the way sap sticks to skin, spurring each other on in mayhem and nuisance; what one failed to concoct, the other devised. I had to take the twins in small doses; both annoyed me with their continuous punching to provoke each other.

The youngest child, a sweet boy named Arman, had a tender way about him. He reminded me of my brother Caleb in the loving way he gathered wildflowers into a bouquet for his mother. Arman showed no interest in becoming a soldier. Jaleh, their oldest child, was the only girl – a younger daughter had died of disease while an infant.

As time passed, Goliath and Simin accepted me as one of the family. When off duty, Goliath taught me, along with his sons and other interested boys, the necessary skills needed for combat. He had learned the art of warfare from his father, Ralf, who soldiered near the end of the Peloponnesian War when Persia supported Sparta against Athens. He then served in the Corinthian War.

A dedicated student of martial sports, Goliath thrived as a soldier and fought for Mausolus during the Revolt of the Satraps, then again when Mausolus fought in Lycia and Ionia. Inexperienced and young at the start of the revolt, Goliath fought with the other tyros on the frontline of the battlefield – a menial post where the least trained soldiers learned to fight hard or die fast. Placing the lesser fighters at the front saved the skilled fighters from making the final assault. Several times injured, Goliath continued to dominate, fearless in the thick of battle. He advanced through the ranks by improving his strength and skill until becoming a strong presence on the rear lines.

After the war, Mausolus commissioned the most courageous soldiers to serve as his special guards. Goliath, an immensely proud warrior, earned his prestigious position as commander of the Carian Guard. Protecting the satraps was an enormous privilege and his ultimate duty.

Soldiering or not, Goliath wanted us boys to learn self-defence for every situation we may encounter. He instructed us to use the bow, and throw the javelin, and also for close-range combat with knives and swords. Using lightweight training swords, we practised in mock duels.

During training drills, he yelled, "Surroundings! Take notice! Who stands beside you? Survey! Stay aware!" We sometimes trained for hours, but our resolve to care about our surroundings – or anything else – disappeared when fatigue weakened us. Relishing those moments of slothful disregard, Goliath launched his legendary surprise offensive.

Out of nowhere, his lieutenant, Thuxra, would appear and pounce. Grabbing his intended target from behind, he lifted his prey off the ground in a tight wrestling hold and body-slammed the hapless victim onto the sandy soil. I failed to perceive any humour in such raids – of course, when I put the same move on Cas, I found these blitzes hilarious.

Equipping us to champion in unarmed combat, Goliath taught wrestling and a new fighting art called boxing. This form of weapon-less combat gained enough popularity to become an Olympic event. Wrapping thongs of ox-hide around our knuckles, we ran into the training pit, waving to an arena filled with imaginary fans cheering us on to Olympic victory. We trained wearing only a schenti or a loincloth pleated in front, but Goliath said the Macedonians practiced their training drills completely naked.

Aiding and depending on each other in battle became a tenet we learned by drilling in the wall of shields. Invented by the Athenians, the wall formation became the winning tactic for victory over the Persians at the Battle of Marathon. Goliath called the formation a phalanx – a massive front line of sparabara, or shield bearers, overlapping shields with the man standing beside him. One shield covered his left side and the right side of another man. A properly formed phalanx, looking like slithering scales along a serpent's back, utilises the power from combined strength to push the enemy off balance, break through their line, swing around, and strike from behind.

Pushing into the wall and shoving against its constant pressure required tremendous body strength. When Goliath yelled, "Wall!" we boys merged, overlapping our spara shields, marching forward in unison. "Shield arms up! Stance! Lean in!" he shouted. Sometimes engaging us himself, he would strap on his massive shield, shove our line backward, penetrate the wall, swing around, and with a thud from his wooden sword, announce, "You are dead, Ethan."

Certain death awaited any soldier who fell in the wall formation if he failed to get back on his feet in a hurry. I remain most appreciative that the sandy training arena provided a soft landing since Goliath knocked me to the ground with no mercy countless times.

Training did provide victorious moments of joy. For example, when accurately employing the phalanx formation by combining our strength, we boys had enough muscle to shove Goliath backward, push him off balance, rush in with our mock swords, and finish him off. Overpowering the giant became an incredible victory, after which we raced into the house, eager to tell Simin of our grand triumph.

Drills included instructions on using stabbing weapons such as the akinaka. This cubit-long double-edged blade is used with a rapid thrusting motion with three quick moves – grip, pull, and stab. Practising with the akinaka explained the ugly wound I cauterized in the assassin's leg. Queen Artemisia inflicted a terrible slice by driving her akinaka into the man's calf. Realizing how close she got to him and how skilfully she used her blade to fight him off only deepened my hopeless admiration for her.

Goliath taught me to move my feet as if dancing -quick and light. He insisted I learn skills in both combat styles – fighting with a weapon and fighting with my hands. The giant devoted much of his time to our regimented teaching and expected excellence from his students regarding the art of knife defence. He taught technique, manoeuvrability, and a forward stance while maintaining balance with proper weight distribution between the feet.

Knife in the right-hand left-hand protecting. Goliath called the left hand the 'guarding hand.' He demonstrated how to keep the guarding arm across the chest, protecting the heart while using the guarding hand to protect the neck and face. It could also be used as a distracting hand to deflect attention and set up an attack. Here I had an advantage. Working with masonry tools sometimes required me to switch hands to carve different angles, so I became competent in using both hands equally well. During our mock knife fights, I smartly wielded the knife switching between hands. In my mind, this fancy knack contributed a dramatic flair to my exceptional fighting skills. Goliath merely shook his head at my puffed-up opinion of my ability.

Sometimes he observed drills from a distance to appraise our form and refine our style. Watching us practise with wooden knives, he yelled commands to help us perfect our moves and defensive countermoves. "Step in, close the gap! Block! Get that guard hand up! Sever a artery! Show me some sweeps. Good! Reverse your grip on that hilt!"

Drills involved striking toward each other's heart or neck, stepping around in counterattack, hitting an arm, or disabling a hand. We learned deadly striking points: liver, heart, arteries.

I found our mock battles amusing, mainly when I managed to gain the upper hand on Cas by tricking him with my fancy hand-switching manoeuvre. As I held my knife in my left hand, Cas positioned himself before me, expecting a particular move. But, by changing hands, I caught him off guard and struck the artery in his neck or his heart. Sometimes, I pretended to drive a wicked plunge into his lung. I fooled him every time.

As valuable as Goliath's training was, I had no plans to become a soldier. Nevertheless, knowing how to handle myself in a confrontation gave me a certain amount of confidence. In truth, I viewed training as a time of play instead of an earnest endeavour to become proficient at knife, sword, or endurance in the shield wall. Soldiers have likened fighting in the wall to a harrowing walk through Hades, a distasteful encounter I intended to avoid.

Ho, to be sure, my education became serious in a hurry the day Goliath carried out real knives. "Rely on your training, Ethan," he told me. "Control your breathing. Avoid shallow breaths; chest breathing makes quivering hands." Then, shifting his feet into a fighting stance, he faced me, holding his knife. Bending his front knee, elbows into his body, and hands up with his guarding hand positioned in front of his neck, he moved with effortless skill.

Smiling an enormous grin, I formed my fighting stance and bounced from foot to foot. Then, circling each other for a moment, I found my opening and stepped in to close the gap.

Goliath struck in a flash! He pitched forward, sliced my arm, and I dropped my knife! Then he grabbed me by my face, threw me to the ground, knelt on my chest, and pretended to kill me with a lethal slice to my neck. "You're dead, Ethan." My first fight lasted five beats – maybe four. Stunned, I lay flat on my back, blood streaming from my arm.

Showing no pity, he scolded, "A knife fight is viscous! It is not some joke to approach with a stupid grin. Ethan, if you want to stay alive, you must believe combat is a serious kill or get killed competition. What did I say about using your first weapon?"

I said, "Your body tells the knife what to do. Use your body as your first weapon, and the knife will follow as your second weapon."

"Is that what you did?"

I answered by holding up my bleeding arm.

"Get used to bleeding, boy!" he scolded. "Carrying a knife indicates a willingness to fight with a knife, so be prepared to get cut with a knife. Use any object at hand and any manoeuvre necessary to win because neither combat nor death follows the rules. And pouting your little boy feelings after dropping your weapon will only get you gutted - stem to stern." He finished our first lesson of hand-to-hand combat by saying, "Have Simin stitch your arm, and we will try again."

The humiliating incident changed my outlook; I no longer viewed training as a time of boyhood amusement. Instead, I accepted Goliath's drills as earnest lessons in self-preservation. I stored his wisdom deep in my heart and used it to become a proficient contender in self-defence, including wrestling. Although initially I resented injuries and hard lessons endured under the giant's tutelage, I later came to appreciate Goliath's genuine care for me. He thumped me hard like a hammer thumps a nail because he wanted me to stay alive.

Before leaving Halicarnassus, Goliath and I would fight side by side, defending those we loved while opposing murderous adversaries of the empire.

Chapter 21

Assassin at Large

Simin's greatest joy was caring for her household. An industrious woman with a tender spirit, she had a way of absentmindedly brushing sand or dust from my clothing or pushing a wayward curl off my face. Of course, I missed my mother, but Simin became a loving substitute. To repay her kindness, I often helped around the house. Sometimes I did errands, gathered vegetables from the garden, or ran to the agora for certain spices or herbs. But, I admit, watching the boys for her was the supreme test of my fondness.

Arman preferred our trips to the sea, where the boys enjoyed floating miniature sailing vessels they crafted from wood. Cas, Farzin, and Gulzar had plenty of friends their age to muck about. Boys in the barracks played war games with wooden swords and small wicker shields. Chasing each other like feral warriors racing through the streets of the commons and along the beach, their final attack came in the training sandpit, where they pounced and wrestled each other, sending sand flying into the air with all the gusts of a windstorm.

Young girls delighted in neighbourhood war games but avoided battling with swords. Instead, they played the role of peltast; confined to the sidelines, they pelted beach stones at the boys – most pebbles missed their mark. Jaleh blushed when I asked if she had spent her childhood loping after the older kids, throwing rocks while boys clobbered each other with shields and swords.

Under the watchful eye of Simin, Jaleh and I enjoyed each other's company, laughing and talking away the days. Sharing personal stories, I told her of my family and life in Jericho and my work in Jerusalem. I shared incidents from my journey to Halicarnassus, the caravans, and the settlements I had seen. I described the Uxians and explained the political views I learned from the Egyptians. On and on, I talked, telling of my dangerous trek through the Cilician Gates and how I found my way to the Meander River. Clinging to my every word, she considered me the bravest, most daring traveller of the Empire.

Jaleh shared her life in Halicarnassus, her love of weaving, and her frustrating struggle to improve. She dreamed of having a business of her own, along with owning a workshop to employ free women she trained in the art of weaving. They would produce high-quality wicker items, filling special orders for export to distant countries. She imagined selling her wares in every major port across the world.

I loved her for her ambitious dreams and worthy goals. I loved her eyes, how they sparkled when she talked or turned dreamy at special times. I loved the way she laughed with abandon at something I said. I loved how hard she tried and how sweetly she sang without realising she was doing it. I loved her beauty and wholesome spirit. Jaleh was a delight; I called her Jaleh Joon – Jaleh, my sweetheart.

Accompanying me to functions at the palace thrilled my Jaleh Joon; we occasionally attended the theatre, or I invited her to my favourite bakery for a treat of fried dough on yogurt. I tried teaching her to play the game Technê, but abandoned the idea after realising she had no capacity for strategic thinking.

Goliath must have considered me a proper fellow since he permitted me to walk alone with Jaleh one evening. Beneath the gentle light of the moon, we strolled through the public gardens; the intoxicating fragrance of gardenias swirled around us, wrapping us in amorous wonder. Our hands, at last, found each other and embraced. Ho, to be sure, her soft skin was warm and her touch tender. Passion and anticipation sent an orchestra of butterflies dancing in my stomach. Her soft eyes whispered, "Kiss me." To be sure, I intended to kiss her plenty until a small voice whispered: "Her father is a giant!"

I wavered and suggested we continue strolling. When we arrived at the scraggly mound in the middle of the city, I mentioned how building something grand on the spacious ground might enhance the city and become financially valuable to the district. To her, the area looked like nothing more than a drab field she passed on her way to the agora, but she became delightfully attentive once I began to speak of the space.

I said, "If I reigned as satrap, I would build a tall structure in this area: a sanctuary or a shrine. Something monumental." I hoped that when something was built there, she would be impressed by my insight.

"Yes," she said. "Something pleasant." Casting her eyes toward the neglected hill, I doubted she could visualise any admirable construction. "But for what purpose?" she asked.

Ho, to be sure, women ask the oddest questions. "The purpose! Why, to stand forever, for looking grand and magnificent. To let the entire world know the greatness of a king and his queen!"

"To be sure," she said. "A structure enhancing our avenue is a decent idea." Tilting her pretty face ever so gently, Jaleh looked at me. Then, her voice changed to a serious tone. "Ethan?"

Oh no, I thought.

"Do you have plans for leaving Halicarnassus?"

"No plans. I wait for my brother."

"As you say, but something other than a brother seems to occupy your thoughts."

I grew uncomfortable under her shrewd scrutiny. "Something else? I occupy myself with nothing else."

"Will you return to your home anytime soon?" Jaleh asked.

"One day, I plan on returning to my home in Judah, but I live here for now."

"What will you do in Judah?"

"I will resume my trade. I am a stonemason. In my country, stonemasonry is an honourable profession and provides a lucrative income, especially in a city the size of Jerusalem."

"Will you marry after returning home?"

"Marry? I suppose someday I will marry, a long time from now."

"Ethan, why not remain here to work as a stonemason and marry in Halicarnassus." Her head tilted the other direction, and her eyes, soft as a doe's, blinked softly.

Confused, flustered, and unsure of how we had jumped to the subject of marriage, I struggled to restore my equilibrium. I had intended to convey my brilliance and profound insight, but when Jaleh moved closer to nuzzle my neck, I forgot what I was saying. Fragrant as honey dripping from the comb, the scent of her skin unleashed another flurry of butterflies, sending beads of sweat trickling down my spine. So naïve and simple was I, but I intended to please her.

Smiling at her face, I brushed away the wisps of hair a gentle breeze had blown across her rosebud lips. And then, a streak. Movement in my peripheral vision caught my attention. *Goliath!* was my first thought.

Turning slightly, I spotted a stealthy figure wearing a black cloak moving between the buildings, making his way to the harbour. I recognised him. Prodding her by the arm, I forcefully moved Jaleh backward into a shadow. "Jaleh Joon, stay silent and come with me."

Confused and disappointed by our lost moment, she demanded an answer. "Ethan, did I say something wrong? Why do you push me? Let go of my arm!"

I pressed her forward. "Hush, Jaleh! I must speak to your father."

"My father? Ethan, what is happening?"

"Jaleh, please! No questions! Come with me now; we cannot delay!" Picking our way past the gardens, I used darkness as a cover to avoid detection. Unsure if the reddish man had seen us or if he had companions lurking nearby, we kept to the shadows, working our way to the house. "I will wait here," I told her. "Go! Tell your father to come out at once!"

"Ethan, do you act this way because I spoke of marriage?" She acted puzzled.

"Jaleh, please! Go find your father!"

Goliath came out, tamping tobacco into his pipe. Fright caused my voice to tremble. "The peltast! He is here! I spotted him in Halicarnassus heading toward the harbour."

Stepping back into the house, Goliath returned dressed as a soldier armed with a spear and shield. Fastening his scabbard belt while sprinting across the yard, he roused his men. His soldiers reported battle-ready in record time, wearing military gear and carrying weapons.

As he shouted orders, his men obeyed. "Thuxra, go to the palace and inform the sentry. Protect the queen! Ethan, come with us but stay behind the troops. We may require your identification of this man. Do you have your knife?

"Yes," I said.

"Do not be afraid to use your weapon if necessary." Then, he motioned his men to move out. Following the detachment, running to maintain their quick pace brought back memories. Making no sound, the soldiers followed their commander, clambering through the streets of Halicarnassus, occasionally stopping to listen, cautious to avoid an ambush or a dead-end path. Goliath took a shortcut to the beach by accessing a tight passageway he knew of. We squeezed through the narrow slot scored between high walls one at a time, then fanned out across the beach, moving away from the city.

The commander stopped to listen for sounds in the blackness. When he motioned with his hand, we dropped to our stomachs. Far ahead, two men helped a third man climb aboard a skiff, his black cloak blowing behind him. The strangers pushed away from the shore. Digging their oars into the water, they struggled to escape the onshore winds.

"Hold position!" he whispered. "I doubt they have detected our presence, but we must avoid letting our enemy know we have discovered his return." Listening to the waves washing in and out against the shoreline, I lay in the darkness, smelling the tang of wet sand. With the slap of the sail, the boat disappeared into the blackness of the sea. The assassin had again slipped through Goliath's grasp.

Returning empty-handed to the palace, Goliath reported the incident to Mausolus. The king burned with anger. "Tell me every detail, and may the gods strike you dead if you hide a single detail from me."

Acting both powerful and fragile, the renewed danger against his wife sent the satrap into a rage. Then, in an act of madness, he exploded, charging from room to room, removing every possible hiding place by tearing down draperies and wall coverings throughout the palace.

Chapter 22

The Barbershop

News and gossip flowed in and out of the city through the barbershop. This location provided an excellent opportunity for spying. A waft of lemon oil hit me as I walked into a crowded establishment filled with chattering patrons. Busy barbers cut and styled hair or tamed beards into any arrangement a person desired. Persian men devoted several hours daily to tailoring their facial hair, trimming, shaping, oiling, and curling with various instruments to force coarse whiskers into irregular shapes.

Considering my struggle to grow a beard, I intended to keep every hard-won whisker and rejected the absurd notion of curling them. I had enough trouble with curls without using hot rods to produce new ones. So instead, I requested a haircut and a beard trim – straight and tight along my jawline the way Mausolus wore his beard.

Setting me on a comfortable cushion, the barber placed my feet on a feather bolster and leaned me back until my head reached a shallow basin for washing. First, he kneaded my scalp with warm scented balm and worked a strange ointment through every strand outward toward the ends.

Next, in preparation for shaving, he applied a layer of lavender emollient and covered my face in hot towels. Then, with a master's skill, the barber swished and whisked a copper razor under my nose and around my cheeks, then along my neck without the slightest tug or nick.

Tsk-tsking while combing through my tangle of curls, the barber introduced himself as Landers and asked where I had come from and my purpose in Halicarnassus. I told the rehearsed story about waiting for my brother. Landers said he came to Halicarnassus five years ago from Greece. He was light-complected and clean-shaven with sandy-coloured hair cut around the ears and combed frontward, almost touching his grey eyes. His straight nose had a bit of a bump on the bridge, and the shape of his body reminded me of a long, thin zucchini. Waving his long thin arms as he talked, he extended his little fingers when styling hair or grooming beards.

I guessed him to be ten years older than me. The boyish texture of his skin gave him an effeminate impression. I imagined such softness came from applying regular emollient treatments. Another reason; Landers was known to drink at the Spring of Salmacis.

Barbering is an art form and a prestigious profession in Halicarnassus; the occupation requires creativity and a sense of style, and Landers had both.

An assortment of utensils and various gadgets lay on a table at his station; I noticed jars filled with perfumed lotions, scented oils, and dusting powders lining the shelves. One jar labelled DYE sat off to the side. Trying to appear inconspicuous with my questions as Mausolus had cautioned me, I asked about dye. He explained that applying lye soap mixed with wood ash and goat tallow would alter a person's natural hair colour.

"How much of a difference will dye produce?" I asked.

"At least several shades lighter or darker, depending on the look the patron wants to achieve," he told me.

"Ho, to be sure. But do many people seek such a service?"

"Once or twice a year."

"Any recently?"

"Not lately with me, but I think Stavros has. Stavros!" he yelled across the shop. "Have you recently dyed someone?"

"To be sure, once last week," Stavros answered. "A reddish man came in seeking a new look."

Chuckling, I pretended to enjoy the entertaining story. "How long will the new colour remain?" I yelled back.

"A few months at the most. Dyes fade, and hair grows, allowing the natural colour to return. Do you want your pretty dark curls dyed?"

"No!" I said, causing everybody in the shop to laugh.

"Imagine!" I told Landers. "Changing one's hair to a different colour."

Landers yelled across the room. "Tell us, Stavros, how did he look afterward?"

"Ho, to be sure, the man transformed before my eyes," Stavros said. "He came to me awkwardly reddish – tatty and raggedy. But once I worked my charm on him, the fellow looked polished as an aristocrat with a dark chestnut mane. He left prancing like a Nisaean stallion. A satisfied patron makes a regular patron."

"And creates a swaggering barber," Landers said. Patrons laughed at his jest.

Landers finished and handed me a glass to scrutinise myself. This barber undoubtedly had a gift for cutting curls. My well-groomed appearance pleased me enormously, with shiny hair behaving and pampered skin glistening in the glass. Before leaving, I purchased a yellow headband to keep the wind from mussing my new style.

I exited the shop and, as if getting caught in a swift undertow, was sucked into the congestion of busy Artemis Street, pulling me along in a hectic tide. I tussled through the traffic flow, making my way to the agora. Hair dye was valuable information; I may have walked past the assassin without noticing him since I was only looking for a reddish. I spent the afternoon conducting a thorough search around the vendor booths in the likelihood the man sought to purchase something more to further his disguise, but I did not see anyone matching his description.

An attempt to mute his appearance convinced me this hired killer had devised a plan of some sort, and he did not want to risk drawing attention to himself – a reddish would stand out in a crowd of dark-haired Persians. After revealing the information to Goliath, we chose to withhold the news from Mausolus; neither wanted to contribute further to his anxiety.

Chapter 23

Mehregan

The assassin's late-night appearance near the harbour unnerved Mausolus. He wore apprehension around his neck like an almpatrós. Worry and distraction prevented his full attention on administrative issues, and he fell behind in his duties. He spent most of his executive time making inquiries, investigating suspicious people, or imagining former allies as possible suspects. Habitually glancing over his shoulder, he remained alert, trying to discern if someone was following him. But, not knowing what else to do, he hovered around Artemisia, smothering her with his fears.

Summer had faded into autumn as Carians prepared for their largest harvest celebration of the year, Mehregan. The agriculturally significant holiday was mandatory for followers of the Zoroastrian religion. Before long, countless people would arrive in the city to spend the feast week with family and friends. Depending on social status, people either partied on the hillsides, at the theatre, in the Stoa of Aegea, or with large groups filling the commons areas. The privileged and most influential citizens celebrated with the satraps in the palace apādana; their admittance required a written invitation. The population of Halicarnassus tripled during Mehregan, which meant the upcoming week would bring risks and dangers and be challenging to monitor.

The autumn sky made me homesick for my province since we also celebrate the harvest. Sukkot, observed during the month of Tishri, is one of three mandatory pilgrimages to Jerusalem and the busiest time of the year, summoning a flood of visitors setting up shelters in the capital city to worship Yahweh. Jews celebrate this week by recalling God's past blessings on his chosen people in the wilderness, his continued care at present, and, most importantly, his promise of the Messiah, our future Saviour.

My family celebrates this festival heartily because my parents met during Sukkot. Millions of pilgrims filled Jerusalem, praising and worshiping at the temple that year. Despite throngs of people squeezed together in the confines of a narrow city, my father, rising from his prayers, said he spotted an angel standing in the crowd. "Your mother was the prettiest girl in the Land of Israel," he always told us. Both fathers approved the match, and before long, a wedding followed.

Warm autumn weather heightened the joy of Mehregan's outdoor activities. Artemisia reasoned Ahura Mazda, the creator of the sun, order, and light, sanctioned this celebration by sending warm rays of splendid sunlight to drive away blackened clouds seeking to ruin the spirited week.

Persians across the realm enthusiastically celebrate Mehregan with days of drunken revelry, excesses in food, eroticism, chain dances, and shameless merriment throughout the streets. Even the great kings of Persia danced and celebrated with reckless abandon during Mehregan.

The holiday brings carnivals, much praying, pageantry, coloured ornaments, and the throwing of seeds. Citizens in Halicarnassus dress in new clothing and parade through the streets, handing out gifts to each other, strangers, and the poor. Devout worshipers pray at altars; some offer animal sacrifices. Tethered streamers of multi-coloured silk, flapping directionless against the breeze, hang from buildings and homes. Priests walk through the streets reciting Gathas from their holy book, Avesta. A woody aroma of frankincense overwhelms the city after days of continual celebration.

The thundering roll of drums followed a long blast trumpeting from a ram's horn, formally launching the week of Mehregan. A grand parade of costumed citizens left the Stoa of Aegea, zigzagging across the city in a spirited procession. Celebrating in wild bacchanalia transformed Halicarnassus into a town of senseless fools performing outlandish acts. Artemisia revelled in passion and flair, laughing at brazen citizens with her network of friends and associates. Carians partied the week away, uninhibited, never considering an assassin might be lurking in their midst.

Ever in fashion with the lavish lifestyle of royalty, Artemisia outdid herself this year by commissioning famous Persian singers, instrumentalists, and dancers from distant parts of the empire to perform at the palace. And she somehow managed to retain MehrDokht, a professional actor from Ephesus known for his lively and animated performances. His birthday fell on the last day of Mehregan, making him the most sought-after thespian of the season.

So Artemisia requested a Sun Day performance at the theatre and asked MehrDokht to recite the epic poem, *Shah Nameh*.

Mausolus believed this year's celebration endangered the queen; he expected the assassin to take advantage of the commotion and unruly crowds. And as with the celebration of Zeus Labrandenos in Labraunda, Artemisia refused to cancel the holiday and overruled any mention of altering or postponing any portion of Mehregan. Losing an opportunity to entertain a select group of elite Zoroastrian priests was asking too much, especially when their visit promised special blessings of love and friendship for the satraps, the district, and Halicarnassus. And she adamantly rejected public disgrace from cancelling an élite appearance by MehrDokht.

Strategizing with Goliath, his generals, and court officials, Mausolus arranged additional troops from Mylasa to protect his wife. He stationed guards at the harbour, along city walls, watchtowers, gates, and beaches. Others mingled undetected throughout the city dressed as visitors. Guardianship of the queen became the sole responsibility of the king's elite guards under the command of Goliath. Preceding the holiday, the commander spent days pushing his men into shape by practising aggressive movements, blitzes, and specific defence tactics until their reactions became a mindless reflex.

All understood their assigned positions; we had rehearsed our roles and believed ourselves to be as prepared as possible. Troops guarded the interior and perimeter of the city, Dathaba stayed close to the king and queen, and my responsibility as the lookout meant I needed to remain alert to the people in the apadana. Mausolus did have one tremendous advantage; the assassin had not considered my involvement. I doubted the man remembered the boy he robbed in the wilderness, nor would he recognise my face. He would be surprised to discover I had given the king vital information for his capture.

The noise and enthusiasm of Mehregan-week climaxed with considerable frenzy. Sun Day, the grandest and most celebrated day, involved dramatic ceremonies, showy worship, sacrifices, and prayers. Guests of the satraps concluded the week's activities with a palatial feast in the apadana. By evening, the palace overflowed with merry guests.

Musicians played energetic tunes on stringed instruments accompanied by the flute's sweet whispers and the drum's infectious beat. Young women dressed in scanty vests of colourful velvet exposed their bare midriff while dancing light and carefree, twirling streamers of flowing silk from their waists. Nude arms and sensual shoulders swayed like elegant spires of grass, rippling in a soothing breeze. Fluid as a gentle stream, their bodies moved in exotic sashays while nimble fingers jingled chalparas overhead, gradually circling them lower, drawing attention to the spread of their ample breasts. Tiny slippers barely touched the floor as they whirled and swayed, then ducked beneath silken sashes before leaping across the room with the grace of a seabird soaring through the air.

Dance of this sort is an integral part of the Zoroastrian faith, even performed in the ceremonial courts of Achaemenid kings. Mausolus' guests delighted in the enchanting talent of sensual entertainers, myself included. I had no trouble enjoying attractive young women frolicking around the hall, exhibiting bare tummies while shimmying their seductive hips. When I was able to turn my attention away, I saw Mausolus mindlessly fumbling with wayward wisps of his eyebrow. He forced a smile and applauded at times, attempting to play his part as the merry king, but I feared his strain might give away our plan. Artemisia, though, brimmed with rapt astonishment. Keeping her safe had exhausted us all, and after days of intense surveillance, we found no indication of an assassin anywhere around Halicarnassus. I wondered if we might have overplayed the danger.

Zoroastrian priests were dressed in flowing robes of white linen with matching headdresses; each wore wide golden sashes wrapped several times around the waist and a long cloak suspended from their shoulders. Several priests wore pointy-toed shoes while the majority walked barefoot. A residue of white ash, still visible on their foreheads, meant they had participated in the afternoon's purification ceremony. Joyful dancing enthused the holy men, inspiring them to sing sacred Gathas.

A temporary altar, or a fire pit, built on the patio of the apadana, held the Flame of Zoroaster. Central to Zoroastrian worship, this very flame, ignited by Prophet Zoroaster long before the reign of Cyrus the Great, had burned continuously without interruption for centuries. Because of Artemisia's influence, priests carried a portion of Zoroaster's eternal flame over 400 parasangs to commemorate Mehregan and honour Halicarnassus.

The evening continued with much merriment, and the loud clamour of pleasure echoed in a dizzying fashion. I delighted in watching the Fire Dance, the Wine Dance, and the Sword Dance. But, determined as I was to remain vigilant, the ecstasy of music and the contagious enthusiasm of euphoric guests lured me into heedlessly joining their chain dances, where we formed a line much like camels in a caravan. Dancers held onto a long cord, licentiously frolicked about, wrapping the room in one long train of tremendous exuberance.

Whirling and swirling, I got a bit crazy and ended up tumbling off balance into a dancing priest. Embarrassed, I apologised heartily but happened to detect an unusual feature, the slightest tear in the flesh of his earlobe, a ragged saw-toothed scar. Fear washed over me as his lips parted, revealing a familiar row of crooked yellow teeth.

Crying out for Goliath, my voice fell to the ground against the noise of the party. Attempting to prevent his escape, I grabbed his arm. Shoving me backward, he broke free, and I fell into the line of rowdy dancers, knocking the crowd over like tumbling dominoes. The commotion caught Goliath's attention, but he considered us dancers drunk and unable to stand. Fighting out of the pile of laughing people, I screamed to Goliath, pointing at the counterfeit priest heading for Artemisia. The rowdy upheaval and jovial noise from people pulling each other over, trying to stand while laughing and spilling drinks and food, distracted the Dathaba. Unaware of the advancing imposter, guards focused on the comical scene of disorderly partiers.

Unnerved by the sudden breakdown in security, Mausolus stood to survey the room. Guests stumbled, laughing, trying to help others to their feet, except one man, a priest, who kept advancing toward the satrap couple. Bounding into action, Mausolus grabbed Artemisia, forcefully pulled her off her throne, and covered her with his body.

At last awakening to the threat, guards formed a wall of shields protecting the satraps as Goliath climbed over the top of the fallen crowd shaking off partiers seizing his legs. Breaking clumsily through the crowd, Goliath advanced toward the assassin as he forced his way toward the patio. Pausing, the killer wrapped the golden sash of his priestly costume several times around his hands, leaned into the altar, and shoved it over with a mighty heave, scattering pieces of flaming wood and glowing coals into the apadana. Celebrators, seeing the fire, panicked, causing complete chaos and disorder. Before guards could react, terrified people fell upon them, trampling and stepping over each other, trying to escape down the stairs into the courtyard.

Pushing their way against the crowds, the shocked priests yelled, "Daeva!" while racing into the flames, scooping precious fire into their sacred pots. Cursing in madness, their haphazard running about worsened the situation.

Raging like a violent storm, Goliath roared headlong into the flaming barricade, knocking over several priests, causing them to drop their consecrated vessels, and sending another cascade of sparks skittering into the apadana. Goliath arrived on the patio as the assassin was stepping over the balcony. Their eyes locked. With a slight nod, the killer winked and wrapped his arms around the polished column as if hugging a giant tree, slid to the ground, and disappeared.

Enraged, Goliath bounded over the rail and plunged off the balcony. He hit the ground hard and rolled onto his feet before realising his hair had caught fire. Swatting out the flames burning his head and neck, he tore off his tunic, threw the burning shirt to the ground, and continued his pursuit of the barefoot priest. A large crowd of partygoers danced in the commons. Desperate, Goliath grabbed people, inspected their faces, and threw them off as if they were small fish unfit for keeping. In the bushes, he discovered a discarded heap of priestly garments. Again grabbing people, Goliath asked if anybody had observed a man dropping the robes, but drunken revellers laughed in boisterous disregard for his frantic inquiries.

With shield and sword, Mausolus moved Artemisia to a secure location. At the same time, his soldiers spread throughout the apadana, focusing their efforts on extinguishing the raging fire, which threatened to burn the entire city.

I ran into the city trying to find Goliath, but the celebrants blocked every street. Like a caravan sentinel, I hollered, "Get out of the way! Move right! Move right!" but with little effect. When I finally caught up with him, he sent me out as a runner, sprinting from post to post to sound the alarm and muster troops for an intensive search. By morning light, the painful truth became apparent; the assassin had escaped our grasp.

Furious, Goliath headed to the apartments at the palace where the Zoroastrians lodged. Bursting through the door with an angry bellow, he demanded to know how a stranger, dressed as a phony priest, moved freely among their group entirely unnoticed.

Mausolus stepped in to defend the oblivious priests, informing them his perimeter guards discovered the nude body of a murdered priest lying beside the Myndos Road. In truth, knowing each priest was impossible due to the sheer number of holy men in the Zoroastrian league. The assassin had chosen a clever disguise.

Chapter 24

Reproach and Reprimand

Mausolus boiled with rage, screaming profanities at the top of his voice. "I want this órrhos in chains! I want him sawn asunder! I will feed his corpse to the dogs! His body will become manure on the ground! What koprophágos son of pórnē dares treat my wife in such a manner?"

The room smelled of burn salve – a tincture of honey, aloe, and tannic acid – yet Mausolus ignored its implication. Neither did he acknowledge the silk bandages wrapping Goliath's head and neck. Instead of honouring the bravery of his faithful commander, the man who ran headlong into a wall of flame, the king ignored Goliath's obvious pain.

He shouted, "Why? Why? Why? I want to know every detail about this vlákas? I want to know where he is from; I want his name. What is his mission, and who sent him? Who is this sodden man, and why does he seek to kill my wife?"

To Goliath and the Dathaba, he scolded, "One man! Did I say an army of men? No, I said one man – a lone renegade! How does a single man gain the advantage over my most elite troops? Shall I discharge you fools and hire the little children I watch running through the commons, battling each other with mock swords?"

He spoke most harshly to me, "A simple assignment, Ethan. All I asked was, 'Stay alert and be on the lookout as you alone know the identity of this man,' and yet you failed me. You would have recognized him at the door if you had been doing your job instead of dancing. Your ineptness jeopardised the queen's life."

Mausolus' disappointment fell hard like a harvester's scythe, cutting a wide swath across my soul. In truth, I never considered the assassin would pose as a Zoroastrian priest, but I remained silent and accepted his cutting rebuke.

The king humiliated us all for the Mehregan disaster. We failed mightily despite weeks of preparation, believing the advantage belonged to us. No one knew precisely when the counterfeit priest arrived; worst yet, had he slept in the palace? How close did he come to the queen? The possibilities were frightening.

Mausolus questioned his wife privately, trying to unravel the illogical assaults against her. Artemisia acted as confused as everybody, denying she knew the motive behind such violence. Instead, she dismissed the entire ordeal as petty niggling.

Goliath swore retribution. Embarrassed by the assassin's flagrant mockery, he vowed to pay it back tenfold. Three times on Goliath's watch, this good-for-nothing foreigner had come into the city, then disappeared without a trace. To be sure, he was no amateur and serious about killing Artemisia; we had gravely underestimated the cunning skill of this resourceful mercenary.

Amid the panic and commotion erupting on the last night of Mehregan, the satraps' guests failed to grasp the situation. With minds dulled by overindulgence, they supposed an inebriated celebrant crashed into the fire altar, spilling flames into the room. No one suspected an assassin had come into their midst, intent on killing their queen. Mausolus ordered the matter to remain quiet. Hysteria in the district would dilute the effectiveness of his troops, redirecting their focus away from this one-man army.

Citizens carried on life as usual, never questioning the heightened protection accompanying Artemisia. She continued downplaying the necessity of security, and Mausolus remained convinced this threat pertained to his father, King Hecatomnus.

The weeks passed in tiptoeing silence; no one dared to draw attention to themselves for fear of receiving another rebuke of scathing swear words from the king. When I tried to find a way to get near him, to speak the right words of apology, the opportunity failed to present itself, and an excruciating silence remained between us. I understood his seething anger was a combination of irritation fostered by a wide range of matters extending beyond my amateurish mistake. Still, I wanted to make amends. The fact that I had disappointed Mausolus was unbearable.

Goliath compensated for the fiasco and his embarrassing defeat by making his face hard as flint. Family dinners turned into hurried, prickly evenings treading softly around the giant. Jaleh and I continued seeing each other but met at prearranged locations away from the house. We walked together at the beach or around the commons, consoling one another. Jaleh struggled to understand the adverse situation affecting her family, and despite twinges of deceitfulness, I did not explain.

The painful impasse with Mausolus lifted one evening when he sent for me. Desiring a distraction, he requested my company for a game of Technê. Playing against me had become a challenge, requiring him to pay close attention whenever we faced each other.

Before coming to Halicarnassus, I was unfamiliar with this game. Only a few people knew how to play it, with even fewer possessing the prowess required for its method. Mausolus taught me the art because he sought a worthy opponent willing to dally away the evenings in front of carved armies, annihilating each other. Once I comprehended the game, I became proficient in no time. I laugh as I write, remembering the comical look on Mausolus' face the first time I beat him; he sat speechless, studying the board, and then looked up at me, then back at the board again, shaking his head. Afterward, whenever I won, he considered my victory a compliment to his brilliant teaching.

Hecatomnus failed to learn the game, but he understood kings played it and that it required battle competence, stratagem, policy, and discipline. He approved any game involving army versus army, one king outmanoeuvring another king. On the day Mausolus returned home to Caria, Hecatomnus presented him with a magnificent cedar box holding skilfully carved playing pieces made with two different colours of marble to differentiate armies.

During my life, I have taught many students how to play – how to engineer opportunities for advantage and then outmanoeuvre oblivious opponents. I have played with beginners and most worthy adversaries while using Mausolus' most cherished set of figures gifted to him by his father.

Mausolus' apparent anger had yet to subside. His tolerance was forced and awkward; I was unsure how to approach him or what he expected of me. I feared he intended to ask me to leave the district because of my mistake. I did not want to leave but practised a cordial goodbye speech.

For the longest time, we sat in silence, moving and capturing figures from each other's army – chariots, cavalry, foot soldiers, or generals. Then, at last, Mausolus spoke. "This morning, I gazed into my looking glass, and a stranger's face glared back at me. An angry, aged stranger. Has this glass lied, or am I the man whose face I observed? Has anger taken hold of my life? Have I allowed joy to die while I await another attack from a stranger? What do I leave behind for a new generation of Carian, an angry, quaking king who lost his realm to a lone mercenary?"

His frailty made me uncomfortable. I sat without stirring, unsure if he knew I had taken my turn. Finally, when I found the courage, I spoke. "Your move."

"My move? Indeed, it is my move! I have no choice but to move!" I sensed his words had nothing to do with our game. "Ethan, I am neither a young man nor an old man. This assassin has forced me to acknowledge something I previously chose to avoid – I am running out of time. Decisions of a satrap carry endless weight. I can face personal choices unafraid and accept their outcome. But decisions about the satrapy reach far beyond today; a satrap must look to tomorrow and rule for the future.

"Has my reign disappointed the legacy of my ancestors or unwittingly hindered my loyal subjects? Have I done enough for the district's unborn lest I impede future generations with my lack?"

Listening to private matters weighing heavy on my hero's heart was awkward and felt too intimate. Knowing a hired killer threatened the most vulnerable part of his life shook Mausolus to the depths of his soul. The emotional struggle prompted unpleasant memories of personal failures and regrets. To himself, the satrap criticised his years of leadership, which I felt were imagined and inaccurate. Simpleminded in my response, I asked about travel. "You and the queen might enjoy a voyage or an expedition to the jungle. An absence may refresh your outlook and provide clarity upon your return."

"You, Ethan, have an advantage over me; you have not yet viewed the entire world. As a young boy, I travelled to the most prominent places in Persia and sailed beyond her borders to remote territories. I sailed through the world's most sophisticated harbour into Carthage, wintering among its wealthiest citizens while studying at the citadel Byrsa.

"I have gone on pilgrimage to Egypt, floated into the Red Sea through the canal of King Darius. When visiting the Giza plateau, I climbed the world's highest structure, Khufu's pyramid, and sought a blessing while standing between the paws of Hor-em-akhet, the enormous sphinx.

"In Kush, I visited palaces built by the Black Pharaohs. Theseum Hill and the Acropolis of Athens hold special memories for me, and several times, I viewed the Olympics from the platform at the temple of Zeus. I grew up in the glazed palaces of Susa, Babylon, Ecbatana, and Parsa, and worshiped in Pasargadae, kneeling before the world's most humble shrine, the tomb of King Cyrus the Great. "I have seen your temple in Jerusalem, visited shrines of India with their gopuram gate towers, toured the Musasir Temple of Armenia, and stood at the tomb of Midas of Phrygia myself touching the Gordian Knot. Have you heard of such a knot, Ethan?"

I managed a slight shake of my head, indicating no.

"There exists an intricate knot tied by Gordius, the ancient king of Phrygia; its undoing is impossible except by one man - the man destined to rule Asia."

I acknowledged this with a polite nod.

"Together, the queen and I travelled to Xanthos in Lycia to visit the Nereid Monument. We viewed the construction of Lycian tombs being excavated in the high places, and spent time in the mysterious city of Derinkuyu, a town much more extensive than Halicarnassus, carved through solid rock, existing entirely underground.

"Travel? Young Ethan, we are veterans of the world, but shall I content myself admiring another man's legacy? Shall I borrow another man's dream? Never may that happen! Tell me, what remains in this world so I might possess it as my own? What structure remains unbuilt, so I might be the one to build it? What aspirations remain undreamed so I might be the first to dream them?"

When his thoughts circled back to the assassin, his mood blackened.

"Fear of this assassin has reduced me to a stagnant man. This mercenary, both a stranger and a scoundrel, has rendered me immovable. Am I a statue, motionless as Zeus in Labraunda, or immovable as Aries in his temple? I am going mad as conflicting thoughts thunder inside my mind."

"You built Halicarnassus. That is a remarkable achievement for you. Such a feat is nowhere near madness, my Lord. Carians love their city, and Persia handsomely profits from your district." I felt juvenile in my thinking.

"True, Ethan, I built Halicarnassus, but other men have built remarkable cities. Is there no significant contribution remaining for me to donate to my world? I am the heir of the Hecatomnid Dynasty, does such a birthright amount to nothing?"

I was out of my depth and could not fathom the complexities he spoke about – particularly the far-off places he mentioned. So, I asked a simple question. "Which place do you remember most fondly?"

"This, too, becomes a hindrance, my boy, for I cannot choose. I find I hold a passion for many places. By the gods, I fear I live at a time when nothing new is conceivable and nothing more is left to accomplish. The world has reached its threshold of possibility."

Once possessing the merry rhythm of a beating drum, the darkness of his mind overruled his jovial personality, and now Mausolus felt like a stranger. He had grown tired and forlorn, wrestling against himself, and I felt ashamed of my contribution to his suffering. To be sure, the underhanded task Artemisia gave me of manipulating him into building her sanctuary for the privileged added weight to his burden. Months earlier, I came to loathe the deceitful assignment I had agreed upon, but I continued my dishonesty despite the pangs of my conscience.

I continued with it because Artemisia reigned as the queen and because I loved spending time around her. Selfishly I stayed because I enjoyed visiting the palace, laughing with high-ranking officials, talking with my favourite cohorts, and joining Mausolus on important administrative assignments. Each time famous aristocrats or celebrated philosophers visited, the satraps included me when entertaining them at the palace. Giddy in my Persian luxury, I became proud of my expensive clothing and hair treatments. I anticipated delicious cuisines, exciting entertainment, theatrical sensations, and those special times when Mausolus invited me to participate in sports, hunting, or accompany him on his travels. I even had a passport allowing me to stay at every inn in the empire.

Not so long ago, a quivering dolt made his first appearance at the palace, yet now I lived an abundant life of sophistication and wealth with influential people who listened to me, laughed at my quips, and asked my opinion on matters of importance. I received much attention everywhere I went, and I craved honour and praise from others, mainly when they referred to me as Son of Mausolus or called me Caria's Prince.

Chasing allurements had turned me into a fraud. As Mausolus wondered who he had become, I, too, barely recognised the paltry Hebrew boy who blithely camped for Sabbath in the Persian wilderness. Did I still exist, or had I bargained away my soul?

Chapter 25

Sketches for a Sanctuary

Restless and edgy, I gathered the rough sketches I had prepared and headed toward the city's neglected hill. Once past the trees, I stopped to admire the sea. If I never looked upon another object of splendour, I would be satisfied knowing I had seen all that is beautiful after beholding the spectacular sunrises and sunsets over the Aegean Sea. The array this evening presented radiant tentacles, orange as ripe papaya, stretching endlessly across an azure expanse.

My profession of stonemasonry frequently compelled me to imagine creative structures. Like a mental hobby, I assembled buildings, arcades, verandas, and unusual abodes – any architectural edifice my mind could imagine. This time was different; my aspirations were genuine, so I used ink and sketched a possible creation onto papyrus.

I ignored the prompting by the queen. Instead, I considered the personal reflections Mausolus confided in me about living unafraid, his incomplete legacy, the future of Halicarnassus, and imagining the unimaginable. I hoped to challenge his cynicism. I wanted to convince him a man's dreams live eternal in the depths of his heart. He needed reminding that buildings begging to be built whirl in the recesses of our minds until accomplished. I wanted to remind him the world, with its insatiable hunger, will forever sanction curious contrivances and distinctive designs. The world gives birth to architects, obligating them to capture a moment in time by creating an ageless testament for the future.

Combining personal details Mausolus mentioned with the memories he shared, I conceived a building proposal of my own, an architectural design I found original, attractive, and plausible, one appealing to the sensitivities of the king.

Standing before the scrubby parcel of land in the centre of Halicarnassus, I again contemplated its size, mentally recalculating the math. Just then, my focus wandered to a spiny hedgehog that cautiously peeked out from behind the leafy branches of a laurel shrub. He seemed unaware of my presence as he grunted and snuffled; no doubt the little fellow sought friends to join him on an evening hunt for slugs and toads.

Louder squealing rang out from another cluster of shrubbery, causing me to laugh at the curious little face peering out. So occupied was I watching these creatures emerge I failed to hear Mausolus walk up behind me. "The gods favour Halicarnassus tonight with a striking sunset." His greeting caused me to jump two cubits straight in the air.

The king had a great chuckle at my expense. Then, pointing to the mound, he said, "Idrieus has plans for this hillock. Notice here?" He unrolled a papyrus with architectural drawings his younger brother had given him several months ago. Mausolus motioned me closer. "Tedious, dull, and repetitive, similar to the temple in Kerkyra. Classic Doric structure has dominated the standard for over a century. My appraisal? Entirely too predictable.

"I delight in frieze panels as shown here, but notice the column heights, less than five times their bottom diameter, and observe the distance between adjacent columns – overly traditional for a distinctive city like Halicarnassus."

The drawing almost knocked me over; it showed features similar to what Artemisia explained to me that day in the garden. So, she had also secretly manipulated her brother, Idrieus, to influence Mausolus. I wondered if there were any others out there working on him.

Mausolus surveyed the mound, visualising and mentally trying to transport the structure from Idrieus' papyrus into reality, but I sensed the plans displeased him. "No Doric structures! To be sure, the notable architect, Pythius of Priene, disparages the Doric order. I say build Ionic. Until deciding on the perfect structure, I will delay my long-time desire of erecting a distinctive monument on this hill."

I said, "Perhaps this time of danger is the wrong time for dreaming dreams. Your delay is wise, my king, at least until the apprehension of the peltast. He may strike again while you are preoccupied with construction."

"Ethan, my boy, this is the absolute best time for dreaming dreams. I will no longer sit as an idle target, allowing this mystery man to intimidate me. Am I to wait like a star hanging above the Earth? Preposterous! Nadir versus imperial birthright; I refuse to linger in this state of uncertainty, acting like his timid servant. Halicarnassus is my city! My enemy must now watch out for me; indeed, I am sure he has not forgotten the stinging pain inflicted by my wife. Together we reign, so together we fight.

"To be sure, this man cannot prevail. Every soldier in Caria hunts for him; my men will apprehend this kovalos who dares threaten an imperial vassal of the empire. In the meantime, our Carian way of life will continue unabated."

"As you say, my King. Your thoughts are wise and fill my soul with happiness. May I speak freely?"

Mausolus gestured with his hand while nodding as he did when granting permission.

"The King of Caria serves King Artaxerxes III, the head of the most powerful empire in the world. Invincible Persia receives applause the world over for her astonishing engineering feats and spectacular cities. With the snap of your fingers, my King, you are entitled to unlimited resources from the empire's storage locker, including its most innovative builders. So why limit yourself in any way, particularly by building one design – by choosing either this or that architectural style?"

"I am lost, young Ethan."

"My King, imagine a structure here, combining your favourite designs from the different places you have seen in your travels. I call it an all-in-one design. No architectural category claims such an arrangement. A structure with no specific style remains non-existent anywhere in the world."

"You suggest I create a monument with no style?" he chuckled.

"Exactly! Create an original, distinctive style by creating no style, then no man will ever duplicate the pattern without the entire world knowing the original master plan stands here in Halicarnassus, built by an unrivalled creator, Mausolus, Satrap King of the district of Caria in the Empire of Persia. Ho, to be sure, such a new idea will be distinctive, forcing the world to recognise the style of Mausolus."

He laughed at my foolish idea. "You propose I create no style called the style of Mausolus? Will history write accounts of the satrap who built a hodgepodge, perhaps building a Parthenon teetering on the point of a pyramid?" He laughed at the absurdity.

"My King, a Parthenon will by no means teeter on the point of a pyramid; you will!"

"Me? Ethan, now you have tangled my mind with your youthful riddles."

"If it pleases the King, reflect with me for a moment. The primary advantage of building a structure on this hill is the available land. A parcel of this size enables extensive construction in four directions, depth, length, width, and height. With that, the options are endless for creating a great masterpiece. Anything you desire, extravagantly daring or unexceptionally modest."

Risking embarrassment, I unrolled my drawings. "After visiting this site on several occasions and taking measurements, I studied the shape of the hill. Next, I sketched a possible structure combining your favourite architectural designs, from your most esteemed world travels to your most admired foreign cultures. Finally, I arranged each style into a single, original structure designed specifically for this hill. Fresh and original, unique architecture without equality will become your legacy."

His pleasurable expression came as a relief; I continued with renewed confidence. "Imagine something in the architectural tradition of Xanthos or the palace at Pasargadae, any similar structure using a sturdy foundation merging with a pedestal platform. Considering this parcel's full dimensions, your platform can be much more extensive than those structures. Even with a large pedestal base, there is still plenty of room for paved walkways and spacious gardens – a true parádeisos skirting the base. And see here?" I directed his attention to my drawing. "I have placed the ornamental entrance in this area to correspond with the harbour." I walked over and stood in the exact spot.

He studied the details on my drawing, turned toward the harbour, then toward the mound. He thought a moment, then turned back toward the port again. "Continue," he said.

"As you know, my King, five sections arranged horizontally fail as a remarkable feat. Notice my drawing; the distinction comes from building five sections vertically."

"To be sure, you mock me!"

"Simple mathematics. I calculate a base pedestal will be strong enough to accommodate these vertical sections." Next, I drew his attention to the second area – the structure resting atop the pedestal section. "Perhaps this area best serves as a lofty porch outlined with the row of Ionic columns you mentioned – if you think a porch will please the queen." (I already knew this idea would please her since she described it to me.)

"A second floor! And what about the pyramid?" he asked. "Does this piece sit beside the pedestal?"

"To be sure, my Lord, not beside anything. No, I suggest surpassing the conventional standards of today by building a pyramid as the roof! Notice where I have drawn a pyramid above the open porch."

"A pyramid roof? Oh, how I would judder the sensibilities of rulers by building an Egyptian pyramid on Persian soil." Mausolus calculated my scribbled measurements in his head. "The height shown here equals eighty pank'a dva."

"We Hebrews call the measurement cubits, but to be sure, I approximate the structure totalling a height of eighty cubits."

"Eighty cubits! Remarkable! The statue of Zeus in Olympus only rises twenty-nine cubits, and the collapsed Temple in Ephesus was thirty-nine cubits. Eighty cubits! Impossible! Admirable indeed, but a structure with such height will topple when built on this hill."

"Likewise, a concern of mine, my King. Considering the irregularity of the slope, notice where I sketched steps graduating into the hill ranging from two cubits to seven cubits, establishing the base depth at ten cubits. A stepped footing of roughhewn greenstone bound with iron clamps will provide ample strength for supporting my proposed height – I believe even greater height is possible."

"Greater height! A mind lacks the capacity for imagining what you describe."

"I speak the truth, my Lord." I showed him my plans. "A lofty and wide structure will endure when applying the fundamental theory of structural engineering, 'height depends on depth'. Anchoring into a rock substructure allows for constructing anything you can imagine and as high as you desire without collapse. With the appropriate foundation, your legacy to Halicarnassus will endure for a thousand years. For two thousand years!"

"Your drawings intrigue me. Proceed."

Pointing at my draft, I explained, "Here, I list the five sections. First is the underground foundation. Consider it the backbone which knits into the structure of the second section - the pedestal. Above that, the open area of columns becomes the third section; the pyramid roof serves as the fourth section."

"You mentioned five vertical sections."

"Section number five is a non-structural piece, but I consider it the most significant."

"How so?"

"I refer to this part as the crowning ornament, a royal diadem resting on the top of the pyramid. This piece is you, my King!"

"Me?"

"Indeed! I envision a grand marble statue of your likeness, large enough to view from the harbour – from parasangs in every direction!"

"Name an architect willing to place such an object atop a towering building. No one!" Mausolus said.

"No one yet, my King, but why has no one attempted such a feat?" Without considering its architectural possibility, I included this apex statue as an intriguing idea, a drawback to dreaming dreams on papyrus.

"Captivating idea of yours, Ethan. May I view your plans?" Examining my scribbles, he again questioned me. "My biggest concern is the design's height which you indicate in this rudimentary drawing. Have you rechecked the math?"

"My King, the empire has mathematicians and architects knowledgeable in these specifics. They understand limitations in engineering matters. These skilled men visualise the impossible and erect the incredible. Men with innovative minds, perhaps Pythius of Priene or Satyros." (Artemisia gave me those names; I was glad Mausolus failed to ask me how I knew of such people.)

Turning again toward the harbour, he paced off the distance measuring his footsteps. Then, talking to himself, he paced extra lengths, turned, and headed back toward me.

"Young Ethan, I will investigate your sketch and determine its structural likelihood, but I find your idea refreshing – you are a youthful source of inspiration veering me away from the monotonous. Three massive storeys with three separate designs! Indeed historical! You possess the aptitude of a creative and gifted engineer; no structure like this exists anywhere in the world. I must talk to the queen at once. Considering her lively imagination for compositions, I assure you, your astonishing idea will intrigue her."

Oh, I imagine it will, I thought to myself.

Taking my drawings, rolling them with the plans from Idrieus, Mausolus tucked the cylinder under his arm and hurried toward the palace. Considering the quickness of his gait, I expected the king eagerly sought to share my proposal with Artemisia.

In my mind, I imagined Artemisia attentively listening to her husband share my unique idea. She would marvel at Mausolus' aspirations for building a sanctuary and congratulate him for desiring to perfect the city. She would no doubt offer to handle the procurement of necessary items, freeing him to manage the affairs of the satrapy.

I imagined her saying, 'Fine white marble is lovely for building. I may know where to obtain this stone. Perhaps we can procure the help of Pythius of Priene – if he is available. He may know of other accessible craftsmen.' Queen Artemisia may have added, "Genius! Nooré cheshm-am, your desire for an epic sanctuary far exceeds my limited imaginings, but perhaps I can add a few ideas to enhance its beauty."

Regardless of her pretence, I succeeded in my assignment, thus concluding an awkward arrangement with the queen. Before returning to my quarters, I walked along the beach. I needed to get away and reflect on things by listening to the rhythm of gentle waves washing in and out.

Ho, to be sure, with Mausolus and Artemisia combining their penchant for boldness and overstated glamour, I predicted the Halicarnassus project would grow to extreme proportions. They would include every manner of indulgence, magnificence, and luxury, requiring fifty years to complete. With the king and queen designing and creating, and no doubt trying to outdo each other, Halicarnassus would become a household name. This structure would become their signature.

Chapter 26

The Original Plan

From the onset, false starts plagued construction as, time and time again, Artemisia veered off course from the original design. On papyrus, the architectural drawings promised to deliver a daring structure. My minimal part in its inspiration earned me an invitation to join architects and builders in discussing with Mausolus and Artemisia the different phases involved in building a structure of such magnitude – a feat intended to endure throughout history, immortalising the satraps' lives and the glory of Halicarnassus.

Pythius of Priene built an exemplar, or a replica model, displaying the structure at completion. Hinges opened the mock-up, revealing fancy interior rooms with pillars and stairs. Ho, to be sure, the magnitude of this sanctuary captured the embodiment of Caria's wealth, culture, and power. At Pythius' unveiling, every person in the room clapped with amazement, realising a tremendous achievement of this sort would bring them all great status.

Papyrus drawings were one thing, but seeing this exemplary in vivid detail meant the Halicarnassus project was official, and construction would soon begin. But there were delays. Extreme opinions about structural refinements voiced by the queen sparked intense discussion and debate among architects. Her first significant point of contention focused on the building's ground-level entrance. Artemisia said, looking at Pythius, "Such a basic entry solicits languor, wearisome and tedious languor." Then, in her lyrical sense of style, she explained, "Arriving at the entrance of a sanctuary of this magnitude necessitates a voyage; a skyward journey; the quest for a spiritual pilgrimage; an ascension on a Diadromí Theïkós – a divine path. Does this boring ground-level entrance convey ascending a divine path? Of course not."

Raising the entrance required building a colossal staircase. Here, the queen insisted on a flight of steps wide enough to hold statues of valiant lions heroically guarding the voyagers' vertical passage on their sacred climb upward toward the ornate entrance. From such heights, the azure sea combined with the panoramic view lent to the spiritual inspiration Artemisia sought to provide.

Agreeing with her sentiments, Pythius restructured the entrance. Afterward, Mausolus displayed the completed exemplar on a table in the Stoa of Aegea for the townspeople to view. Construction of this dimension involved the entire district and would forever change the fabric of Halicarnassus. The last I knew, Idrieus had this exemplar moved to Mylasa, but I will briefly describe its features, section by section. I will also explain the sanctuary's transformation and how it ended as something remarkably different.

Pythius' final exemplar showed a solid underpinning of greenstone stepping into the hillside and the pedestal – the first of three above-ground sections. Those two parts knit together, becoming the stalwart upon which the above sections rested. The rectangular pedestal lacked exceptional architectural features; its intended purpose was singular, to provide centuries of unshakable support. Pythius' display showed the pedestal in the centre of a square courtyard at least twice the size of the foundation area. A low wall with intermittent gates surrounded the courtyard. Faux greenery represented a perimeter parádeisos. Each section was given a name; Pythius called the bulky base the Váthro Persis, Greek meaning a Persian Pedestal. The shape reminded me of a large, stout box on which to stand. The beauty of the Persian Pedestal came from its polished white Proconnesian marble walls and the surrounding courtyard.

With miniature statuettes representing visitors, the exemplar showed people trekking upward along a lion-guarded staircase leading to the entrance of the Persian Pedestal. The elegant entry opened into a decorative gateway lined with muscular columns. Once through this vestibule, visitors found themselves standing inside the first room of the sanctuary (the first public room; rumours suggested a hidden chamber below. I imagine Artemisia did add a secret compartment, possibly two or three, within the lower portion of the Persian Pedestal, but I cannot guess her intended purpose). Pythius called this first room Aíthousa Lapis or Lapis Room since Artemisia intended to decorate the walls with semi-precious, deep blue lapis lazuli. At completion, this Lapis Room would serve as the couple's magnificent parlour for entertaining.

Artemisia did not want the members of her club to merely visit; she expected her sanctuary for the privileged to become an experience they would long remember. The initial stage began in the courtyard with a quiet stroll through the gardens, allowing time to enjoy the vegetation while viewing statues and frieze panels. This private worship time was intended to settle one's thoughts and bring celestial peace.

After traversing upward on the Divine Way, the spiritual sojourn led guests into the Lapis Room - the sanctuary's introduction, an appetiser to whet their appetite for the wonders yet to unfold. When ready, guests ascended a spiral staircase. Labouring through an interior rock-cut passage, breaking free from darkness, and entering the light of the veranda symbolized a rebirth. Rebirth was an integral part of the sanctuary experience. The spiritual crossing culminated in walking onto a stunning open-air veranda surrounded by statues and thirty-six fluted columns supporting a Pyramid Roof.

Pythius named this roof section the Stégi Pyramís –the part most loved by Mausolus. Thin horizontal marble slabs lay in a graduated rise, forming twenty-four steps. Posed figurines represented guests dining in the middle section he referred to as Théa Megaleiódis or Grand View since such height provided impressive vistas in every direction. The Greek-style veranda was Artemisia's dream, a place for her guild to retreat in a bright and breezy garden floating above the Aegean Sea. Her colonnaded patio in the clouds would be like no other.

What a wonder! I imagined no place on earth more extraordinary to share with Jaleh. Together we would undertake the complete journey as Artemisia envisioned, then with the world's most respected artisans, composers, poets, diplomats, heroes, and aristocrats, dine in the clouds far above the city while viewing the sea and faraway mountain peaks.

A curious feature of the building's design was its gradual tapering. Picture a mountain wide at the bottom and graduating to form a peek at the top. Similarly, the sanctuary had a broad base, and each rising section became narrower than the one below. The most expansive area, the foundation, supported the Persian Pedestal. Then the pedestal supported the mid-sized Grand View, which supported the smaller Pyramid Roof. This ingenious tapering was pivotal to structural soundness, but more noteworthy is how the shape produced broad horizontal planes at every level. Like shelves hung in the house and filled with baubles and expensive gewgaws, these planes ran around the circumference of every tier, providing plenty of room for frieze panels and sculpture. A lot of statues! Pythius overly decorated the ledges of his exemplar with mock figures making these shelves the sanctuary's most exceptional exterior feature. Built to scale, Pythius marked the height of the Persian Pedestal at 40 cubits, the Grand View at 25 cubits, with the Pyramid Roof rising another 15 cubits.

Even though Artemisia later revised and adjusted various aspects of the original plan – and several were significant – her alterations did not affect the building's taper or exterior height. But change comes with a price. It seemed that as Artemisia dreamed bigger, she veered further and further off course destroying the objective of her dreams and replacing it with the aspiration of her vanity.

Chapter 27

The Chariot Monument

The structure's first significant change was born on a cloudy morning at the quarry. The foreman had his crew out to evaluate the amount of dimension stone he expected the pit to yield. I was curious myself, so I joined them. We busied ourselves cutting channels and lever sockets, but with the sun hidden behind grey clouds, such a dreary morning made it hard to work.

Mausolus and Artemisia took advantage of the coolness of the day to enjoy a romantic drive through the countryside. Mausolus, passionate about Olympic quadriga races, chose to handle his team of quadriga – handsomely groomed, muscular purebreds, proudly galloping four abreast held in check by black harnesses of polished leather. In an era when kings did not drive, and queens did not ride, the couple's passion for the chariot revealed another layer of their uncharacteristic lifestyle.

Waving to citizens from their custom chariot, polished to a sparkle, adorned in thick gold trim, Mausolus held the braided reins as Artemisia stood hugging his arm. Side by side, the couple sprinted through the Aegean scenery, thundering along in a transient blur of majesty and fame – the envy of the district.

Anxious to learn the results of our findings on the dimension stone, Artemisia planned their day trip to circle past the quarry. A rumbling like roiling thunder juddered the terrain beneath our feet as bodyguards mounted on massive Nisaean horses charged into the pit area. The king and queen followed, a grand spectacle in their elaborate chariot. Horses with flared nostrils danced in place, pawing the ground and tossing their lathered heads.

At this moment, the strangest phenomena occurred. The clouds broke open, allowing soft golden rays of sunlight to push past dark billows and encircle the satraps, capturing them in a halo of light as if they were radiant flickers cast in bronze. The peculiar aura lasted several moments. The incident was remarkable enough that those witnessing it questioned its significance.

Later in the evening, I set up the board to play Technê, as Mausolus sat deep in contemplation – an observation confirmed when I dropped a chariot. The playing piece skittered across the floor, yet Mausolus remained motionless, staring at the new pipe he had purchased from a tobacco vendor. Studying the ivory bowl carved into the head of an Arabian stallion, he trickled strands of fresh tobacco leaf into the basin, tamped the sprigs, and puffed a series of shallow puffs while Moza held a fire stick. Wisps of silvery smoke began swirling around his head, the king's attention returned, and we prepared to play.

As the evening progressed, I explained the appearance of the light radiating on him and the queen at the quarry. The strange phenomenon seemed to elude his interest, but I suggested he commission a frieze panel showing the king and queen driving radiantly through the sky.

"Consider this idea for the sanctuary," I said. "A prominently placed frieze panel – maybe above the entrance – depicting you as a satrap couple, riding side by side in your famous black chariot, with the sun's rays bursting around you. Gleams of light would create a startling effect.."

Townsfolk had bombarded Mausolus with suggestions and opinions after he announced the erection of the upcoming sanctuary. Intrusive citizens, most were well-meaning, a few not, inundated him with ideas for ambitious features. Some warned him of drab features he needed to avoid, or folks encouraged embellishments seen on other monuments or trimmings they deemed pleasant; others ostracised any ideas not to their liking.

Merchants complained the excessively tall building might collapse and ruin the city. People living on nearby residential streets complained drainage would cause problems for their homes and the town below. People said the cost was too high, the disruption too severe, the noise unbearable – on and on, their comments and complaints flowed. Offering my recommendation about the chariot felt equally as rude; I could have kicked myself for adding to his troubles. The king dismissed my suggestion saying he would consider the idea. I quieted, and we played Technê.

Days later, a commotion erupted at the building site. Swift as a fire moving through the brushwood, rumours circulated. Some people said there was a plan for a monument, something colossal to grace the Pyramid Roof.

Others said statues representing Mausolus and Artemisia on an endless voyage across the sky would stand side by side on the sanctuary's apex. I also heard about plans for a grand marble chariot pulled by a quadriga of Nisaeans. A trick of the eye included adding highly polished bronze reins, wheels, and trim pieces to attract sunbeams, emitting shafts of light radiating from the statues as if the couple eternally watched over their city.

To my surprise, it was all true. The queen's joy overflowed. Beaming happier than ever, she said, "An enormous chariot statue high in the sky will become the sanctuary's most exceptional feature, an unrivalled feat visible parasangs in every direction!" Artemisia's insistence on placing a sculpture of herself standing beside her husband in his triumphal chariot shocked the cultural standards of her era. A woman! Such a crass idea was unheard of, but Carians intuitively acquiesced to their queen's stance on female equality. They praised Artemisia's boldness, calling her a freethinker with a one-of-a-kind disposition for challenging the confines of women.

Meanwhile, the queen's half-knowledge of structural capabilities stunned architects. Artemisia's new dream was to place more than a hundred tons of marble on the top of the Pyramid Roof, creating a nightmare - worse, an architectural impossibility!

Her insistence on placing the zenith monument would require significant reinforcements. Like a line of dominoes tipping over, adding the massive top piece would require altering every section below, including the projected size of the interior rooms, lighting, and ventilation. Additional rows of interior greenstone would be needed to shore up the Persian Pedestal and the Grand View. Pythius would have no choice but to streamline the size of the Lapis Room from a large parlour into a modest area, 42 cubits by 35 cubits.

The rock-cut staircase could remain, but the Grand View would require extensive remodelling. Thicker walls would be needed to stabilize the roof's weight, meaning there could no longer be an open-air veranda in the sky. Architects would be forced to enclose the porch, making it into a relatively small room, about 25 cubits by 16 cubits.

Bargaining and haggling continued while Artemisia negotiated with engineers. She wanted the Grand View to remain open, she wanted the Lapis Room to be a large apadana hall, and she wanted the chariot piece, including the quadriga. Most of us agreed with Pythius' suggestion to place the chariot statue in the spacious courtyard, but Artemisia vehemently disagreed. She argued that beholders must observe her masterpiece from the mountaintops, the sea, the Myndos Road, and the Mylasa Road.

Once she had received her husband's signature of consent, Artemisia's dreams bounced in every direction with want and improvement, imaginings, and daily changes. Mausolus let others sort out those details, but the monument argument left him no choice; he had to take a stand for logic. Using Artemisia's pride against her, he explained the miserable humiliation she would suffer when the tonnage of her latest contrivance toppled her sanctuary within months, crumbling her treasure in front of the entire world.

Artemisia's insistence on having her way stalled construction, defusing the excitement whirling throughout the district. People's enthusiasm for the project dwindled as if the queen had snuffed out a torch's flame. Builders grew impatient while labourers contemplated moving elsewhere, hoping the Ephesians had organised their rebuilding efforts. Becoming a stumbling block to herself, Artemisia had one of two choices, chariot or veranda – wealthy people picnicking high above Halicarnassus on a floating patio or an enormous statue of herself on the roof.

Pythius recognized the risk involved in attempting this architecturally unexplored procedure. Placing the enormous chariot statue would require genius. Yet, the impossible feat, if successful, could elevate his fame. At the same time, he had a reputation to uphold and would not suffer humiliation by building a ruin. He refused to proceed until Artemisia agreed with every critical revision needed to correct the instability.

Artemisia had to choose one or the other, her dream or her vanity – an insufferable position for the highborn queen of Caria. Mausolus, the builders, architects, sculptors, and artisans, stood frozen, waiting for the queen's decision. A deathly silence filled the room; a feather would have boomed as a thunderclap had one fallen to the floor. Rescinding her concept of a sanctuary for the privileged, Artemisia finally pointed to the modified illustration opting for the chariot, a decision giving birth to an all-new structure.

Over time, the chariot section exceeded everyone's wildest aspirations becoming an engineering spectacle so extraordinary the world fixed its attention on the architectural genius of Pythius of Priene, applauded the Halicarnassus project, and honoured Artemisia and Mausolus with the highest distinction. The satraps shone like luminaries.

Chapter 28

Breaking Ground

Once groundbreaking for 'the temple' got underway, Halicarnassus exploded in momentum and a flurry of activity. Since plans for a sanctuary for the privileged fell through, Artemisia recalibrated her original aspirations and formulated a different purpose, making the project all the more financially advantageous.

Using the word 'temple' was a business decision. The queen reasoned the fascination for divinities held drawing power. Therefore, she would provide a single location for many gods, drawing scores of people to Halicarnassus to pay homage to their particular deity.

During a gathering at the Stoa of Aegea, she announced what she called 'the improvement'. "My joy exists in this improvement, offering pillars for the gods. To be sure, gods require rest from their spiritual labours; therefore, I have invited each god to rest in our city and dwell in a magnificent temple. Athens boasts its Altar of the Twelve Gods; I anticipate their twelve gods coming to Halicarnassus and inviting other deities to perch alongside them on our stately pillars and dwell together within chambers of jewelled splendour."

Terms changed, and diagrams required adjustments, but Artemisia's motive never wavered – she resolved to build a historic landmark in Halicarnassus impressive enough to generate a steady income from visitors. The loss of the veranda in the clouds altered how she chose to regale her affluent guests.

Her vision expanded beyond the privileged to include all people regardless of status. She would impose a toll on visitors depending on which part of the temple they wanted to enjoy. For example, strolling through the parádeisos on the outside of the curtain wall required lesser payment, allowing the middling folk an affordable place to revere their divine benefactors.

Individuals desiring to walk through the courtyard would pay a slightly higher toll with an increased fee for approaching the temple, touching the walls, and nearing its statues and panels.

Aristocrats, affluent enough to enter the temple, would pay a steep sum for lingering in the richly decorated galleries. So Artemisia determined to transform both inner chambers into worthy spectacles for enticing the wealthy.

With delays, glitches, and snags out of the way, construction on the temple finally commenced. The primary assemblage required nine distinct phases. Phase I – lay the stepped foundation. Phase II – erect the internal greenstone core of the pedestal and the Grand View. Phase III – overlay greenstone core with marble blocks and slab. Phase IV – attach the staircase. Phase V – anchor thirty-six columns around the Grand View. Phase VI – set the Pyramid Roof. Phase VII – hang frieze panels, and place statuary. Phase VIII – place the chariot monument. Phase IX – finish the courtyard with its enclosure wall and parádeisos.

Decorating the interior chambers was a non-structural undertaking and could begin after the completion of Phase II. Artisans accessed the chamber areas before the staircase was built by climbing ladders and scaffolding.

Phase I, the least exciting yet most extensive stage, dragged on for months. The gruelling task included digging a massive crater, adding drainage, laying hundreds of foundation blocks, and clamping them together. Next came Phase II – laying the internal framework by placing more greenstone blocks was no more exciting than Phase I. Phase III – adding the pretty exterior - now, that stage generated tremendous enthusiasm. Imagine the temple as a hen's egg; the exterior marble would be like the egg's glossy white shell and the greenstone framework would be like the yoke.

Phase III brought momentum and a fresh interest to the worn-out workforce. Excitement filled the air, and crowds of applauding citizens gathered to watch stone-laden ships sail into the harbour. Mausolus was on business in Mylasa when the merchandise arrived in Halicarnassus. I suspect Artemisia intentionally waited, hoping to avoid unwanted questions about Athenian ships bringing marble. Also, without raising suspicions, the queen employed extra security measures by anchoring the vessels in the Naval Harbour and positioning additional guards shoulder-to-shoulder around the waterfront.

Artemisia stood on the dock, shouting orders and giving commands, directing stone blocks and slabs to their designated locations while warning workers to be careful. White, polished, smooth, and perfect, the magnificent stone was the best Grecian marble on Earth.

Hand-selected dock workers unloaded freight using a system of pulleys and oxen. Once loaded onto carts, drivers hauled the items to their proper destinations. Delivery destinations meant certain pieces passed through town while others proceeded to worksites outside the city. Dockhands also unloaded an abundance of the sculpting stone – limestone, ivory, and granite – which went to an assigned area west of town.

Crafting three-dimensional statues, frieze panels, precision fluting of pillars and columns, notching beams, cutting mitre joints, and detailing capitals created tremendous noise. Mausolus alleviated commotion and costly intrusions on the city's commerce by designating sculpting sites outside the city walls.

Hundreds of skilled artisans needing work flocked to the town, lugging their tools and families with them. The influx of immigrants concerned Mausolus; he expected the assassin to attempt to access the city by posing as a labourer. Anticipating the trick, he established a fail-safe measure by appointing a shrewd overseer to maintain a rigid hiring procedure. Dathaba provided security during sign-on days, and Mausolus ordered me to join the hiring overseer at his booth outside the Myndos Gate to monitor all workers desiring employment. Fearful of failing Mausolus again, I remained vigilant, scrutinising each person applying for work – and I did not rely on hair colour or costume. Strangely, though, after the Mehregan debacle, the assassin vanished without a trace.

Signs posted on the beach prohibited erecting household tents along the shoreline. But the invasion of workers needed accommodations. Sculptors, masons, goldsmiths, potters, brickmakers, metal workers, black smiths, carpenters, weavers, and painters had families. Tending to their needs required establishing a temporary city north of Halicarnassus below the burgeoning mountain town of Pedasa. The populated area became known as the Pedasa Slope. Labourers worshipped and shopped in Pedasa, only coming to Halicarnassus to work. While restrictions tempered noise and commotion in Halicarnassus, I cannot say the same for Pedasa, not with such a rowdy bunch enjoying their leisure time up the hill.

Lodging in the palace was reserved for Leochares, Bryaxis, Scopas, Timotheus, and architects Pythius and Satyros - their lavish quarters included meals with the satraps and a personal attendant to meet their every need. As the world's foremost sculptors lived like royalty, Artemisia sought to make money by taxing the baseborn people along with their agora and every new business sprouting up in the Pedasa Slope area. She aimed to refill the depleted coffers of her empty purse by devising a plan for levees and tariffs, but Mausolus opposed that scheme.

When dealing with people, Mausolus earned a reputation as a fair manager of men. He gained his humanitarian views from the Charter of Human Rights, a manuscript of just policies conceived, written, and utilised by King Cyrus the Great. Adopting the conqueror's ethical principles, Mausolus neither enslaved individuals through high taxation nor demeaned them through cheap payment for labour, and he paid women labourers the same wage he paid the men.

Referring to the charter's creed, Mausolus told me, "Fair-minded thinking elevated Cyrus to the status of the greatest ruler; if his sound ideology benefited an empire, imagine how much more it will benefit my small district. Favourable treatment increases productivity, and a fair wage yields a sense of dignity. Avoiding an uprising from humiliated workers or hungry families is cost-saving enough." He added, "As the Greeks say, pleasure in the job puts perfection in the work."

The boomtown on the Pedasa Slope operated like any other community in Caria. To live there, occupants had to comply with district edicts and decrees. And to keep the peace, Mausolus posted a Dathaba unit, and to appease his wife, he appointed a city manager with two administrative officers to oversee the area.

One legal avenue did exist for acquiring free labour. Anyone in the district delinquent in taxes, imprisoned on a civil matter, or otherwise indebted to the satrapy became eligible for appropriation. Indentured labourers became known as the drudgery team since they were given menial tasks with extended shifts during the heat of the day.

Old men on the drudgery team were responsible for tossing ground stones under sleds and rollers, feeding the draft animals, and cleaning up the messes they left behind. Stronger men assisted surveyors with digging, filling, clearing, and setting stakes for the architectural grid lines. The drudgery team did most of the foundation work by removing dirt, quarrying greenstone, and hauling rock. They cut and hauled trees, then built scaffolding and ladders.

They lashed poles to beams constructing frames for lifting devices. Their tasks included the back-breaking work of excavating slopes for drainage channels and digging deep holes to anchor giant cantilever cranes. At day's end, when work ceased for others, they prepared for the next day by resupplying sand and picking up shards of marble left behind by the sculptors' chisels.

Mausolus spared no expense on this project; he purchased bronze and iron digging tools and modern machinery, even commissioning necessary qanat construction. He added cubits of piping to the existing ductwork along with extra joints and fittings to meet construction demands and supply the masses with water. Enormous amounts of water were needed to keep sand and the splitting wedges moist and to operate the revolutionary hydraulic trip hammers. Ho, to be sure, this innovative hammer mechanism from the Orient made swift work of otherwise time-consuming tasks.

Qanat construction was expensive to initiate but gradually grew into impressive profits. Persians excelled in the science of hydrology, enabling them to build well-watered cities in barren deserts. Moreover, Achaemenid kings attached attractive incentives for qanat specialists, allowing profits to remain in families for five generations.

Another labour team, the pull squad, used draft animals to pull counterweights and wooden sleds to transport stone along inclined tracks to dressing stations or uphill to the construction area. The brake team worked alongside the pull squad; their responsibilities required aligning heavy stone blocks on sleds and operating a braking mechanism to prevent the load from shifting or rolling.

The lift team had a long list of duties. They operated the leveraging towers and pulley cranes needed to lift heavy stone blocks into position, winch frieze panels, and hoist statuary to upper levels. They also built tall columns by stacking marble drums one section at a time. Columns were not one solid piece. Instead, the marble was sliced into thick sections then stacked by lowering individual drums one on top of the other. A metal peg or wooden dowel in the centre of each piece secured them in perfect alignment. This operation required meticulous proficiency for hoisting marble drums above the vertical dowel, lowering them onto the drum below while calibrating the rod precisely through the hole without breaking or bending it. Pythius said the technique gave columns 'licence and fluidity' to remain standing in the event of an earthquake.

Aligners were my favourite team. After the tampers laid a coat of mortar, the lift team moved in to lower the next row of blocks, then hurried away, making room for the alignment team.

Pythius, or a trusted assistant, plumbed different points to calculate alignment. If the block tested out-of-true, he smeared red clay targeting the precise area for striking. The alignment team forcefully rammed the block into perfect position by swinging a leather-tipped ramrod back and forth, similar to a pendulum. The motion generated enough striking power to nudge heavy stones into position.

Pythius again measured; if satisfied with the block's placement, he moved on and plumbed the next one. Swinging that giant ram back and forth, smashing it into blocks of stone, looked like great fun, and I wondered if the team would allow me to join them for a few whacks. I abandoned that idea after reconsidering Pythius' impatience and sharp tongue.

Concerning his work on the temple, the famous architect stated, "I tolerate neither faults nor incongruities. This masterpiece of my genius is the endowment to a future generation. Men in a forthcoming time will one day look upon us with awe and laudable wonder." Therefore, aligners were required to strike their heavy ramrods despite the number of necessary swings - the task was not complete until Pythius determined every stone had settled into perfect vertical.

Once given the go-ahead, aligners moved aside, and tampers hurried back in, pushing mortar into crevices and cleaning off the excess by dragging sanding plates along the surface.

Before hoisting another row of blocks, labourers from the metallurgist team stepped in to perform their job. After the tamping, plumbing, and ramming blocks, metal workers cut rectangular-shaped furrows across the tops of parallel blocks and filled them with molten iron. These iron-filled furrows hardened into a strong bond, seamlessly hugging two blocks tight against each other.

On and on, day after day, this process continued – mortar, block, tamp, ram, anchor – higher and higher, piece by piece, thousands of men laboured, building this wonder, a sophisticated one-of-a- kind phenomenon.

Metallurgist and blacksmith teams stationed on the east side of town near the beach received regular ore supplies from the plateau mines of Anatolia. Furnaces, confined to shore, burned nonstop. Metallurgists extracted and processed metals, and the blacksmith team crafted tools and hammered out the thousands of iron anchor clamps needed for cranes and lifts, carriage pulls, rope fasteners, and to secure exterior art displays. Imagine the thousands of copper clamps required to bolt the pyramid steps in place and hang frieze panels when Pythius ordered one clamp placed every cubit.

Ships arrived with containers of volcanic ash collected from the nearby island of Santorini. Kilns burned day and night as the drudgery team mixed the ash with powdered limestone churning out top-quality Pozzolan mortar. Nothing compares to the integrity of this superb volcanic mortar, especially in regions with pervasive moisture like Halicarnassus.

An army of skilled Jewish woodworkers cut, placed, and carved Lebanese cedar panels for the double-barrel ceilings in the temple's interior rooms. Sturdy frames supported posts and beams joined together with mortise and tenon joints crafted of thick fir and olivewood. Jews also fashioned elaborate archways, furniture, altars, boxes, utensils, and platforms.

Minor disruptions in town flared daily, but merchants had no legitimate cause to complain. Their businesses garnered huge profits, growing their purses fatter than the cows of Bashan. Still years from completion, the Halicarnassus project had already strengthened the city's economy, shaped personal fortunes, and generated tremendous revenue for the entire district.

Chapter 29

Sculpting

Organised construction bustled along, and Artemisia's obsession with details became a ritual. Thinking nonstop about the temple project, she constantly interfered by altering or adding to plans previously established. The root of every dispute? Engineering logic versus vain imaginings. The queen could not work as part of a team and failed to appreciate engineering basics, frustrating supervisors as she tried directing matters with no fundamental comprehension of physic. Keeping workers and keeping the peace required Mausolus to intervene numerous times.

After settling one squabble, another rose, with moaners running to Mausolus to negotiate a policy for harmony. But the time-consuming clashes flaring up between prominent artisans required a bit more tact. Passionate about their particular ideas, styles, and designs, sculptors refused to work together.

As if they were naughty children, Mausolus separated them. Placing Bryaxis on the northern side of the temple, Mausolus assigned the entire wall to him alone. Timotheus sculpted the southern wall, Leochares received the west side, and the responsibility for the eastern wall belonged exclusively to Scopas. This brilliant solution renewed peace, and construction again proceeded at a vigorous pace.

In hopes of diverting his wife's attention away from structural matters, Mausolus invited her to oversee the progression of frieze panels. Here Artemisia excelled with creative and ingenious embellishments. By rejecting tedious, static-looking profiles typical in Persian reliefs, she created life-like three-dimensional characters staged in dramatic poses, wearing elegant costumes with animated features, and engaged in bold action, particularly in historical battle scenes depicting the Amazon warriors. And she insisted on at least one equestrian grouping to honour the Amazons for inventing the cavalry.

To my surprise, something about my appearance captivated the artistic eye of sculptors. My face, physique, or general expression struck them as creative, and each wanted to sculpt me. So, I became a model. Originally I revelled in their compliments, believing myself to be an exceptional specimen of a man. But, before long, I loathed the tedious job of sitting as a model.

Frozen in awkward positions uncomfortably arranged by sculptors, I sat for hours – a full day at times – as artists chiselled my likeness from chunks of stone. Jaleh occasionally passed by and stopped to watch stone cutters at work, carving out their masterpieces. She pretended to be intrigued, but I heard her sarcastic sniggers. Modelling as an Amazon warrior was the worst; I tried dismissing Jaleh with my eyes, but she acted unaware of my distress. Ho, to be sure, had I been permitted to move, I would have shooed her away along with her insufferable heckling.

Another problem I faced was that sculptors constantly fought over me. They called me a prototypical model, and each stone worker demanded pieces of me – the angle of my face, arms, or posture. I would sit for the rough-out stage of one sculptor, then move along for something else with another artist. Every time I stepped out, a different model stepped in for the detail and the finish.

I sat. I leaned. I reclined. I raised a spear. I stood as the victor; other times, I fell, overpowered, moments from slaughter. Finally, I begged Mausolus to rescue me from squabbling clashes and the hours of tedium, but he just laughed a deep belly laugh and told me to figure it out.

A lower frieze panel wrapping the circumference of the Persian Pedestal depicts a bloody battle between Greek warriors and Amazon women. One section of this display portrays a bearded Macedonian intending to slay a fallen Amazon. Beneath his helmet, he frowns with a fierce scowl while poising his right arm to plunge a sword in a vicious death blow. To be sure, the rough-cut of the prone Amazon woman, defenceless and unable to rise to her feet, is me. Secretly, I enjoyed posing as an Amazon woman because I hoped it would make me appealing to Artemisia, but she failed to notice. Instead, she remained occupied by staging battle scenes, positioning fierce Amazon women, and rearranging their weapons. She posed models to make scenes more violent. For example, she adjusted the woman's spear in one pose by placing it deep within the Macedonian's side. In another, she had an Amazon striking her battle axe downward into the body of a fallen Greek soldier who could not raise his sword in defence. She insisted the Macedonian's face express both recognition and defeat.

My favourite is the hunting scene where I am sculpted pursuing a leopard; I enjoy this piece the most because I wear trousers. Parts of me – of my physique anyway – became etched in one form or another on every frieze panel surrounding the temple. Still, my greatest pride came from sitting for Leochares as he sculpted Mausolus' statue for the chariot piece. Generally unavailable, Mausolus missed posing sessions due to district responsibilities. To stay on schedule, Leochares enlisted me for help. He sculpted my arms as Mausolus' holding the quadriga reins and used my feet wearing a pair of Mausolus' shoes. The statue's muscular chest and handsome head belong entirely to Mausolus.

Leochares carved the chariot sculpture of Artemisia from a single block of Pentelic marble, but quarrels abounded after the queen found fault with his work. She disapproved of the silliest issues – the look of her hair or the cut of her dress. She despaired over her cap and criticised the shape of her jewellery. Her main disappointment – in her own words – was "the gross lack of proficiency in capturing the authentic aura of my face." Ho, to be sure, spirited disputes erupted between those two.

In truth, Leochares' statue resembled Artemisia so precisely that I secretly wanted to kiss it. He expertly captured the beauty of her pillowy lips, the height of her cheeks, the tilt of her head, and the triple row of curls she wore for special occasions. He shaped the himation accurately pinned over her shoulder just as she wore it. Yet, Artemisia dismissed the quality of his craftsmanship. She once scolded the artisan, "This debauchment of unbecoming and average features bears no resemblance to my physical expression!" Over and over, she argued with Leochares telling him to capture her exact appearance.

"This statue is my eternal legacy. My form will endure as you fashion it," Artemisia continued. "Perhaps you care nothing of your reputation or future conversations concerning your poor abilities and sloppy craftsmanship, but I care about my status. Look at me, Leochares! Look at my face! Do I have the nose of a dolphin as this statue does? Are my hands thick like the hands of a slaving miner? The clumsy hands on this statue look nothing like mine. I want my sculpture exact! I am the queen of Caria; properly honour me by designing me like a queen."

169

No one found fault with Leochares' excellent portrayal of the queen; the legendary sculptor's error was that he failed to decipher precisely how Artemisia viewed herself. Intervening once again, Mausolus made weak excuses for his wife and begged Leochares to continue with the Halicarnassus project. As a further step for preserving peace, he forbade Artemisia from examining any of her sculptures except at a distance. Keeping Leochares on the project was vital; his name carried the temple's reputation. For that reason, Artemisia managed several polite words of apology but later moved on, commissioning Scopas to sculpt her other portraits.

Surprisingly, Mausolus assigned me the position of construction supervisor. Under the direction of Nash, an assistant to Pythius, I organised and directed the team responsible for building the grand staircase. Grand indeed! Twenty-two cubits wide, perfectly centred to the Persian Pedestal, with twenty-four graduating steps harmonising to the rise of the Pyramid Roof. Embellishments required building extra deep steps – the average person required two complete strides to cross one step. A marble lion stood at the edge of each stair, looking like a frozen sentinel guarding visitors making their skyward climb on a sacred path.

Stonework requires brute strength, which I had. I enjoyed the swell of my muscles when swinging the hammer in a broad arc. Sakeri taught me where to plant hard blows for minimal breakage and ways to cut smoother edges by spinning the subbia between strikes. While I possessed a knack for physical labour, working as a supervisor required entirely different skills, ones I had yet to learn. Younger than most men (and two women) under my direction, I doubted Nash or the other labourers would have given me a chance without an endorsement from the king.

Wishing to be worthy of Mausolus' confidence in me, I adopted his advice as my guideline: "Your good actions will give strength to yourself and inspire good actions in others." Gradually, I earned the respect of my crew, and together, we produced a spectacular staircase gracing the grandest structure in the world. The management skills I learned as a young man in Halicarnassus proved invaluable throughout my life, benefiting me in countless ways. Mausolus had a particular way of blessing people's lives like that.

The rhythm of everyday life kept me busy working on the temple as a construction supervisor and assisting the hiring overseer. In addition, I often modelled. I visited my friends, continued to train under Goliath, travelled with

Mausolus, went to parties at the palace, and regularly played Technê. I also continued my covert mission of spying. This meant I scarcely found time for Jaleh except at mealtime with the entire family. When in a pleasant mood, Goliath regaled us with exciting tales and wild adventures about his life and his father's military campaigns.

Simin had already heard most of her husband's stories, but she listened politely while sewing garments for her family. Jaleh sat beside her mother weaving various items, and the boys, wide-eyed and tense, sat in rapt attention, immersed in their father's tales of travels, battles, and covert assignments requiring clandestine meetings with mysterious foreigners.

Carving occupied me while I, too, listened spellbound. I found a chunk of ivory discarded at one of the sites. The shape of it inspired me to try my hand at sculpting. So, while listening to Goliath tell of danger and intrigue, I meticulously fashioned a replica of an elephant with a small tail and massive tusks protruding past the trunk – I planned to gift the carving to Mausolus.

Despite this busy schedule with many distractions, I kept the assassin foremost in my mind, searching and speculating where he might be hiding. I worried about his strange disappearance, but worse, I agonised about his imminent return.

Chapter 30

Lysippos

Supplied with flaky apple pastries and a lime drink, I found an outlying bench near the library where I could eat while discreetly surveying people coming and going. After a few moments, a disgruntled gentleman requiring rest approached and sat on the seat beside me.

I spoke first. "Have you come to the city to work on the temple?"

"Quite the opposite, my boy. I have come to protest the temple!"

"What possible reason might you have for protesting this historical work?"

"Historical work? Bah! You mean a historical scheme. She is both criminal and iniquitous."

"She?" I asked. "To whom do you refer?"

"The queen, of course! She is the one who has carried out this intolerable crime. She is no innocent victim, nor is she ignorant of her offences, which is why she refuses me an audience with her husband, the king." The man fumed with anger.

He told me his name was Lysippos and said he came to Halicarnassus as an envoy from the people of Rhodes, hoping to talk sense into Artemisia.

"Lysippos?" Unsure if I heard him correctly, I asked again. "The head of the art school at Argos? Lysippos, the famous sculptor?" I practically fell off the bench.

"Steady yourself, boy," he spat back.

Curious, I asked, "Why does a man of your expertise miss an opportunity of contributing to this legendary work of art? Is not this a most coveted ambition for any artisan?"

"Thievery!" he said. "Why should I involve myself in this thievery and gross misuse of power? Your queen has foolishly planted poisonous weeds in the garden of her own household."

"Pardon me, sir, for my confusion. Please, clarify this grievance you have against Artemisia."

My stomach turned, listening to Lysippos describe the malice behind Artemisia's dishonest actions to acquire a monument for herself. I learned that the superb white marble being expertly dressed and hoisted into place to create the most celebrated temple in the world – this noble tribute to the king and queen of Caria – was, in fact, stolen property. Commandeered. Wrongly appropriated. Annexed from the people of Rhodes, who had procured the marble to build a temple to their god Helios. Worse yet, Rhodians had already paid the exorbitant cost, including fees for transporting ship-loads of materials from Athens to their island.

According to Lysippos, the queen waited in the sea for the slow-moving Athenian cargo ships to pass, then ordered her marines to over-run and seize the vessels. Once in control of the helm, she sailed the entire shipment of stone and other building materials away to her prearranged hiding place. Worse still, in an attempt to conceal her identity as the mastermind behind the extortion, she disposed of the crew by casting every man overboard, believing both the Athenians and the Rhodians would blame Cetus or another sea monster when their vessels failed to arrive.

"The lone monster in the sea that day was a woman named Artemisia," Lysippos spat.

"To be sure, my Lord, you are mistaken. Perhaps a band of pirates did attack your vessels, but how can you accuse the queen? How do you know for certain Artemisia was involved?"

"Because she stood on the deck and ordered the sailors thrown overboard. Able-bodied men tried swimming; most drowned, but a few stayed afloat until a passing ship rescued them. Under oath, each man gave an identical account of the incident. To be sure, my boy, their testimony regarding the ruthless queen's mercenary crime is how I know who is responsible for such a shameful act.

"Rhodians are not keen on war," he added. "Their request is simple; they want their property returned. They will not seek retribution for their citizens' deaths. They will forego the penalty for theft and will not involve the Shahanshah. They merely seek the return of their stolen property, promising to forgive the incident as an unfortunate misunderstanding. And yet, the queen refuses."

Lysippos' words came as a lamp illuminating a moonless night. I had sensed inconsistencies with Artemisia, but when I tried pinning down specific discrepancies the basis for my suspicions became like bubbles floating just beyond my grasp.

In one instance, after Mausolus signed his signature of consent, building supplies miraculously emerged almost overnight. And the reddish man; I now realised why he was hired to kill the queen. This discovery explained her glib reaction to his threats.

Artemisia already had these stolen supplies hidden away when she hired me to manipulate Mausolus into building her sanctuary. Mausolus was taking too long to decide, and Artemisia feared the discovery of her hidden ships. Giving the impression the project originated with her would cast suspicion in her direction, so she got me to involve Mausolus, then swore me to secrecy to ensure her scheme remained as airtight as an earthenware jar. She deceived Mausolus, me, and the entire district, and now the angry Rhodians sought righteous revenge.

I previously imagined the peltast as a slobbering, merciless beast unworthy of running with the dogs. I gave him no acclaim beyond pure evil. Perhaps this peltast acted as an instrument of justice, righteous in his actions against Artemisia.

Conjuring sympathy for such a man was dangerous; compassion put me at odds with the empire and the district's rulers, yet sweeping away Artemisia's piracy and callous murder was no small matter. But, despite justified retaliation, assassinating an imperial vassal was not the answer either; the act would lead to war. Innocent people would die.

I asked Lysippos, "Have you taken your complaint to the king? I know him as a fair and even-handed man."

"Listen, boy! I am telling you, the queen has blocked my way! I have travelled a far distance seeking an audience with Mausolus, but the queen barred me. Or is he also a conspirator, thieving along with his wife?"

"Mausolus did no such thing! I assure you of that, my Lord. Of course, I cannot speak for the queen's motives, but I assure you, King Mausolus remains entirely unaware of this deceit you mention."

"As I surmised."

"What do you intend to do?" I hoped he would mention the assassin sent to Halicarnassus by the Rhodians.

"Reasoning has failed; I wash my hands of this matter. I have a school to manage with eager and brilliant students awaiting my return. I cannot help the Persian couple now; this shadow of iniquity falls on Artemisia's head."

Playing a role in this betrayal obligated me to apologise. "My Lord, I am truly sorry and regret this terrible incident has happened," I said.

Regarding me as an ignorant boy of no consequence, he asked, "Why would you apologise?"

Fighting back the tears, I told him, "I cannot explain my apology, but I remain profoundly ashamed."

Privileged Artemisia, born with subsidy and opportunity, dwelling in life's most favourable circumstances, aspired to higher honours than being the wife of Mausolus or a warrior queen. She treated accolades for military prowess and praise for leading Caria to an independent lifestyle as meaningless drivel and spoken rubbish, calling oral history "A lifeless world of one-dimensional words. Invisible lyrics, slipping away unnoticed from broken memories struggling to survive in the emptiness of space."

She sought physical identification, a noticeable and tangible narrative to regale the world over and over, century after century, reaffirming her worthy life and exceptional contributions. When future generations viewing the temple asked, "Who built such a wonder?" she wanted her name spoken, "Artemisia II, Queen of Caria, built this!"

Suffering financial insolvency with no viable revenue, yet desperate to satisfy her burning hunger for a matchless legacy, she chose a foolish course and trusted in her cunning and position to escape penalty. But, as if opening Pandora's Box, Artemisia's actions were sure to end badly for Halicarnassus.

Barely able to stand, I walked away, leaving Lysippos alone on the bench. Fearing I may encounter Mausolus or come upon Artemisia, I side-stepped the construction area. Neither did I want to see the sickening sight of the Rhodians' marble being applauded as a mighty Persian temple. Taking narrow side streets, I slipped through yards, past back doors, and climbed over terraced walls to skirt the busy commons area until arriving unseen at my quarters.

Chapter 31

Sailing on the *Trojan Hector*

Work on the temple halted temporarily during the rainy season. Still, the unseasonably warm winter blessed Halicarnassus with sunny days, allowing construction to maintain a steady pace, keeping us ahead of schedule. Silence from the peltast unnerved me, but the news I had learned from Lysippos felt like a tinderbox waiting for the smallest cinder to ignite a vast woodland. Whenever I considered Artemisia's actions, my stomach churned, and my arms felt heavy. Unsure of what to do or how to proceed, I elected to do nothing and continued to perpetuate the lie – the false narrative Artemisia declared to the world. I dismissed Lysippos' words, ignored their implications, and conducted myself as usual.

The pace and progress of the Halicarnassus project pleased Mausolus. He allowed others to deal with production worries, freeing himself for district matters and time to handle his real problem: Artemisia. She was overly eccentric and barely slept, and she continued inserting herself into every aspect of construction without knowing the fundamentals.

When an invitation arrived to attend the first birthday celebration of Prince Alexander III of Macedon, Mausolus saw it as an opportunity to refocus his wife's attention elsewhere and, at the same time, satisfy his curiosity about the colt he had sent to the young prince the year before.

Artemisia resisted leaving her essential position of oversight in managing the temple project. Still, an opportunity to visit her friend, Myrtle, presently known as Queen Olympias of Macedon, convinced her to relinquish control of construction issues for several weeks.

Household servants and personal attendants prepared the necessary supplies for travel to Pella. Then, astonishing me beyond my wildest dreams, Mausolus requested my presence. Me! Traveling across the sea to Pella to meet the king and queen of Macedonia! Ho, to be sure, I was swept away.

Jaleh anticipated spending extra time with me when she heard her father would be away on assignment guarding Mausolus and Artemisia. When she learned I was to join the entourage to Greece, she grew miffed and failed to share in my excitement. I appeased her annoyance by promising to bring her a special gift. The idea thrilled her immensely. Asking Simin for advice on an appropriate item, she suggested a colourful epiblema for Jaleh to drape over her shoulders when we walked together on chilly evenings.

The king's marines readied four triremes for our voyage. Of course, these days, double-sailed triremes are mostly obsolete. Still, during the reign of King Artaxerxes, powerful triremes ruled supreme as the deadliest naval weapons, and Mausolus owned more than one hundred such vessels. Master shipbuilders at the Isthmus of Corinth built Caria's entire fleet from the wood of ripened fir lumber or oak cut down precisely on the seventeenth day of the moon's age when the sap ran ripe, thus preventing rot or worm plagues.

The ghastly chore performed by rowers was nothing I sought for an occupation. However, Nature eased their labour once winds grew favourable, and they could exchange oars for sails. Watching the wind catch, unfurling a grand Faravahar with wings spanning from one side of the sail to the other sent shivers up my arms. Ho, to be sure, nothing compared to the remarkable sight of a Persian fleet spanning the mighty Aegean, with overfilled sails harnessing the wind to pilot the world's premium ships in a majestic cadence across the sea.

Mausolus named each naval vessel in his fleet but distinguished his four personal ships with names he found in a poem he identified with, *The Iliad*, written by a man named Homer. The lyrics tell of a city called Troy. Mausolus read Homer's poem many times, considering it an epic tale about a tremendous clash between ancient cultures. "To be sure, Ethan," he told me, "Homer's tale moves beyond war at its cruellest to expose the human heart at its most authentic." He gave long, passionate explanations of Homer's poem, possessing the raw elements of real life: intervention of the gods: courage on the battlefield, personal glory, betrayal, lust, infidelity, honour and wealth, blood, war, and ultimate destruction.

He named one ship *Scamander* after the river flowing through the plain where the Trojan Army mustered for war. Another he devoted to the story's ever-conflicted hero, Achilles – a Greek warrior, the son of a nymph, and king of the Myrmidons. The third ship, the *Helen*, was named for the beautiful wife of Spartan King Menelaus. While still married to Menelaus, Helen eloped with another man, Paris, and together they built a life behind the fortified walls of Troy. Unfortunately, her deceit and cunning launched 1,000 ships, followed by a ten-year war, collapsing the once powerful Trojan culture. Helen's vain attempt at happiness cost her a lover, his family, and every inhabitant of the city.

Mausolus named his private ship *Trojan Hector* after the story's champion and his favourite of all the acclaimed Trojan warriors. The character of Hector represented Mausolus' ideal of heroism, the personification of courage. Hector passionately loved and defended his wife and placed his people and city's welfare above himself. Mausolus explained, "Tragically, Hector's death sprang from treachery carried across the sea by another. Dying is made worse when delivered by the hands of betrayal, but no death is eviler, no heartbreak deeper than betrayal at the hands of a loved one."

Achilles savagely battled with Hector, avenging a wrong committed by Paris, then killed him in a gruesome death witnessed by the entire city. After rituals and funerary rites, the grief-stricken Trojans wept as their champion disappeared in the cremation flames of loss. Troy never recovered from the profound loss of Hector. Mausolus told me, "Young Ethan, despite the passing of many centuries, this warrior's integrity and bravery continue to stir the sensibilities of men. Indeed, Hector achieved everlasting honour, the greatest accomplishment possible."

Mausolus treasured Homer's legend, inspiring him to acquire enough artifacts from the battlefield of Troy to fill an entire room at the palace. He possessed armour, helmets, shields, swords, spears, and knives. The sea air corroded some abandoned items, but many pieces buried beneath the sand remained in decent condition. Mausolus placed labelled objects in a specific order according to the location of their discovery and which army owned them. Then, he built something he called a diorama – a representation simulating a miniature battle zone showing Troy's palace with figurines of tiny soldiers staged in various fighting scenes. He rearranged the Greeks and Trojans several times yearly into different battle sequences. The Trojan War happened long ago. The entire area was laid to waste for centuries until being rebuilt into what is today known as Ilion. Yet Mausolus determined to one day stand on Troy's sacred ground where his ancestors once stood, but I believe he meant where his hero Hector once stood.

I previously mentioned that centuries after Troy, the Persian King Xerxes campaigned against the Greeks with Hydarnes, who enlisted the 10,000 Immortals. Ho, to be sure, Xerxes held a grudge. Strangely, he bore the loss of Troy as a personal insult and a slap in the face to Persia, regardless of the fact the Empire of Persia did not exist until centuries later. No matter, before advancing against Greece, Xerxes stood on the area known as Thicket Ridge and vowed to avenge the malicious attacks on his Trojan ancestors.

History has a strange way of repeating itself. – or maybe it is people who repeat themselves. As we blithely sailed toward Pella on the *Trojan Hector,* none of us could have predicted how world events would play out. In the future, this birthday child we were traveling to meet, Prince Alexander, would also visit Troy. The young warrior would stand on the area called Thicket Ridge, wearing the armour cast aside after the war with Troy – perhaps the armour belonged to Agamemnon, or maybe it was the suit worn by King Menelaus. Yes, on the ground where King Xerxes stood swearing vengeance, the man Alexander would stand, vowing to re-enact the glorious victory against Troy and snatch the world away from Persia.

Mausolus' favourite four vessels received elaborate embellishments. Solid oak rams plated with bronze tips, rising slightly above the hull, were powerful defence weapons for striking and piercing other ships. Above the ram, a ship's stem typically exhibited carvings of horned animals such as a boar's head, a markhor, or the head of an ibex, but the *Trojan Hector* bore no horned animal. Instead, the stem displayed a horse head –Mausolus' imagining of the famed Trojan horse.

Sternposts were the most decorative piece of a ship, curving in a slight sweep, rising higher than the stem. Ship owners prided themselves in the fascinating designs they created for their sternposts: horses, lions, griffins, gliding falcons, gods, and goddesses. Mausolus' private vessel, stem to stern, rivalled all other ships, from the Trojan horse head to vividly painted battle scenes running along the sides to the Zeus Labrandenos chiselled in the sternpost, holding a lotus-tipped sceptre in his left hand and a labrys, the double-headed axe of Queen Penthesilea, over his right shoulder.

The city of Labraunda (where I stayed before starting my journey to Halicarnassus) housed the Hecatomnid dynasty's sacred ancestral shrine. Holy Avenue wound through a forest of plane trees connecting Mylasa to the Temple of Zeus Labrandenos. On a pedestal in the centre of the temple, King

Hecatomnus placed a marble statue of Zeus holding the double-headed labrys formerly owned by Penthesilea, the wise and famous queen of the Amazons killed at Troy.

Her dexterity in wielding a double-sided weapon became legendary, earning her the reputation of a mighty warrior. She died honourably in a battle to the death against Achilles. (Artemisia owned an ancient collection of painted vases depicting their famous fight.) After killing Penthesilea, Achilles seized her famous labrys as a trophy. The item worked its way throughout history until arriving in the Lydian dynasty. Centuries later, the satrap ruler of Lydia, namely King Hecatomnus, acquired the labrys as a gift and commissioned a grand statue to allow Zeus the opportunity of holding the sacred axe. Mausolus admired the work of art and had it engraved on Carian coinage.

How proud I felt standing on the deck of the *Trojan Hector*, voyaging among the elite entourage of vessels, sailing beneath giant Faravahars, coursing our way across a mighty sea.

Chapter 32

Crossing the Aegean

Refreshing temperatures provided excellent visibility for our Aegean crossing, but a contrary wind sometimes whipped up rough tides. The open sea invigorated Mausolus as he stood at the bow, inviting the wind to blow hard against him. Throwing open his arms, he echoed the words of Sophocles: 'Wonders are many, and none is more wonderful than man; the power that crosses the white sea, driven by the stormy south wind, making a path under surges that threaten to engulf him.' Ho, to be sure, as the crew made a path among the surges threatening to engulf me, I hung over the side spewing.

Goliath noticed my predicament. He touched my shoulder and asked, "Do you have anything left?"

"I ran out a long time ago," I said. "Being out here in this bottomless basin of blue water is awe-inspiring, yet terrifying. To be sure, I would not wish to fall overboard."

"Can you swim?" he asked.

"Some, but I prefer water where my feet touch the bottom. Can you swim?"

"Like a stone!" he said. "Falling overboard is part of sailing; drowning is always discouraged, so keep your head above water if you go in. Each ship has a rescue team. They are swift to extend an oar. When you see one, grab it! Or, if you are too far out, they will form a human chain to reach you."

"Can Mausolus swim?"

"Like a dolphin, but I do not think he would appreciate getting wet, so I advise against falling overboard."

"Acknowledged," I said.

Tiny islands peppered the sea, but I gave them little thought. To me, they resembled nothing more than tedious specks haplessly flung across the water. Yet, as we sailed through straits and passed different regions, Goliath took time to describe exciting details about each one, their societies, prehistoric cultures, and historical legends.

"They look like jumbled slabs of rocky ground to me," I said.

"Ethan, appreciate these islands for their resilience. They may appear insignificant, but in truth, they are one vibrant community sharing a common heritage of foreign occupation, blockades, disputes, and domination by one realm after another in a cycle of ever-changing sovereigns."

He pointed out distinctive geographic features: grottos and granite or limestone cliffs and explained how wealthy islanders owned exclusive export businesses, shipping vases of black steatite across the empire. Some profited from agriculture or the luxury industry with paradise resorts and vacation hideaways attracting aristocrats, mostly Egyptians.

I enjoyed the dramatic tales about savage battles with Leviathan, sneak attacks from Amazons, encounters with centaurs, and the fearsome Minotaur. I wished I had been born an islander just for the chance to clash with a monster.

"Despite centuries of conflicts and seizures, these communities have preserved their cultural identities and histories by celebrating life, honouring their legends and myths, assaults and battles, losses, and victories," he said.

"What about that one?" I asked. "The high cliffs are covered with windmills. Do you know anything about it?"

"Depending on which country you associate with, this island is named Patmos or Litois. For example, people honouring Neptune call the isle Patmos, and people worshiping the goddess Artemis refer to it as Litois," he said.

"This slab, as you call it, Ethan, is the most unique of all islands. Legend has it that centuries ago, the island sank for no explainable reason. It disappeared beneath the surface, whirling and plummeting haplessly into a bottomless cavern. Then, hearing pleas for help, the goddess Artemis dove into the water. With assistance from her twin brother Apollo, they retrieved the island and relocated it on the mountainous pillars where it presently stands."

Ever since Mehregan, Goliath unconsciously touched the burned area of his neck whenever he felt agitated or stressed. A large part of his scalp behind the right ear remained bald, and the skin of his neck healed lighter in colour with a mottled texture. As scars go, his was particularly unsightly and painful. At night, Simin plastered the area with a soothing salve of cannabis and milk.

When I saw him fidget with his neck, I asked, "Anything else?"

"Somewhere on that island is the unmarked grave of my uncle."

"I did not know you had family living out here in the sea," I said.

"Not living here, Ethan, only dying here. It happened during the last stages of the Peloponnesian War. My father – Ralf was his name – and Omid, his brother, along with other Persian soldiers fighting on the side of Sparta, became shipwrecked. They swam for the closest island to escape the Athenians' brutal sword—that one – Patmos.

"My father survived, hiding for months until it was safe to leave. But, unfortunately, many comrades, including my uncle, perished at the hands of the enemy."

He avoided telling me the gruesome detail, so I did not ask.

"I almost died before I was even born. While my father was hiding on Patmos, fending for his life, my pregnant mother was alone, trapped in the war-torn city of Byzantium. Byzantium held split loyalties between the Athenians and the Spartans – both sides fought to profit from established trade routes, the fertile region and gain control of the Strait of Bosphorus. Untold people died in that fight at Byzantium, but the women in town aided my mother in birthing me despite the dangers. I am here because of them."

"To be sure, that is some story," I said.

"After the war, Father found his way to the ravaged city, located my mother, and finally met me. I was but a few years old; I do not remember those days."

"You grew up in Byzantium?" I asked.

"No. My father moved us inland, where he became a farmer in Persian-dominated Lycia. He said farming was the most important labour of man. He served as a hatru whenever the empire required temporary military aid, but he called farming the only civilised life. My parents lived together for many years and raised a large family – all sons. Most became farmers. I miss them all." He touched the mottled scar on his neck.

Goliath finished ruminating about the time we docked for the evening. For some reason, Artemisia insisted on spending the night on Skyros – that is the island where Achilles grew up. Before going ashore, I asked, "Do you think the assassin knows the satraps left Halicarnassus?"

"He knows," Goliath answered.

"Do you think he will make his move in Pella?"

"I would," Goliath said. "Unless I was injured or dead."

Chapter 33

A Taste of Mead

Mausolus, Artemisia, and their attendants moved ashore to comfortable lodgings. During the evening, Goliath stayed near Mausolus, and Mausolus stayed near Artemisia. The rest of us slept on the ship or under the stars on the beach. Marines and crew seeking food and recreation alternated shifts going ashore. Neither a member of the crew nor part of the vassal's entourage, I was free to explore on my own.

The island smelled sweet from the bounty of figs, grapes, honey, flowers, and herbs, and the night sky shone with a thousand stars twinkling overhead. I strolled through the city wearing my Persian finery - comfortable silk trousers with braided tassels hanging from the waist, a matching vest, leather shoes, and fashionable silver-filled bazuband bracelets on each arm. In those days, I wore saffron and brown, the official colour for Goliath's Dathaba. Before sailing, I visited Landers. He trimmed my beard and polished my hair, again accomplishing a miracle with my curls. Now, finely groomed and quite fetching with my yellow headband accentuating my professionally styled hair, I ambled about, taking in the sites.

By the many statues around, I surmised the locals worshiped Dionysian but also Poseidon, whom they claim protected these waters with his mighty trident. His gem-coated palace of coral is said to lay nearby on the floor of the Aegean Sea. Numerous hostelries dotting the coastline overflowed with marines, soldiers, and locals. Festooned women lingered, laughing with gaiety and brio. Each establishment served an assortment of food, much wine, mead, and wheat beer.

After walking a distance, I stumbled into one attractive hostelry filled with laughing women and a crowd of men sloshing goblets of beer while singing songs and playing board games. Not Technê, like Mausolus and I played, but I did recognise games in my land – Petteia and Mancala.

One unusual game I saw piqued my interest - I heard someone call it Weiqi. The game was played with black and white stones. The player who used the black stones moved their piece first to begin the game, and afterward, each player took turns placing one stone on an empty intersection of the vertical and horizontal lines carved into a polished board. The player capturing the most territory wins. Before long, the men invited me to join their game. I was swept away when the fellows allowed me to move first with a black stone.

My ability to make new friends pleased me immensely. I learned the rules of Weiqi in no time, and I won every game. Not surprising, considering I had acquired much knowledge and expertise by associating with Mausolus, philosophers, and Halicarnassus' esteemed members of the nobility.

Someone ordered a round of juice for our table; they called the strange drink mead. Sniffing at my cup, I identified an aroma of honey heightened by curious spices and fruit. Suspicious, I lifted the tumbler to my lips and permitted the slightest drop of tipple to roll over my tongue. Ho, to be sure, mead was delicious juice.

Soon a different man ordered another round for our table, and my second goblet tasted as incredible as the first. I enjoyed drinking mead and ordered the next round for our table. Playing Weiqi and drinking mead, the raucous evening passed as I laughed and sang with my new friends. Finally, someone suggested we put money on the table, betting on our games. That suggestion brought enthusiastic clapping, and soon, the festooned women gathered around to watch.

One festooned woman asked me to buy her a goblet of beer. Suitably I agreed, which produced wild applause from my friends, who slapped me on the back and cheered when the woman sat on my lap and began kissing my ears. Of course, I would have enjoyed Jaleh kissing my ears, but Jaleh was not around, and the festooned woman, smelling of sweet perfume, seemed most fond of my ears.

I recall loud cheering, laughing, and shouting as the fellows urged me to down another goblet of mead. Craning my neck, I kissed the ears of the festooned woman still on my lap. Everybody laughed with much merriment throughout the evening.

Here is where my memory gets fuzzy. I cannot recall much of the evening after that. The next thing I remembered was waking up face-down on the beach, and it was morning. Sand was in my mouth and glued to the sticky mead, which had dribbled down my chest. I tried moving but found the task impossible. Waves brushed against the shore, sounding like clashing cymbals pounding in my skull, and the sun's unusual brilliance hurt my eyes.

Laying prone on the beach, resting my head on the cold sand, I caught a familiar scent wafting past – myrrh and cassia. Raising my head the slightest bit confirmed my worst fears; Mausolus! And Goliath stood beside him! Appearing larger than ever, Goliath folded his monster arms across his muscular chest, shaking his head at my pitiful state. Ho, to be sure, I honestly wanted to rise and give a proper greeting, but strangely, I could not move. From Mausolus' expression, I suspected he had once laid face-down in the sand.

Grabbing my arms, the two men stood me up, steadying me before I tried to walk. Woozy, as if hanging over the side of a rolling ship, I spewed several times. That is when I became aware of the strangest thing; I was naked - no shoes, vest, or fancy trousers with braided tassels at the waist. I stood bare as the day of my birth without so much as a yellow headband. And my purse was missing, every daric I had brought to buy Jaleh a gift.

I glanced over my shoulder and saw the men on the *Trojan Hector* watching from the deck. Asking me about my night plunged them into hysterics; they slapped each other on the back and bent over with colossal belly laughs. Embarrassed, I tried explaining the situation to Mausolus, "I only played a game of stones with my new friends and drank a goblet, maybe two goblets, of juice, made from honey. But the part about my clothes – I have no idea what happened to my clothes!"

He and Goliath pitched me into the sea, prompting more gales of laughter from the gawking crew. Praying Artemisia was nowhere near to observe my unseemly condition, I stumbled awkwardly, heaving in the early morning rollers. I spat several more times while standing in waist-deep water, begging the current to carry me away from the humiliation.

Stumbling my way to the ship caused lingering sand to grind into my private crevices. If Goliath had his way, I fear he would have left me nude for the entire trip, but Mausolus extended mercy by allowing me to warm myself in the forecastle.

Before sailing for Pella, I visited a friend, Karim, a metallurgist working onsite since the temple's commencement. Earlier, I had fashioned a wax and clay cast of a Nisaean warhorse and asked Karim to pour the design in bronze whenever he had a bit of metal left. I intended to give Alexander a modest gift for his birthday, so I fashioned the horse big enough to impress a toddler and made the hooves larger than scale, hoping the animal would stand unsupported.

Karim poured up the mould, and the finished product turned out more beautiful than I expected. Karim agreed. He gave me a piece of buff cloth to finish the polishing. Now, sitting in my shame in the forecastle of the *Trojan Hector*, Karim's gift proved providential. Avoiding the crew's constant heckling while dodging the silent reprimand of Goliath, I occupied myself polishing Alexander's toy.

Arriving on the second day, rowers guided us through the narrow inlet of the Thermaic Gulf into the Port of Pella.

Chapter 34

Pella, Kingdom of Macedon

Pella was a destination city, a dazzling place enjoyed by royalty, aristocrats, generals, and noblemen. Pella was already a remarkable place at the time of my visit – the largest city in the kingdom of Macedon, with the wealthiest port and the world's largest agora. But today, owing to the world fame of Pella's son, Alexander, the entire region has grown exponentially into the most affluent society in the world.

Before Alexander was born, extensive remodelling of the palace converted the royal home into a sprawling structure of sturdy marble and exhaustive detail work, rising in majestic splendour atop a mountain crest. The surrounding landscape grew thick with olive groves and citrus orchards, and dense forests of cypress, oaks, and yellow-flowered acacias.

Steep hills became terraced gardens of showy green foliage and bright yellow flowers, blossoming with clusters of oyster thistle and rows of pink oleander. Sweet-scented vines crept up walls and rock faces, attracting honeybees, butterflies, and flitting hummingbirds. Walkways wound among reddish-orange trumpet flowers where fleshy leaves of agave and aloe grew beneath a canopy of silk trees, heavily laden with clusters of soft pink flowers.

King Philip strengthened his Macedonian realm by building numerous cities to breed and train horses. His most expensive renovations went into expanding stable blocks and refurbishing chariot depots. Ancillary remodelling included new guest quarters, a private library, and a personal gymnasium for the king. Fountains, pools, and shaded verandas wrapped the palace offering panoramic views of the vast plain, the sea, and surrounding mountains.

Damp air rising off the rivers smelled of fish blended with the musty tang of silt. Early settlers wisely founded this city on these fertile deltas, where vast river systems ensured an endless freshwater supply. Every aspect of nature possessed religious significance to the Greeks, especially water. Therefore architects and artisans incorporated waterworks into the development of the city.

The rectangle dominated Pella – every Greek settlement in Macedon and those communities along the Persian side of the Aegean Coast, including Halicarnassus, built rectangular buildings. Greeks admire the rectangle as the only genuinely harmonic proportion. Engineers termed this architectural style the Divine Quotation. The temple in Jerusalem embraced this aesthetic design, as did Artemisia's burgeoning temple – a rectangular structure in an open courtyard.

Aristocracy in Pella was worshiped as an art form, an attitude punctuated by overstated buildings, ornate temples, and showy two-storeyed homes. Stone mansions built with massive oak doors, glaze-tiled roofs, wall frescoes, and gurgling fountains in broad colonnaded courtyards made Halicarnassus look like a paltry borough filled with humble cottages.

The daily effort to sustain Pella's size and exquisite elegance was an impossible feat save for one element: slavery – and far more slaves lived there than free citizens. Natural-born Macedonians are proudly free people who enjoy a luxurious existence. Their culture teaches that people exist for two purposes – to be a slave or rule slaves – and Macedonians heartily protected their right to rule.

Thousands of slaves served at the palace, the royal stables, in the agora, as domestics, factory workers, shopkeepers, farmhands, crewmembers, and baggage carriers. Barbarian women, captured in far-off lands, became public property and worked in the brothel industry, serving as pornai, while their menfolk slaved in the dangerous mining trade.

Mosaics flourished as the favoured art style for adorning floors, walls, and courtyards. Imagine an art involving millions of tiny pebbles. Insignificant and lacklustre nuggets collected from riverbanks emerged as masterpieces. Most atriums located throughout the city used nothing but pebble-mosaic for paving. Sap: I am guessing tree sap was a secret ingredient in the strong adhesive used to secure mosaic pieces in place.

Intricate mosaic scenes represented status with one neighbour trying to outdo another by acquiring more prominent and elaborate arrangements. One grand mosaic captivated Mausolus, a scene from Homer's *Iliad* showing Paris and Helen locked in a passionate embrace. He stared at the picture for the longest time while Artemisia became absorbed in the mosaics of battling Amazon women. I, too, remained fascinated with this marquetry art form, curious how simple pebbles created dramatic scenes with life-like dimensions.

Pella was easy to navigate because city planners integrated the grid system, a concept invented by Hippodamus of Miletus, the Father of Urban Planning. Streets were paved with large stone blocks. Wide avenues following the north-south axis contained governmental agencies, libraries, physicians' offices, and the royal palace. At the same time, temples, civic centres, and businesses ran on an east-west axis. Residences built in adjacent zones afforded the peace of seclusion while remaining near the agora in the town's centre. Mausolus structured Halicarnassus as much as possible using Hippodamus' urban design, except the city's clam shape prevented an actual grid.

The guests of King Philip spent their first couple of days in Macedonia immersed in political discussions, playing Technê, viewing the city, and engaging in athletics at the king's gymnasium. Philip also arranged a special exhibition to flaunt the latest in Grecian technology. Immensely proud of his scientists and inventors, he was anxious to give world leaders a look at the machinery of the future.

One contraption was a long-range communication system – a hydraulic telegraph. The device moved water under pressure in a confined space to send coded messages to distant receivers. King Philip called it a hydraulic semaphore.

Another invention, the three-pulley crane, did not interest me because at the moment, Halicarnassus was bursting with three-pulley cranes. But the best invention, one I could not stop thinking about, used a cogged mechanism with gears, pointers, and planetary dials to identify one's earthly location using the five planets, Mercury, Venus, Mars, Jupiter, and Saturn. I was blown away. Imagine the intellect needed to contrive such devices. This dial could transform the world.

Mausolus took these marvels in stride. Raised among Persia's most distinguished innovators, experimenters, and advanced designers, he had no trouble fitting into the environment of Pella's greatest minds. (Artemisia struggled to find commonality with the exceptional, the accomplished, and those of royal breeding.) Compared to King Philip II of Macedon, Mausolus and Artemisia were marginal leaders and ancillary governors in a small region – a disparity inconsequential to Mausolus.

Olympias had sent a personal invitation to the Persian satraps requesting their presence at the prince's birthday celebration. Before his death, King Neoptolemus I of Epirus would layover in Halicarnassus when traveling on business. At the request of Artemisia, he several times allowed his daughter, Myrtle, to join him and then remain as a guest of the satraps in Halicarnassus while he continued his travels. Despite their age discrepancy, the two women grew close in friendship. After her marriage, Myrtle received the royal title Queen Olympias to commemorate Philip's equestrian victory at the Olympics.

Guests of Olympias spent their mornings enjoying soaks at the thermal spas, receiving massages, manicures, and beauty therapies. Considering Artemisia's natural splendour, I questioned her need for such treatments.

With Goliath working and the vassals occupied in their endeavours, I again found myself on my own, so I embarked on a journey of exploration to discover the marvels of Pella. Mausolus gave me a minimal advance on my pay which made my visit more pleasurable, but I did not have enough to buy Jaleh a gift, as promised. Ho, to be sure, I dreaded the trouble waiting for me when we returned home to Halicarnassus.

I first set off on an outer path running past a sizeable commercial workshop filled with smiths creating attractive objects from metal, clay, cloth, wood, and stone. Locals had an endless supply of exceptional items, but most of these products fulfilled consumer orders from cities worldwide.

Curious hammering and clanging echoed ahead. I followed the sound to a booth belonging to a master swordsmith working in a secluded area away from prying eyes. Blade-making is a confidential process comparable to owning a secret pie recipe; special skills and techniques are trade secrets, staunchly guarded and passed on within families from generation to generation. The weaponry occupation is both honourable and financially prosperous. Since Greeks believed the gods were actively involved in blade-making, forging smiths received the highest esteem as deific craftsmen. This reasoning stems from the four elements necessary to produce a weapon: earth, air, fire, and water. The fifth element is an endorsement from the gods.

Customers stopped to admire the flawless swords with sophisticated grips and pommels. I ached at the thought of owning such a remarkable weapon. Imagine the prestige and envious looks I would receive wearing such a fine blade. I asked the merchant about its cost and then acted casual and nonchalant when he told me, hoping red ears would not divulge my embarrassment. Nodding my head up and down as if still contemplating a purchase, I said, "I will consult with my father," then turned and walked away, pretending to be excited about his offer.

Typical shops selling clothing, shoes, and household items did not interest me. But I did want to find a barber to purchase a new yellow headband, then a fruit vendor to get an apple. I also bought a fuzzy-skinned fruit called a peach. The fruit was delicious, but biting into the skin made my teeth feel itchy.

Continuing my journey past administrative offices, document offices and storage warehouses, I greeted several Halal merchants selling lawful foods to Pella's growing Jewish population. "Shalom berakah we-ṭobah." I said.

"Shalom berakah we-ṭobah," they answered back.

In the distance, a bell rang at the docks announcing the arrival of freshly caught fish. Following a footway in the direction of the clanging, I neared the harbour and noticed an increasing number of hostelries. The smells of strong drink wafting out their doors produced familiar nausea, which I did not enjoy remembering.

The docks, seedy places bustling with hooligans, trading posts, and state-funded brothels required a constant presence of astynomia - these were publicly owned slaves used to maintain peace on the streets of Pella. King Philip placed them under the command of his epilektoi, a special war-trained branch of Hoplite.

Today, Hoplites are citizen-soldiers, but once were famous warriors called the Chosen Few. They earned their reputation as an élite force when a minor detachment of Hoplite fighters defeated 6,000 armed Persians at the Battle of Marathon, a victory preserving the state of Greece.

At least one unit of astynomia remained on patrol at the waterfront, with a second unit joining them after sundown. From what I know of hostelries at night, I imagined these men stayed quite busy.

Slave traders conducted business at the docks. I heard businessmen calling out, "Ennoia pros polisi! Doulos! Doulos! Pornai! Pais!" announcing the public sale of slaves. Curious about the process, I followed the sounds of their publicising to a filthy square. Here newly arrived shipments of humans – men, women, and children – endured surveying, scrutinising, and inspection.

Observing from a distance, watching the organised sale of human beings, I became aware of something touching my shoulder. Turning, I noticed I had carelessly positioned myself near a holding pen filled with captured women, stripped naked, and overcome with despair. A woman, stretching her hand through the staves, begged me for mercy. With no words spoken between us, her pleading eyes and limp posture told the story of a forsaken human, fated to become the property of a stranger seeking to improve his lifestyle by purchasing an abducted soul held against her will. Having no comfort to offer, the utter helplessness of the situation caused me to walk away as the bidding for bodies continued.

I followed a different footpath back to the agora and sought a particular vendor. I allowed my nose to show me the way. Ever faithful, my snout led me to the baker. Despite the Doric Greek's strange dialect, I found a way to communicate which tasty delicacy I wanted - the syrupy walnut bun and a fluffy crunch loaf. The lovely Grecian girl wrapping my items had soft olive-coloured skin highlighted by dancing brown eyes. A single ribbon gathered bouncy tresses of her golden hair into a ringlet trailing from the side of her head, reaching her waist. Perhaps her father owned the bakeshop; with laws forbidding slaves to wear long hair, I assumed she was a free citizen. Handing over my order, she inadvertently brushed her hand against mine while giving a suggestive gaze – I recognized the action as one frequently used by Jaleh. My face grew hot. Flustered, I took my items and moved along. Why do young women tilt their heads and blink their eyes in such a mysterious manner?

I found a shaded bench to sit and enjoy my bakery treat but was interrupted when a platoon of proud astynomia filed past. These armed men, dressed like Hoplite - marched through the streets in brisk unison, three rows, four abreast, bright sunlight glistening off their bronze shields and breastplates. Watching their manoeuvres fascinated me, but my previous experience with ill-humoured soldiers prompted me to move along, avoiding unwanted attention.

Congested, animated and colourful, with decorative art, sculptures, fountains, monuments, and mosaics, the agora required countless slaves to clean and maintain its beauty and serve in the public baths and húdōr buildings. I mentioned before the enjoyment of using a luxurious húdōr house. Pella's agora had several fabulous húdōr facilities with attentive slaves rinsing and delivering dampened sea sponges for a patron's cleansing.

Beyond the agora, near the public gymnasium, a colossal statue of Asclepius stood beside a physician's office. Statues of Asclepius, the son of Apollo, served as a sign indicating medical and healing facilities.

So, it is true. Goliath was not joking. Greeks do train naked. When I stepped into the gymnasium, I saw unclothed men absorbed in rigorous calisthenics, sparring with fists and wrestling each other. Afterward, they wearily retired to thermal spas and steam rooms where attendants kneaded out cramps and massaged sore muscles. I planned to thank Goliath for allowing us to train in loin coverings.

Wandering further, I encountered a most unusual business. It was like a barbershop with couches beside basins of water and side tables lined with specialised tools, except citizens visited this establishment when they had problems with their teeth. Patrons received poultice remedies for pain or chewed on cleaning sticks while waiting for beauty cures; others allowed specialists to bond jewelled inlays onto their teeth.

Typically, the cure for toothache requires pulling out the painful tooth, but in this office, the craftsman skilfully worked a bow drill back and forth, removing infected bits of a tooth, then repacked the hole with linen and beeswax. I wanted to suggest bonding a mosaic pebble into the hole as a permanent replacement but did not. After watching the specialist pack teeth with flakes of gold and use silver as a solution for loose or fractured teeth, a genuine terror prompted me to leave before they perceived me as a patient.

Following a footpath away from the agora to the outskirts of town, I entered a tomb garden lined with hundreds of monumental sepulchres. Walking among rows and rows of stately graves, I recalled Mausolus' words about the flaw of life. "Tombs filled with wealth amid a magnificent estate where gardens are alive with beauty, art, and architecture in a world that continues despite the pain of its greatest losses."

My brother Sakeri lies in such a tomb. It is nonsensical to insist death is a natural part of life. Overwhelmed by this sadness, I left Pella's tomb garden and continued my excursion in the other direction.

Chapter 35

The Library

Exploring a different route led me to a splendid building of modern architecture, surrounded by marble and bronze statues of famous conquerors and celebrated intellectuals: the public library.

Ho, to be sure, Pella had a grand library; I was astonished at the many scrolls of papyrus, parchment, and sheepskin stowed in one cubicle after another, on shelf after shelf, reaching wall to wall and floor to ceiling. Perhaps hundreds - maybe thousands - of texts were organised by a system consigning particular focuses to particular sections, separating one from another according to language and subject material. Literary treasures, political guidance, battle strategies, legal information, financial summaries, academic focuses, philosophies, histories, fictional epics, mythology, and religious texts were all under one roof.

My presence in this house of learning drew the attention of its patrons. Well-groomed intellectuals deep in introspection perused, pondered, and piously roamed from shelf to shelf, climbing ladders, selecting specific scrolls before descending, and returning to their couches eager to extract profound words of wisdom.

I decided to join the intellectual circle of knowledgeable men by selecting my own scroll. Appearing scholarly, I studiously roamed past overstuffed cubicles until ascending a ladder as if to scan a collection of documents on an upper shelf. After a few moments of browsing, I moved to a different section, fully aware of curious patrons following my movements. I acted oblivious as I climbed another ladder. Midway up, I pretended to spot a particular text and leaned with a broad stretch to obtain it. From my perch, I briefly examined its contents. Shaking my head, I scowled and returned the papyrus like a disapproving academic, discovering inadequate information. Making my way down, I moved to another area and surveyed the lower shelves. With knitted brows and narrowed eyes, I maintained the shrewd pose of a thinker well-versed in the art of logic. Holding my hands in front of my chest, thrumming the tips of my fingers together, I passed each shelf, studying my choices.

I roamed. I thrummed. I stopped. I thrummed again while roaming from shelf to shelf. Another stop. This time I tapped the tip of my forefinger several times against my pursed lips while discerning which morsel of insight I sought for the day.

After making my final selection, I crossed to an empty couch near a statue of Athena, the goddess of wisdom. Situating myself, I removed the ring, unfurled part of the manuscript, and had no clue what language it was. Several men in particular, no doubt the thinkers of Pella, scrutinised me. Pretending to be unaware of their critical gazes, I unrolled the papyrus further. Running my finger under the line of text as if reading every word, I stopped on the longest word, patting it a couple of times before nodding in agreement with the ideas illuminating my mind. Pausing, I cast a penetrating stare of deep meditation out of the window toward a distant mountain peak.

Still ruminating and dreamy-eyed, I nodded, rerolled the scroll, attached the ring, and returned it to the shelf while double-tapping my palm against my heart as if the rest of my life had suddenly improved in some mysterious way. Still acting oblivious to their disapproving glares, I strolled, unhurried in my genius, directly past Pella's most celebrated scholars. Onward I moved, thrumming, examining scrolls, casually edging my way closer and closer to the door. Finally, after making an arrogant departure gushing with supreme intellect, I rounded the corner and ran.

My route back to the palace took me through Pella's temple district. Most deities were unfamiliar to me, but I quickly identified Aphrodite; she is not difficult to recognise with her exposed bosom and flimsy scarf barely covering her naked body. I also saw a statue of Alkidemos, the official benefactor of Pella, and the trident-wielding Poseidon, whom I recognised from Skyros.

Flamboyant worshipers spilled into the streets, creating a bottleneck that blocked my route, causing me to navigate flailing arms and skirt swaying and dancing bodies. Wailing devotees fell to the ground, rolling side to side as if suffering a stomach ailment. By the time I escaped the congestion and returned to the palace, hundreds of servants had already begun scurrying about in an excitement-filled frenzy, preparing for the grand birthday feast to honour Macedon's favourite prince.

Chapter 36

The Celebration Feast

The summer banquet hall overflowed with guests spilling onto spacious verandas overlooking mountain vistas, where remarkable water gardens sprayed fine mists of water in every direction. Elegant flower arrangements throughout the gallery accentuated statuary, bronze figurines, reliefs, marble sculptures, and busts. Woven tapestries hung along inner walls. Grand mosaics showed King Philip, daunting in his battle gear; another portrayed Apollo, silver bow in hand, shooting an arrow at the sun. The newest mosaic, commissioned specially for the feast, pictured Queen Olympias, stunning as a goddess, tending to her infant son.

Smooth flooring of white marble cut at perfect angles displayed a rayed Vergina Sun consisting of 16 points. Guests, reluctant to walk across the sacred symbol of the Argead dynasty, avoided the centre of the room, but as the evening progressed, merrymakers paid no attention to such matters.

Prominent members of society comprised the guest list, from elite officials of Macedonia to administrators of the Aegean coastal regions and significant rulers from Carthage, Egypt, Kush, Armenia, Bithynia, Cappadocia, and China. King Philip welcomed every guest regardless of political views, and the evening remained peaceful, with interest in feasting instead of political discussions. Debates may follow later during a symposium or at the gymnasium, but the birthday event continued jovial and undisturbed.

The hot month of Garmapada required dressing for abundant sunshine. Macedonians wore superbly designed clothing from Megara, richly coloured in deep reds, bright yellows, or shades of blue. Their ensembles, accented with jewelled ornamentation, stood out compared to other national costumes. Royalty alone wore purple, a colour to distinguish sovereigns from others (as governors, Mausolus and Artemisia were ineligible to wear this hue).

Mausolus and I dressed in fancy silk trousers with matching knee-length coats that slipped over our heads and fastened stylishly around the waist with a kamarband. Tight sleeves ran the length of our arms, and bazubands hugged our wrists. His colours for the evening joined lime-green with a rose-coloured kamarband embroidered in golden thread and his favourite fawn leather shoes. He wore two jewelled rings on one hand and a collar of twisted gold around his neck.

Macedonian adorners styled, polished, and combed Mausolus' hair away from his face. Keen on arraying his distinctive blue eyes, the women decorated him with shades of green outlined by a smoky mist. Artemisia resented the domestics' interest in her husband, but wherever Mausolus went, women swooned over him, particularly his eyes.

My apricot-coloured clothing included a blue kamarband fringed by darker blue tassels and ornamented in light blue stitching. Mausolus placed a golden collar around my neck and honoured me by allowing me to wear his ruby ring. I kept the ring from slipping off by wearing it on my thumb. I allowed limited adornment to my eyes and tried not to giggle as adorners fussed over me. Mausolus called me a most handsome Persian prince.

Artemisia wore a long, voluminous dress, rose-coloured, gathered at the waist with a silken girdle of deep red embroidered by lime-green and golden threads. Sheer sleeves touched her bedecked wrists, which jingled from her usual array of bracelets. She wore golden hoop earrings, a gold collar, several jewelled rings, and one on her toe. Adorners illuminated her eyes with enhancing colours and, at the corners, applied tiny sparkles. Glittering and gorgeous, she smelled of blossoming flowers. Three rubies set in a golden ornament held her thick braids in an attractive sweep. On her feet, she wore petite sandals woven of silvery strands that produced a sensual jingling when she walked.

Mausolus considered her the most stunningly attractive woman in the room and amorously gazed at her throughout the evening. I avoided glancing in her direction for fear of betraying my fondness.

As we entered the banquet hall, official presenters proclaimed our arrival. Artemisia and Mausolus stood together in an archway covered in bluish wisteria blossoms; the presenter introduced the couple as governors of the district of Caria in Anatolia. When they entered the room, I nervously stepped forward and stood beneath the archway, waiting for my introduction. Finally, proclaimers announced, "Ethan, son of Mausolus, prince of Caria." A grand moment to be sure. I beamed with tremendous pride. Throughout our stay, people honoured me as a highborn prince.

Royal guests wore their national costumes and jewelled crowns – diadems, circlets, wreaths, headbands, or tiaras – each distinctively ornamented with gold, gems, glamor, and style. For example, King Philip II wore a tunic of deep purple, high sandals laced above his calves, and on his head sat a simple wreath of shiny gold with interlocking branches sprouting leaves of laurel.

Trumpets sounded, and we stood as Queen Olympias made her grand entrance carrying the toddler prince. Perplexed by the pomp and ceremony in a room crowded with applauding people, the scared little fellow clung fearfully to his mother. Unaware the most influential people in the world had travelled hundreds of parasangs to worship him, bestow gifts upon him, and feast with his parents, the birthday boy hid his face, pressing it tight into his mother's neck.

This child was the privileged prince of Macedon, yet I pitied him. A fine-looking boy, but at first glance, I predicted a future plagued with frustration; to be sure, the child had a full head of rebellious golden curls.

Prince Alexander's eyes generated much conversation – one was brown, and one was green. People said the oddity represented a kiss from the gods, marking young Alexander for fame and fortune. Others considered the quirk a curse of the gods, shaping a brief life fraught with turmoil and controversy. Yet, King Philip called the anomaly pointless, declaring his son Alexander could accomplish whatever he wanted with his life.

Queen Olympias, a girlish-looking twenty-year-old, handled herself with self-assured poise and majestic grace. Intoxicatingly beautiful, the orphaned daughter of King Neoptolemus I of Epirus caught the attention of Philip the moment he saw her while visiting the island of Samothrace. He proudly proclaimed his undying love for the foundling, and a wedding immediately followed. The young teenager became the fourth of Philip's seven wives.

Olympias, the proud mother of one-year-old Alexander and noticeably pregnant with her second child, looked alluring in a flowing purple tunic cinched with a gem-studded belt above her swollen belly - bare feet peeked beneath the hem. Her flawless skin displayed one dark freckle on the left side of her chin, an exotic feature heightened by fabulous chestnut hair. Olympias' crown was the most distinctive of all the royal headpieces that evening - it swayed with floating strands of gold, each covered in golden leaves of myrtle and accents of delicate blossoms.

After viewing the enchanting demeanour of her mosaic, I expected to meet a woman endowed with a delightful spirit and a divine nature; instead, I found Olympias to have a most bitter countenance, earning her the widespread reputation of being arrogant, headstrong, and meddlesome.

Possibly born of resentment, her unpleasantness may have stemmed from her singular value in the Argead dynasty – to produce Alexander, the male heir Philip desperately sought. On their wedding night, Olympias dreamed a thunderbolt struck her womb, causing a small fire to burst into flames and spread across the land before finally subsiding. Many speculated Alexander might be that fire.

While married life in Pella started grand, Philip found Olympias' reverence for her deity, Dionysus, unbearable. Although he found no fault with the god of wine and merriment, his annoyance and the apparent tension between the couple rose from the Queen's insistence on inviting poisonous snakes into their bedchamber.

After kissing his son on the cheek, King Philip placed a small crown of golden leaves on Alexander's head, raising thunderous applause. Alexander resisted and threw the circlet off, but at his mother's insistence, he tolerated the headpiece at least during the salutes, tributes, and pledges. Then, after rounds of personalised words, praise, and promises, feasting commenced with sweet melodies played on the double-piped Aulos, accompanied by the lyre, flute, and tambourine. But, of course, no Greek festival was complete without a flute, the instrument played by their god Apollo.

Musicians traded off during the evening with actors appearing on stage, holding masks with exaggerated facial features to demonstrate the emotion of each scene. Guests applauded as actors randomly moved on and off the stage after performing brief satirical parodies – comical scenes based on everyday affairs in Pella. People laughed plenty, particularly King Philip. I was ignorant of most issues being mocked but enjoyed watching the actors and laughing when the others did.

An arc of large serving tables teemed with exotic foods. There were mounds of hot meats such as cattle, lamb, and slow-roasted goat smelling of mountain herbs and imported spices. Fish occupied another table; platters of shrimp, squid, octopus, and bowls of mussels, cockles, and limpets.

Busy servants carried trays of broiled fish drizzled with olive, yogurt and honey sauce, also roasted hare, pigeon, chicken, and thrush. Others set out vegetables cooked with hen's eggs, peacock eggs, and iris bulbs marinated in vinegar. Bowls filled with mushrooms and truffles sat beside dishes containing hot boiled horta, asparagus, fennel, and pickled nettles.

Fruit bowls overflowed with grapes, apricots, figs, apples, pears, and pomegranates. I counted ten varieties of baked bread and an assortment of pastries. Naturally, I avoided the foods my culture considers forbidden, but I had no trouble finding enough lawful foods to gorge myself.

Wine, drunk from silver goblets, flowed throughout the evening. King Philip drank hardily from a phallus-shaped rhyton.

Luxurious reclining couches allowed comfortable dining. Low tables and footstools arranged beside each divan adjusted to varying ranges to easily lift food or drink. In case of a miss, simple napkins of bread dough offered a quick clean-up.

I suffered several food mishaps, but my biggest problem was my balance – my silk trousers slipped against the cushions causing me to slide downwards into a most lopsided pose. I wiggled my way back to a comfortable reclining position, but the moment I relaxed, I slid down again, tilting off-centre. Copying other guests, I used big pillows to prop myself. After struggling and tussling to position each pillow for bracing, I finally figured out a suitable technique for relaxed lounging. Once situated, I smiled and glanced around the room. Two men sitting across the room whispered back and forth while observing me. I broke eye contact after recognising the pair as the disapproving men from the library.

Ignoring their glares, I initiated a conversation with the men reclining on either side of me. Neither was my age nor my status, but both received me graciously. When detecting the sneering glances coming my way, the older man leaned toward me and said, "When men speak ill of you, my boy, live so nobody may believe them." I nodded politely.

Mausolus sat away from me during the evening; he had been seated beside two young men, a Phocion named Aristobulus of Cassandreia, and Agnaptus, a Greek gentleman from the Peloponnese Peninsula. Educated in architecture, both men were aware of the Halicarnassus project, and when asked, they were able to answer Mausolus' questions about air quality in the temple's interior rooms. The satrap's thirst for knowledge was one of his most admirable qualities; he was polite when others shared what they knew. I smiled, watching his rapt expression as the engineers explained their techniques for adequate air circulation.

Although women of nobility rarely joined men in their raucous festivities, ladies cordially attended this celebration to honour Alexander. They clustered around Olympias in a tight group off to one side. Goliath stood against the wall with the other bodyguards – these men had a knack for standing nearby while remaining out of sight. Standing with his massive arms crossed over his chest, I saw him shake his head while observing my attempts to keep from slipping off the dining couch. I refused to acknowledge his gaze as I did with the other critics in the room.

Aristotle, the man to my right, travelled to Pella from Athens with his friend and teacher, Plato, the older gentleman to my left. Plato contributed much to the elevated mood of the evening. I sat spellbound, listening to his tales of a lost city named Atlantis. He said there were few clues as to its whereabouts, but when the wealthy city sank to the bottom of the sea, unimaginable treasures and enormous riches sank with it. According to Plato, whoever finds Atlantis will become wealthy beyond measure.

Talented and versed in numerous subjects, Aristotle intrigued me with his knowledge. On several occasions, I heard Mausolus make mention of this young philosopher, but I never expected to meet him. After watching one theatrical performance, Aristotle commented, "The Dorians lay claim to the invention of both tragedy and comedy in theatre. In truth, comedy has its beginnings with the people of the coastal state of Megara here in Greece, while tragedy became introduced by certain Dorians of the Peloponnese."

"Remarkable," I responded. But, of course, I had no idea what the man was talking about, so I knitted my brow and narrowed my eyes, feigning enlightenment.

Drunken King Philip bellowed to Plato during the evening, "Know this, my friend. One day I will steal Aristotle away from your precious academy and employ him as a tutor for my son, Alexander."

"Yes, my King. We must talk over the subject of the boy's studies." Plato remained polite.

"Studies?" the king shouted from across the room. "You mean war!" He staggered to his feet. "My son will be a student in the art of war. Combat and swordsmanship will be his text. He will learn the courage of heroes." Holding up his phallus cup, he announced, "I will teach my son, 'Go east, that the world may witness the annihilation of those fire-worshiping Barbarians'." He drank, and the Macedonians clapped wholeheartedly, cheering at his words.

I knew of no barbarians and failed to grasp the meaning behind 'go east'. The Empire of Persia lay east, nothing else. So I dismissed his strange statement as drunken gibberish and forgot to ask Mausolus about the comment.

"Yes, my Lord," Plato responded cautiously, considering the king's drunken state. "The beginning is the most important part of the work, and the direction in which education starts a man will determine his future in life."

"Mà tòn Diónyson !" King Philip swore. "You speak the truth!" The banter dropped off with Plato allowing the King to have the last word. When no further discussion passed between them, Plato turned toward me and whispered, "Rhetoric, my boy, is the art of ruling the minds of men." He winked.

Later I learned the names of the disapproving men from the library, Agathocles, an intimate friend of King Philip and part of his council, and Lagus, another aristocrat. Apart from their apparent judgments of me, we had no formal introduction, but I did meet the young son of Lagus, an older playmate to Alexander named Ptolemy.

Salutes and tributes continued throughout the evening, and with each homage, servants refilled our wine goblets to the brim. I enjoyed drinking the wine, but as the banquet progressed, the beverage changed. Mead! I spent the rest of the evening taking mock sips, holding my breath not to smell that nauseating aroma of spiced honey. After my unfortunate episode on Skyros, I never again drank mead.

The feast wore on and on long after the young prince had gone. When women entertainers and dancers entered the room, drinking games began. Olympias, accompanied by her female guests, retired to a different banquet hall to avoid the spectacle of boisterous men embarrassing themselves while groping dancers and playing Kottabos. Curious game, Kottabos. After drinking a goblet of wine, contestants would fling the lees or the particles of dregs still lingering in the bottom of the cup at a particular object without losing a grip of the goblet. Hitting the object earned a point. Whoever collects the most points wins the game and is sorely drunk.

For one fleeting moment, I visualised my brothers and me laughing and carrying on in a game of Kottabos, throwing lees at objects in our mother's kitchen – at once, I swept the scary image from my mind.

My head throbbed from music, songs, dances, performances, abundant laughing, food and drink, and the endless conversation followed by copious applause and cheering. I was done celebrating. I managed to slip out of the hall unnoticed, found my quarters, and dropped into a deep sleep.

Chapter 37

The Boy, Alexander

The following day, I awoke with a severe headache, but my growling stomach sent me in search of breakfast. Busy servants in the eastern garden prepared tables with hot teas and barley cakes, peacock eggs, porridge, grapes, myrtle berries, and figs, but I had the place to myself since guests staying late to play Kottabos missed both breakfast and lunch.

The pleasant chirping of songbirds filled the morning air as I ate my fill. Later, a nurse came into the garden carrying young Alexander for his playtime. He studied me with suspicion, so I tried disarming him with a little wave and a smile. Someone had tamed his curls, but in no time, the wind whipped his crown of ringlets into a tangle.

The prince broke away from his caretaker to stumble and wobble in my direction. I witnessed similar staggering the night before with the drunken men at the banquet, but Alexander looked adorable learning to walk. Faltering and falling, he moved toward me, anxious to investigate the new person invading his play area. He reached for me with outstretched arms, and I scooped him onto my lap. Holding him reminded me of my youngest sister and how I enjoyed playing with her. The nurse acted concerned, but I calmed her fears saying the child was welcome.

Full of energy and curiosity, Alexander bounded with the joy of a boy discovering the world around him. If destiny had determined his lot as a slave, he would soon be entering a life of servitude and hard labour. But, instead, the lot fell in his favour, appointing him as ruler, a prince to reign over a mighty nation. Already he commanded an army of servants whose sole purpose was tending exclusively to his needs.

The young prince studied my face briefly, then reached up and pulled my headband over my eyes. I put it back. He pulled it down. I pulled it up and made a silly face bringing howls of cute baby laughter. Next, I pulled the band down and said, "Hoot!" He startled and then roared with delight. Again, I said, "Hoot!" and we both roared with laughter.

Once the headband game grew dull, Alexander watched as I tossed crumbs of bread onto the lawn, attracting a cluster of hungry mountain finches. I gave the exuberant toddler a morsel to throw, but his best effort landed the titbit on his foot.

We romped in the garden and played chase and a hiding game until the nurse produced a ball. Tossing the ball to Alexander, I said, "Catch!" Unfortunately, he failed to lift his arms, and the ball hit him square on the forehead. The nurse shrieked in horror, but Alexander laughed and chased after it. Watching a slight lump and purplish bruise develop above his eye prompted me to modify the sport into a rolling game.

Ptolemy later joined us for a game of Ephedrismos. Alexander was not interested in knocking over the pins, but he enjoyed the part where he rode around on my back, pretending I was a horse. Laughing and playing away the morning, the tired prince finally gave out, crawled onto my lap, and I rocked him to sleep. Then I passed him over to the nurse, who carried him to his bed.

After our initial meeting, Alexander stretched out his arms for me anytime I came near. The nurse handled him gently and cautiously, treating him like fragile glass for fear of breaking the future ruler of Macedon. Not me! I played rough with him the way boys play. We enjoyed rowdy scrambles in the grass, clambered on rocks, and waded in the fountain pools. Alexander earned his first bloody knee roughing with me in the garden. Despite obvious pain from falling, he got to his feet and continued playing.

Mausolus came out to the garden one morning for breakfast and was surprised to see the young prince sitting on my lap. He smiled, but Alexander glared and drew tight against me. I said, "Perhaps he thinks you are an outlandish creature from the jungle and comical to look at." Mausolus chuckled at my jest.

The satrap had arisen early that morning to keep an appointment with Leonidas, the groom responsible for Bous – the colt Mausolus sent across the sea as a gift for Alexander. Leonidas arranged a tour of King Philip's famous stables and an inspection of the herds to see the Thessalian foals born last spring. Mausolus invited me along. Unwilling to release me, Alexander joined us. So did his nurse and Ptolemy. We all squeezed into the coach and raced across fields to the horse shelters.

Hundreds of horses grazed in pastures or stood in divided paddocks. Immaculate stables with over one hundred stalls in each building required scores of servants to care for the animals in exercise, grooming, watering, and cleaning. Most humans never experienced the level of nurturing King Philip's horses received daily.

After attaching a lead rope, Leonidas walked Bous out of his stall – he had taken to calling the horse Arion-Bous. The name suited him. Arion was a divine horse of Greek mythology known for swiftness, courage, and immortality. Moreover, the myth says Arion conversed with those he deemed most worthy.

Amazed at how remarkably muscular the colt had grown, Mausolus took the rope and continued leading Arion-Bous through the gate and into an arena. Holding the prince in my arms, I pointed to Mausolus as he worked the animal through different equine moves. "See?" I said. "That is your colt, Bous. Can you say Bous?" Alexander watched intently. As his eyes followed the horse, he pointed his chubby finger and spoke something in baby gibberish.

Mausolus and Leonidas discussed specific points about Arion-Bous. Unable to hear their words, I watched the groom draw back the horse's top lip to show something of interest. He next pointed to the predominant oxhead coloration and then mentioned something about the knees before leaning into the animal's shoulder, forcing him to surrender his front hoof. Leonidas continued pointing and discussing noteworthy points as Mausolus beamed with pride at the precious gift he had given the boy.

Mausolus signalled me into the arena, so I brought Alexander. The nurse protested. Leonidas held his hand up to the nurse, and I proceeded. Mausolus lifted him from my arms, placing the willing child on the yearling's back. Ho, to be sure, Alexander gloried. Mausolus held him steady as Leonidas led Arion-Bous around the enclosure. The nurse fretted, Mausolus and Leonidas glowed, and I laughed as Alexander squealed with a child's delight. Trying to remove him brought crying and kicking, so Alexander rode around the enclosure a second time and a third. By the fourth time, the mesmerised child had enchanted everyone, including his fussy nurse.

Mausolus stared at the toddler sitting on my lap on our return to the palace. "He sits well on a horse, obvious athletic ability. Did you notice how fearless?" he said of Alexander. "Good balance, too, for a youngster. I foresee a great equestrian in this boy."

Turning to Ptolemy, Mausolus began to regale the youngster with fascinating tales of Lailapás, his high-spirited Nisaean back home. Persians were proud of their Nisaean breed and thought them divine. "Imagine the velocity of a sea storm on four legs," Mausolus bragged. "Why when Lailapás last competed in the games at Labraunda…"

To be sure, I wanted to jump out of the coach. I had listened to Mausolus raving over this horse far too many times. So fond was he of his prized stallion, he memorialised the animal by commissioning a marble statue of wild-eyed Lailapás rearing back with hooves pawing the air. Mausolus intended to use the figure as a prominent feature at the Halicarnassus temple.

Years later, I again saw Alexander - Ptolemy, also. That was the day the Macedonians rode into Jerusalem as victorious conquerors. Alexander, dressed in royal armour, approached the city riding a magnificent horse displaying a white star on his brow and the marking of an ox head on his rump. The hefty stallion, obviously sired by Arion-Bous, possessed the spirit of a fearless warhorse. Alexander had named the tall, black stallion Bucephalus, a combination of Bous, ox, and kephalē, head.

Mausolus died before learning Leonidas sent Arion-Bous to Thessaly as a breeding stallion. The story goes that one afternoon, herdsmen assembled a herd of wild horses into an enclosure for assessment and evaluation, a process of scoring them against an exhaustive checklist to determine their usefulness in King Philip's cavalry.

One horse, muscular and matchless in height, presented as particularly untameable and ill-mannered - riotous to the point of defiance. No one dared approach the dangerous beast, and trainers decided to slaughter the horse before it injured or killed someone. Twelve-year-old Alexander intervened. After observing the animal's behaviour, he recognised the problem; the horse feared his shadow. Turning the stallion away from the sun to position his shadow behind him, Alexander spoke soothingly, stroking the horse's face. The animal calmed, and to the surprise of the trainers, the young prince grabbed a tuft of mane, swung onto the horse's back, and rode away. The two were inseparable after that; historically, Bucephalus became as famous as Alexander.

Mausolus had recognised Alexander's pronounced equestrian abilities, and with Bucephalus' exceptional aptitude for battle, the two became a legendary duo.

Chapter 38

My Gift to a Prince

After two glorious weeks of living as a sophisticated Macedonian, our departure drew near. My sentiments fluctuated. On the one hand, I missed Halicarnassus. On the other hand, I dreaded saying goodbye to Alexander.

Playing with him one last time, romping through the garden, he sensed something was different. His nurse held him as I walked out the gate, waving goodbye. Squirming to break free, he cried and held out his arms, pleading for his rough and tumble playmate to stay. I refused to leave in such an underhand manner, so I returned, lifted him onto my back, and we raced around the garden.

The bronze Nisaean warhorse I had crafted was still in my satchel. Considering the priceless gifts figureheads from across the world bestowed upon Alexander, an inferior homemade toy struck me as absurd. Still, I decided to present my humble offering and allow him to determine its value.

Intrigued, the toddler knelt beside me as I rummaged through my bag. I removed the cloth-covered object with a measure of suspense, laid the mysterious lump on the ground before him, and patted it several times. He flashed an inquisitive expression causing me to laugh. Unfolding the fabric, layer by layer, I finally revealed the shiny bronze stallion. Alexander's eyes lit up, and he smiled a grand smile showing several cute baby teeth.

Whinnying, I galloped the horse around in a circle before stopping in front of him. I said, "Charger. That is his name," then galloped around again while whinnying and snorting. I stopped and said, "Charger. Can you say Charger?"

Alexander laughed and struggled to copy me, "Charger!"

"Yes, Charger! You said it!" I told him. He beamed with pride.

Then came the moment of truth; I removed my hand, and ho, to be sure, the horse remained standing. Alexander pointed as if asking permission. "Go ahead," I told him. "You can touch it." He stroked his chubby fingers across the horse's polished withers. "Pick him up," I said.

"Charger," he said and tried duplicating my whinny sound.

My heart swelled watching the young prince of Macedon play with a toy fashioned from Halicarnassus bronze. Ptolemy later came into the garden, and I asked him to occupy Alexander with Charger so I could slip away unnoticed. Before leaving, I removed my headband; Alexander snatched it from my hand and tried putting it on his head. Ptolemy and I both laughed at his struggle. I hugged Macedonia's prince one last time, surprised at how fond I had grown of him. Preoccupied with his new toy, I tousled his curls and crept away unnoticed, feeling like an immense trickster.

Looking back over those special days in Pella still amazes me with the wonder of events. I saw no hint, not the thinnest warning, nor even the slightest imagining; nothing to suggest the empire where I and millions of others lived, was headed for a bloody defeat at the hands of that curly-haired boy.

Our return trip grew smoother after catching the Etesian winds. Stopping again in Skyros, I spent the evening on board the ship playing games I learned in Macedonia – checkers, knucklebones, and backgammon. The following afternoon we sailed into the Port of Halicarnassus. Standing in silence on the bow of the *Trojan Hector*, Mausolus, Artemisia, Goliath, and I watched our fair city come into view.

A thousand men systematically grouped into teams worked at a double-quick pace on the most ostentatious building in history. Scaffolding loomed on all sides of the Persian Pedestal, which appeared remarkably close to completion.

Men moving around the site resembled ants scurrying across a hill. Watching tiny figures climb scaffolding and swing on ropes from one plank to another brought Sakeri to my mind. My brother climbed faster than any man; he purposely swung from dangerous heights, making women shriek, and older men hold their breath. While he acted carelessly, Sakeri was no fool. He checked and double-checked his harness, knotting his line and inspecting its connection to the anchor plate. He met Huldah, his wife, by climbing on scaffolding, I should say by falling off a scaffolding.

The shy young girl lived with her family in the hill area – the Hill of Ophel. Sakeri was working near the Sheep Gate on the wall at the Hill of

Ophel when he first observed her. Every day he watched from above as she walked below, going to the agora, the public well, or chasing after her roguish younger brothers. He had a birds-eye view, but she failed to notice him perched high above, pining away in love.

One day as she neared the gate, Sakeri feigned slipping, shouting, "Yhoaaa!" Every person looked up. Swinging back and forth, missing one plank while flailing his legs to find the other, he moved through an assortment of comical antics, attempting to return to the scaffolding. From side to side, he dangled as his crew howled with laughter at his prank. Playing the part of a buffoon worked. Huldah watched with the crowd forming below, and, as if removing a veil from before her eyes, she finally beheld the handsome young stonemason.

Making his way to the plank, Sakeri turned and gazed into the crowd. Their eyes met. He bowed. Sliding his hand inside his coat, he pulled out a clump of buttercups tied with a crimson cord and released the bouquet so it fluttered to the ground before her. After this romantic gesture, the two anticipated seeing each other every day.

Once Sakeri met her father, a wedding followed. We welcomed Huldah as the first newcomer to our family; my mother especially adored her. This marriage of the firstborn son freed Caleb to leave home and pursue his career as a translator.

I loved Sakeri. As a child, I followed him around doing whatever he did. I adored his prankster side, but he also possessed a deep godly character. He prayed regularly at the synagogue and studied under the tutelage of Rabbi Efrat. Sakeri was a devout worshiper of the Mighty One of Israel.

Considering the times he played at falling, I never imagined he would fall. I worked at a different site the morning of his accident, which spared me from witnessing his death. When I heard the news and arrived at the gate, a group of men had already carried Sakeri away. In my imagination, Huldah and Caleb had a child, a son for Sakeri.

Nudging me out of my daydream, Mausolus pointed. "You have a problem, son." Eagerly waving us into the harbour was Jaleh. Goliath glanced over at me and shook his head.

I attempted to linger behind, helping the attendants with the baggage, but Goliath grabbed me by the elbow and encouraged me to disembark down the gangway. I sensed the men onboard watching as I greeted Jaleh.

"Jaleh Joon. Delbar-am! You are the one who has my heart!" Focusing my eyes on the weathered planks of the dock, I explained the unforeseen problem I encountered on Skyros at the hands of a murderous band of thieves. (I embellished a slight amount for my safety.) Annoyed, she turned and stomped away. I hollered, "I almost died!" but she continued walking.

The crew watched from the deck and burst into howls of great laughter, melting my face with embarrassment. I looked at Mausolus for a reprieve, but he shrugged his shoulders and held his hands up in surrender. Goliath, with arms crossed, stood shaking his head.

Chapter 39

A Tangled Web

Embarrassed and foolish-looking, I lacked the maturity to make proper amends with Jaleh. My solution was to avoid her. I decided to forego dining with her family and occupied myself with projects at the temple. I focused on building the staircase and continued with modelling assignments, most of the time for Scopas. Jaleh no longer passed. Goliath failed to notice my absence since managing the extra people coming in and out of town escalated his duties.

Artemisia wasted no time immersing herself in the clamour and commotion of construction. She busied herself by talking with architects or suggesting new ideas to sculptors while slightly repositioning models. Weary expressions followed as she moved out of view to critique another group.

Mausolus spent those first weeks back from Pella catching up on administrative issues. Regardless of the extra work generated by the masses moving into the area, the satrap kept abreast of all district affairs. Caria could not have asked for a better man reigning over them, but sadly, Mausolus possessed a fatal flaw. His Achilles heel. A blind spot. Artemisia was the invincible enemy he failed to conquer; he remained oblivious to her ploys and the schemes she birthed in the dark places of her heart.

Earlier, I described Mausolus as two people combined into one body; I suspected the same about Artemisia. To be sure, Artemisia was intense. She passionately supported the arts and regularly commissioned entertainers, musicians, and artists to perform in the theatre of Dionysus. She ruled Caria as a forceful leader with a warrior's heart but did not possess Mausolus' spontaneous spirit. Her social interactions came off as spurious, like performing before an audience at the theatre.

Nor did she fully embrace the attention her husband showered upon her. She was proud of him and his accomplishments. She honoured his management of the satrapy, but like Pixodarus, she often snapped, scolding Mausolus for no apparent reason. Perhaps her barrenness. Possibly guilt. For some reason, she appeared standoffish and often acted bored with her husband's silly gestures and spontaneous affection. She seemed more comfortable occupying herself with frivolous entanglements and distracting ventures.

Artemisia was kind enough to the townspeople but quickly grew bored, drifting in and out when listening to the pedestrian class. She reminded me of her cat, Miut – both were watchful hunters, cunning, alert, aloof, and scarcely tolerant. They had the same lithe body, graceful and exotic, with agile footfalls barely touching the ground. Regardless of her inner character, her outer beauty and the periodic attention she bestowed upon me proved irresistible for my enamoured heart, and I remained hopelessly enchanted.

The assassin had vanished without a trace, not so much as a whisper since Mehregan. Possibly our heightened security scared him away, but I was not about to relax my efforts. Changing investigative tactics, I formulated different routes taking me to other parts of the city and alternated days and times. I backtracked if, by chance, someone had followed me. I lingered, listening to conversations in the húdōr. I dallied, pretending to shop in the agora. Finally, I rested in the Stoa of Aegea, waiting until the water clock twice emptied before continuing along the docks and around the barracks. Casually strolling behind people, I listened to conversations, keeping track of vital information. I took careful notice of who drank from the Spring of Salmacis. And whether needing a haircut or not, I stopped to visit the fellows at the barbershop, convinced any prattle concerning the mercenary would come through there.

Artemisia remained unaware of my visit with Lysippos. How would she react if she discovered I knew of her piracy? If she saw me as a threat, she may deem it necessary to have me killed to protect her secret. Mausolus remained ignorant of two crucial facts: the queen had used me to manipulate him, and I knew the answer to his questions of who and why. The king of Caria did not realize Pandora's Box had opened in his beloved city; he remained unsuspecting and ill-equipped for the calamity his ambitious wife set into motion.

Despite the web of lies, secrets, and deceit, temple construction continued at a steady pace. Everyone in Halicarnassus prospered; even the commoners gained wealth. Scores of labourers kept their families fed, and wives raved over their husband's earnings. Commerce thrived. The port financially boomed. Middling folk enjoyed the prestige of participating in history. All creation raved about the world's most magnificent structure with its incredible engineering accomplishments. Pythius' reputation grew; Persia publicised him as a true genius. Letters of applause arrived regularly from the Shahanshah, and Mausolus gloried over his temple legacy.

Besides interfering with history, exposing the queen by coming forward with the truth would end it all: livelihoods, prosperity, growth, commerce, happiness, and Persian pride. I contemplated my options; examining all sides of this ethical quandary felt more like walking in a circle than solving a problem – I was not getting anywhere. In the end, I ignored her transgressions against Rhodes and opted to keep Artemisia's theft and murders a secret. The truth behind the Halicarnassus project would remain hidden in darkness unless I found a reason to speak.

Chapter 40

The Temple Exterior

Pella changed Artemisia. The wealth and power she witnessed in Macedonia unfurled a relentless gnawing in her soul – she wanted more and desired more, believing she deserved more. (She even went so far as to have goldsmiths fashion her a crown of myrtle leaves floating on strands of gold as Queen Olympias wore.) Her love of luxury, extravagance, and indulgence increased, merging inspiration with innovation to design a legacy beyond the grasp most people fancied in their wildest dreams. One idea led to another; before long, more became less, and bigger grew smaller as she incessantly reshaped the project.

At the same time, the temple seemed to have aspirations of its own – or perhaps an anonymous force mocked the careful plans of our mortal ingenuity. With designs drawn by the best architects and engineers in the world, scurrying humans resembling tiny insects, piled marble on top of marble as the legendary structure emerged, and then one pleasant spring morning, Artemisia's temple tragically revealed its true identity.

People around the world discussed the mountain of priceless marble and fabulous pillars for the gods.

"The size is grand!"

"The gods are pleased!"

"The adornments are magnificent!"

"They build a wonder!" visitors would say.

Travelers lodged an extra day or two in Halicarnassus to watch the historical production. Returning home with first-hand reports of the Halicarnassus project garnered them much prestige, especially if they returned with souvenirs from creative vendors buying scrap marble for crafting distinctive gifts.

Real honour came from sitting for prestigious artisans – celebrities in stone eternally adorning the most renowned architectural undertaking the modern world had ever known. For the right price, a person's likeness could become part of this famous achievement, forever tying them to history and elevating them to the status of a god. Prominent individuals, both men and women, came from across the world, throwing considerable amounts of money at Artemisia, begging for the honour to be sculpted for this opportunity of a lifetime.

Members of the Hecatomnid family and influential nobles who financially contributed to the project earned the right to sit for sculptures. Besides people, remarkable statues of a muscular sentry mounted on a Nisaean warhorse sat atop each cornerstone, along with a cavalry of Amazon warriors. (The fabulous sculpture of Lailapás, intended to adorn the temple entrance, did not happen since Artemisia wanted the statue to stay closer to Mausolus.)

Most ingenious was how architects placed larger than life figures on the uppermost ledges, with slightly smaller statues on the rows below. Descending sculptures grew more diminutive until the life-sized carvings stood at ground level. The beholder on the ground perceived every figure as the same size. Pythius called the technique a trick of the eye or optical refinement.

Ornamenting the temple exterior took years to finish. Aristotle once told me, "Happiness is the meaning and the purpose of life, the whole aim and end of human existence." Artemisia was happiest when expanding and highlighting every layer of her masterpiece. This building was the aim of her existence, but I knew she would never reach the end – she would never look upon the temple and be satisfied.

Unfortunately, none of us saw its completion. Therefore, I can only share what was projected - the hoped-for outcome laid out on the architectural plans Mausolus showed me. Ho, to be sure, the completed parts I did witness were astounding and remain alive in my memory. By closing my eyes, I can visualize the vivid details of beautiful statues and see animated frieze panels highlighted in garish colours. I feel the sun's warmth glistening off marble walls and bronze adornments. I even remember the enormous testicles Pythius sculpted on the stallions of the quadriga. I imagine those things are still generating much conversation.

I saw the Grand View nearly completed - now that was a phenomenon! Genius! An ornate stratum of greenstone overlaid with polished marble slab accented by blue limestone. Soon, every lifelike statue of gods and heroes would be standing in its assigned place between one of the thirty-six fluted columns. Each statue was massive, measuring seven cubits (my height measures a morsel over three cubits); they seemed to peer down on the city from their location beneath the Pyramid Roof.

Mausolus and Artemisia personally selected the gods and heroes most qualified for watching over Halicarnassus. But, out of fairness, each picked two sides of the temple to decorate in their particular fashion. Mausolus chose first since he wanted the side facing Troy – he wanted travellers to see this array as they approached the city, so he commissioned Leochares to sculpt his beloved characters from the *Iliad*.

Artemisia placed her heroines above the grand staircase, facing the sea. She commissioned Timotheus to create the bravest Amazon warriors beginning with defiant Queen Penthesilea holding her labrys. And she commissioned Scopas to create Olympian gods and goddesses on the east side.

When Mausolus needed to select the final characters for Bryaxis' north side, he first chose Heracles. Ho, to be sure, an unpleasant outburst followed that suggestion. Artemisia quashed his choice. "Hero or no hero, I hate the man responsible for killing my beloved Amazon sisters. I allowed your statue of Achilles because he did love Penthesilea, but I must refuse the presence of the murderer, Heracles, near my temple."

To goad his wife for insulting Heracles, Mausolus suggested Hades, then watched as she erupted in a fury. "What! The god of death perched on my fabulous temple! Save Hades for the tomb garden in Mylasa; keep him away from here." Acting perplexed and in a quandary, Mausolus held back his laughter and allowed his wife to make the final choice. She chose Elpis, the spirit of hope.

Another exceptional feature of the Grand View was the ceiling. The intricate engraving required years to complete. Cephisodotus the Younger and Timarchus, under the guidance of their father, Praxiteles, carved a fighting scene of the Greek hero, Theseus, attacking the fire-breathing bull of Marathon and killing a Minotaur.

The temple's most prominent feature became the Pyramid Roof. Lauded for its distinction and ingenious motif, the Pyramid Roof escalated this temple from a fascinating building into an entirely new dimension of architectural genius. Travelers coming upon Halicarnassus from any direction - the Myndos

Road or the Mylasa Road - beheld a sight of pristine beauty, looking like a radiant, pure white pyramid floating on a distant cloud—another one of Pythius' clever optical tricks earning additional applause from the Shahanshah.

Bryaxis' commission included thirty-six enormous Pentelic marble lions for the lower ledge of the Pyramid. Painted in striking ochre yellow, the procession of prowling beasts alternated right and left gazes as if keeping guard from all angles.

The temple's crowning glory, touted throughout the empire as 'the most triumphant decoration in history,' was the chariot monument. Designed by Pythius of Priene, intended to be visible from parasangs away, the gigantic chariot monument was only a few cubits shy of the height of the pyramid roof. Bright, bold colours highlighted every detail, from the quadriga to the highly decorated double-sized cart supporting realistic statues of Mausolus and Artemisia.

Placing the chariot monument elevated the entire structure to its maximum height, a staggering 93 cubits, dwarfing the city by its grandeur, size, and glory. The entire site harmonized - the temple was situated perfect-centre in the courtyard, the grand staircase was perfect-centre to the temple, and the double bronze doors were perfect-centre to the stairs. The chariot monument sat in perfect-centre to it all.

The enormous courtyard dwarfed the temple base. Four access gates in the boundary wall restricted entrance into this sacred ground. A grand parádeisos around the wall's outer edge provided an ideal place for visitors to stroll along arcades of white marble, refreshing fountains, and shaded benches positioned among beds of plants, flowers, and exotic grasses. This area offered a stirring vantage point for viewing the picturesque Aegean Sea and watching the harbour's endless parade of ships.

Witnessing the birth and triumph of the temple in Halicarnassus filled me with a sense of pride. I dreamed of the future when Jaleh and I would stand together admiring its completed splendour. I imagined our children climbing on marble lions in the courtyard. Perhaps we would have twin sons – I would name one Thomas, which in Hebrew means twin, and the other Baruch after Mausolus, whose name means 'muchly blessed.' Thomas might point to Penthesilea on the Grand View and ask, "Mother, what does that lady hold in her hand?" Seeing the heroes from Troy, Baruch may ask, "Father, why do you stare at Hector? Is that your favourite statue?" Perhaps they will race skyward on the grand staircase, yelling, "Our father built these steps!"

I imagined us as a family strolling beneath sweet-smelling blossoms in the parádeisos. Then, like Goliath, I would tell stories to my children about building the remarkable wonder standing before them. Oh, how I would regale them by pointing out my images on frieze panels and directing them to statues of King Mausolus and his wife Artemisia. I would tell them, "When I was a boy, these were the rulers of Halicarnassus; they became my Persian family and I loved them."

Dreams are not prophets. Unbeknownst to me, a cruel wind was astir, bringing with it my unwarranted departure from Halicarnassus.

Chapter 41

The Temple Interior

Cellas, or interior chambers of the temple, affirmed Artemisia's talent for unusual design and pattern. It would be impossible to estimate the cost she paid for countless gemstones used as exquisite adornments – arrays of priceless gewgaws inset throughout. But she spared no expense. "Aristocrats expect opulence, excess, and wealth," she said. "This profusion of rare gems promises a true temple experience. Privileged-society will want to return over and over again."

After the ritual of ascending the grand staircase and stepping through the foyer into the jewelled Lapis Room – which was like a grotto except Artemisia softened the shape with ornate arches and dome ceiling - guests would discover a glistening interior bedecked with precious ultramarine lapis lazuli and trimmed in gold stone called chrusolithos. Splashes of topaz, amber, and red-jasper inlays ornamented pillars.

Krustallos, arranged throughout, generated an extraordinary sparkle by capturing the glow of burning lamps and then bending firelight outward to illuminate other gems, which created a scattering of blended colours. Imagine walking into the heart of a rainbow; stepping into the Lapis Room produced the same dazzling sensation.

Artemisia intended this room as an exclusive hostelry for the privileged – a place with drink and soft music where it would be safe to relax and share thoughts while escaping the confines of the world.

The experience continued for guests once they traversed the circular stairway to the core of the Grand View – this upper room was once the planned open-air veranda. Here, walls with turquoise accentuated white, red, and black striped sardonyx. Red Odem stone and rare refracting stones imported from the ancient Indus Valley punctuated the ceiling. Artemisia referred to the glittering nuggets as diamonds and accurately named the room Aíthousa

Adámas' or Diamond Room. Light from lamps illuminated each diamond, flickering them like luminaries borrowed from heaven – another sensational trick of the eye.

Two lifelike white onyx carvings positioned between large support columns held hands – Mausolus and Artemisia standing together, forever united beneath a blanket of twinkling diamond stars. This room also had elegant furniture and was intended as a dedicated chamber for prayer and worship or could be rented to conduct private business.

Construction of the cellars required armed guards supervising vetted artisans. Secrecy was paramount. The extraordinary wealth meant production was carried out in stages – a tactic Artemisia contrived to conceal the full magnitude of the gallery's treasures.

First came assembling the Diamond Room using a group of craftsmen to place the turquoise and sardonyx. Afterward, Artemisia dismissed that crew and hired another group to prepare the ceiling. Once that was completed, she dismissed that team and hired a different group of artisans for another task. After completing the embellishments of the Diamond Room, the queen prevented curious labourers from entering by posting a guard at the foot of the rock-cut staircase. Decorating the Lapis Room followed the same process of utilising and discharging craftsmen.

The excellent outcome of this inner world, this treasure trove of rare gems and sparkling jewels, overjoyed Artemisia. Each flamboyant feature validated her sophistication and undeniable talent for original style. She was excited to unveil her marvellous exhibit to the world, but not before Mausolus experienced the first official tour.

Carians blamed the Fates for thwarting Artemisia's plans for jewell-studded pillars in grand and glitzy rooms. They accused the sisters of working together, colluding to hamper the human spirit. As Clotho spun silken strands of destiny, Lachesis determined their length. Then Atropos snipped. One snip is all it took, and Artemisia's jewelled chambers went unnoticed by the world she had so eagerly pursued.

Chapter 42

Painting Day

With no further attempts from the assassin, the queen assumed Rhodes had accepted the supremacy of her Persian rule and dropped their grievances before bringing trouble upon themselves. She dismissed her piracy as inconsequential, confident her deceit passed with impunity while life in Halicarnassus continued skirring along. Temple construction moved forward at an astonishing pace, and Artemisia, soaring high as an imperial eagle, rejoiced in the wonder of all she had accomplished.

Barely able to contain her excitement, she was most anxious for Mausolus to experience the heart of the temple – those phenomenal rooms she had designed – yet she strictly prohibited him from entering. Not yet! She required his patience until the placement of the final marble lion on the grand staircase. She wished to safeguard his skyward journey, then overwhelm him with her incredible spectacle of bejewelled chambers. Unsentimental, Mausolus played along because he wanted to please his wife.

I will never forget this day; oh, what an occasion! It was painting day, and enthusiasm ran high! Everyone in town had patiently waited for the day when decorating the temple exterior could begin.

Deep-cut, three-dimensional frieze panels would soon come to life in garish hues of porphyry red, vermilion, ochre, indigo, and aquamarine, resonating against a backdrop of glistening white marble.

That morning, the satraps planned to examine the worksites, visit the quarry, then watch the painters. A sense of excitement filled the air, and everyone in town turned out to see famous Ephesian artisans at work.

Proficient at painting pigment over stone, this coveted group of artists had recently decorated the multi-coloured pillars in the Stoa of Ephesus. A woman mixing paints greeted the eager crowd in the usual Ephesian manner. "Great is Artemis of the Ephesians!" She engaged inquisitive spectators by explaining processes and sharing several unknown facts. "Earth tinctures, mined from your quarry here in Halicarnassus, provide the rich iron-oxide content needed for heightening hue intensity, causing yellows to glow brighter and reds to glint deeper, particularly when contrasted against bright blue backgrounds. Beholders will have no trouble viewing details, even on the uppermost friezes."

Onlookers asked questions about techniques and listened as the assistant explained. "We use different methods to achieve different depths and shades. Typical instruments are feathers, twigs for outlining, and horsehair brushes. Sometimes, the artist will use their palm or fingertips depending on the desired result. This hollow bone is used when seeking softer touches for clouds, flesh, or around the eyes; the tool allows the artist to blow thin mists of paint across the surface." As the assistant engaged the audience, more townsfolk gathered, and painters, absorbed in the bliss of their profession, continued dabbing, smearing, and palming colourful pigments, adorning the temple's splendid frieze panels.

Imagine this idea, what if you could choose to stop time? What if you could remain living in your favourite moment or on your happiest day? If such a thing were possible, I would have stopped time and remained forever immersed in that spectacular morning when Halicarnassus burst with zeal and wonder. On that day, life was exciting, and my happiness overflowed. On that day, I trusted in a benevolent world.

Contagious enthusiasm from the crowd fed Mausolus' sense of humour, inflating his boyish nature with playful mischief. Carians found their king's spontaneous revelry refreshing. Leaving the painting station, he and Artemisia picked their way through the temple's cluttered courtyard to inspect and view completed sculptures. Mausolus laughed in his usual light-hearted manner while talking to sculptors and greeting citizens (the women openly swooned, and he pretended to be unaware of their girlish rapture). His blue eyes sparkled while inspecting the evolvement of his legacy, Halicarnassus' masterpiece, the heartbeat of the city, and the final jewel in its crown. Goliath led the bodyguard detail. He spotted me, and we nodded.

Smiling his rascal smile and overcome with a sudden urge to tease, Mausolus pretended to examine the staircase my crew and I built. Then, playing ignorant of my presence in the crowd, he stomped his foot several times on the bottom step, jumping around as if testing its soundness. Recognising his jest, I laughed.

Ascending and descending several steps, he walked as if one of his legs was shorter than the other. He said to no one in particular, "These steps appear sorely crooked. Perhaps the stonemason crafting them knew nothing of masonry." Whopping laughs rose from the crowd as people rejoiced in his antics. Then, continuing his lopsided caper, he clomped up and down the next few stairs, producing another round of laughter. Mausolus enjoyed people's reactions to his funny antics, and my side hurt from laughing at him.

Impulsively he blurted out, "Ho, to be sure, I cannot wait, not another flash! I must see the inside of my enchanting temple this very moment!" Light-hearted, he bounded up the steps, skidding to a stop when Artemisia shrieked. Laughing with the townsfolks delighting in his antics, Mausolus turned toward Artemisia, trying unsuccessfully to stifle his amusement. Failing to appreciate the humour in his performance, the queen marched straight up the stairs and duly scolded him for walking onto the staircase before his first pilgrimage. He bowed a sweeping bow and said, "As you decree, Mesia."

Still unmoved by her husband's teasing, Mausolus amorously seized his beautiful wife in his arms, whirled her around, then stopped with a jolt. Unamused by his affectionate display, Artemisia glanced away, bored with his childish frolicking. Standing momentarily, Mausolus held his wife – immobile and silent – then relaxed. As if collapsing in slow motion, he began sinking lower and lower, then crumpled in a heap on the stairs. Artemisia screamed at the sudden limpness of her husband's body.

Bounding at lightning speed, Goliath and the Dathaba covered the imperial couple with their wicker shields. My mind froze; what prank did Mausolus play? I heard whirring, then a thud followed by screams as an arrow penetrated the barrier of shields, grazing Artemisia's thigh. Mayhem exploded. Panicked citizens ran in confusion, Artemisia screamed, and red blood rolled across the polished white stairs.

Scanning the tree line past the temple site, Goliath yelled commands. "Thuxra, come with me; the rest of you secure the queen." Then, placing their shields in front of their bodies, he and Thuxra ran forward in violent fury, heading for the trees.

When I ran toward Mausolus, the Dathaba pushed me away, but I could see him lying on the steps, an arrow lodged deep in his back. Lifting the queen, soldiers hurried her toward the palace as she hysterically screamed for her husband. Ignoring her protests, the men kept moving. I needed to do something, so I foolishly hollered, "I will stay with him." I ran back to Mausolus and told the soldiers to let me through.

Stunned and shaking uncontrollably, I sought a place to spew. Mausolus' head lay motionless on the grand staircase, awkwardly twisted to the side with both arms folded under his body. A look of confusion seemed frozen on his face. His empty eyes stared at nothing. I nudged him with my foot, but he was dead. I heard screams, "No! No! No!" finally recognising them as coming from my mouth. "No, Mausolus! Wake up! Mausolus!" I cried, hitting my fists on the side of my head. I felt dizzy and isolated, as if I had suddenly been sucked into blankness, captured inside a monotone – a hum droning neither high nor low, just steady humming in the mournful timbre of desolation.

Like silken sheets, my legs became too flimsy to support me. I sat in a dull stupor beside my king and watched his flowing blood cascade down temple steps, forever tarnishing the pride I once felt for the magnificent staircase I helped create.

Priests arrived and, without a word, placed Mausolus on a cot and carried him away to a holy dwelling privately accessed by Zoroastrians. I remained on the steps, unable to move, numb with shock, and waited for Goliath and Thuxra to return. Scanning the distance, I anticipated Goliath coming into view, dragging the body of a red-haired man thumping and bumping behind him. But, instead, the men returned empty-handed.

If possible, I would have remained in those precious moments before Mausolus' death, forever reliving that day when Halicarnassus burst with zeal and wonder, and I trusted in a benevolent world.

Chapter 43

The Flaw of Life

When Mausolus died, Halicarnassus died, and an eerie silence enveloped the land. Mausolus' family left the palace in Mylasa and hurried toward the capital city. Work on the temple stopped. Laborers stayed home with their families. Shops closed, and the harbour shut down. Artemisia languished out of her head with grief despite surviving her physical wound.

I was angry. I was angry when the sun decorated the sky with glorious streaks of brilliant orange, shining gaily on a mesmeric sea where white flecks danced across the water in joyous celebration.

I was angry when the moon rose, dazzling beneath an array of twinkling stars, casting the land in a poetic light. I was angry when a soft breeze stirred by the sea brushed its pleasantness against my skin. How dare the world stay the same when nothing is the same, nor will it ever be?

Lying awake on my bed, racked with pain and drowning in grief, I dreaded the morning. If the sun rose with exceptional beauty, painting the blue sky in glorious arrays of pink and violet, its splendour would be an insult. The glorious dawn of a new day would mean the world continued unchanged, and Mausolus' life was of no consequence.

I was angry at the world and angry at myself. Mausolus died, murdered right before my eyes. I wished I had done something. I wished I had died. Me, the lowly peasant from the Land of Israel, I should have an arrow in my back instead of the king – not Mausolus, not my friend.

Goliath blamed himself. Over and over, he relived the moment when, under his command, the satrap king of Caria died, murdered – shot in the back with a sniper's arrow as the vanguard of his army stood smiling, lulled into safety, watching the admiration their king showed toward his wife. Distraught with failure, his inexcusable error plunged him headlong into the darkness of hate. Rile washed over Goliath like a violent torrent. He would settle for nothing short of savage vengeance.

The following day I awakened angry, afraid, and still stuck inside that same relentless droning of no distinguishable rhythm, just a stale monotone of emptiness. I curled into a tight ball and buried myself beneath comforting blankets, hoping to stop the room from spinning. Thuxra entered. Shaking my shoulders, he forced me from my protective nest. "Bathe yourself and dress; the queen desires an audience."

Attending physicians had applied herbs and salves before bandaging the queen's wound. They forced her to drink medicinal teas steeped with Powis Castle foliage. Yet, despite sedation, unrelenting waves of pain overwhelmed her. As I entered her darkened quarters, she at once extended her arms to me, crying in broken defeat. "I am unable to endure this sorrow! Ethan, Mausolus no longer lives! I no longer live, yet how is it that I am still alive?"

As I held her in my arms, she wrestled against the crushing pain in her heart, struggling for words of lament. Her racking sobs prevented speech. Once leaning against my chest, she went limp as a doll sewn of rags.

I guided her to the sofa, covered her shivering body with velvety sheets of Egyptian linen, then sat beside her holding her hand in mine. I stroked her rumpled hair and said, "Indeed, my Queen, this day is cruel. The entire district mourns with the deepest grief. Mausolus' subjects await your arrangements; we must discuss plans for his funeral."

I sensed she struggled to tell me something important but instead produced blubbering sobs of fitful breathing and confused mutters. Fading in and out of coherency, Artemisia rejected any discussion of burying Mausolus. Finally, risking possible repercussions, I took charge and sternly directed her as Mausolus would have. "My Queen, if you remain undecided on this matter, others will plan the king's interment. He will be laid to rest while you lament here alone in the darkness. Put weeping aside until later; this moment must be for Mausolus."

Inaudible words followed, yet her eyes indicated she understood.

I asked, "Who did Mausolus most admire? Tell me about his hero. Tell me of the man Mausolus hailed as life's truest hero?"

Again sobs followed imperceptible noises.

"Prince Hector," I said. "The greatest warrior of Troy. Mausolus chose to model this champion by the way he lived. Perhaps you should allow the king to do the same in death. Remember how passionately Mausolus spoke of Hector's funeral? Has the king ever glorified a public cremation the way he gloried over Hector's spectacular funeral?"

More sobs.

"True, he did not anticipate his early demise, so we do not know his wishes. Therefore, as his most trusted companion, the best interest of Mausolus falls to you. This funeral is your opportunity to honour Mausolus as he would want. How would you feel about recreating Hector's farewell? My Queen, what do you think of such a bold idea?"

Hiding from her loss, the queen attempted to disappear by retreating to a safe place within her mind. I shook her by the shoulders and refused to allow her to drift away from her obligations. Practically scolding her, I said, "At this moment, you must consider Mausolus and the extraordinary life he lived. Respect his noble character along with the pursuits he loved. Plan a ceremony to honour his accomplishments, my Queen. Halicarnassus will be pleased to honour Mausolus in such a grand fashion; they will praise you for arranging it."

Believing such a ceremony would please Mausolus, she agreed, even though the Zoroastrian religion held no account for cremation. Hearing of these plans shocked her priests and administrators. They protested and firmly sought to block her decision, refusing to allow her to incinerate her husband's body.

I was proud of the mulish way she handled them once she unleashed her ferocity and the sharpness of her tongue. I refused to hide my satisfaction as she rebuked the strident men back into their places. I imagined Mausolus throwing his hand up in surrender while chuckling with knowing laughter.

Taking her demands one step further, she requested Mausolus' body be brought into her quarters to remain with her until his funeral. Trying to prevent the unusual request, her priests and physicians again objected. Finally, after levelling another barrage of sharp words at them, his body arrived.

Priests exclusively serving the Hecatomnid dynasty had performed specific rites and rituals of cleansing and equipped Mausolus for his journey with a perfuming sacrament. After selecting his clothing, Artemisia instructed Moza to dress her husband. She wanted him entering his new life clothed in royal finery, acknowledged as a king in his brown silken trousers and saffron tunic embroidered with golden thread and adorned with stones of garnet and green Peridot. Next, she laid out bracelets, rings, and twisted collars of gold and handed Moza stockings of white along with Mausolus' favourite fawn-leather shoes.

For the last time, weeping adorners decorated his eyes – now forever closed. Moza then wrapped him in a robe of splendid purple. Sitting beside her husband, Artemisia removed an ivory-handled brush from her dressing table and began brushing Mausolus' hair with long, loving strokes. Blankly, hour after hour, she tended to the waves of his thick dark hair. Brushing and weeping, brushing and weeping until overcome by exhaustion, she curled beside him and slept.

Impossibly true and too painful to imagine, the first event held on the temple grounds was Mausolus' funeral. Winding through the streets of Halicarnassus, a grand parade carried the bedizened body of their king. Everybody in town turned out, lining both sides of Achaemenid Street, lowering their heads in silence, whispering goodbye as his corpse passed. I recognised labourers from the Pedasa Slope, people from the barbershop, the agora, the barracks, and the docks. Charioteers came to perform Olympic-style quadriga races in honour of Mausolus' generous contributions to sustain the art as an Olympic event, and a touching play called *Mausolus*, written by the tragic poet Theodectes of Phaselis, was read to honour our fallen satrap.

Looking limp as a bruised reed dazed from a tincture of opium joy plant, Artemisia rode propped against silk-covered laths on a lavish cot carried by servants. Also following the corpse in a slow march toward the temple were her family, Zoroastrian priests, the queen's physician, General Orontobates, Artemisia's guard, and her attending maidens. Goliath's family also walked in the procession, but he was nowhere in sight. He, instead, organised a district-wide manhunt to search for Mausolus' killer. Dathaba and infantry forces executed grid searches in the villages; marines patrolled the water while foot soldiers combed the woods and mountains. Expecting a swift arrest, angry citizens focused on the king's funeral.

Simin and I shared a glance of sympathy. The boys behaved as well-mannered young men, and Jaleh wept with her face buried in her hands. Still estranged, I could only mouth to her, Delbar- am, you are the one who owns my heart.

Speaking at Artemisia's behest, the funeral ceremony featured reflective words from the orator Theopompus. He delivered a pleasant discourse passionately expounding on Mausolus' most significant achievements. Recalling the king's once vibrant life brought renewed weeping.

I wished for Theopompus to continue talking. I wanted the priests to speak with endless lyrics and grieving citizens to prattle on and on, voicing gracious words concerning Mausolus' life, because I knew that once their adulations stopped, the priest would drop his fiery torch onto the tinder holding my dear friend. The agony of losing Mausolus caused me to realize the flaw of life is death.

A Zoroastrian priest concluded the ceremony, "To the air, to the water, to the soil, to the fire. In releasing these four elements of life, I release Mausolus, ruler of the district of Caria. May your spirit become a god, traveling safely beyond the river which opens to the universe. May everlasting peace be yours, dear King Mausolus."

Several priests stepped forward, lowered his body further into the pyre, and added more brushwood over the top of him. Then, brandishing a flame, suspending his torch above the timbered pile, the priest mumbled inaudible words. I watched, holding my breath, and wished for a way to extinguish the fire, but then his cruel hand unfolded. The burning torch dropped into the dry sprigs cradling a king.

Nothing happened! A dream? Possibly I was asleep, unable to rouse myself from a terrible nightmare. Any moment I expected to awaken and find Mausolus laughing at my fright. But then I noticed it, a slight waft of rising smoke. Steadily it grew until becoming a heavy swirl of flame. Fire finding its fury, surged and lapped at timbers. Crying howls of anguish filled the courtyard as hurting citizens watched the blaze feed itself on mounds of dry brushwood. Dark grey smoke spiralled heavenward as wailing citizens filed past. As though grasping reality for the first time, Artemisia screamed, "Mausolus, my half-and-half!" Then she fainted.

Chapter 44

Life Without Mausolus

Priests delivered the urn holding Mausolus' ashes to Moza, who accepted them on behalf of the queen. She remained secluded in her quarters, refusing to venture out or even sit on her veranda to enjoy the sea. Moza delivered meals, encouraging her to eat, but she refused food. Instead, she scooped heaps of ashes from her husband's urn, stirring his cinders into her pomegranate juice. Long and deep, she drank, hoping to return Mausolus' life to her soul.

Adorners and maidens had a difficult time keeping her clean. The queen turned away her physicians, remained in bed, and accepted no visitors. She turned me away, and when Simin called on her, she impolitely turned her away also. Wanting nothing to do with General Orontobates, the man she had thrown out as he tried warning her of this moment, Artemisia refused to supervise the district.

Attempts to ease her emotional pain proved futile, and Mausolus' widow remained inconsolable, a broken woman shuffling under the ache of her thigh and the break of her heart. People in the district displayed overwhelming pity for their grief-stricken queen, saying, "Artemisia's sun has blown out even though it is daytime."

Unrelenting sorrow refused to relinquish its destructive grip on her wounded heart. Tortured, exhausted, and sequestered in her quarters, she passed the moments, the days, and the weeks in conversation with Mausolus apologising, explaining she intended to honour him, never to harm him.

Deeper and deeper, she sank into the blackness of her mind until one morning, in the darkest hour before dawn, she emerged hysterically. Running unkempt through the palace corridor, consumed by anxiety, and babbling nonsense, she summoned her scribe. A fiery impulse rose from the abyss of her broken spirit, and relentlessly pursued her mind.

Artemisia began rattling off incoherent words before the groggy scribe could set out his ink. "Hearken, Sisters of Fate, you are not my gods. You have failed in your conspiracy against me while I have prevailed in my victory over you. Reckon my words; I will replace your tragedy with a glorious tribute."

Afraid and unsure how to handle the muddled transcription spilling from the wild woman who was once his forceful queen, the scribe had no choice but to ask her to repeat the proclamation. Then, with all urgency, she rattled off a blasphemous diktat.

"Curse the day this marble came to Halicarnassus. We have not built an exclusive sanctuary for the privileged, nor even a temple with heavenly galleries. Sorrow destroyed that vision the day Mausolus' blood flowed across its polished steps. My humble presentation, my gift of holy marble with stately pillars for you gods, has been met with scorn. How dare you renounce my generous offering by turning this place into a house of lament.

"To be sure, the loss is yours because I now reclaim every marble block. I revoke the gods and remove every one of your statues to present this temple as a gift to Mausolus. This structure belongs to him now as his official burial chamber. It is a place for honouring Persia's favoured satrap king; no one in the world will rest more adorned or be in a finer ossuary of stone than my husband. Hades tried, but death cannot erase Mausolus of Caria. This glistening marble will not allow that. Indeed, Mausolus lives. He endures forever.

"Gods will come, and gods will go; that is my curse to you for rejecting my gift. But not Mausolus! The world will remember him now when viewing this sacred structure. As a testament to his life, these exquisite marble stones will outlive Persia, forever echoing the voice of Mausolus, satrap king of the Persian Empire and ruler of the district of Caria. Time and eternity hold no sanction over this Mausoleum of Halicarnassus."

She concluded her diktat by prohibiting the word 'temple' when referring to the Halicarnassus project, replacing it with a new term – Mausoleum. Once written, she used Mausolus' signet ring, stamping and sealing her ramblings into official district records. The scribe included the dates of Mausolus' reign – twenty-four years commencing in the twenty-seventh year of Achaemenid King Artaxerxes II, ending in the sixth year of King Artaxerxes III Ochus of Persia.

Placing Mausolus' urn inside a sarcophagus of alabaster, Artemisia, heavy-ladened with sorrow, paraded his ashes through the streets and up the hill toward his final resting place, the Mausoleum. She ordered the jewelled chambers filled with her husband's favourite possessions, clothing, and choice foods. She placed his famed sculpture of Lailapás in the foyer and installed a relief of herself crying. She also left weapons, coins, and live animals – lions, doves, oxen, and sheep. Then, hopeful of making amends through a personal sacrifice, she slew her beloved Miut, leaving his fluffy body behind for Mausolus.

Once a joyous site, the temple became a sorrowful place, a Mausoleum filled with precious items most favoured by a king – now cold, dormant objects surrounding an urn of ash resting in a stony sepulchre, ornamenting a stunning city. The fabulous structure acclaimed as the heartbeat of the city became a grave with no heartbeat at all.

I have since seen reproductions using the same terraced style as the Mausoleum. Idrieus built a much smaller version for himself in the tomb garden of Mylasa. Recalling my prophetic words to Mausolus long ago as we discussed a bleak mound of dirt, I said, "History will associate this renowned monument as belonging to Mausolus of Caria." Indeed, a style unto its own, this structure became the world's first mausoleum.

An accidental witness I am to the strange journey of this dazzling marble. Old as the Earth itself, this precious stone remained hidden from sight where it had no experience with death or blood. Once dragged from veiled obscurity and loaded into the belly of sailing ships, the defenceless rock was stolen by hunger and redirected through want. At last, arriving on the other side of the sea, scoring and gouging sculptors sought to bring glory to themselves by forcing lumps of stone into mortal shapes honouring the immortal. But one hundred tons of self-importance moved white marble into a new role: a distinctive centre for worship, jewelled chambers intended to shelter weary gods. Alas, the Fates, commissioning an arrow from across the sea, amending human plans, assigned this faultless rock to hushed repose. Today, the Mausoleum of Halicarnassus sits in deafening silence.

Do humans decide how the Earth's frame should look once dragged into the light? Possibly, our world's most fantastic architectural feats received direction from unseen forces. Will these forces, one day in the future, prompt the sacred marble blocks of the Mausoleum to reinvent themselves as something altogether different? Perhaps, but for now, this building remains my fondest memory and most profound loss.

Chapter 45

The Tenth Step

After an extended period of mourning, the citizens of Halicarnassus eased back into the routine of life. Construction resumed. Much talk circulated about the king's murder, and Carians wanted to know why such a horrible tragedy happened at such a grand moment. The entire district was on edge, knowing a killer was at large.

Artemisia prohibited the removal of Mausolus' blood from the stairs, but the weather eventually washed away the ugly reminder. Even so, the tenth step, where Mausolus died, became the forbidden stair. No one was allowed to touch it. Artemisia forbids anyone from standing there.

Citizens incorporated the tragedy into cautionary adages. "Be careful," folks would say, "avoid your tenth step." Or, "The gods determine the day of your tenth step," or "Pray the gods to guard your tenth step." The irony was, Mausolus got no closer to his legacy than that tenth step.

Several weeks before Mausolus died, Artemisia rewarded me for keeping our secret arrangement. Unbeknownst at the time, her gift became priceless. The queen invited me on a personal tour through the interior chambers, anxious to flaunt the marvels and nuances she built into her jewelled rooms.

She gleamed with pride, watching me explore every detail of those treasured cellas; she even encouraged me to enter through the maintenance door and venture onto the Pyramid Roof. Ho, to be sure, my strides were tentative as I climbed each pyramid stair toward the uppermost pedestal, the place designated to hold the chariot monument once completed. Treads, grooves, and weather joints with thousands of copper cramps joined marble planks, anchoring twenty-four steps to fortify them against possible earthquakes. No shuddering was going to loosen those pyramid slabs.

The platform measured my height five times in both directions. At such an elevation, I stood as the highest person in the world. Into heaven, I hollered, "Yhoaaa," believing my voice circled the sun. Gazing upon human ants scurrying below, I wished Jaleh, Landers, or Goliath had walked by. Especially Goliath! I would call his name and watch as he looked around, trying to discover who spoke.

Disorientated by the height, I felt lightheaded and sat down before toppling over the edge. I viewed the landscape in every direction, and from such an elevation, I am sure I saw the mountains of Pella. Being on that platform produced conflicting emotions: amazement and terror.

I laid on my back, listening to the silence. The wind blew across my face as billowing white clouds paused to survey my intrusion into their realm. Clouds alone bear witness to that moment, the day I stood high above Halicarnassus, hollering into the wind from the pinnacle of Mausolus' grave.

Fearful of relaxing too much and rolling over the side, I moved through a cursory inspection of the top frieze panel, the tiles, and the lion's head gutter spouts while working my way to safety on the ledge. With nothing to hang on to, I sat on my bottom and sidled step by step. After dropping through the maintenance door, I acted bold and unafraid to Artemisia as if I had run carefree to the temple's summit and back down again. Few people in history have had the privilege of viewing Artemisia's jewelled galleries; fewer still know of their existence. And save for me, who can boast of standing so close to heaven they could reach out and touch the face of God?

Artemisia never revealed the actual location of Mausolus' ashes. However, some people speculated she placed him in a secret compartment within the Lapis Room or beneath the Persian Pedestal. No, Mausolus is not there. Instead, the priests carried his gilded urn up the rock-cut staircase to the highest level, into the Diamond Room. I feel confident of this because of Artemisia's Zoroastrian beliefs.

True, the religion resists the custom of cremation, but as with King Cyrus, and other Achaemenid kings, Artemisia wanted her beloved husband elevated above earth and soil. Zoroastrians place their dead in high dakhmeh towers, towers of silence. I feel certain Mausolus rests beneath a spray of diamonds, high above Halicarnassus in his tower of silence, overlooking eternity beyond the Aegean Sea.

Chapter 46

Goliath's Fury

Agony. The days following Mausolus' death were unbearable. I suffered from periods of sadness, loneliness, and sleepless nights. The lively agora became a place of dread. Instead of experiencing my usual joy, I felt anxiety in the presence of others.

During those early days of grief, I was most comfortable aimlessly wandering along the beach where I could openly cry, and with no one around, I allowed my anguished crying to become screams. A tinny emptiness in my heart reminded me daily that Mausolus was gone. My body ached and felt stiff; even the simple task of walking became a weighty effort as if trudging through a bog.

One day I thought I saw Mausolus walking along Achaemenid Street. Another time, I thought I saw him at the building site, strolling casually among the equipment. Once again, I observed him sitting beside the water clock at the Stoa of Aegea. But my mind was playing a mean trick on me, and each time the person turned out to be someone else. Mausolus seemed to be everywhere in our midst, but Mausolus was nowhere.

Grief is painful to endure, but the pain becomes unbearable when faced alone. Artemisia kept me shut out, and with Goliath constantly gnashing his teeth, he became a person best avoided. Jaleh and I had not yet reconciled. Others in the community endured their mourning by relying on family and friends; everybody had somebody to hearten them except me. So, like a bird without a nest, I wandered alone.

Moza had served Mausolus since the satrap was five. Mausolus was like a son to him. But, unfortunately, the grief was too much for the aged attendant; he never fully recovered. Without his routine and daily expectations, Moza grew disoriented like a ship that had lost its rudder.

No one suffered more abysmally than Goliath. He, too, had served Mausolus for most of his life; he was the king's most dependable soldier, a trusted ally, and a constant escort. Goliath would have taken the assassin's arrow to protect Mausolus; he expected to die in that fashion, but he never expected to stand idly by as Mausolus lost his life to a coward's arrow.

Whispers and opinions circulating throughout the district contributed to Goliath's crushing humiliation; the worst moment of his military career became a matter of public scrutiny. Disgrace and self-reproach dug into his soul like an insect burrowing under his skin. Such bitter resentment caused insufferable hardship for his family.

Respecting his need for privacy, I avoided the temptation to contact him, but when weeks became months, and he still ignored me, I chose to push open the door he needlessly shut. Simin and I discussed Goliath's darkening mood and withdrawal from family activities. With tears streaming down her cheeks, she feared her husband might vanish into a caldera of despair. We arranged a risky intervention for the following evening, and scared out of my wits I arrived as planned – at mealtime.

Wiping sweaty palms across my vest and clearing my throat, I knocked on the door. Simin answered and invited me in. My heart pounded like hailstones hitting a rooftop. The twins ran over and greeted me, becoming instant pests by jumping on my back and touching the pommel of my new sword. Cas nodded from across the room, sad and subdued. His father's withdrawal caused a confusing void in their strong bond. Arman clung to his mother, but Jaleh's smile brought me incredible joy. I had missed her. Before we could speak, Goliath walked into the room; the giant looked haggard and ten years older. Stunned by my presence, his reaction showed he was unhappy with my visit. In a mean voice, he grumbled and cut me to the core, "Ethan, leave my home. We have nothing to discuss."

Simin came near, attempting to intercede on my behalf as her husband tried to bully me out of the house, but I did not require her rescue. Instead, I stood straight as a temple pillar. I held my ground and refused to tremble as if a puny grasshopper.

Goliath had taught me, 'Once a man pulls his sword, he throws away his scabbard until winning the battle.' Indeed, I had drawn a sword on my teacher. Then, eyeing him directly, I held my head high and set my jaw tight enough to snap a tooth.

"No!" I said,

His head jerked back as if someone had yanked it with a cord.

I continued, "You have no reason to treat me in this harsh manner. I have done nothing against you, and I hold nothing against you. Besides, Simin invited me here, and the family welcomes my visit. So if you must disparage my presence, you go away because I am staying."

I saw a vein bulge in his muscular neck, and his eyes grew round with anger. Every instinct in my soul begged me to turn and run. The giant stiffened his hands; he seethed at my audacity, but I refused to budge. I did not blink. A feather would have sounded like a thunderclap had one fallen to the floor. But I had stepped into the heat of battle and would stand my ground.

I told him, "You have a family who welcomes you back home in the evenings, yet you have excluded me, flicked me off your vest like an insect. Your coldness forces me to suffer all the more. You served Mausolus for many years, and I respect the bond you two shared, but I loved him, too, and I miss him every day. You give yourself the blame for his death, but you remain unaware of certain matters. I must be allowed to talk, and you must listen."

Nobody dared speak. Farzin and Gulzar looked at me, then at their father, and back at me again, fearing to release even the softest breaths. Neither of us broke the stare; our eyes remained locked. Finally, realising my determination, Goliath motioned for me to sit at the table. Incredible relief washed across the room, and my shoulders dropped away from my ears. When my jaw slackened, I heard a slight pop.

Praise be to Yahweh; the people I called my family again opened their hearts to me. Simin smiled and squeezed my hand several times throughout the evening. Jaleh wanted to be near me, something I, too, desired, but repairing our relationship would have to wait. After eating, Goliath and I stepped into the garden.

"What I have to say is painful and difficult to confess. I warn you; the truth is not in the queen's favour," I said.

"You risk being arrested with such a statement, thrown in the Tower of Ash," he snapped.

"Which is one reason I refused to come forward earlier. Instead, I sat idle until I became culpable in Mausolus' death."

"What have you to do with it?" Goliath acted confused.

Like a raging river escaping its banks, buried words and maddening frustrations gushed as I confessed every secret.

"You are aware Mausolus hired me to spy. And you know he prohibited me from telling the queen. Did you know, also, the Queen hired me and forbade me from telling Mausolus?"

His look of surprise led me to believe he knew nothing of it.

"The queen tricked me, and my infatuation for her prevented me from realising it. She hid a terrible secret from Mausolus – from you, from everybody. In hopes of creating a decoy, she used me to entice Mausolus into building her temple."

"Foolishness! Why would she need to play such a game?"

"Tell me, whose idea was the Halicarnassus project?"

"To be sure, King Mausolus'. From the rubble, he created a capital; this temple would complete its fame."

"Artemisia has concealed her wrongdoing by accrediting the Halicarnassus project to her husband."

"Ethan, you are naïve and know nothing of such matters."

"Did you know plans for this project had been set in motion before Mausolus signed his signature of consent? Artemisia already hired Pythius and the others. Before I arrived in Halicarnassus, she had acquired the building materials, including the marble. During the special inspector's visit, Artemisia used her charm and feminine manner to credit Mausolus for the ambitious proposal. Somehow, she flipped the situation, manipulating both men until they begged for her consent."

"To be sure, I agree there may be some truth in what you say, Ethan. Continue."

I shared the information I learned from Lysippos regarding Artemisia's piracy and how the outraged Rhodians sought revenge. "The queen knew who sent an assassin and why. Over and over, Mausolus asked, 'Why now? Why her? Why a mercenary?' She knew the answer all along. She did not speak out, though. The discovery of her offense and drastic measures would have nullified her plans. Exposure would publicly humiliate her, and she could not endure Mausolus' disappointment. What would Mausolus have done had he known of her piracy?"

"We both know the answer; the king was a man of honour; if he learned the truth, he would insist his wife return the marble to the Rhodians, with compensation. Huge compensation in hopes of averting a war."

"In which case, Artemisia would forever lose her legacy. She tricked me into believing if I told the truth, I would humiliate Mausolus. I had grown far too involved by the time I learned all the facts; therefore, I ignored the entire affair. Not knowing the proper course of action, I opted to sweep the situation out of my mind."

Goliath fumed. He paced back and forth with rage. By the time I ran out of words, I was exhausted. Goliath said nothing. He continued pacing. Unsure of his reaction, I feared the truth doomed me to the Tower of Ash.

At last speaking, his voice had softened. "You have endured a strange dilemma, Ethan; you were right to tell me these things. Your secret will remain safe with me. What you say clarifies my suspicious – twisted facts and confusing explanations, which never quite lined up. The king loved his wife; he never questioned her, but how did I not discern this dangerous situation happening right before my eyes?" With nothing else to say, we sat in silence, both reproachful of our failures.

Curious, I asked about the arrow used to kill Mausolus. Goliath removed the missile from its hiding place in the garden shed and motioned me over. Seeing the blood-stained instrument used to kill my friend caused my head to spin. Unlike the cane arrows of the Dathaba, this arrow, one forged of different metals, used one kind for the tip and another for the shaft.

"To be sure, a foreign-looking arrow," I said.

"Crossbow. Popular in the warring states of Zhongguo. I have seen this weapon before, but never in Western regions. Built with a trigger mechanism for rapid-fire, the draw weight combined with flexible arrows means they can hit their target from a distance of thirty daca trayas without losing speed. That second arrow penetrated our shields as if piercing linen." Goliath's eyes dropped to the floor as he fidgeted with his scar.

"I replay that awful morning over and over again," I said. "Each time I suffer deeper, and my anger grows stronger. The day would have ended differently had Mausolus not acted in such silliness. Perhaps the queen would have died on the steps. Neither choice carries a desirable outcome, but an innocent man does not deserve to die in such a demeaning manner."

Goliath acknowledged my logic. "I shudder at such a theory; if Artemisia had died as intended, Caria would now be at war. Mausolus would have called out his navy; he would raise an army to kill every Thracian and Rhodian in sight. Persians would unite to decimate the island, spilling innocent blood on both sides. Perhaps with his death, Mausolus unwittingly protected his people in a manner extending far beyond our grasp."

Like Hector, I thought to myself. "To be sure," I said. "One life in exchange for many. A curious thought I had failed to consider; a saviour, selflessly dying to protect the people he loved. We both know Mausolus would have sacrificed his life for Caria. To be sure, Mausolus unknowingly died a hero. The world deserves to know his death was not without good cause."

"Ethan, we must swear an oath to keep the honour of Mausolus's death a secret. True, it is a loathsome burden to carry, but we must. The facts may one day be revealed, but our focus must now be devoted to the current situation. The queen! This assassin has, by now, learned of his failure. To be sure, he will try again, anxious to fulfil his contract and collect his payment. But, considering he has the blood of a king on his hands and a substantial bounty on his head, the man has nothing to lose. Therefore, his attempts will grow bolder."

"To be sure, he has by now fled the district."

"No, Ethan. I fear this man lurks somewhere nearby. He will remain until succeeding in his mission to kill the queen."

"What do we do? How do we find him?"

"He will be impossible to find. But, Ethan, we do not need to find him. We need to make him find us."

Chapter 47

Attack at the Harbour

Temporary leadership of Halicarnassus fell to General Orontobates. With Mausolus gone and Artemisia bedridden by depression, Idrieus made threats from Mylasa, saying care of the government must now pass to himself.

"Perhaps she scorns me by taking advantage of my patience and the tolerance of our loyal subjects," Idrieus said to Orontobates. "I have afforded my sister a lengthy period to grieve, yet she remains dispirited. She must decide to rule or transfer the district into capable hands.

"I have secured a room for her at the sanatorium on Cos," he informed the general. "To be sure, the island's medicinal centre will care for my ailing sister with professional treatments to ease her malady. However, remaining disagreeable with this provision will leave me no choice but to petition the special inspector. Once he discovers how the queen's negligence endangers this lucrative satrapy of the Shahanshah, he will have no option but to establish me as king."

The strain of a domestic war would tear the district apart. Her darkened state did not permit Artemisia to recognise the jeopardy she placed on herself or how the sudden loss of leadership affected the satrapy. Plagued by fears, remaining out of touch, and absorbed in her guilt, Artemisia lived as a slave to her secret and the penalty Mausolus paid in her place.

A persistent nightmare tormented the queen. Shortly after falling asleep, faceless people emerged in her dream, lashing her to the bow of the *Trojan Hector*. Constricted, immobilised, and reproached, she was powerless as the ship sailed faster and faster through the darkness. Unable to free herself and unable to calm the sea, she fought helplessly against the tide. Deeper, she plunged until her death was imminent, then upward the bow rose, allowing a single gulp of air before dropping again beneath harsh, unforgiving waters. The bow rose for another brief moment before dipping again below the surface. The nightmare continued with turbulent waves breaking across the bow – submerging, climbing, plunging, then rising, in and out of the jagged torrent; frigid waves angrily slapping against her face. Then suddenly, the waves changed form and became a hostile volley of bloody arrows, suffocating her in Mausolus' blood. Each time she tried screaming, Mausolus' blood filled her mouth, choking her until she woke in a panic, blankets wet with sweat and her maidens trying to calm her.

Every nightmare sent her out the following day, hurrying up the hill to the Mausoleum to make amends with votive objects – Mausolus' cherished possessions: his silver horse bridle, clothing, jewels, his circlet crown, and his Persian Arabian head pipe, a marble replica of his battle helmet, vases, boxes, and weapons. Then, believing Mausolus would find joy in their presence, she released his falcons to fly among the cellas.

Next, the queen placed her cherished possessions beside her husband's. She included the jewelled necklace and matching tiara she wore at their wedding, her dainty gazelle rhyton, and Queen Bahar's set of ivory doves with silver wings and gold feathers. Further hoping to bless Mausolus, she left her most-loved possession – the alabaster vase gifted to her ancestor Artemisia I by King Xerxes after the Battle of Salamis. Finally, the queen left scroll after scroll of feverish scribbling, penned prayers, and love songs with apologies and sweet expressions from her broken heart.

Trekking back and forth, shuffling along in the stupor of an emotional crisis, crushed by the unexpected consequences of her deceit, the warrior queen lingered on edge, feeble and shaken. Useless as a damaged pillar, her contributions to the district ebbed – until Pisinah came to town.

Word of Artemisia's fragile emotional state had circulated throughout the district. People believed her unfit to rule. Finally, Admiral Cyberniskos of Rhodes learned of her frailty. Assuming the gods had given him the perfect opportunity to exact justice against the arrogant Hecatomnid dynasty, he strategically planned a revenge attack. And the festering resentment against Persia generated plenty of supporters.

Years earlier, Mausolus had installed an armed garrison to subjugate the island and funnel a significant portion of its natural resources to Caria. Grappling under a Persian presence, struggling to remain viable, powerless Rhodians silently endured the yoke of oppression – until the day Queen Artemisia stole their marble. To entitle herself further, to help herself to the remnants of the earnings they scraped together to build a sacred temple, this heartless act drove islanders to their breaking point. Vengeance without mercy would follow.

Pisinah, a Persian soldier stationed at the Rhodes garrison, had slipped off the island and sailed across the sea to warn General Orontobates of a budding conspiracy. Rallying in anger, incensed Rhodian dissidents plotted a seditious attack against Halicarnassus.

General Orontobates feared burdening the queen with the threat of insurrection, but Persian law obligated him to inform her of the potential hazard. Afraid an act of terror aimed against the satrapy would overwhelm the fragile queen, he regrettably informed her of the impending doom, explaining the Rhodians were gathering ships to destroy her city, destroy her, and abolish her dynasty.

The news of this sedition outraged Artemisia, shaking her from her lethargy. Like a dried sponge revitalised by water, the warrior queen emerged from her chambers clean, equipped in battle armour, and ready to claim her rightful place as commander and sole ruler of Caria. Assembling her generals, she gathered crucial information and formulated a strategy.

According to Pisinah, Admiral Cyberniskos and his captains hatched a clever plan for an early morning attack. By quietly launching in the dark of night, the admiral intended to glide his ships unnoticed past the island's northern garrison. He would sail undetected through the night and then wait until dawn just below the horizon. Veiled by the morning fog, he would sail his fleet of penteconters into Halicarnassus and capture both marinas and the palace before the sleepy town knew what had happened.

Pisinah's detailed report gave the warrior queen the necessary information to prepare a shrewd counterattack. To Orontobates, she said, "Heed this lesson from Themistocles, 'Battle in close conditions works to our advantage.'" Brimming with the confidence of a sly opponent, she set a plan into motion, revelling in her firm advantage.

Yelling, "Fireship!" Goliath's men sprang into action. Gathering large hydriai jars and every amphora from the citadel, soldiers began fashioning incendiary detonators designed to launch a firestorm. Explosive mixtures of beeswax, olive oil, and animal fat filled the jars, followed by a combustible blend of twigs, timbers, and dry grasses densely compressed into the bottom. Arranged plumes of dried plants served as a fuse. Adding decorative tendrils, fresh flowers, and vine foliage masked their intended purpose. Placing the artistic displays in a delivery skiff gave the impression of floral arrangements awaiting transport to a neighbouring island. A secondary incendiary source of kindling sticks and dried brush, moistened with the oil mixture, lay in bundles around the volatile pots.

A folded sunshade laying across the bow innocently disguised the waiting disaster. The weapon-charged boat sat moored in a slip nearest the harbour entrance. Hidden from sight, a detachment of fire archers waited for their signal. The timing was crucial; Artemisia needed to catch the invaders off guard, trapping them and their ships in the Commercial Harbour.

Merchant ships remained docked to avoid suspicion, but military vessels, save one trihemiolia, sailed out of view. Remaining hidden on the other side of the city's forested peninsula, they awaited their signal – a marine watching from the hilltop would alert the warships by waving a red attack standard once he heard the go-ahead: three long trumpet blasts coming from the watchtower. This signal meant 'sail into the Gulf and seal off the channel.' At the same time, the remaining military vessel would move into the mouth of the Naval Harbour, barricading the inner marina. Persians operating signal drums and different coloured attack standards waited in the watchtowers, ready to herald Goliath's troops hidden nearby.

In case this initial tactic failed, and the battle moved beyond the perimeter of the harbour, Goliath stationed me with ordinary citizens on the ground just beyond the pier. Breaching the Persian barricade was doubtful, but in such an eventuality, our orders were to defend the passage between the harbour and the city, blocking the Rhodian warriors from gaining access to the streets. Behind us, several units of Dathaba remained concealed for a lethal ambush.

Selecting a position, I glanced around to get my bearings as Goliath had taught me. At first, I failed to recognise the soldier standing on my left with a black band tied around his head and yellow cosmetic smeared in streaks across his cheeks. Landers! He winked at me as he slipped on his vest armour of thick silk and secured his scabbard. He carried a distinctive secondary blade, an iron xiphos with a green gem fixed into the midrib of the cross-section. Indeed, a fancy knife for a fierce-looking barber.

Townsfolk, without effective weapons, received swords from the arsenal; I used my sword, but Goliath gave me a shield, and a kopis battle-ax. And I had Ajax – the name I had given my dagger. I learned about Ajax from

246

Mausolus' tales of the Trojan War. Ajax played a significant role in the Battle of Troy. I felt naming my weapon after a strong fighter seemed altogether fitting. Ajax came to my rescue on several occasions. I gifted that Persian dagger to my son; he later passed the blade on to his son. I no longer know the whereabouts of Ajax, but I live today because of that dagger.

Marines had set their trap at sea, soldiers set their trap on land, and we townsfolk waited. The silence set me on edge; I felt skittish, hiding in the fog, anticipating the Rhodians' arrival. Goliath bolstered his eager troops while reviewing possible tactics the enemy may impose. I noticed his posture and the set of his jaw; he moved among his men like a god, breathing courage into each man. Goliath governed his troops like a battle-wise master deserving of respect regardless of current events involving the peltast.

Sparring with Cas, a combat form I viewed with great amusement, hardly prepared me for the scrimmage I was about to face. My mind flashed to possible scenarios of a gruesome nature, causing beads of sweat to form across my brow. Goliath approached me. "Relax and think, Ethan. You have rehearsed battles and developed valuable skills, but I warn you now, these Rhodian soldiers are coming here with one purpose. They intend to kill you, Ethan. Rely on your training, stay aware of your surroundings, and use your breathing rhythm." He squeezed my shoulder, conveying assurance with his firm voice.

Quiet. Gentle waves lapped against the shore as a small army of Persian soldiers waited out of sight. At first light, Rhodian vessels sailed into the harbour, floating in perceived secrecy beneath a blanket of morning fog. The convoy glided into a sleeping town and moored at docks in the Commercial Harbour. Holding our positions, we waited without moving, listening for the trumpet blast. My pounding heart echoed in my ears as I watched the enemy disembark in quiet stealth – I felt a strong urge to visit the húdōr!

Creeping onto the docks, the Rhodians failed to notice a single vessel slipping away from its mooring, floating directly into the narrow mouth of the channel. Archers stationed in watchtowers loaded their bows and lit their arrows. The men watched with iron nerves waiting for their commander's signal. Goliath raised his hand, suspended motionless in midair, waiting for the precise moment.

The intruders mobilised on the docks and prepared to enter the city. Goliath dropped his hand, releasing a flash of arrows whistling through the air. Projectiles swishing overhead scattered the Rhodians. Diving for cover, they failed to notice the dry fuel igniting in a blaze of skyward flames. Persian archers rained another barrage of arrows onto the invaders. Unfurling signal flags from the watchtowers followed three long trumpet blasts.

The battle for Halicarnassus had begun.

General Orontobates ordered the remaining trihemiolia to close off the inner marina while sending his foot soldiers to the pier.

Pop! Pop! Pop!

Fire pots in the drifting merchant vessel ignited, exploding into an inferno of oily globs spreading across the surface of the water, closing off the enemy's escape. As blazing water burned in an impenetrable slick of flaming oil, the wind carried thick smoke, blinding the invaders as the noxious cloud seized their lungs.

Choking, Cyberniskos yelled, "A trap!"

The troops scrambling away from the smoke provoked another trumpet blast sending the sparabara marching forward in a Wall of Shields to prevent the Rhodians from breaking past the marina. Nervously, we townsfolk stood at the ready.

As the smoke dissipated, hand-to-hand combat erupted. Scuffling at the waterfront shook the wooden planks with the rumble of an earthquake. Iron smashed against iron, then shouting and yelling, followed by splashing as the wounded or dead fell into the harbour.

Cyberniskos sought to gather his men in retreat. "Back to the ships. Move the ships into the open!" The frantic command came too late; directly past the sinking fire-boat Persian naval ships waited in the sea. With no place to run, fighting dwindled and at last ceased.

The brief struggle ended when the sparabara corralled the rebels. That is until Landers stepped up and provoked a wild new storm by mocking the Rhodians' embarrassing loss. Landers flicked a girlish wrist at the defeated men and said, "Kriòmyxos!"

The laughter produced by the insult of comparing the failed Rhodians to stupid rams refuelled their humiliation and rekindled a new fury. Savage fighting again erupted as Cyberniskos' men, intent on hurting Landers, fought their way through the sparabara toward us common-herd citizens. Bravery favoured the Rhodians; with execution awaiting them, they had nothing to lose by fighting. Infuriated by falling into a Persian trap, enraged at Lander's effeminate taunt, the foiled soldiers revelled in the opportunity to inflict as much damage as possible before dying.

Combat escalated with ruthless momentum, spilling into the Stoa of Aegea, advancing up tiers and toward the city – the area I was to defend. The uproar sent Goliath into action. Pointing in our direction, he rallied the troops sending reinforcements on the double-quick.

Shouldering my way to the front, I joined the wall, pushing my shield against the blitz. Quick with the blade, I struck low, keeping my axe hidden until I found an opportunity. Agonising sounds of battle rang in my ears – shouting and cursing, bodies jarring and dropping, swords and axes clashing, iron meeting iron, shield meeting shield, followed by screams of hatred mixed with the foul stench of blood and bowels.

Our line thinned as people fell, wounded. Wielding his xiphos, Landers remained beside me, his windmill arms sweeping, swift, and uncatchable. We blocked incoming blows by joining shields, but I lost my balance when tripping over a fallen soldier. An angry Rhodian locked his eyes on me as I struggled to rise. Goliath spoke the truth; I knew this man intended to kill me. Landers, unable to break free, left me vulnerable and exposed.

The Rhodian raised his arm, aiming his weapon at my head; as he stepped forward, I scooted backward, looking like a fleeing crab. My hand touched something – it was the dead man's spear. Without time to think, I grabbed the shaft, lifted the spear with both hands and swung. The broad motion caught my opponent's heel, sweeping his front foot out from under him. He tried to recover by widening his stance, but I swung again fast striking his shin, taking out his rear support leg. As he began to topple, I shoved the butt end of the spear upward, catching him under the chin. His head snapped back, and he went down. I got to my feet, advanced, and lunging forward, thrust the sharp point into his stomach. Doubling in half, he groaned then his arms fell to his sides. I froze - my foot pressed hard into his chest.

The battlefield had become eerily quiet. Men still fought, mouths moved, and swords clashed - except in silent, slow motion. I watched in a dreamlike state as soldiers moved with measured strikes like whirling dancers pivoting and arching in a performance of perfect melodic unison.

"Ethan! Ethan!"

I looked around.

"Back in the line, soldier!" The commander's voice brought me out of my stupor.

I returned to the battle and fought for Halicarnassus until Admiral Cyberniskos' final surrender.

Victory belonged to Persia; Artemisia had orchestrated the entire ambush, watching the battle unfold from her vantage point on the trihemiolia. Now General Orontobates awaited her further instructions.

Indignant at the Rhodians who dared to profit from her grief by launching an attack against her, the enraged queen barked her next orders. Eyeing Admiral Cyberniskos and his captured men, Artemisia commanded, "Remove their clothing!"

Heads turned in her direction. Nobody moved. Orontobates questioned whether this order came from a mind damaged by grief or whether Artemisia issued an actual command. Blankly staring, her soldiers stood motionless.

"I said remove their clothes! I will give this insurgent group of pompous islanders a Trojan horse they will not soon forget."

The Rhodians resisted the disgrace, but well-placed blows from the blunt end of a spear quelled their hostility, and the defeated troops stripped down to an indecent condition. Adding to their humiliation, Artemisia stood on the dock, refusing to avert her eyes.

After they had been relieved of their weapons, battle gear, uniforms, and sandals, Thuxra ordered three details of Dathaba to escort the band of conspirators to the jail. Revolt against the empire doomed rebels to certain execution. This group would march to Mylasa, where they would plunge into the Tower of Ash.

Admiral Cyberniskos' request to join his men in the Tower was denied. Instead, he received a horrible fate; Artemisia ordered him tortured in the Triple Death. Dispensing a skilled torturer, she sought to gain vital information regarding the murder of her husband by torturing and reviving, torturing and reviving him three times before finally killing him.

Speaking in an authoritative tone, Artemisia commanded the next part of her vengeful plan. "Persians, undress!" Astonished, General Orontobates thumped his right arm across his chest, turned to his soldiers, and ordered them to disrobe. Again no one moved. "You heard me! Undress!" Orontobates commanded.

Brilliantly, Artemisia ordered her army to dress in Rhodian uniforms and to decorate their pentecenters with victorious laurel wreaths. Then, initiating the second half of her plan, Persians sailed in enemy vessels back to the island. Disguised as victorious Rhodians, Persian soldiers sailed undetected into the harbour. The entire town turned out cheering in triumph, gathering at the docks, shouting congratulations as their fleet returned home from a successful mission of destroying Halicarnassus and the greedy queen of the Hecatomnid dynasty.

Pisinah rode on the lead ship; Goliath waited below deck with Artemisia. I stayed on the second vessel with orders to follow Pisinah, whirling the Persian battle standard, signalling our troops at the garrison for help.

Unsuspecting crowds of Rhodians waved and cheered as the fleet glided into the berths. The disguised Persians disembarked at the pier and quickly assembled in battle formation. Unsure of the situation, the confused crowd quieted and looked around. Then their nemesis, the hated queen, stepped mockingly onto the deck, dressed in protective armour, brandishing her sword.

Shrieking in protest, sneering islanders launched into a riotous uproar, but Artemisia screamed above the din, "Curse the Fates; they are the gods who have delivered you into my hands. Now shall you learn what might wells up in the breast of an Amazon. With my blood is mingled war!"

As she waved her hand in a subtle flick, Pisinah unfurled the standard, shouting a wild Persian war cry, "Verethragna! The god of certain victory sustains us!" I loosened my flag, as did the masquerading Persians on the other captured vessels. We all shouted, "Verethragna!" and pandemonium exploded.

Recognising the deception, the Rhodians advanced with force, unsheathing their swords, but the Persian garrison attacked from the rear, squeezing the rebels between themselves and Artemisia's soldiers. For the second time in one day, Queen Artemisia II of Caria outsmarted and humiliated the insurrectionists of Rhodes. In her revenge, Artemisia ruled the islanders with unbridled sovereignty, gaining more political and financial superiority than Mausolus had before her.

Chapter 48

A New Rhythm

Artemisia's historic win over the Rhodians began to fill the depleted coffers of her grief-stricken soul. News of her clever Trojan horse offensive spread across the empire, earning her tremendous respect. Citizens of the district paralleled her fearless military prowess to the life and daring escapades of Artemisia I. Catchy new songs and innovative poems recited in the Stoa of Aegea commemorated the queen's incredible victory. Townsfolk dedicated the day as an official holiday, 'Níki Níki Artemisia. Victory for Artemisia.'

To punctuate her absolute authority, Artemisia commissioned a bronze statue of herself posing as a warrior queen, wielding a hot branding iron, scorching the hind ends of puny Rhodians. She erected her silent threat on a circular platform in the square at Rhodes Harbour – a constant reminder of their absolute powerlessness. Then, she passed a law with deadly consequences if her statue suffered any harm or removal. I heard rumours the Rhodians hid the sculpture behind a towering fence. I can only imagine their joy when craftsmen later melted that offensive reminder along with other bronze items to build the Colossus.

After learning of the uprising and the ingenious ruse their sister employed to crush the rebels, Artemisia's family in Mylasa left her alone, abandoning their efforts to steal the throne. Ignorant of their queen's deceit and shameful treatment of Rhodes, the citizens of the district never learned the reason behind the attack against them. Instead, Carians marvelled at Artemisia's show of power by quelling an unprovoked insurrection with minimal loss to Persian life or property. In the process, she gained a handsome fleet of penteconters. Selling the ships replenished the city's dwindling treasury, convincing citizens the queen served the satrapy for their ultimate benefit.

Surprisingly, the weeks following the harbour battle produced a season of refreshment, like abundant rain falling on parched ground, healing us from our loss and the drudgery of grief. Work on the Mausoleum of Halicarnassus resumed with renewed vigour, and life crept forward again. What is interesting is the way the community came together. 'Defend Halicarnassus!' had been the battle cry met by every able-bodied citizen. An army of civilians coming together in one collaborative effort to protect their native soil united neighbourhoods and forged a community bond previously lacking. Obstacles and class barriers disappeared the day neighbours and strangers fought side by side to defeat a common enemy.

Goliath's leadership during the Battle of Halicarnassus redeemed his credibility. He received applause from the district and a commendation from the Shahanshah, who called him a valuable asset to the empire.

I also benefited. After realising the danger I faced from the Rhodians, Jaleh softened, admitting she still had affection for me. She stopped being angry and apologised for mishandling her disappointment. Embracing once again, we held on to each other and promised our undying love. I passionately kissed her with no fear of her father.

For a time, Goliath and I avoided discussing the marina battle. But Cas and the twins eagerly talked on and on about the attack. They constantly pestered me for gory details. "How many did you kill? Did you see guts and brains? Was there lots of blood?"

After dinner one evening, Goliath and I retired to the garden to smoke our pipes. Sitting in peaceful tenor, we listened to the distant trill of a melancholy nightjar, perhaps warbling for a companion to join him on his lonely perch. Goliath, at last, broached the subject of the Rhodes battle. "You fought bravely, Ethan; I am proud of you. You have proven yourself a worthy student with the qualities of an excellent soldier." Ho, to be sure, his words warmed me to the depths of my soul. I thanked him for his teaching, and for the first time, Goliath shook my hand.

Halicarnassus had become my home; I was part of a family and belonged to a community. Seeing Landers and Stavros at the barbershop, Karim at the kilns, and visiting Thuxra and other Dathaba always provided goodhearted camaraderie. And I could not imagine life without Simin and the boys.

Strangely, I still loved beautiful Artemisia, but differently now. I loved her as one cares about a wilted rosebud withering on a dried branch. I pitied her wanting heart and mercenary spirit that had unleashed a crisis of exquisite agony. People admired Artemisia as the Great Warrior Queen of Caria, yet despite their lauds and praise, and regardless of her glistening tower of marble, the vindictive arrow killing Mausolus emptied her, leaving her destitute and aching with internal poverty.

Goliath remained my mentor. My nervousness around him diminished (mostly diminished) once he congratulated me for my courage in battle. I had proven my mettle and earned my place beside his daughter – my Jaleh Joon. The time came for me to have a serious conversation with Goliath about the future.

Romance aside, Goliath and I had one last obligation to fulfil. The marina battle had distracted us for a while, but now we needed to find a killer and avenge Mausolus.

Chapter 49

Cleon

Delivering Admiral Cyberniskos to the torturers proved most informative. The tasteless punishment of the Triple Death revealed the name and whereabouts of the assassin along with his connection to Queen Artemisia, and the Hecatomnid clan and much more torturers persuaded him to divulge.

We discovered the assassin, a man named Cleon, hailed from Thrace. He was the youngest son of General Xenophon. Mausolus had been right; there was a connection between the killer and the Hecatomnids. Years ago, when Artaxerxes II became king of Persia, his headstrong brother, Cyrus the Younger, hired someone to kill him – namely General Xenophon, supported by his Army of Ten Thousand Greeks.

Cyrus the Younger and his band of renegades gathered at Sardis with Xenophon and his army and began their march toward Babylon. In great secrecy, Cyrus the Younger and Xenophon planned every detail of their sure-fire overthrow; their surprise attack had all the markings of success. If not for the vigilance of one Persian satrap, Artaxerxes would have died, and Cyrus the Younger would have become the supreme ruler of Persia, establishing Xenophon as his second in command. By chance occurrence, Tissaphernes, a close friend and predecessor of Hecatomnus, discovered the seditious plot and reported the news to Artaxerxes II.

Tissaphernes' information gave an army of Persian loyalists time to strategise, and in a sneak counter-attack, they collapsed the revolt. Artaxerxes II killed Cyrus the Younger, and the Army of Ten Thousand Greeks scattered. Xenophon returned home to Athens, expecting a hero's welcome; instead, he suffered banishment for his mercenary efforts. Artaxerxes II prevailed and continued as the legitimate Shahanshah for another 50 years. Tissaphernes gained distinction, position, and wealth from added territories for his allegiance.

During the reign of Hecatomnus and later Mausolus, Xenophon lived in disgrace in Thrace, where he seethed with resentment. He spent his days writing historical accounts about wars, which included blaming all his woes on Tissaphernes. His ire expanded to encompass the Hecatomnid dynasty as well. Xenophon's oldest son, Gryllus, served with the cavalry, but when he died at the Battle of Mantinea, the much younger son, Cleon, joined the Greek infantry, becoming a peltast.

Due to his extended absences, as was typical of military life, Cleon arranged for his family to live with his mother – an Akkadian-speaking Babylonian whom Xenophon met in southern Mesopotamia. She now lived on Rhodes Island. He would join them there during his layoffs. Several years ago, Cleon secured passage from Thrace to Athens while going home for a visit. At Athens, he was hired as a guard, protecting a large cargo fleet carrying marble and construction materials destined for Rhodes.

Along the way, Artemisia intercepted the convoy, commandeered the ships, and put every last man overboard, including Cleon. Discovering a Hecatomnid had orchestrated the atrocity rekindled a simmering family hatred. His contempt for Caria and the unworthy successors of Tissaphernes escalated to a new level when considering the casual manner in which the arrogant satrap disposed of him and the rest of the crew.

Once safely ashore in Rhodes, Cleon approached Admiral Cyberniskos with a proposal. Aligned with no particular nation or king, Cleon sought personal vengeance. Considering his valuable military training, he saw an opportunity to grow wealthy by providing a beneficial service; at the same time, he would garner the admiration of his aging father. Cleon's driving force for eliminating Artemisia was revenge, respect, and wealth. With a mother, wife, and two young daughters to support, Cleon wanted to finish the lethal assignment, collect his money and put the Hecatomnid dynasty behind him forever.

Under torture, Cyberniskos revealed Cleon had departed Rhodes with his family and moved to a remote region near Labraunda. The pieces began coming together. I now understood why I crossed paths with this man in the wilderness; the injured mercenary must have spotted my campfire as he travelled home. I left Labraunda, heading for Halicarnassus, while he fled

Halicarnassus, trying to reach Labraunda. No doubt Cleon was resting comfortably at home as Goliath was dragging me away in the opposite direction.

Locating Cleon in the vast mountainous area around Labraunda would be difficult, but Goliath had a plan.

Chapter 50

The Confrontation

Goliath set up an information post and offered a reward for any reliable reports concerning foreigners settling in the vicinity. Finally, one trustworthy source came forward with important news; he knew of a foreign family living in the hills east of Labraunda.

Cleon would have heard of Admiral Cyberniskos' capture and moved his hideout; at least this information gave Goliath a starting point. The commander promptly organised two units of Dathaba to conduct grid searches in Labraunda and two more to scout out the hills to the east.

My strategy involved making a casual stop at the barbershop. Perhaps someone had a piece of vital information that would unknowingly reveal a helpful clue.

Animated as ever, Landers tended to a client while flailing his windmill arms, wagging tongue in unison. Waiting for my turn, I pottered around, chatting with customers and laughing with friends.

Stavros busied himself cleaning his station after his last client. Finally, I hollered out, "Stavros, how goes it with your hair-dyeing methods? Have you mistakenly used an extract of murex shell and given an unfortunate soul purple hair?" Everybody laughed.

He said, "I have time to dye your pretty curls. Come over here and have a seat on my couch."

"No, thank you, Stavros. I plan to keep the colour God intended for me. Whatever became of your last casualty, did he have to shave his head and move away to a remote island in the Aegean?"

"You, Ethan, have no confidence in me. That man did return and asked specifically to see me. To be sure, my reputation exceeds what you or Landers are willing to admit."

"Tell me, Stavros, has he an appointment today? Perhaps he lingers nearby, gathering courage for another visit?" Again the men laughed at our banter.

"If you must know, he left Halicarnassus. Seems like..." gazing upward as he thought, he continued. "Oh, I know, it was after Mehregan. Yes, a servant from his father's household came looking for him. His elderly father had fallen ill and sought his son's company to settle the family business before his death. Zeus knows the man will never get a decent shave among those disorganised Thracian barbarians."

His comment incited abundant laughter from the men in the barbershop. Of course, I laughed also, but I had learned vital information. After my visit, I reported to Goliath.

"This information explains much," said Goliath, "and clarifies the long interval between attacks. We anticipated a strike at the groundbreaking for the temp—" He came near to saying the word temple but caught his error. "While we were breaking ground for the Mausoleum, the man was far away, occupied in Thrace. During our trip to Pella also. I wonder if his dying father riled him further against the Hecatomnid dynasty.

"It makes sense that after his father's passing, Cleon returned to Halicarnassus, where he mistakenly killed Mausolus in an attempt to assassinate the queen. He will know we learned of his identity from Cyberniskos' torture. In Persia, he will live the life of an animal, hunted by men seeking to collect the bounty placed on his head. Desperation will drive him harder to fulfil his contract and leave."

Establishing the search grid proved valuable because a Dathaba unit returned with three prisoners: a woman and her two young daughters. Cleon's family. Pressing Cleon's wife for information was an effort in futility; if she did know his whereabouts, she would die before betraying her husband. However, Goliath had another idea; he would use the man's family as bait.

The woman and her children were detained overnight in a secure holding cell on the prisoner block of the courthouse. Merciful, the commander gave guards strict orders to respect the prisoners and provide fresh food, plenty of drinking water, and a comfortable sleeping pad. Early the following morning, we moved them away from the city to a more secure location – the windmills.

"Cleon has proven his ability," Goliath said. "He is resourceful, but now that we have his family, he will come out into the open. Ethan, we will fight our final battle with that man on this ground." He touched the taut skin of his scarred neck. Hate spurred the giant to fight; he relished the idea of a showdown.

Shackling our prisoners inside the mill sat ill with me. The oldest daughter, who I estimated to be five years old, spat at me when I secured her chains to the wall clamp. "Ktínos," she hissed. Kicking at me, she hissed, "Ktínos! Kovalos!"

Ashamed of my actions, I unconsciously glanced over my shoulder, half expecting to see the disapproving glower of my mother. While we had no plans to hurt the children, we did intend to kill their father.

I agree this action was cruel, but bear in mind, regardless of his righteous indignation, once Cleon decided to assassinate a vassal of the Persian Empire, he signed his death warrant and endangered his family. Sending his wife and children away months ago may have protected them, but he took no such precaution; perhaps, with his stealth and convincing disguises, he considered himself too clever to get caught. Who would suspect a shy family man of treason? His ingenious plan of living in plain sight under the nose of the Dathaba may have succeeded except for one reason; he came into my camp one Sabbath evening.

As a soldier and sworn defender of the empire, Goliath's duty obligated him to exact justice against the treasonous man. At the same time, we considered manhandling the children a terrible act. However, restraining the woman was a different matter. She fought us and had already scratched one guard and bitten another. I had compassion for her plight; she sought to protect her family as a she-bear protects her cubs. I admired her combatant spirit, but we gave her no margin for escape – thus the shackles. While we had no intention of punishing his family, we required hostages for our plan to succeed.

To keep the children warm and comfortable, we secured the family upstairs on a wooden platform instead of forcing them to sit on the cold stone floor. This second-storey location kept them out of harm's way if a battle ensued.

The dome-shaped roof did not connect with the frame of the mill; this gap allowed light to stream through the open area under the eaves. Bundles of cane stalks, attached to a central shaft by horizontal supports, held jib sails of triangular cloth attached to each arm. Once the wind caught these sails, the arms rotated on an axis and moved the cogs. Depending on the internal mechanism, these mills either pumped water or ground grain. We were in the larger mill used to grind grain from nearby villages. It smelled good inside, a mixture of dried grain, a sweet and powdery scent, with the slightest aroma of honey from the beeswax coating the wooden cogs. A thick timber door provided entry on the lower level, with another smaller door on the second-storey - Goliath locked that from the inside. Anchoring the mill arms required a brake mechanism to prevent moving, and then releasing the brake allowed the wind to fill the sails and again turn the cogs. I enjoyed the mill's clanging rhythm, but such clamour obstructed sneaking and inching noises, so Goliath ordered his men to restrain the arms. Besides the wind's natural ebbs and flows, our first night was uneventful, with no sign of Cleon.

Twelve of us remained on duty throughout the night: ten soldiers with the Dathaba unit, their commander Goliath, and me. Twelve against one, the odds favoured us. Goliath stationed four mobile guards around the perimeter and four stationary guards around the mill. Majid and Roozbeh remained inside with Goliath and me. (Interesting how things change. Once, those two men threatened to cut my ears off, and now we were comrades. I recently attended the feast given for Majid and his wife after the birth of their fourth son, where he again joked about cutting my ears off. That time it was funny.)

A replacement company of Dathaba arrived early the following day. Majid and Roozbeh remained on duty inside the mill while Goliath and I stepped out for fresh air, to relieve ourselves and then instruct new troops. A brief commotion occurred when the units overlapped with guards coming on duty and others going off duty. Men crawled out of hiding places, and others oriented themselves to the layout before moving into their assigned positions. Goliath glanced over his shoulder at one guard knocking on the mill door. The door opened, the man stepped through, the door closed again, and Goliath looked away.

When the new arrivals had settled into their positions, and the tired troops descended the forested hill, Goliath stepped into the woods to tend to personal business as I filled buckets with fresh water for our prisoners. No one had counted the number of incoming soldiers in the flurry of shift change. Instead of the expected ten soldiers, an eleventh soldier arrived unnoticed.

Majid and Roozbeh fell to the floor before either had time to greet their replacement. Cleon, dressed in the saffron uniform of the Dathaba, dragged their bleeding bodies away from the door leaving the soldiers in a heap under the staircase. Then, removing keys from the hook, he raced to the platform and unshackled his family while hushing their joyful cries.

As he carried his daughters down the stairs, the children clung to their father's neck, oblivious to the slaughter he had unleashed moments earlier. Then, at the door, Cleon instructed his family.

"Hush now, my daughters; you are safe. These Carian soldiers mean you no harm; they seek only me. Girls, would you like to play a game? Can you pretend to be bunnies running quietly through the woods? No, I have a better game."

"What game is that, Father?" The older one asked.

"Let's pretend a jinni lives in the woods. You can catch him if you run to the bottom of the hill. Catching a jinni means he must grant you a special wish. Would you like to receive a special wish?" "Yes, Father," she whimpered. "But we want you to chase the jinni with us."

"I know, my daughters. And I will, but first, I must stop the soldiers from scaring our jinni. I will hurry them away and send them down the hill and back into the city." He kissed the top of their heads with loving tenderness.

To his wife, he said, "I have created a distraction in the woods, giving you time to flee. When I open the door, stay close to the wall, and work your way around behind. If it looks safe, move across the clearing and escape into the thicket. Keep making your way down the hill until you reach the shore. Once there, remain hidden until you see my brother, Diodorus, in a small merchant vessel. He will be disguised as an aged man. Wait for him to signal before you approach. Dress the girls in the clothing he provides. No one will suspect a family traveling with an older man and two young boys. First, sail to Cnidus; from there, go to Thrace. You will be safe at my father's estate, and I will follow soon."

"Come with us now. Forget about this Persian family and let us sail for Thrace together," she begged.

"I cannot," Cleon told her. "What will become of my honour if I do not take revenge on my enemies? Do not ask me to suffer humiliation by refusing to exact vengeance on the man who dares to touch my family."

"My sword is strong, my husband. Ask Diodorus to escort the girls alone; I will stay here and fight the ktínos with you. Do not ask me to leave your side, not when I am begging to stay," his wife said.

"You must not! Go with Diodorus to protect our daughters. We shall be together within the month. Wait for me in Thrace, agápi mou. I will think of you every moment we are apart.

"Once you pass through this door, keep moving. Do not stop to rest. Do not look behind. Girls, obey Mitera and hold her hand. Can you be my brave girls?"

"Yes, Father."

Crying and hugging, Cleon affectionately kissed his family. Then, he told his wife, "I requested this assignment to please my father and to secure our future. I did not expect my mission to endanger you and the girls. I hope you can forgive me."

Crashing logs thundered from the lower woods in front of the mill, followed by yelling and the stampede of soldiers rushing to investigate. Cleon opened the door a crack. With no guards in sight, he pushed the door open further, kissed his wife, and sent his family out. They stayed close to the wall, crept around to the rear of the mill, and then bolted, disappearing from the ridgetop. Once they were out of sight, Cleon closed the door.

Combing the woods, Goliath and his men discovered a log snare set to ambush them. No doubt the device released prematurely. Concluding the ruse had failed, Goliath believed he remained one step ahead of the assassin and ordered his men to return to their posts.

He and I collected the buckets – each carrying two–and returned to our position inside the mill. Goliath set his bucket down and pounded his thunderous fist on the door. We waited for a response. The door opened halfway, the buckets were collected, and we slipped into the darkness of the mill. The door shut behind us, and I heard the latch slide across the jamb. Leaving bright sunlight behind, we needed a moment for our eyes to adjust to the dark.

Flash! White powder hit us square in the face, stinging our eyes and blinding us. I heard the swish of a sword leaving its scabbard, trailed by a distressed snarl coming from Goliath. Water splattered onto the floor, and I heard scuffling, but I was choking, and my eyes stung with burning pain.

"My eyes! I cannot see!" I yelled!

I heard Goliath's agitated breaths. "Use the water, Ethan!"

Tussling footfalls shuffled back and forth on the stone floor, and I heard the sound of a sword slicing through the air. I was like a blind man searching for his cane, padding around on my knees until my hand touched the bucket. I splashed its entire contents on my face, soothing my stinging eyes. My vision returned, but I was baffled by what I saw. One of the Dathaba from our unit stood in the centre of the room wielding Goliath's sword against him. Drenched in water with patches of congealed flour stuck to his face and uniform, Goliath had blood streaming from his right arm. Backing away, weaving and bobbing, he dodged the deadly blade brandished against him by one of our own.

I yelled, "Ho! You there! Stop! You mistakenly fight the commander!" I needed to bring daylight into the room, so the man would recognise he had attacked the wrong person. Fumbling my way to the door, I found the latch was stuck, jimmied from the inside, preventing the door from opening. Soldiers on the outside rattled the latch and pounded on the door. I yelled, "Find a log! Smash the door!"

Goliath shouted, "Ethan!" I wheeled around. "Ethan! Find me a sword!" The crazed man then honed in on me and moved sideways, keeping Goliath between us. When he turned toward me, I recognised his face: Cleon! He had trapped us inside the mill. Filled with a sickening dread, I realised we had once again underestimated the talent and stealth of this cunning adversary. Cleon had incapacitated us both the moment we walked into the darkened mill – he locked the exit, blinded us with flour, and disarmed Goliath while inflicting a slicing glance on his combat arm.

"Ethan, a sword!" he yelled again.

I drew my sword from its sheath, yelled, "Catch!" and lobbed the weapon toward Goliath. He caught the hilt mid-air, but his wound sent a stream of blood past his wrist, making the hilt too slippery to control. Transferring the blade to his left hand, he stepped back into the fight, brutally returning Cleon's blows, slashing and chopping toward him.

I hurried to the staircase, rolled Majid slightly, and removed his sword from the sheath. He moaned and called my name, but I had no time to assist him. "Do not despair, Majid; I will return for you."

My heart pounded, thumping in my ears like a water trip hammer as I advanced, also engaging the enemy. Cleon quickly overwhelmed my ability with the speed at which he slashed and combatted my weapon. Iron smashed against iron. I fought mightily to counter his moves, but he expected little competition from me; fighting me was more of a lark than a serious threat.

Keeping Goliath in his peripheral focus, Cleon toyed with me as I concentrated on the deadly blade of a killer's sword. I skittered from side to side, looking for my chance.

Use your body as your first weapon, Ethan; the blade will follow. Remembering Goliath's words fortified me like a bronze wall. I stopped reacting and leaned in to Cleon's strikes. I became the weapon.

The assassin moved swiftly, lite on his feet, handling his blade with uncanny precision in this two-against-one battle. Finding an opening, he struck hard against Goliath's hand, lopping off a finger. The giant's weapon fell to the stone floor with a loud clang. Sneering, Cleon raised his sword for the kill, but I moved in to protect Goliath. Cleon spun and knocked my sword away with a terrific strike. My thumb snapped, immobilising my right hand with stinging numbness.

Still far from his sword, Goliath grabbed a water bucket. Holding the rope, he whipped the bucket around and around at Cleon's head while inching closer to his weapon. Then, pounding the bucket downward while towering over his opponent, he targeted Cleon's head and the back of his hand. Around and around, Goliath whipped the heavy bucket, gaining momentum with each swing. Goliath's pummelling kept Cleon's attention off me, so with my left hand, I unsheathed Ajax.

Cleon broke away, lifted his sword, and swung – colliding blade against bucket – sending pieces of wood flying across the room, leaving Goliath holding a limp piece of rope.

Out of range from his weapon, the giant wound the rope around his hands and pulled it taut. Cleon thrust his sword forward. Goliath pivoted on his front foot, side-stepped, and came in from an angle to grab Cleon's wrist. With one hand in control of his opponent's sword arm, Goliath used his other hand to encircle the rope around Cleon's neck like a spider wrapping its prey in a web.

Cleon countered by pivoting his sword toward Goliath's neck, and then, with a sweeping motion, kicked Goliath's foot out from under him. The giant went down on one knee, allowing Cleon to regain control. The assassin had found his moment.

With both hands gripping the hilt of his sword, he raised his arms, preparing for a heavy strike to hammer the deadly blade through Goliath's skull. I had one chance. Leaping forward, I screamed, "Yhoa!" and reached toward Cleon's throat with my dulled right hand.

As I expected, he turned his head slightly, lifting his chin away to dodge my grasp. Then, with a slight twist of his shoulders, he stepped back. This move allowed me to come around with my left hand and plunge Ajax into his side.

I thrust the shaft hard, sending it deep between his ribs, causing a hissing sound. Pinkish blood foamed from the wound. His body contorted off kilter. He coughed. As blood ran from his mouth, Cleon's eyes grew wild with fear. Instinctively, he shoved me off, smashing me against the wall where I slid to the floor. Dropping his sword, he pulled against the hilt of my dagger protruding from his side!

Goliath retrieved his weapon. Wrapping his fingers around the hilt, he secured his second hand under the first and, with the furore of an Olympic discus thrower, spun around shouting a thunderous yell, "For Mausolus!" Extending his arms, he connected the sharp blade against Cleon's neck with such force the man's head became entirely severed. His legs buckled, and his lifeless body crumpled to the floor.

Scrambling away from the mess, I found my sword, broke off the door latch, and pushed it open. Soldiers ran in while I stumbled out and collapsed, spewing several times. After a while, Goliath emerged blood-soaked, missing a finger, and rubbing his red, swollen eyes. Shaking from the rush of battle, he came over and stood beside me, where I sat shivering, unable to speak.

Using his trouser leg, he wiped Cleon's blood off my dagger. "We did it, Ethan! We got him! You fought well, son." he said laying Ajax on the ground beside me while squeezing my shoulder. I nodded while trying to steady my breathing.

"We have to help Majid and Roozbeh," I said.

"Majid died, Ethan. I sat with him. He was able to explain what transpired inside the mill. He said Roozbeh fell instantly without suffering."

Replaying the battle in his mind, Goliath said to no one, "The water saved us. If not for silly wooden buckets…" His voice tapered off, thinking of our narrow escape.

"When did you develop such skill for bucket combat?" I asked.

"I have an assortment of skills. Secret moves. Perhaps I will teach you someday."

"I look forward to the day when bucket battles become an Olympic sport."

Levity ended when the Dathaba carried out our dead comrades, laying their corpses side by side on the ground. Troops returned to the mill and collected the headless body of Cleon, son of Xenophon, husband, father of two young daughters, peltast, and mercenary hired to assassinate the satrap queen of Caria - the slayer of Mausolus.

Staggering to my feet, I entered the mill, found a basket, and dumped out the remnants of grain. Then, grabbing a shock of messy red hair, I placed the severed head in the container and secured the lid. I carried it down the hill, into the city, and entered the Harbour Garden. Finding a bench beside the quiet path winding in front of a gurgling fountain, I set the basket in a visible location near Artemisia's favourite flower bed.

"Today, we exacted vengeance for the death of Mausolus. May you now find peace, my queen," I whispered, then walked away.

Chapter 51

A Second Funeral

Sound asleep beneath a tangle of soft, warm blankets; I was startled awake when Goliath burst into my room. Throwing my vest and trousers at my feet, he said, "Get up! Something has happened!" One leg in my trousers, struggling with the other leg, I tried to keep up. By the graveness of his voice, something serious had happened. Running after him, I held my vest in one hand and sandals in the other. The new day dawning in twilight hues of purple and orange offered defused light as I followed him from the barracks into the city and toward the Mausoleum.

A courtyard lion chilled me as I supported myself against its cold body to tighten my sandals and straighten my clothes. Fussing at the grand staircase attracted my attention. Several guards stood whispering amongst themselves while looking at a pile of linen, white and discarded, perhaps left by someone during the night. To be sure, Artemisia's wrath would blaze against someone for breaking her decree concerning the sacred tenth step.

Struggling to understand the situation, I studied the horizontal shape. *What is all the fuss?* I wondered. Then, a whisper kissed my cheek as a gentle breeze enveloped me in a familiar scent –ginger oil.

Then I saw them: tiny bare feet protruding beneath a luxurious dress of white fabric. I froze with sickening dread once recognising painted violets and a sash of matching silk wrapping a dainty waist where rested manicured fingers intertwined over a dagger housed in a jewelled sheath. A purple robe wrapped the figure's arms. Flakes of sparking gold trailed along her neck and chest. Without consent, my disobedient eyes continued looking until I perceived the lovely face of Artemisia II, satrap queen of the district of Caria.

Dazzling braids of thick dark hair, woven with a string of pearls, cascaded from beneath her head, resting on the exact spot where Mausolus last held her

– the tenth step where her husband fell and bled and died. Beside her lay an empty vial of lethal conium.

Artemisia had left us. In a daring escape to end her misery, she hastened her journey to join Mausolus somewhere across the Dark River in the kingdom of Yama.

Through streaming tears, my stare locked onto the dainty earrings, tastefully accentuating her loveliest feature, her ears. When one guard moved away to speak with another, I spied, to my horror, a familiar basket – the container holding Cleon's head, the one I brought from the mill and placed in Artemisia's favourite garden. The world spun. I lost my footing and collapsed. My gesture of love had killed Artemisia.

Unable to look away, my eyes fixated on the scene. Artemisia looked peaceful, as if she had laid back to watch the twinkling stars and then fell asleep, but I knew better.

Goliath stepped between me and the queen to block my view. He stood me on my feet. "Do not consider her death your fault, Ethan. Let go of this burden; her death has nothing to do with you." He took hold of my shoulders, dwarfing them beneath his giant hands. I looked at Artemisia again, but he turned me away from the sight. "Look at me, Ethan." Struggling to obey, I tried focusing my eyes, but light-headedness caused Goliath's face to appear blurry, like a melting candle. Finally, concentrating on his warped face, I watched the movement of his lips, garbling words strangely distorted and drawn-out.

"Ethan!" he snapped at me. "Her death belongs to her and no one else. Your act was a gift so that Artemisia could leave in peace. Permit her spirit to go free. The queen lived life her way and on her terms. Today, she chose to die her way. Her flight from Earth is hers alone to bear." Clasping my shoulders, he shook, bringing me back, insisting I acknowledge his words.

Dathaba murmured about the basket left on the step without grasping the significance. Before anybody peered inside, Goliath distracted them. "I will tend to this item. You men, notify the priests. Thuxra, stay with the queen, post a barrier to keep people away, and somebody, bring a robe to cover her body." He walked away with the basket, and I never inquired of its fate.

As priests had once arrived to collect Mausolus' remains, the same men now lifted the lifeless body of Queen Artemisia II of Caria onto a cot and carried her away. As is the custom, she received preparation rituals for her long journey. For the second time in two years, priests built a funeral pyre in a courtyard once intended as an exclusive gathering place for the world's most privileged. Again construction stopped, and Halicarnassus gathered to bid farewell to their queen.

Onto the pyre, priests lowered the body of a woman – the once graceful queen with dancing eyes and pillowy lips. That fetching diplomat, perfumed and sensual, wearing jingling bangles of gold whose tiny feet barely touched the ground as she walked.

Priests layered brushwood and tinder sticks, tucking fuel around her frail body. Again I heard prayers and gentle words as the priest tortured me with his suspended flame. "To the air. To the water. To the soil. To the fire."

And then his hand slackened, releasing the fiery torch of destruction. First came a slight waft of smoke followed by an all-consuming pillar of combustible rage stealing Artemisia from us. Scorching flames leaped higher, forcing priests to move aside.

Public moans of emotional pain floated in echoing cries through the air. While sadness filled me, it was different than with Mausolus; I did not join in with broken-hearted weeping as others did. Watching grey smoke rise heavenward, swirling past fluted pillars for immobile gods, I finally understood Artemisia's last words to me, "The gods have turned me into a beggar." What would I have done differently had I known I would never see her again?

On that Sun Day, I visited her in the Harbour Garden. She had experienced another one of her nightmares and fought an intense depression. Staring into nothingness, shadows of pain darkened her face. I held her hand as we sat in silence beneath a canopy of shade. Musical chimes tinkled nearby. Finally, she spoke. "I envy you, Ethan. Your life is simple, and the God you worship sustains you. I worship many gods, yet I have lost confidence in them all. You have an accord with your God while I have become a beggar to mine."

Nonsense, I thought. Artemisia, the graceful queen, living in a luxurious palace in a legendary city adorned by a world-renowned masterpiece reaching heights beyond the clouds, how could she consider herself a beggar?

She continued, "The gods have turned me into a beggar. I implored them, but they refused me an audience. They have granted me no clemency despite my grovelling pleas for mercy. Therefore, my sin knows no cure; no medicine can heal my shame. Instead of soothing me, their cruel silence only deepens my wounds."

Artemisia worshiped many gods; I did not know which of her gods was the god of redemption. I wanted to tell her of David's Prayer, 'O God of unfailing love, cleanse me from my sins,' but instead I remained silent. *Best saved for another time*, I thought.

She continued, "I have nothing left to offer and no words to speak. Once the assassin's arrow plunged into Mausolus' back, the Fates condemned me to a life of suffering. Shame and guilt, like twin gods from Hades, have taken me captive, tethering me to my crime. Despite my endless pleas, I cannot escape their whispers."

Covetous ambition had set into motion a machination as merciless as Leviathan conjuring up an unbearable rubric. Artemisia, powerless to stop the whirlwind, could not rein back the creature she had unleashed. Its growing mutiny treated the queen as valueless; as a shard of broken clay while wielding cruel tricks of its own. Death became her only escape from persecution, and I imagine she perceived taking her own life as a noble gesture, following in the footsteps of her heroine, Artemisia I.

In sorrow, I allowed Artemisia to float away in peace. Flames danced, lapping against the mounds of tinder, indiscriminately consuming the corpse of a satrap queen. Kissing my fingers, touching them against my broken heart, I felt the polished chert she had once given me. Rubbing its smooth surface, I pondered her words: "Should you find it necessary to communicate with me or if you have important information to share..." At that moment, I did want to communicate with her. I wanted to see the wind blow wisps of hair away from her face as she strolled through her garden, a bundle of tulips filling her arms. Artemisia's stone remains in my pocket, ever near my heart.

After the pyre cooled, Moza swept the queen's ashes into a golden urn while preparations got underway for another event at the Mausoleum – a commemoration service.

On this upcoming memorial day, a priest would bring Mausolus' alabaster urn out of the Mausoleum and place it on the presentation table outside the bronze doors. After much prayer and ritual, the chief Zoroastrian priest would join the ashes of the satrap couple together into one vessel, binding their souls for eternity. After securing the jewelled urn inside the Mausoleum, the bronze doors would close, and according to Artemisia's decree, a massive stone would seal the entrance. Forever beneath a spray of diamond stars, the spirits of Mausolus and Artemisia would hover in quiet solitude between panelled walls of turquoise, accentuated with white, red, and black striped sardonyx and red Odem stone.

This upcoming commemoration service required a plan, and I needed help from a trusted friend, Landers.

The area around the courtyard and parádeisos resembled a debris field with pieces of stone and scattered equipment. Workers cleared a path through the rubble, providing room within the courtyard for a handful of citizens to stand. Others observed from a distance while privileged guests, nobles, city officials, family members, and a few friends, along with myself, stood at the top of the grand staircase just outside the bronze doors.

I gradually inched my way forward, careful not to draw unwanted attention, moving as close as possible to the presentation table. Casually I fumbled with the cord dangling from my neck, which held a pouch hidden inside my vest, its mouth stretched open and waiting. The urn containing Mausolus' ashes lay two cubits before me; the container holding Artemisia rested beside his. The anxious priest acted as if removing the lids might cause the satraps' imprisoned spirits to escape. He wasted no time initiating funerary proceedings with loud, flashy prayers.

Townsfolk bowed their heads, muttering private words to themselves; others wailed at the top of their voices, arms pleading, outstretched toward the heavens. Landers stood in the crowd, awaiting my signal – bringing my yellow headband down to my neck and then putting it back in place. Perfect timing was the crucial factor in determining my success.

Waiting. Waiting. The priest, at last, moved far enough away from the presentation table, allowing me to move into position. I pulled my headband down as if nonchalantly straightening my hair and then put it back again. Landers caught my signal and ran to the stairs alive with energy and enthusiasm. Sidestepping the guards in a dramatic episode of uncontrollable grief, he convulsed and wailed, rolling around, kicking his legs in the air.

Landers was a Halicarnassus landmark; he tended to most aristocrats, court administrators, and guards. I anticipated his behaviour would be considered non-threatening and accepted as a strange part of his effeminate manner. As predicted, his dramatic performance became hugely believable; I felt tempted to stop my task and watch him myself as he wailed, twisting and rolling. The priests turned and moved toward him as people rushed over to soothe the pain of a grieving citizen.

With enormous trepidation, I approached the open containers while Landers distracted the crowd. Seizing one handful of Mausolus' ashes and one handful of Artemisia's ashes, I put their cinders into my pouch, pulled strings closed, and returned to my place. When no one discovered my act, I congratulated my stealth with a long sigh of relief. After consoling Landers, people turned their attention back to the ceremony, none the wiser to our scheme.

Priests resumed the combining ritual of joining Mausolus and Artemisia for eternity, then carried their joint urn into the Mausoleum. After returning, a few more words were spoken. The double bronze doors closed. I heard the mournful sound of a bolt sliding across the jamb, connecting with gears. Then, a metallic click. The priest tested the bolt. Locked.

The lift team hoisted an enormous stone, securing it tight against the entrance. And with that, the Age of Mausolus came to an end.

Chapter 52

Goodbye Glorious City

After the interment ceremony joining Mausolus and Artemisia, I delivered a basket of fresh pastries to Landers, congratulated him on his impressive performance, then headed to my quarters at the barracks. I stopped mid-stride. My personal property sat out front, and Thuxra came out the door carrying an armful of my clothes. The look on his face indicated he disapproved of the task given to him.

"Orders," he told me. "King Idrieus and Queen Ada have taken over the district, and Idrieus wants you moved out. I am sorry, Ethan; my Lord Mausolus treated you as a son, as did the queen. The troops enjoy having you here as well. This harsh treatment against you is unnecessary, but we must obey orders."

"I understand, Thuxra. I appreciate your friendship." Then, gathering my property into a bundle, I departed, seeking accommodations in the city.

Idrieus and Ada – the new vassals. Since first meeting them, Ada had treated me with kindness and open acceptance, but I cannot say the same for Idrieus and his absurd jealousy. Chiding and suspicious, he used every opportunity to find something wrong with me. The more Mausolus took me under his wing, the more Idrieus fumed. He especially did not appreciate my presence at family activities and had a way of looking past me as if I were invisible. But, when he did acknowledge me, his glances carried cruel overtones.

Ho, to be sure, his arrogant dismissal became open abhorrence once people of the district counted me as Mausolus' son. He boiled whenever citizens referred to me as Caria's prince. Mausolus had chosen me to become his student, and I became an eager apprentice of his governance, yet Idrieus' cynical mind conjured up baseless suspicions, questioning my intentions.

With a large crowd of visitors in town for the satrap's memorial, I found no vacant rooms in Halicarnassus for lodging. I accepted the last available space in a billet hut on the Pedasa Slope. As if I had devoured too much food, life changed faster than my mind could digest. The world was spinning out of control; I needed to catch my balance and organise my thoughts. I found respite by spending several days alone in the solitude of the hill country concealed beneath the forest canopy, eating fruit from the trees, drinking water from the streams, and napping on pine needles carpeting shady nooks.

Beloved Mausolus and Artemisia had departed, yet I was obligated to continue living despite my terrible loss. And I wanted to continue living with Jaleh. I loved her and wanted to marry her. Confident she would marry me, I formulated a plan for our future, which I believed Goliath would approve. I would support his daughter by resuming my position as a stonemason in Jerusalem. We would live in my parents' home until we found our own place. His daughter would always be provided for, cared for, and loved. So, with joy in my heart, I returned to Halicarnassus.

Along the way, I practised my speech. "Commander, I must discuss a matter of most importance…" No, too aggressive. "Commander, you no doubt realise, Jaleh and I…" No, too assuming. Perhaps, "Commander, I love your daughter and want to marry her." Curious stares from passers-by had little effect on my verbal preparation – the most important conversation of my life; I wanted to get it right.

Standing at Goliath's front door, mentally outlining the main points of my proposal, I ran my fingers through my windblown hair, steadied myself, lifted the latch, and walked in. Thuxra stood in the living room with his family. His children ran through the house, and his wife smiled, her arms holding a bundle of kitchen utensils.

Thuxra said, "They left, Ethan."

"Has the new king moved the commander to a larger residence?"

"No, Ethan, they left Halicarnassus."

Stunned, I asked, "Left? No! Why would they leave?"

He explained, "Idrieus. He has wrongfully blamed the commander for the death of his brother and accused him of negligence in protecting the queen. He sent the entire family to Persepolis."

"What assignment was he given? No doubt guarding the Shahanshah or his family." I said.

"The commander will manage the kennels."

"Kennels? What kennels?" I asked.

"Shelters for the king's dogs."

"He will train the king's dogs?" I asked.

"No, Ethan, he will only clean their enclosures." Thuxra tried hiding his embarrassment.

"This is lunacy! Why did no one say goodbye before leaving or inform me of their departure? I would have joined them!"

"Ethan, the commander searched for you, he sent the boys looking everywhere throughout the city, but no one knew where you had gone. The entire family wept, mainly Jaleh. She refused to leave Halicarnassus without you, but her father hoisted her over his shoulder and carried her kicking and screaming onto the ship, transporting them to the Port of Issus."

Sickened by this news, my stomach churned, and my legs wobbled. The room spun, and my arms grew limp.

"The girl left a gift for you."

Thuxra handed me a miniature basket woven by Jaleh. I removed the lid and nestled inside was a loop of her thick black hair tied in a bow of spear grass. My heart leaped at her message. Jaleh and I used the excuse of collecting spear grass to go off alone, but instead of collecting grass, we spent hours kissing. Simin must have suspected when we returned home with big smiles, carrying few sheaves.

Like water running through my fingers, I felt powerless to keep those I loved from slipping away. In the blink of an eye, my entire world had vanished, taking my purpose and belonging with it. I felt abandoned. What reason did I have for remaining in Halicarnassus now?

For the first time in years, home beckoned; I needed to return to my province and my people. I would tell my family about Jaleh and my life in Halicarnassus. Then, after a time of rest, I would travel to Persepolis, find Goliath, and marry his daughter. Imagine the joy on Jaleh's face when I walked through the door. I would take her in my arms and again kiss her rosebud lips. Then, I would reach inside my vest and take out a bundle of buttercups tied with a crimson cord as Sakeri had done. With Jaleh by my side, we would have a wonderful life together in Jerusalem.

Halicarnassus lay still and quiet as I walked her precious streets one last time. A cloudless sky promised a superb day for sailing. The sun rose in soft rays glistening across marble stones. I protected Jaleh's basket between layers of Persian clothing tucked inside the travel satchel Mausolus had given me for our trip to Pella. Then, using a robe, I cushioned Mausolus' game of Technê, the one his father Hecatomnus had given him. Artemisia gifted it to me after he died. She said she wanted me to have something Mausolus especially loved.

If Idrieus discovered I had this precious heirloom, he would call me a thief and arrest me. Who remained to vouch for my character or attest that Artemisia bequeathed the set to me? Idrieus would enjoy watching me fall into the Tower of Ash; he may pull the lever himself. Sensing an urgency, I chose to leave the city without delay, but first, I needed to say goodbye.

Walking toward the Mausoleum of Halicarnassus, I picked my way through the vast courtyard, skirting cranes and carts, blocks of stone, and other construction materials. Greenstone blocks overlaid in stucco were evolving into the courtyard wall, and several completed sculptures stood in line for hoisting. By nightfall, the mounting team would have these statues installed on blue limestone bases, standing for eternity on the ledge around the Grand View. I ran my hands across each stone face chiselled perfectly by the famous sculptors I had befriended. Tipping my head back to absorb the monument's fantastic height, I recalled the day I hollered into the sky from its uppermost platform. With a new look, I appreciated the colourful frieze panels capturing antiquity's most acclaimed moments. Every dull session I endured posing and modelling as a famous character now became a sense of pride. I felt stirring gratitude for the privilege of contributing to their story.

I climbed the steps to the massive stone in front of sealed bronze doors – no one would ever enter that sacred dwelling. I once heard Artemisia tell Idrieus and Ada, "Mausolus and I built this city, and we built this Mausoleum. You may have our city and take our palace when we are gone. Yes, enjoy every one of our exceptional possessions, but the Mausoleum remains mine to enjoy with Mausolus; it belongs to us alone so that our love may transcend death."

I pressed my hands against the enormous barrier, hoping to feel the presence of my friends resting on the other side. I thanked Mausolus for the privilege of knowing him and for treating me as a son. Then, pressing harder into the stone, I said out loud, "Know this, my Lord, your efforts will not go in vain; I promise to uphold the valuable lessons you saw fit to teach me. As I am today, I will forever be your son, and you will be my noble Persian father." I told Artemisia I loved her and wished her life had ended differently.

277

Wiping tears off my face while heading down the grand staircase, I wondered if I would ever again find my way back home to Halicarnassus. Once proud of my contribution to this Mausoleum, I no longer felt sentiment in my handiwork. Standing on the tenth step, the exact spot where Mausolus' blood flowed, the place Artemisia chose to die, I questioned the Mighty One, the God who holds the wind in His fist. Why had He allowed these tragic deaths? In my exquisite sorrow, I expected the sun to grow dark and the stars of heaven to burn out and fall one by one into the sea. A sad and lonely world closed in around me.

I removed the elephant I had finished carving from my satchel. Since I could not gift it to Mausolus as intended, I hid the ivory piece within the partly assembled wall so no one would discover it. If Mausolus knew of this gift, he would jest at my attempt to carve the large-eared beast. I imagined him looking over my sculpture, saying, "Ethan, you are a genius! Look how masterfully you have sculpted my prized stallion, Lailapás!" I laughed out loud.

The sun rose higher in the sky, and the city began awakening to another day. Turning my back to the Mausoleum, I descended the terraced steps into the agora, and greeted my favourite baker.

Anticipating my usual request, he wrapped three pastries without my asking. I also purchased a loaf of almond bread to sustain me on my trip. Next, I stopped at a vendor booth, selected his thickest, most colourful Persian carpet as a gift for my mother, then headed for the harbour where the Paralos III was making ready for its departure to Joppa.

As a young man, I had walked beside this busy harbour, believing slavery on a Persian warship had become my fate. But this time, the threat came from the Stoa of Aegea. Up ahead, I saw Thuxra directing his unit of Dathaba, searching the harbour and the Stoa, looking for me. Idrieus had sent his new commander to hunt me down. Sidestepping, I dropped behind several freight containers, but I was not fast enough, and he spotted me. My heart froze.

Crouched low and peering through a narrow crack, I watched familiar faces – my friends – frantically searching for my whereabouts. Hiding from Idrieus reminded me of something Mausolus said, "Ethan, be wary of weak men. A weak man will seek to push you down; strong men can afford to lift others up."

Thuxra shouted to his men, "To the Tripylon Gate on the double-quick! Perhaps he circled back, hoping to escape to Ephesus!" As his men hurried in the opposite direction of my location, Thuxra turned toward me. I stood to reveal myself. Instead of arresting me, he thumped his arm across his chest; I returned the gesture, and after a moment, he turned and hurried after his men.

I had escaped Idrieus like a bird escaping a fowler's snare. Thuxra demonstrated his noble character the day he spared my life.

Standing on the deck of the Paralos III, watching the familiar red-tiled roofs disappear into the distance, I imagined the waves of the Aegean washing in and out against the shoreline, removing my footprints as if to erase me from the city. To be sure, Idrieus would nullify my contributions to Halicarnassus. I recalled Artemisia's fear of 'slipping away unnoticed from broken memories, struggling to survive in the emptiness of space.' No one would ever remember I was here - me, Ethan, son of Mausolus, Prince of Caria.

But now I had one final task. Lingering about, watching until no one could observe me, I slid my hand inside my vest and removed the pouch containing the combined ashes of Mausolus and Artemisia. Treasuring the affection they once showed me, I wanted to bless them in a special way. I wanted to give them something they both loved: the sea. Untying the pouch, I shook out their ashes and watched as the wind swirled the rulers of Caria high into the air before blowing them across the surface of the water, forever joining their spirits with the greatness of the Aegean.

For a brief moment, two dolphins appeared alongside our ship before changing course, leaping away into open waters. I recalled something else Artemisia told me. "Mausolus is like the Aegean, resilient, constant, and ever-present." Oh, I hoped the spirit of the satrap king of Caria would remain resilient and ever-present in these azure waters of the sea.

Gazing in the direction of Halicarnassus, I ended my Persian life with a low bow of farewell. Then, turning away, I worked my way to the ship's bow and set my sights ahead to the future.

Chapter 53

Jerusalem, Fourth Year of Darius III

For various reasons, my plans changed after returning home to Judah. Instead of regaling my family with fascinating details about my Persian life, I remained silent and scarcely mentioned Halicarnassus. I never did travel to Persepolis to find Goliath, nor did I marry Jaleh.

I dreamed of her often, though. Plato once told me, "Every heart sings a song, incomplete until another heart whispers back." Indeed, Jaleh Joon had whispered back to my heart. Pleasant evenings found me in a clearing on the Mount of Olives stretched out, gazing at stars. I named the brightest star after Jaleh and hoped that wherever she was, she would see it shining from heaven. If we both noticed the same star at the exact moment, perhaps our whispers of love would find each other.

My wistful nostalgia stopped after I married Hadassah. On the first star-filled evening before our wedding, I made my way up the mountain one last time and said goodbye to my lovely Jaleh Joon, vowing never again to speak her name.

I also dreamed of Artemisia. In my dreams, her onyx statue – the one carved by Timotheus, which stood beside Mausolus in the Diamond Room – awakened, and the lovely woman with the star-kissed brow came to me. Smelling of sweet ginger oil, she sat beside me, talking about Mausolus and the halcyon days in Halicarnassus building their monument. Once, she appeared as a warrior queen dressed to fight the Rhodians.

After I quit blaming myself for her death, the dreams stopped. Still, I sometimes struggle with the paradox of my heart – secretly cherishing the exquisite queen of Caria while pitying the wanton ruler who chased headlong after the wind until she ended up alone like a solitary flagpole standing on a distant mountain peak.

At times I found it necessary to wrestle my mind away from the thought of Idrieus relaxing in Mausolus' lounge, drinking from his golden rhyton while puffing on one of his favourite pipes. Sometimes I would visualise the new satrap bragging to his friends about the collection of wild animal hides he acquired from the jungle or pointing out his assortment of poems written by Homer and incorrectly positioning diorama soldiers on the battlefield of Troy.

Goliath had collected the bounty on Cleon and awarded me the money – probably thinking the fortune would secure a good life for his only daughter after our forthcoming marriage. Combining the reward money with the wages I earned working for Mausolus and Artemisia, I paid for schooling and became educated as a water supply engineer. With the remaining funds, I opened a lucrative business in Jerusalem. I named my company Lailapás after Mausolus' horse. 'Hurricane' sounded like a fitting name for a water business. My professional focus revolved around flood control, devising clean water systems, and practical sewage disposal.

As Mausolus had once taken a chance on me, giving me the position of a construction foreman, I paid the gift forward by hiring Hadassah's nephew, Esli, the somewhat reckless son of her brother. He worked alongside my son, Baruch and Skari, the firstborn son of Caleb and Hulda. Together the three boys managed construction projects, repairs, and maintenance, thus freeing me to draft creative water-related designs. For example, I created private plunge pools, household tubs, and steam spas. Using my masonry skills, I designed ornamental water gardens like those I had seen in Pella.

My favourite creation was a double-sided bathroom in my home. One half held a bathing tub similar to the ones I enjoyed in Halicarnassus, while the other half contained my private húdōr. Ho, to be sure, an elegant húdōr remains a respectable extravagance I have no guilt in possessing.

Years after Mausolus and Artemisia died (roughly fifteen years), a young man named Alexander of Macedon set out with his army to destroy the entire Persian Empire. Satrapies crumbled into chaos as Alexander advanced, crushing Persian city after Persian city. I had not anticipated seeing that sprightly young boy from Pella, but I did – the day he and Ptolemy rode into Jerusalem.

When I heard Alexander had crossed the Hellespont with an army, I began paying close attention to their movements and used my maps to plot the advancement of his troops. Alexander's first stop on Persian soil was visiting

Troy to honour his hero, Achilles. Standing on Thicket Ridge, the young conqueror threw his spear into the ground, signifying he accepted Asia as a gift from the gods. After anointing himself and offering sacrifices to his fallen ancestors, he marched his army north to engage the Persians.

Gathering an army to fight the Macedonians proved more difficult than King Darius III imagined. By consensus, Persians trusted in their superiority. They assumed disbanding Alexander's menial army would require minimal effort and saw no threat from the tiny nation of Greek inferiors. Trained mercenaries put together a small militia under the leadership of local satraps, hoping to stop this petty invasion at the Granicus River.

The Macedonians' attack was swift and brutal, causing the unprepared Persian cavalry to retreat. This collapse of bravery struck fear into the infantry, who also withdrew. The outcome of Alexander's first battle? The Persian death toll was high, while the Macedonian victory at Granicus River became legendary, reflecting the military cunning of a genuine threat: Alexander of Macedon.

His next strike was at the neighbouring town of Sardis. Terrified citizens never forgot the day Persian King Darius I destroyed the city as a punishment for their resistance. This time, Sardinians humbly surrendered, and the Macedonians spared them. Alexander led his army city by city, advancing further, liberating the Persian-held settlements along the Aegean Sea, which landed him at Halicarnassus.

How would Mausolus have dealt with the invading Greek army? The satrap was Grecian at heart, Persian in duty, with Hector as his paragon of leadership. Alexander's hero, Achilles, killed Mausolus' hero, Hector. Would the descendants of these two men again battle over a city, or would Mausolus avoid ruin by handing over Halicarnassus to protect it? Would he pledge alliance with the Macedonians, retaining power by serving as a vassal to Alexander? I know that history would tell a different story had Mausolus lived long enough to take part in the invasion of the Macedonians.

Survivors from the Granicus River Battle regrouped inside the protective walls of Halicarnassus along with several hazarabam of the 10,000 Immortals. Alexander predicted an easy defeat, razing Halicarnassus with minimal exertion, but failed to anticipate Mausolus' fortified walls. Alexander never lost a battle, but he came close to losing this one. Trying to destroy

Halicarnassus dealt a hard blow to the overall strength of the Macedonian army.

After acquiring Halicarnassus, the army continued destroying Persia's naval bases along the Aegean coastline before traveling inland to Gordium in Phrygia. Remember the knot I previously mentioned tied by King Gordias? Alexander wanted a go at untangling it, so he visited the oracle at Telmissus. After carefully studying the mysterious gnarl from all sides, he removed his sword and sliced the knot in two.

Next, he sneaked undetected through the Cilician Gates, gaining an invaluable military position near Issus. The battle-ready Greeks eagerly anticipated their first engagement with the Shahanshah, Darius III. Codomannus – the name Macedonians gave Darius III – woefully outnumbered Alexander two to one.

Undeterred by numbers, Alexander attacked, annihilating Persia's troops, including a regiment of 10,000 Immortals. King Darius fled the battlefield after seeing tens of thousands of his finest soldiers massacred.

Jews were anguished in paralytic fear, and inhabitants throughout the Judean countryside prayed for Alexander to take his troops eastward into the desert, leading his soldiers away from the land of Israel. After the victorious Battle of Issus, the young conqueror fought the urge to advance his men in an easterly direction toward Babylon, Ecbatana, and Persepolis. He was anxious to achieve his celestial mission – kill the fire-worshiping barbarians.

As their leader, Alexander cared about the safety of his men. Before continuing east to Persia's epicentre, Alexander thought it best to protect his rear troops by negating the power of the Persian Navy, including threats coming from Phoenician coastal cities. So he marched south along the Mediterranean coastline toward the land of Israel, accepting submissions from towns along the way.

The wealthy citizens of Tyre put their confidence in the strength of its Persian naval base and did not submit. Instead, the Tyrians demonstrated their refusal for a peaceful surrender by brutally killing the Macedonian messengers relaying Alexander's reasonable terms. The disrespect enraged Alexander, launching him into a vicious 'show no mercy' campaign. A brutal conflict followed.

Callous Greek invaders destroyed the coastal city of Old Tyre. Then they spent seven months piling rubble into a makeshift causeway inching their war machines closer to the island of New Tyre. When the angry Macedonians finally breached the walls, Alexander's soldiers demolished the city, killed countless Tyrians outright, and executed others, impaling them on stakes along the beach.

Again Jews waited. Where would the Greeks strike next? Anxiety filled the land as Alexander continued his southward march. But instead of veering toward Jerusalem, he advanced his army along the Mediterranean coast, setting his sights on the city of Gaza.

When foolish King Batis of Gaza scornfully refused to yield, Alexander's men accepted the insult as an invitation for war and surrounded the city. On discovering a weakness in Gaza's southern wall, Macedonian generals established a perimeter of siege weapons. At the commencement of a long and bloody battle, Alexander shouted to King Batis, "Holy shadows of the dead, I'm not to blame for your cruel and bitter fate. Blame the accursed rivalry which brought sister nations and brother people to fight one another."

Ultimately, the Greeks razed the city, put surviving men to death by the sword, and sold women and children into slavery. I intentionally avoid mentioning the grisly manner in which Alexander executed Gaza's King Batis.

The world's most profitable resource, physical labour, prompted greedy slave traders to follow Alexander's campaigns. After a battle, brokers wasted no time amassing survivors, negotiating prices, and filling orders for affluent Greeks back home requiring miners, domestic slaves, and brothel property – an exchange I well remember watching in Pella.

After wreaking havoc along the Mediterranean shoreline and inflicting appalling horrors on Gaza, the battle-weary army required a place for rest, fresh supplies, and distractions. So Alexander turned his attention toward the largest urban municipality still standing, Jerusalem.

Panic spread. Farmers, shepherds, and townspeople feared for their livelihoods and families. Finally, after much prayer and fasting, High Priest Jaddua received divine instructions through a dream. The Mighty One of Israel instructed him to befriend the new ruler by appearing vulnerable, exposing himself in a peaceful demonstration.

Jaddua ordered the city gates to remain open. Then, after organising a dignified procession of affluent residents, temple priests, musicians, and donkeys laden with precious gifts, he led a parade of white-clad citizens into the open beyond the safety of the city's protective walls. Because of my position of respectability, I joined other affluent citizens and ventured out to greet the conqueror.

In the distance, I observed a lone rider astride an eager horse, spirited and proudly prancing in our direction. My heart stirred, watching the warrior draw near. Behind the forced smiles on Jewish faces, an aura of fear and thick tension hovered over our welcome parade as I struggled to hide my pride at the sight of Alexander. The child I met in Pella had grown into a tall, muscular man, carrying himself in stately confidence as if never imagining any possibility of failure.

Wearing a headdress of lion skin, he wore a purple linothorax fortified with bronze, silver, and gold armour; his breastplate bore the star of the royal house of the Timenids, along with a golden image of Athena. Gilded embellishments decorated his leather skirt.

Receiving the conqueror with outstretched arms, High Priest Jaddua stepped forward, dressed in priestly garments of purple and scarlet clothing, a mitre on his head, and a golden breastplate bearing the name Yahweh. With one voice, we saluted Alexander. Jaddua identified himself and explained no Jew wished war with Macedon. The land of Israel, as with other countries, merely accepted its lot of subjugation under Persian rule. Jaddua's words fell agreeably, and the conqueror spared Jerusalem.

The Macedonian army camped on the hills surrounding the city while Alexander and his officers stayed at the palace – including Ptolemy, one of Alexander's seven bodyguards. From my office, I observed Greek soldiers moving about the city. Their presence raised concern over the safety of my map collection, a valuable discovery for any advancing army. How well I know baseless accusations of treason can transpire out of thin air. Knowing their existence would lead to suspicion and confiscation, I packed my atlases into clay pots. Then, with the help of night-time shadows, I travelled in stealth to the tombs north of the city and concealed the vessels in an empty stone chest inside our family burial chamber. After the Greeks left for Egypt, I successfully retrieved them.

Alexander had received a severe injury at Gaza – an arrow pierced his armour. The warrior grumbled at having to nurse a shoulder wound. His angst had nothing to do with the excruciating pain; sitting idle was his agony. Alexander was the restless sort who sought constant challenges and extreme trials. He wanted to race his horse, draw his sword, and wrestle with his men, but his physician emphatically prohibited any such activity. If the warrior ever planned to use his arm again, Alexander had no choice but to rest. Reluctantly, he filled his days soaking in one of my mineral spas, dining on our lawful Hebrew food, listening to musicians, drinking with his men, and playing Technê.

Chapter 54

The Man, Alexander

"Is no one in this city of the Jews able to oppose me in a vigorous game of Technê?" Alexander hollered.

Jaddua, the High Priest, answered. "My Lord, I know of one such man, Ethan, son of Zuriel. He lives past the eastern wall near the Garden of Gethsemane below the Mount of Olives."

"Send for this man at once," the conqueror demanded.

Sitting across the table from young Alexander, conqueror of the world, struck me as comical. I thought, *Behold the mighty conqueror who holds life and death in his grip, yet he still cannot manage the rebellion of his wayward curls.*

Alexander studied the foreign-looking Technê pieces I arranged on the board. "Jewish?"

"No, my Lord. Persian, from my Persian father."

As though seeing me for the first time, he asked, "Who are you again?"

"No one important, my Lord, merely an Israelite promising you a rousing game of Technê."

We played several games throughout the evening. Not to blow my own horn, but I won the first match. A unified gasp filled the hall. Both Greek and Jew moved away, anticipating the drawing of swords. Leaning back in my chair, I crossed my arms and waited for Alexander to study how he walked into my trap. Intrigued, he reorganised the board for our second game.

Ho, to be sure, the man played like a strategic genius, but he had not learned from Mausolus. Sitting across the board from the ruler of the world, I imagined the satrap proudly smiling as I whipped Alexander at Technê using moves he showed me long ago. Ironically, with this same set of Technê, I played against the two owners of Halicarnassus– first Mausolus, now Alexander.

Alexander and I looked forward to our evening matches, and regardless of our vast differences, we forged an unlikely friendship. Being a Greek, he believed himself the son of his god Zeus – virtually equal to Zeus. I considered myself a servant of my God, Yahweh. The behaviours deemed ordinary by his gods amounted to abominations by my God. We both held worship rituals of prayer, washing, and incense, but I worshiped one God, and he worshiped many.

My invisible God forbids worshiping carved images, while Alexander venerated nothing but carved images. He sought to conquer the world while gathering hordes of attractive women along the way, and I wanted a quiet life with one woman, Hadassah. To be sure, I had acquired an excellent education. Still, Alexander received extensive schooling, tutored by the world's most brilliant men – Leonidas and Lysimachus. Yes, King Philip did steal Aristotle away from Plato to be one of Alexander's most excellent teachers.

Throughout the passing weeks, we grew comfortable around each other. Once the invisible wall of our differences collapsed, we found a commonality in being men with hopes and dreams, loves and losses, plans, and regrets. Talking openly and enjoying each other's company, we found unexpected insight from each other's knowledge and perceptions about life.

As our respect and trust grew, I risked forwardness. "I feasted with your parents many years ago. Please accept my condolences on the recent loss of your father. To be sure, he transformed Macedon into the most powerful state on the Greek peninsula. And your mother, Queen Olympias? I trust she is well."

"Your words of comfort are appreciated. My father accomplished much and might be the man sitting before you today had he not misconstrued a prophecy from the Oracle of Delphi. Indeed, his murder saddened every Macedonian. My dear mother resides in Pydna; to be sure, she is well."

"During your childhood, were you able to spend much time riding Arion-Bous?"

Alexander flashed a surprised glance across the board. "How do you know of this horse?"

"I have many memories from a happier time long ago."

"Tell me these memories," he demanded.

Fearing I may cross a line, I asked, "Do you know of Charger?"

Alexander hesitated for a moment. "My horse?"

I measured the span of my hand. "About this tall?"

"How do you know of this? I command you; tell me at once!"

"I fashioned him from Halicarnassus bronze as a birthday gift for a young prince."

"And what do you know of Arion-Bous?"

I told the story of Mausolus sending Bous across the sea, and the day a Persian satrap gave a toddling prince his first riding lesson. I included Alexander's youthful exuberance when riding Arion-Bous around and around the arena. Finally, I discussed the ox-head marking, seeing the same one on Bucephalus. Alexander said two other foals turned out with the same inherent coloration.

Smiling, I recalled playing Ephedrismos with Ptolemy in the garden and how much the toddler enjoyed watching me unwrap Charger. He eyed me strangely when I apologised for throwing a ball in his face, but after a moment, he burst into laughter. Alexander appreciated learning facts about his young life as much as I enjoyed sharing them.

Time plays tricks on the mind. Was it not just last year the satraps and I visited Pella, with Mausolus playing sports in the king's gymnasium and me playing the wise scholar in the library?

Alexander and I had many philosophical conversations during the weeks of his recovery. One such discussion included prophecies by a Jewish prophet named Daniel, a resident of Jerusalem, before being taken captive by the Babylonians. The strange story of Daniel fascinated this Macedonian; he respected the courage of any young prisoner upholding his faith by saying "No!" to the king of the world.

I told him how Daniel honourably served in the court of King Nebuchadnezzar and the succeeding kings. He also recorded dreams and visions foretelling the rise of other kingdoms. The Jews speculated the world's third conqueror would arrive from the Greek nation. Alexander accepted this reference to prophecy; it explained the mysterious adulation Jews had for him.

Alexander admitted he, too, had a dream. He explained he dreamed of a white-clad procession streaming from the gates of Jerusalem. Leading the parade was a man dressed in purple and scarlet clothing. On his head, he wore a mitre and a golden breastplate engraved with the name of his God. In his dream, the man (who he now realised was the High Priest Jaddua) blessed him with victory and conquest. Despite a scolding from Ptolemy, this vision prompted Alexander to approach our procession alone, adore the name Yahweh, and humbly salute Jaddua.

The idea that Yahweh determined triumphant events involving Greeks agreed most heartily with Alexander. Still, I did not appreciate the casual way he included Yahweh in with the long list of other gods he believed endorsed his mission to defeat the Persians.

If, by chance, the two sovereigns clashed in battle, I felt it my duty to elaborate on the Messiah for whom we watched. "We have faith in a coming Messiah who will rule as an extraordinary leader. A descendant of our ancient ancestor, King David, he will govern the entire world in the End Days, reigning as the divinely anointed king. This future king, well-versed in Jewish laws and God's commandments, will inspire others to follow his worthy example. As a grand military leader, he will win battles for Israel, thereby restoring the lost nationality of the Hebrews. After that, he will rule as a righteous judge over all the world."

I continued. "This man, the Messiah we have awaited since the dawn of time, we expect will arrive soon."

While Alexander remained fascinated by my declaration, Ptolemy disapproved, hovering and growing more resentful of our deepening friendship. (I recalled Mausolus' words about weak men and wondered if Ptolemy would remain loyal to his ruler.) Finally, Alexander said, "When your Messiah arrives, He will no doubt want to meet me. I, too, shall enjoy meeting Him."

I heard rumours the Macedonians were making plans to depart for Egypt. Time was running out. I had to learn all I could about the fall of Halicarnassus, and Alexander possessed the details I sought. So one evening, I took a chance and probed for more information. I first opened up about my personal life in Halicarnassus and Mausolus. I included training under Goliath and fighting in the Wall of Shields during the battle with Rhodes. He admired me for having soldiered. I knew tales of Cleon would impress him further, but I remained mute on that subject. I congratulated him on traversing the Cilician Gates and explained my trip through the pass. Because of our friendship, I warned Alexander about engaging the Uxians in the Zagros Mountains. I added, "Offering figs is a bad idea." He laughed, listening to my harrowing moment with the Uxians, calling me a jellyfish. My ears began to glow red, and I changed the subject. Jaleh never laughed at my near-death misadventure with the Uxians; she thought I was immensely brave.

Alexander knew of Mausolus and was familiar with his philosophies and accomplishments, but it surprised him to learn he had met the satrap. Before delving into vivid details about his gruelling battle against Halicarnassus, the Macedonian esteemed Mausolus with a heartfelt tribute. "I am not afraid of an army of lions led by a sheep; I am afraid of an army of sheep led by a lion; King Mausolus was a formidable lion."

Alexander explained that Persian naval domination along the Aegean coastline threatened his army. Sensibly he subjugated every seaport and naval harbour to protect his rear flank. Mausolus' state-of-the-art double harbour posed a substantial threat. As if merely employing a strategy to move Technê pieces across a board, Alexander told how he launched a battle to incapacitate Halicarnassus, one of his bleakest moments since Mausolus' walls proved too resistant for his war machines. (My heart soared, but I did not reveal it.)

Weeks of bloody back and forth attacks continued with no end in sight. When the Macedonians gained the upper hand by felling two towers and toppling sections of the outer wall, a Persian leader named Ephialtes retaliated. Taking 2,000 troops, they crept out of the city at daybreak. Undetected, they got close enough to set fire to the Grecian siege engines. Persian archers on the walls rained a barrage of missiles on top of Macedonian troops as they struggled to extinguish the flames. Finally, Alexander's oldest soldiers, the Macedonian Guard, rallied and broke through the city walls at the Myndos Gate.

Incredibly, the man fighting to save Halicarnassus, General Memnon, was a mercenary from Rhodes. Alexander previously confronted him at the Battle of Granicus River. He said Memnon issued the command to abandon Halicarnassus. Terrified citizens retreated to Cos. Persian soldiers themselves set the city ablaze before fleeing, refusing to allow the Macedonians any benefits. The town burned in mere hours, helped by a strong wind blowing off the sea. Imagining beautiful Halicarnassus suffering such deadly destruction felt like a dagger to my heart.

I learned Idrieus reigned seven short years before his untimely death, and, not surprisingly, Pixodarus deposed Ada, banishing her to a life of exclusion in the inland city of Alinda. He then established himself as the new satrap. After the Macedonian siege, with Pixodarus dead, Alexander allied himself with Ada, reinstating her as Halicarnassus' rightful satrap. He maintained control over Caria on the merit of Ada's loyalty to him.

Alexander gave the impression of genuine regret, wishing the Carians had surrendered, leaving Halicarnassus intact. I thanked him for valuing Mausolus' grave, and what he said next profoundly touched me. "A tomb now suffices him for whom the whole world was not sufficient. Perhaps I shall leave instructions for my burial tomb to resemble the magnificent design of Mausolus' tomb."

Fascinated by the Mausoleum, Alexander questioned me regarding depth and height, drainage concerns, construction problems, estimated cost, labour, and time. He asked about the selection of marble and the location of the mines. I told him I had no details other than the Proconnesian stone was mined in Marmora, and the Pentelic marble came from Athens, but the Parian pieces came from Paros. I held my face in check to not look guilty thinking about Artemisia.

Explaining the stepped foundation required me to use papyrus and ink. While drawing the complicated layering system and assemblage of the underground tiers, I chuckled to myself when Alexander scooted closer the way he did in the garden of Pella when I laid a mysterious gift in front of him. Finally, after answering many questions and satisfying his curiosity, I handed him my diagram. Alexander rolled it into a cylinder and held it over his shoulder. Ptolemy stepped forward, seized the scroll, and placed it in his pouch.

I was not forthcoming in every aspect of the Mausoleum. To be sure, visualising his generals cracking it open like a massive geode, I avoided mentioning Artemisia's jewelled cellas.

Alexander considered us linked, joined like brothers. After hearing of my fond relationship with Mausolus, he said Ada had adopted him as a son. Yes, by the time Alexander left the land of Israel, I, too, regarded him as my brother. Ho, to be sure, people either loved Alexander or hated him. Jews accepted him as God's instrument, Persians called him Alexander the Accursed and sought to kill him, while the Egyptians declared him pharaoh of Egypt.

I stayed abreast of his travels, tracking his miraculous victories, plotting his conquests on my maps, and privately celebrating his many accomplishments. Yet, I cringed hearing the latest in his long list of wounds – serious injuries, any one of which should have stopped him dead.

He received a slash to the head, a catapult missile to the shoulder, a sword to the thigh, an arrow through the leg, a stone strike to the head, a dart through the arm, an arrow in the ankle, and an arrow through the lung. No man can boast of surviving such injuries. But, as Daniel had dreamed, Yahweh had a plan for Alexander, proven by his success and miraculous recovery from every wound. I fear victory became an excessive burden, too heavy for Alexander. He won battle after battle while nation after nation worshiped him as a god. He sanctioned their adulation, believing his destiny had grown beyond Persia, and his ordination now expanded across the world. His relentless ambition stressed his army to the breaking point, causing mutinous divisions within the ranks.

One morning while working in my office, I heard a commotion on the street outside my window. News of something significant spread across Jerusalem like a torrent of rushing water. More and more people filled the streets gesturing in wild agony, lamenting and tearing their garments. I stepped out the door just as a young boy raced past. Scooping him up, I held him around the waist and inquired about the fuss. His words left me speechless. "The great Alexander is dead! He has died of disease in Babylon!" After marching his army to the ends of the world and surviving every wound, his stolid death was an utter humiliation. The daring and fearless military commander, undefeated in battle, had died in bed.

Returning to my office, I bolted the door and closed the shutter. Opening the false bottom of my map cabinet, I pushed away a wooden box containing my private belongings, including a small woven basket holding thick dark hair tied in a bow of spear grass. Tucked in the far corner, protected by a bundle of cloth, I retrieved one of my most precious objects. A courier from Alexander delivered the item to me several years after the Macedonians left Jerusalem. It was a gift from Alexander made of pure Babylonian gold fashioned into a perfect replica of Charger, my amateur offering to a young prince decades ago.

I again read the note accompanying his remarkable gift, a message written by Alexander's own hand; it said:

'From my earliest memories, Charger was my fondest joy. Your brother always, al-Eskandar Μακεδόνια.'

Epilogue

"Captain, the crew unloaded the cargo, restocked supplies, and topped off the water jars. We acquired three new passengers, two sailing to Ephesus and the third to Chios. On your order, we set sail," the chief officer Reported.

"Have all the men returned to the ship?" Captain Dareios asked.

"To be sure, Captain. No sailor wishes to remain ashore in Halicarnassus, not in a town for ghosts and jackals."

"Enough then. I will join you in a moment." Captain Dareios dismissed him.

Alone in his cabin, he leaned back, contemplating Ethan's narrative – the fascinating story he had spent the evening reading. Lifting the triangular flap, he replaced each scroll, then secured the bronze ring. Gazing beyond the harbour, he viewed the Mausoleum standing like a majestic throne surrounded by a dilapidated city, still bearing the scars of its burning. Only minor restorations had been done since the Greeks took over more than fifty years ago.

Captain Dareios returned to the deck and summoned his chief officer. "I must tend to a matter in town; we will set sail upon my return."

Leaving the harbour area, he ascended a flight of damaged steps leading into the agora. He paused. Scanning the city in every direction, Dareios tried to picture the shamble as Ethan had described – as a dazzling metropolis glistening in the sun, a favoured resort for the wealthy, a thriving capital city spirited and alive during the Age of Mausolus – but it was impossible to imagine.

He climbed the southern staircase and stepped over fallen stones in a crumbling wall encircling a large courtyard. Leaning back, craning his neck to view the chariot monument, Dareios marvelled, imagining Ethan perched high in the clouds, yelling into the sky. He proceeded to the grand staircase, recalling what he had read about the 'divine path.'

Ascending between massive lions carved of Pentelic marble, he lingered at the tragic tenth step. "They both died right here," he said out loud. Then, looking to the top of the staircase, Dareios noted the large stone still in front of the entrance and considered the tremendous wealth few people knew existed inside.

Surrounding the Mausoleum, statues and frieze panels hung as Ethan had described. Taking his time, Dareios walked around the entire structure studying the art, examining each scene, wondering which images might be of Ethan as a young man. He ran his fingers along the marble block, feeling the smooth, flawless texture, musing over its capture in the sea.

With a need to stay on schedule, Dareios beheld the structure one last time, amazed by its story. Having read the remarkable tale of Ethan's life, learning about Goliath and intimate details concerning the satraps, the captain felt he knew the people involved in its construction. Previously dismayed over Ethan's mariner's grave, Dareios now smiled, imagining a joyous reunion – Mausolus, Artemisia, and Ethan together again. Burying Ethan in the Aegean Sea was the right choice.

Heartened by such an architectural accomplishment, the captain spoke in laudable wonder. "To be sure, this triumph of marble stone, the most expensive garment ever to clothe ambitious mortals, shall endure throughout history. This Mausoleum of Halicarnassus stands as one of the great wonders of our world."

Dareios wandered, following Tyche Street around the harbour, until noticing a statue of Thoth in front of the newly constructed public library. *Perfect!* he thought. *Surely a gift to the public library is what Ethan would want for his chronicle.*

Stepping inside, Captain Dareios observed numerous scrolls on high shelves built throughout the large chamber. An aged administrator, dressed in a knee-length chiton with linen chlamys trimmed in red cloth, busily climbed a ladder to deposit his texts. Dareios stood nearby, hoping to gain the man's attention. Nettled by the intrusion, the administrator finally stopped arranging and climbed down. Tilting his head upwards, looking down his nose through squinted eyes, the scraggly-haired Grecian properly greeted the sea captain, "Kalimera."

Dareios returned the greeting and motioned to the satchel while explaining the scrolls. Recounting their importance, he could not help but brim with passion while sharing their content. "I wish to donate this entire collection to the Halicarnassus Library. These historical manuscripts require protection. Rolled within each papyrus are histories - actual events and sad misfortunes involving Halicarnassus and her citizens years before Alexander. I assure you, sir, no history articulates a grander account."

Again, tilting his head back to view the captain, the administrator squinted with suspicion. "Are you trying to sell me a collection of scrolls?"

Dareios struggled to hide his reaction to the librarian's simple-mindedness and tried again to clarify his purpose. "The safety of these manuscripts has fallen to me; I desire to make their narrative available to every interested reader - scholars, academics, intellectuals, thinkers, philosophers, and whoever else seeks a historical account. These scrolls provide a first-hand look at life in Persia, personal experiences, and unique perceptions about Halicarnassus and its rulers. About that Mausoleum out there, too. Does anyone around here know who is in it?"

"To be sure," said the administrator. "The building is stately and impressive, but trivial matters of the Persians do not concern us. We do not care who is in there. Still, I will evaluate your manuscripts. They do sound marvellous and will undoubtedly make a fine addition to our collection of literature."

"Might I ask, sir, where you will assign them?" asked the captain. "Perhaps in the section you have labelled, History."

"Perhaps, if I find the writings have actual significance," the administrator said.

"Read the chronicles for yourself, sir. You will discover their significance and will not be disappointed by fascinating details previously unknown."

"Thank you again, Captain, for your kind contribution to our burgeoning library." Dareios handed over the satchel.

Feeling unsettled, the captain feared he had made a mistake; he may have failed Ethan. Unsure of the author's intended destination for his writings, Dareios could only guess Ethan desired his manuscripts to return to their origin, Halicarnassus.

Despite his apprehension, Captain Dareios could stay no longer. He had obligations; his crew awaited his arrival; his delay was costly. Pausing by the door, the captain lingered, pretending to look at something of particular interest. He watched from the corner of his eye as the administrator gathered Ethan's scrolls and haphazardly plopped them onto a crowded shelf under the sign: Mythology.

The End

Addendum

The Mausoleum of Halicarnassus stood for seventeen centuries before toppling in an earthquake. Pieces lay scattered across the courtyard until the early fifteenth century when the Knights of Rhodes as if bringing the misappropriated marble full circle, collected the rubble, dismantled the mausoleum remains, and built their castle on the peninsula where the palace of Mausolus and Artemisia once stood. The knights, needing stone to fortify their mortar, pulverized statues of Persian citizens, gods, and goddesses, considering them graven images best destroyed.

The castle is now a museum, yet greenstone, portions of frieze panels, and columns remain visible. Between blocks of Proconnesian stone is mortar mixed with priceless art from the ancient world's most celebrated sculptors – Bryaxis, Leochares, Scopas, Timotheus, and Pythius of Priene.

Artifacts excavated from the site during the 19th century – glimpses of the Mausoleum's splendour – are exhibited in London's British Museum. Interior wealth, looted by the Knights of Rhodes, was never recovered and remains lost to history.

The Hecatomnid Dynasty continues to make world history thousands of years later. In 1989, the tomb of Ada was unearthed in Halicarnassus, modern-day Bodrum, Turkey. Her sarcophagus, remains, and several artifacts are displayed at the castle museum.

For 2,387 years, the tomb of Hecatomnus remained undetected beneath the temple of Zeus in Mylasa, modern-day Milas, Turkey. In 2010, looters tunnelled their way into an underground chamber, discovered his elaborate sarcophagus, and emptied the vault of priceless artifacts. Hecatomnus' sarcophagus is on display at the museum in Milas, as are the ruins of the temple of Zeus.

The ancient ruins of Labraunda, ten miles north of Milas along the one-time Holy Avenue, are open to the public and display the last vestiges of builders Mausolus and Idrieus.

The ruins of the Mausoleum of Halicarnassus, one of the Seven Wonders of the Ancient World, located in Bodrum, Turkey, are open to the public. The Myndos Gate and portions of the city wall built by Mausolus are still apparent in Bodrum. The ancient ruins of Pedasa, about two miles north of Bodrum, are also open to the public.

Glossary of Words

Achaemenid – Persian Dynasty 553–330 BC

Agápi̱ mou – Greek meaning my love

Akkadian – Babylonian dialect

Ahura Mazda – the name given to the Zoroastrian God

Aíthousa – Greek meaning room or gathering hall

Akinaka – a Persian dagger-type weapon

Almpatrós – Greek meaning albatross

Amphora – an ancient jar with a long neck and two handles

Angaros – Persian dispatch rider

Angarium - a Persian delivery system dispatching riders similar to the Pony Express

Antaeus – a Greek god

Apādana – an audience hall in ancient Persia

Astynomia – police force in ancient Greek

Aulos – a Greek wind instrument

Avesta – the sacred book of Zoroastrian scriptures

Aziz – a Persian expression meaning beloved

Cellas – inner chambers

Cetus – a sea monster in Greek mythology

Chalparas – finger clappers, castanets

Chiton – ancient Grecian short tunic

Chlamys – ancient Grecian cloak

Cohorts – colleagues of the king or ruler

Colossus – statue on Rhodes Island, 108' tall, 280 BC - 226 BC

Conium – Hemlock

Cubit – measurement, one cubit = 1.5 feet

Daeva – Zoroastrian meaning demon

Dathaba – a Persian military regiment of 10 soldiers

Doulos – ancient Greek meaning a slave

Ennoia pros polisi – ancient Greek meaning for sale

Ephedrismos – ancient game involving piggy-back rides while knocking over pins

Epiblema – ancient Grecian shawl

Etesian winds – summer winds of the Aegean

Gathas – poems contained in the Zoroastrian Bible

Garmapada – Greek month around June /July

Hatru – a Persian military reservist

Hazarabam – a Persian military regiment of 1,000 soldiers

Hector – a Trojan prince and great warrior of Troy from Homer's *the Iliad*

Himation – an outer garment worn by the ancient Greeks

Hoplite – Ancient Greek special forces

Hypostyle hall – Persian interior space whose roof rests on pillars or columns

Hydriai – Greek meaning water-carrying vessels

Húdōr – Greek meaning water

Ibex –an animal with backward-curling horns

Ikat – a decorative pattern of weaving

Jeegaram – Persian term of endearment meaning my liver

Kairos – Greek mythology meaning an opportune moment

Kalimera – ancient Greek meaning good morning

Kamarband – Greek meaning cummerbund

Koprophágos – ancient Greek insult meaning shit eating

Kovalos – ancient Greek insult meaning parasite

Kriòmyxos – ancient Greek insult meaning stupid like a ram

Krustallos – crystal

Ktínos – ancient Greek insult meaning beast, brute

Kvevri – fermenting vessel

Lailapás – Greek meaning hurricane

Leviathan – a horrible monster

Mà tòn Diónyson - By Dionysos! used as a swear word

Markhor – a mountain goat

Mehregan – Zoroastrian festival celebrated in Persia

Millo – a structure of some sort

Mitera –Greek meaning mother

Órrhos – ancient Greek insult referring to someone as the exterior buttocks, the anus, or the rectum

Pais – Greek meaning a child, children

Parádeisos – large extravagant Persian gardens

Parasang – distance measurement; 1 parasang = 3+ miles

Peltast – Grecian soldier in the light infantry

Phallus – an image of the male reproductive organ

Pillars – A pillar and a column are upright structures supporting a more extensive structure above them. Pillar is a general term, and column is a technical term. Pillars are cylindrical. Columns come in different shapes.

Pórnē – ancient Greek meaning prostitute

Qanat –ancient Persian shaft to transport water

Rhyton – ancient Grecian drinking vessel

Ritó – Greek meaning motto

Satrap – a provincial governor in ancient Persian often called king, serving as imperial rulers, not royal.

Satrapy – a province or state in ancient Persia governed by an appointed satrap

Shalom berakah we-ṭobah – Jewish meaning Peace, blessing, good

Spara – Persian military shield

Shah – Persian royal title for a king or ruler

Shahanshah – King of Kings, Supreme King of Persia

Sparabara – Persian shield-bearers

Stoa – long open ancient Greek building with column- supported roof

Subbia – a chisel

Technê – ancient Grecian philosophical concept for practical knowledge

Theaomai – Greek meaning view, behold, look upon

Thilyprepís –ancient Greek meaning effeminate

Trihemiolia – oared warships used by the Persian Navy

Vlákas – ancient Grecian insult meaning fool, moron

Weiqi – ancient Chinese board game

Xiphos – ancient Grecian sword used as a secondary weapon

Yibbum – Jewish brother-in-law marriage

Zoroastrianism – an ancient religion of Persia founded by the prophet Zoroaster who lived during the 6th and 7th century BC

Glossary of Historical Characters

Aba – Hecatomnus' wife, daughter of Hyssaldomus

Ada – Mausolus' sister born July 29, 390, died 326 BC

Alexander the Great – born July 29, 356, in Pella, Greece – died June 323 BC in Babylon

Amazon Women –5th century BC warriors from Scythia, Thrace, Asia Minor, and the Aegean Islands

Araissis – a political enemy of Mausolus

Ariobarzanes – satrap of Phrygia, Mausolus' political enemy

Artaxerxes II - King of Kings Achaemenid Empire reigned 405 to 358 BC

Artaxerxes III - King of Kings Achaemenid Empire reigned 359 to 338 BC

Artemisia I – first satrap queen of Caria - 5th century BC

Artemisia II –satrap queen of Caria reigned 377 – 351 BC

Bucephalus – famous warhorse of Alexander the Great

Colossus – 280 BC, one of the Seven Wonders of the Ancient World, built by Greek sculptor Chares of Lindos

Darius III - last Achaemenid King of Kings of Persia reigned 336 to 330 BC

Diodorus – son of Xenophon

Esli – included in the lineage of the Messiah

Esther – queen of Persia (her Jewish name was Hadassah)

Fates of Greek Mythology – Clotho, Lachesis, Atropos

Gryllus – Xenophon's oldest son

Hecatomnid Dynasty –Hecatomnus, Mausolus, Artemisia, Idrieus, Pixodarus, Ada. Ruled Caria 395 to 330 BC

Hecatomnus – Mausolus' father, reigned 395 to 377 BC

Holy Avenue – Connected Mylasa to Labraunda

Hyssaldomus – Mausolus' grandfather, priest, and satrap of Caria

Hydarnes – Persian commander of 10,000 Immortals

Idrieus – Mausolus' brother, reigned 351–344 BC

Jaddua – High Priest of Judah at the time of Alexander

Labraunda – a city north of modern-day Milas

Leonidas – a kinsman of Olympias, tutored Alexander in horsemanship

Lygdamis – first satrap of Caria late 6th century BC. Father of Artemisia I

Lysippos – one of the three greatest sculptors of the Classical Greek era

Manites – son of Pactyas, a conspirator against Mausolus and Artemisia

Maath – included in the lineage of the Messiah

Mausolus – satrap of Caria reigned 377 – 353 BC

Mithridates – a political enemy of Mausolus

Olympias – Alexander's mother

Orontobates – succeeded Hecatomnid Dynasty, married Pixodarus' daughter

Penthesilea – Amazon queen killed by Achilles during the Trojan War

Persepolis – a capital city of the Persian Empire, its ruins are located in southwest Iran.

Philip – Alexander's father

Pisindelis – son of Artemisia I

Pixodarus – Mausolus' brother, succeeded Idrieus

Ptolemy – Alexander's childhood friend, general, and bodyguard

Themistocles – a Greek general

Theopompus – a Greek historian and rhetorician who spoke at Mausolus' funeral

Tissaphernes – great grandson of Hydarnes, and satrap of Caria reigned 408 – 395 BC

Thyssos, son of Syskos – conspirator against Mausolus and Artemisia

Xenophon of Athens – philosopher, writer, historian, soldier, mercenary (d 354 BC)

Xerxes - fourth Shahanshah of the Achaemenid Empire, reigned 486 - 465 BC

Yahweh – the personal name of Almighty God

Glossary of Fictional Characters

Admiral Cyberniskos of Rhodes –leader of the rebellion

Arion-Bous – a colt gifted from Mausolus to Alexander, sired Bucephalus

Bahar – Mausolus' grandmother

Caleb – Ethan's brother

Captain Dareios – Greek commander of a sailing vessel

Cas – Goliath's oldest son

Cleon – a Greek soldier, hired assassin, and youngest son of Xenophon and his Babylonian wife

Ethan – narrator 373 – 279 BC

Farzin – Goliath's son – a twin

Goliath – commander of Mausolus' guard

Gulzar – Goliath's son – a twin

Hadassah – Ethan's wife

Hulda – wife of Sakeri, wife of Caleb

Jaleh – Ethan's Persian love, daughter of Goliath

Karim – metallurgist in Halicarnassus

Landers – a barber from Greece

Lailapás – Mausolus' horse

Majid – Dathaba soldier

Moza – lifelong servant of Mausolus

Miut – Artemisia's long-hair Persian cat

Omid – Goliath's uncle killed in the Peloponnesian War

Otis – personal servant to Artemisia

Pisinah – a soldier station at the garrison in Rhodes

Ralf – Goliath's father, a soldier

Roozbeh – Dathaba lieutenant

Roxane – daughter of Hecatomnus and Aba

Ruth – Ethan's mother

Sakeri – Ethan's oldest brother, later his nephew was named Sakeri

Simin – Goliath's wife

Stavros – a barber

Thuxra – Goliath's lieutenant

Zuriel – Ethan's father

Aristotle said, "Pleasure in the job puts perfection in the work."

Plato said, "The measure of a man is what he does with power. His excellence is not a gift but a skill requiring practice. Refuse to act right because you think you are excellent; instead, achieve excellence by acting rightly; then, your good actions will strengthen yourself and inspire good actions in others"

Artemisia quoted Queen Penthesilea's words in the *Iliad* when she said, "Now shall you learn what might wells up in the breast of an Amazon. With my blood is mingled war!"

Description of the Mausoleum

With no two archaeological conclusions being the same regarding the structure's size, design, or interior, *Pillars for the God* uses a combination of findings and discoveries, assigning fictional names for clearer understanding. The exact years of construction, the Mausoleum's entrance, and the precise location of Mausolus' and Artemisia's ashes are uncertain. The most reliable description of the Mausoleum comes from Pliny the Elder, a Roman author (23–79 CE). Never officially excavated until 1856, many of the mausoleum artifacts and ruins are in London's British Museum.

Foundation depth = stepped into the hillside approximately 2' to 10' deep.
Greenstone Foundation = 127' north to south, by 108' east to west.
Mausoleum base = 120' north to south, by 100' east to west.
Base = Marble crossbeams discovered at the site suggest the Persian Pedestal contained an interior room possibly 63' in length. This pedestal section measured 60' high by 120' x 100'. Ledges surrounding the pedestal supported hundreds of statues of actual people living at the time, action scenes, battles, cavalry, and wild animal hunts.

Column section = Steps found at the site suggests an upper room, possibly 38' in length. This colonnaded mid-section was surrounded by thirty-six Ionic columns measuring 38' high—statues placed between the columns measured 10' tall. A vividly painted frieze panel wrapping the ledge below displayed Greeks and Amazon women in battle.

Pyramid Roof = This Egyptian-style pyramid was tapered skyward with 24 steps reaching a height of 22'. A platform measuring 20' x 25' sat on its peak. Frieze panels wrapping the base of the roof displayed Olympian quadriga chariot races. Forty marble lions guarded the chariot on the surrounding ledge above this panel.

The Chariot Monument = The enormous statue was mounted on the platform of the Pyramid Roof, measuring 20' high. This final contribution to the Mausoleum raised its height to 140'. Frieze panels at the platform's base depicted battle scenes between Greeks and Centaurs.